THIEVER

Also by David M Allan

The Empty Throne

Quaestor

THIEVER

DAVID M ALLAN

Elsewhen Press

Thiever
First published in Great Britain by Elsewhen Press, 2021
An imprint of Alnpete Limited

Elsewhen Press, PO Box 757, Dartford, Kent DA2 7TQ
www.elsewhen.press

British Library Cataloguing in Publication Data.
A catalogue record for this book is available from the British Library.

ISBN 978-1-911409-87-8 Print edition
ISBN 978-1-911409-97-7 eBook edition

Designed and formatted by Elsewhen Press

This book is a work of fiction. All names, characters, places, nobles,
rulers, deities and events are either a product of the author's fertile
imagination or are used fictitiously. Any resemblance to actual events,
gods, kings, peers, places, daimons or people (living, dead or
incorporeal) is purely coincidental.

IN JOTUK

THE TWENTY-THREE FAMILIES

House	Person	Colours
Branidh	Lias; Lodesh	Grey and blue
Colnis	Sahnes	Pale blue and dark blue
Dunish	Ilhas	Pink and yellow
Fimigh	Jemol; Ionek	Red and black
Glinin	Pevus	Blue and white
Guesyr	Dunel; Therem	Orange and green
Hivarn	Mianil; Febay	Blue and silver
Jerut	Carilt	Black and silver
Leynik	Esayn	Purple and white
Monost	Rinil	Blue and black
Neyen	Yisul; Muhan	Green and scarlet
Pridhar	Elklis; Hulser	Red and white
Rimled	Feydis	Green and yellow
Shuth	Cuhes	Brown and yellow
Vilost	Frenuj	Green and black
Widhis	Julnaw	Silver and green

THE HOULN

The Dark Fountain	Jemak; Ivarros
The Stone Grasshoppers	Hentro; Yarelk
The Three Flowers	Richak

OTHERS

Osir, a servant at House Neyen
Trusef, Master of the Keys at House Neyen

IN CARREGIS

THE INNER CIRCLE OF
THE DAUGHTERS OF QUARENNA

Belari, a Scratcher
Jaenis, one of the king's advisers, a Feeler
Nuasi, a Sponger
Tilua, a Sponger

OTHER PRIESTESSES

Jilesi, a Seeker
Kemeneah, a Scratcher
Trenyas, a Terromancer

THE BROTHERHOOD OF HULER

Desern, a Seeker
Druciel, an Aeromancer
Grovaen, a Feeler and one of the king's advisers
Jimoth, a Seeker
Rupesc, head of the Brotherhood

OTHER PRIESTS

Raifen, a Feeler

NOBLES

Sulereath III, the King

Aesol, Duchess of Simand
Latisec, Duke of Alrem
Kuranesh, Duke of Voro

Ghendul, Baron of Hemeark

Aness Debennis, one of the king's advisers
Fedic, Commander of the king's guard
Kieret Beghroth, one of the king's advisers
Yertis Pirrosha, judge, one of the king's advisers

OTHERS IN CARRHEN

Anarya, a Sponger
Baram, a Stealther
Corvek, Seneschal to the late Count Graumedel, a Chemer
Daersi, Mistress of the Household to the late Duke Wurauf
Harviel, a possible heir of the late Count Graumedel
Jarik, a miller
Limabur, landlord of *The Seventh Step* in Verenthe
Melauthua Minobis, owner of the *House of Silken Delights* in Hemeark
Nasuren, secretary to Praukel Vecsin
Nurmed, a possible heir of the late Count Graumedel
Praukel Vecsin, a rich merchant, a Chemer

THE GODS

HULER
GOD OF MEN

His aspects:
Boy, Warrior, Judge, Craftsman, Grieving Parent, Avenger, Pardoner, Good Companion

QUARENNA
GOD OF WOMEN

Her aspects:
Child, Maiden, Wife, Mother, Warrior Maid, Friend and Comforter, Helper, Guardian

KEHSIEH
ONE OF THE CONFINED GODS

MAGIC

Name	Ability	Aura
Aeromancer	Affinity for air	White
Aquamancer	Affinity for water	Pale blue
Chemer	Prepares potions	Gold
Daimoner	Controls daimons	Dark blue
Feeler	Empathy	Green
Lifter	Telekinesis	Red
Pyromancer	Affinity for fire	Purple
Scratcher	Casts spells by word or gesture	Yellow
Seeker	Can find people and things	Pink
Sponger	Duplicates other's abilities	Rainbow
Stealther	Invisibility	Brown
Terromancer	Affinity for earth	Violet
Thiever	Steals other's abilities	Black
Voyanter	Sees and hears at a distance	Orange
Whisperer	Communicates at a distance	Grey

Stealther is an exclusively male skill, Sponger exclusively female.

CONTENTS

CONTENTS

THE TEMPLE OF THE GOD IN JOTUK

Yisul cra Neyen had trouble believing her eyes as she watched her father kill The God.

He stood still for a moment, looking down at the body lying among the shattered remnants of the throne. Blood dripped from the knife he had used to cut The God's throat. Then he straightened up, waved the knife overhead and shouted, "We are free! At last we are free!"

Most of the surviving representatives of the Twenty-three Families echoed his shout and crowded around to congratulate him, gaze at the body and, in several cases, kick it or spit on it. Three others looked stunned and drew back, as if unwilling to be associated with what they had witnessed. One man ran screaming from the ruined splendour of the Presence Chamber.

Muhan dropped the knife and walked over to where his daughter was crouched over the still figure of the woman who had defeated The God in a contest of magic. "Let me get you out of those chains."

Looking at the heavy manacles around Yisul's wrists and ankles, he gestured as if he was cutting something. The restraints fell apart and rattled to the floor. Yisul turned away from him to put a hand on the woman's forehead and frowned.

"Is she alive?"

"Yes, father, but she must have exhausted her talent. I'm worried about her – I've seen her overexert herself before and suffer for it. Can we take her home and let her rest? Give her a chance to recover."

"She deserves that much at least. Who is she? Where did she come from?"

"Her name is Anarya. We met in Carregis. She helped me settle there. We worked together. I don't know how she managed to follow me here – the last time I saw her was in a little town called Verenthe a few days away from Carregis."

Muhan looked quizzically at his daughter, then he turned towards the throne and called, "Feydis! Feydis cra Rimled, come here. I need your help."

A thin man, wearing green and yellow, left the group around the body of The God and walked across to join Muhan. "I'll do anything I can to help the man who freed us. What do you want?"

"Can you Lift this woman and carry her back to House Neyen?"

"Easily," Feydis replied. He exerted his talent as a Lifter and Anarya floated up until she was level with his waist. Muhan and Yisul started walking towards the far end of the room from the throne. Feydis followed with Anarya suspended in mid-air beside him.

A young man with pale blue eyes, a thin moustache and long brown hair joined them.

"Who are you?" asked Muhan. He had no idea who this man was, but had seen him stab The God and distract him during the fight; he had to be an ally.

The man looked blank and said, in an atrocious accent, "*Sitru nela-fis*. I don't speak Sitru."

Muhan repeated his question in Katelish and the stranger answered, "My name's Baram. I came with Anarya to help her if I could."

Yisul turned to stare at the newcomer. *What is he doing here? He was one of those looking for me, wasn't he? Why did he help Anarya? And what's father doing? I'm going to need a long chat with him.*

"Well, I suppose you'd better come with us while we take care of her," said Muhan to Baram and carried on walking towards the south end of the Presence Chamber. "Everybody else, go home."

"Stop, Muhan," called a woman's voice from the group around the body. "I saw Elklis run out that way. You know what he's like, totally devoted to The God; a real believer. I'm surprised he didn't attack you. He might have gone for help. If so, he can get to House Pridhar faster than you can get to Neyen. Be careful."

"I'm sure I can handle Elklis. Go home. All of you go home. We need to arrange for a meeting of the Families. I'll get word to you as soon as I can organise something. First I've got to look after this young woman who made it possible for me to do what I did."

"This young woman's name is Anarya," said Yisul.

Muhan nodded. "Yes. You did tell me and I haven't forgotten. Keep looking ahead of us as we go in case Elklis does try something."

He led the small procession through one of the side doors from the Presence Chamber avoiding the main route to the Family's Door. They hurried along a corridor and round a corner.

"Stop, father," said Yisul. "I can see Elklis. He must have anticipated which way we're going and he's hiding in the Court of Statues. There are three guardsmen with him. He just told them 'we'll let them get well into the Court before we attack'."

"Can you tell me exactly where they are?" asked Muhan.

Yisul concentrated on her talent. The Court of Statues was only a short distance away and well within reach of a Voyanter as strong as her. She could see translucent images of the twenty-three statues in the Court, and the four men hiding there among them.

"They are all hiding behind the plinths of statues. Two of the guardsmen are using the Rearing Horse, one the Faithful Servant's Reward and Elklis is behind the Eagle Landing."

"Typical of Elklis. Of course he'd hide behind the statue his Family donated. The way we're going he'd do better using the Sleeping Lion, but I'll not grumble about his stupidity."

Muhan thought for a moment then pulled a blackwood cane the length of his forearm from his belt and gave it to Yisul. "Have you kept in training? Do you think you can you hold off one of the guardsmen by yourself?"

"I think so, father," she said, spinning the cane through some practice moves. "You taught me well."

"Good. When we enter the Court, I will cast an enclosing spell around the Horse and trap the two behind it so that they can't interfere. Then I'll confront Elklis and leave the last one to you."

"Be careful, father. Elklis is strong. Remember he's always liked to show off how skilful he is."

Muhan told Feydis, "You stay here. Don't move until we return." Then he switched to Katelish and said to Baram, "There are four armed men ahead waiting to attack us. You stay here while we deal with them."

"I can help you," replied Baram. "I'm a Stealther."

"Are you? That's useful." He explained where the men were waiting and asked, "Will you use Stealth and take out the two behind the Rearing Horse? It'll be easier if I don't have to worry about them too."

"I'll do that," said Baram. "I'll shout when they're down."

"Are you ready, Yisul?"

"Yes."

"Go, Baram."

Baram faded into invisibility.

Muhan gestured, preparing a spell as he waited for Baram's signal.

Sooner than they expected Baram's voice yelled, "Now!"

Muhan ran out into the Court of Statues, completed his spell and released it.

Elklis must have been distracted by Baram's shout because he was looking towards the statue of the Rearing Horse, not at their route into the Court. He turned and sent a fireball spinning through the air towards Muhan. It collided with the one Muhan's spell had produced, creating a shower of bright yellow sparks, a loud thumping noise and an acrid smell, but injuring nobody.

The two of them moved towards each other until they were eight or nine paces apart. They stopped there, both gesturing as they tossed spells at each other, shielded themselves, or flinched away from a near miss.

Yisul forced herself to stop worrying about her father. She ran at the last guardsman, forcing him to pay attention to her. She evaded his first attack with ease, using the cane to deflect his thrust at her chest. *I used to be very good with the cane but it's a while since I practiced. I hope I'm good enough.* By the way the guard's eyes dilated when he saw the cane parry his attack she knew he had faced one before and was wary of what it could do in the hands of an expert.

He pulled back slightly but she followed him, aiming a flurry of strokes at his head. Although he was wearing a helmet it didn't protect his face. He retreated until he was pressed against the plinth of the statue he had been hiding behind. He lifted a gauntleted hand to protect his eyes and Yisul changed her point of attack. She hammered the cane into the unprotected part of his forearm, then into the angle between neck and shoulder and back to his forearm. He dropped his sword.

Her cane stabbed upwards under his ribs.

He fell to the ground gasping for breath.

She bent over him for a final, killing, stroke then straightened up and turned to see what her father was doing.

Not being a Scratcher, she couldn't see the spell glyphs they were creating with their gestures. She had to guess what was happening by their reactions and the occasional visible manifestation of a spell. Although she had seen both of them demonstrating their skills on many occasions she wasn't sure who was stronger and she watched them anxiously.

She saw her father take a step back, then another. The look on Elklis' face as he stepped forward was one of triumph. He raised his hands one final time and shouted, "So dies the godkiller!"

He never completed the gesture. Yisul screamed and threw herself forward, her cane slammed end first into his throat crushing his larynx. He crumpled to the ground, hands going to his throat as he struggled for breath.

"Father! Are you injured?"

"No, Yisul. I'm fine, thanks to you. Just exhausted. It was a close thing."

They turned to see what had happened to Baram. He was walking towards them, leaving two bodies in a pool of blood on the ground behind him.

"Let's get home as quickly as we can," said Muhan. "Thank you for your assistance, Baram. Yisul, will you tell Feydis it's safe."

House Neyen in Jotuk

"Wait here," said Yisul to Baram when the procession carrying Anarya reached House Neyen and Feydis cra Rimled had lowered Anarya on to a makeshift stretcher.

Muhan thanked Feydis for his assistance and suggested he went home until a meeting was called.

Four servants carried the stretcher upstairs leaving Baram standing in the entrance hall. He looked around in amazement. Marble arches gave access deeper into the building and to corridors on either side. There were large, delicate ceramic vases decorated with a multicoloured, long-plumaged bird he didn't know standing in the corners of the hall. An intricately carved goldenwood staircase swept up one level before dividing around a gallery and going up another level. Light was provided by windows at ground level and in the dome above the hall. The ceiling was whitewashed with details picked out in yellow. The effect was one of wealth and sophistication, even more so than Graumedel's mansion.

Under his breath he muttered something about the opulence on display and was surprised when Caseir's voice agreed with him. He had forgotten about the piece of wood containing Caseir's spirit he wore at his neck.

Two servants, in green jackets and trousers with scarlet piping, stood at the bottom of the stair and were obviously keeping an eye on him. He didn't blame them, he would have been suspicious of someone in dirty, scuffed leather and smelling of smoke too. *Should I sit? It might put them at ease. On the other hand, it might upset them if they'll have to clean the upholstery afterwards. Better not.*

Baram was still waiting the better part of a chime later and was beginning to get restless when Yisul appeared on the upper landing. She beckoned to him and said "*Jhe golen-ve muterlish.*"

What does that mean? Doesn't she realise I don't speak Sitru?

One of the servants indicated that he should go up the stairs just as Caseir translated for him. "That means 'bring him up here'."

Baram followed the servant up the stairs and along a corridor to where Yisul was waiting for him. She had changed clothes, from the simple, unadorned cotton gown she had been wearing in the temple to a green chambray top and scarlet skirt much more suitable for someone of her rank.

"Sit down," she told him.

"Where's Anarya?" he asked instead of sitting.

"Through there," she said, pointing at one of the doors leading from the room.

"Is she…"

"She's unconscious, but she *is* alive. Come and see, if it will make you happier. Then you need to answer some questions."

She ushered Baram into a bedroom where Anarya was lying unmoving but breathing quietly.

Two women sitting in a corner of the room stood when they entered.

"She's not being left alone for a moment," said Yisul. "The healers think she'll recover but they aren't really sure what's wrong with her. I told them it's talent exhaustion, but I don't think they believe me. Now, will you answer my questions?"

"Yes. I will. Thank you for letting me see her, Yisyena."

"Don't call me that! It's a name I adopted when I ran away to Carregis. My true name is Yisul cra Neyen."

"I'm sorry. I will remember that."

"Good. Come outside again. We'll be told if there's any change."

Baram heard whispered comments from the women servants. He thought one of them muttered '*Dislokcil*' and the other replied *'Pertes'* but he wasn't sure if he had heard the unfamiliar language correctly. "What did they say?" he asked under his breath knowing Caseir would hear him.

Caseir guffawed. "Think you've made a conquest there. One of them called you handsome and the other said you're 'beddable'."

Baram felt himself blush and left the room quickly.

Yisul followed him out and said, "Sit." This time Baram obeyed her.

"I know you're one of those who were searching for me. That's partly why I ran away from Verenthe, you were getting too close for comfort. How do you come to be working with Anarya?"

"I was told to look for you by Count Graumedel. He wanted to send you back here, to Jotuk. The God promised him a lot in the way of trade agreements for your return. Anarya stopped me from finding you, she was distraught with the idea you were in danger."

"Distraught?"

"Cundrasev," said Caseir, and Baram repeated it to Yisul.

"How did you know that? I didn't think you spoke Sitru well enough."

"I don't. Caseir translated it for me."

"Caseir? But he's trapped in the bloodstain in that table in Verenthe."

"After you ran away Anarya discovered that, within limits, a fragment of the wood works as well as the whole tabletop."

"And you have a piece of the wood? Let me hold it."

Baram removed the necklace and passed it over.

Yisul sat muttering to Caseir for almost half a chime while he told her about Anarya's search for her, how it had led to the deaths of Count Graumedel and Duke Wurauf and the release of Baram from his magically compelled servitude to Graumedel.

She was startled when Caseir told her, "Anarya took a terrible risk. She went into the Darkworld and negotiated with a daimon for control of the portal. Then she used it to come here to rescue you. Baram came with her to repay her for freeing him from Graumedel."

"I understand now," said Yisul, inclining her head in Baram's direction and touching two fingers to the base of her throat. "Baram, you have the thanks of Yisul cra Neyen. Be welcome to my home as a Housefriend. If we can be of service to you, you need but ask."

A SAFE-HOUSE IN JOTUK

Osir's stomach churned. He had to keep swallowing to avoid vomiting. *What do they want?*

Four men had surrounded him soon after he walked through the south-western gate from the inner city. He didn't recognise any of them, but he knew what they were, enforcers from one of the *houln*, he didn't know which and it didn't really matter. He wasn't part of one himself and he took great care to avoid antagonising anyone who was. *What do they want? I haven't done anything!*

They hustled him along one of the main streets leading from the gate, round a corner and into a warren of narrow alleys where he was soon lost. It was a part of the outer city he didn't know. A door opened when the leader of his escort knocked on it in a peculiar staccato rhythm. The room beyond the door held another five men. One of them nodded towards a staircase in a corner and said, "Take him up."

The man who pushed him up the stairs reached around him once they got to the top to knock on another door, opened it and said, "Found one of them, boss. This here's Osir." A shove sent him stumbling into the room. The door closed behind him.

Osir recovered his balance. When he looked up he saw a burly man sitting at a desk with an abacus, a small stack of paper, an inkwell, a flagon and a glass of green wine in front of him, and a pen in his hand. A small fire behind the desk kept the room comfortable despite the cold autumnal wind outside.

The man rubbed a scar running over his bald head from just above his left ear. Another scar, across his face, started close to the inner corner of his right eye and pulled up the right side of his mouth into a permanent grimace. The hand doing the rubbing was missing the thumb and most of the first finger. Scars and missing body parts weren't uncommon in the outer city but Osir had heard this man described. From what he had heard, he had no difficulty recognising him as Richak, one of the most feared men in Jotuk. He ruled the *houln* known as the Three Flowers and had done so for over eight years, a very long time in the continuous struggle for dominance within and between *houln*. Osir took a step backwards to get as far away from Richak as possible, and ended up against the door.

"Osir, eh?" said Richak, "You work for Neyen."

Osir swallowed and managed to say, "Yes," in a hoarse whisper.

"Good. I'm told you were one of the Neyen servants who went to the temple two days ago to clean up after the earthquake."

"Yes – but it weren't a 'quake," said Osir, feeling a little more confident because it seemed he wasn't in trouble after all. He had information Richak wanted; it might be worth something. "Appears there was some sort of fight. Don't know for sure but from the looks of it a Terromancer and a Pyromancer must 'ave went wild and did a lotta damage. People got killed."

"Go on," Richak commanded when Osir paused.

"Me an' some of the others was sent to the temple to clear up. Went all the way into the Presence Chamber we did. Was a right mess. Had t'get rid of some bodies an' there were some fires we had to put out."

"How many bodies? Who were they?"

"Ten in the Presence Chamber. Most of them was burnt so bad you couldn't tell who they were. There was one what wasn't burnt and I did know him. It was the Head of the Vilost Family. Looked like every bone in his body was broke. An' there was one I didn't recognise near the throne. His throat'd been cut and there was blood all around him. Then there was that arrogant prick Elklis cra Pridhar and three of his Family's guardsmen in the Court of Statues. Looked like they'd been on the losing side of a fight."

"What about the living?"

"There weren't none. Seems they'd all left before we got there."

"Rumour says a stranger was injured and taken to House Neyen. Who was it?"

"Don't know," said Osir, shaking his head vigorously.

"Did you see this stranger?"

Osir hesitated before saying, "Yes, I did. Neyen, and that daughter of his what went missing, was fussing over an unconscious woman I ain't never seen before. She was brought to Neyen by a Lifter but it was me and some of the others had to carry her up to one of the visitor's suites before we was sent to the temple."

"Describe her," said Richak, sitting back and taking a sip of wine.

"Middle sized, mid-twenties or thereabouts, dark but not as dark as most of the Neyen. Sorta chestnutty-brown hair cut pretty short. She was wearing man's clothes – breeches, and a leather waistcoat what fastened right up to a funny high collar. Never seen that style afore. Good stuff though, even if it was torn and smoke stained. They was calling for a healer to see to her when I left."

Richak sat back in his chair, rubbed his hand across his scar again and said "What happened to her clothes and things?"

Osir looked directly at Richak for the first time and quickly dropped his eyes again. "They got thrown out when they put her to bed."

"Did you get any of them?" asked Richak, adding when Osir didn't answer immediately, "Don't try to fool me. If they were being thrown away I'm sure everyone involved got a share of them."

Osir shivered at the thought of what might happen to him if Richak caught him lying. "Yes," he whispered. "We drew lots for them. Was lucky, I got this." He indicated a pouch at his belt.

"Let me see it."

Osir unfastened the pouch and dropped it on the desk, still trying to keep as far away from Richak as he could.

"Was there anything in it?"

"A few little metal discs with some marks on them. Could be tokens, I suppose, but I didn't know the markings, and nobody wastes metal on making tokens. I don't got them, they was in the draw separate an' I didn't get lucky with them."

Richak examined the pouch. It was made of dark-green leather with a stamped design of interlocking lozenges. It held a kerchief, a comb, a key and a token that would let someone into the inner city.

"These yours?" asked Richak.

"Yes."

"I believe you," said Richak after studying Osir for a moment or two. "You're too frightened to lie."

He tossed the pouch back to Osir saying, "You can keep it. I want to know what happened to the things that were in it. Tell me who got them."

Osir reluctantly named two more of the Neyen servants. *They'll be angry but they'll know I don't have a choice.*

"Got anything else to tell me?"

Osir sighed inwardly. *Guess I gotta tell him. The God knows what he'd do if he catches me lying or hiding something from him.* He took a necklace from around his neck and dropped it on the table. "Got this too," he said. "It talks."

Richak started to reach for it but paused, "What do you mean, 'It talks'?"

"What I said. Touched it an' voice told me it would bring me luck."

Richak's scowl frightened Osir but he found some courage and insisted, "Not lyin'. It did talk. Pick it up and you'll see."

"If it told you you're in luck it was right," said Richak, "you are. You've cooperated nicely so you can have this." He took something out of his own pouch and tossed it in Osir's direction. "It will get you one favour from anybody in the Three Flowers. You can go now. Go on, get out."

Osir scrabbled on the floor to pick up the object Richak had thrown. It was a disc of deer antler with three crosses burnt into one side. "Thank you," he bowed low and repeated, "Thank you, thank you." Then he opened the door and left the room as quickly as he could.

Richak picked up the flagon, poured himself more wine and took a mouthful. He studied the necklace wondering why anybody would bother making an ornament out of a roughly rectangular piece of wood about the size of the last joint of his thumb. It was rough edged and discoloured as if it had been dipped in blood. He picked it up and almost dropped it again when a voice said, "I didn't promise him luck. What I told him was that I could help whoever's holding this."

Richak gasped. His grip on the piece of wood tightened and, in a slightly shaky voice, he asked, "Who are you? What are you? And what do you want?"

"That's a quick recovery," said the voice. "I'm impressed. People can be frightened by hearing a voice without an obvious source."

"I don't frighten easily," said Richak. "I'd never have ended up where I am if I did. Are you a ghost?"

"Not exactly – Don't worry, I'm not the revenant of someone you've killed."

Richak's hand shook slightly. "Then what are you? Tell me or I'll throw this necklace into the fire."

"I'm someone confined to this piece of wood by a daimon's revenge."

"Confined? By a daimon? What's your name?"

"I'm called Caseir."

"Kehsieh," whispered Richak. "Are you really Kehsieh?"

"That is my name. You seem to know it."

"Of course I do. Kehsieh is one of the Confined Gods."

"So you know who I am," said Caseir

Richak raised a clenched fist to shoulder level. "Great One, how may I serve?"

"Tell me what you know of the gods."

"But… "

"I want to know how the truth has become distorted over the years."

With a hand that wasn't too steady Richak reached for his glass and took a couple of mouthfuls before he started speaking. His voice settled quickly into the sing-song cadence of someone repeating a well-known tale.

"In the days before days at the beginning of the world, those who aspired to be gods argued among themselves. Some of them went elsewhere to make their own worlds. Others stayed in this world to contest among themselves for dominance. Two of the strongest, who we don't name, agreed to work together. Their alliance prospered and together they banished many would-be gods into the darkness at the edge of the world to become daimons. Some resisted and avoided exile, living precariously in the gaps between moments."

Richak hesitated, "Your pardon, Great One. I confess I have never understood that part. May I ask how there can be anything between one moment and the next?"

"Don't let it worry you," said Caseir. "I doubt if you could understand any explanation I could give. Carry on with your story."

Richak dipped his head, took another mouthful of wine and carried on speaking. "For many turnings of the world the last of the free gods were strong enough to resist the two we don't name. Then the two chose to give powers to men and made a truce with the daimons. Working together daimons, gods and men succeeded in imprisoning the six free gods. Lohkrah the Crafty was the first to be trapped and the loss of her strength and cunning was the turning point. One-by-one the others fell; Mueliss the Brilliant after Lohkrah; then Pronathu the Stalwart; Yvernis the Swift; Glorious Abrenli; and, last of all, Kehsieh the Great. Thus it has been for turnings of the world beyond counting. And thus it is!" Richak clenched his fist, raised it to shoulder level and bowed his head.

"Well spoken," said Caseir when Richak finished. "It sounds as if it's something you have said many times before. Are you a priest of the Confined Gods?"

Richak looked up and said, "I have that honour."

"Talk to me of the one who ruled here."

Richak spat. "He is no true god… " He fell silent, shook his head and, rather hesitantly, continued, "Your pardon, Greatness. You speak as if he no longer rules."

"His was the body in the Presence Chamber with its throat cut."

Richak gaped for a moment then asked, "Who killed him?"

"It was Muhan cra Neyen who actually cut his throat, although it was the woman Osir described who defeated him and gave Muhan the opportunity."

"Great One, may I ask what she is called."

"Her name is Anarya."

Again Richak clenched his fist and raised it to shoulder level. "She will be revered as a saint by the faithful. She gives us hope that one day we may free ourselves from the domination of the Twenty-three as they have been freed from the rule of the false god."

"You're planning rebellion," said Caseir.

"The followers of the Confined Gods have been planning another uprising for many years."

"Another?"

"Forgive me, Greatness. How is it that you don't know of the previous rebellions?"

"I have been imprisoned and it is only recently I have been able to touch the world in this way. Tell me about them."

Richak drank some more wine, rubbed his scar and said, "The followers of the Confined Gods outnumber the Twenty-three Families and their servants many times over. But they have talents and we do not. We can't stand against them when they attack us with Pyromancers and Scratchers and the like. The last revolt was before I was born but I know the stories of how more than four thousand of the faithful died in an attack on the inner city and managed to kill just five members of the Families and about fifty of their servants. We hope and pray for deliverance, but in reality we have little chance of success."

"You included the servants among your enemies," said Caseir.

"I did. They should be on our side, as should all the people of the outer city, but almost all of the servants, and many of those outside the wall, have abandoned the Confined Gods and now worship with the Families."

"What will they do when they realise their god is dead?"

"Whatever the Families do, I expect. I don't know what that will be," Richak said.

"Hmm. I must think about this. In the meantime, wear the necklace with the wood touching your skin. Nobody else will hear me when I speak to you. I will be able to hear anyone nearby, however quietly they speak, and I will tell you if they say anything of interest."

THE ROYAL PALACE
IN CARREGIS

The quiet taps on the door sounded tentative and, unlike the usual peremptory knock, they weren't followed by someone entering without waiting for an invitation.

Sulereath III was sitting in the most comfortable of the four chairs in the room, close to the fire because the warm day had become much cooler in the last chime and a half. The small table beside his chair held the debris from his evening meal and a carafe of pale wine. Next to that was a rack of scrolls and he had another scroll unrolled across his lap.

The firelight glinted off his bright red hair as he looked up in surprise at the still closed door. He let the scroll roll up and tucked it carefully into its worn leather case before calling, "Come."

The door opened and Sulereath's heart sank as the commander of Duke Wurauf's guard entered. The man copied the contemptuous way the Duke treated him and ignored or snubbed him at every opportunity.

The commander's black enamelled cuirass gleamed. Unusually he was carrying his helmet with the red horsehair plume in the crook of his arm rather than wearing it. He went down on one knee and lowered his head.

Now thoroughly puzzled at this uncharacteristic behaviour Sulereath said, "Stand."

The man obeyed and waited in silence.

He's waiting for permission to speak! What is going on? Is this some sort of game Wurauf's put him up to?

"What is it?"

"Your Majesty, I bring grave news. Duke Wurauf has been murdered."

Sulereath jumped to his feet, narrowly avoiding

knocking over the rack of scrolls, "What! How?"

"It's not clear what happened, Your Majesty. The Duke and Master Jynder went to his study at about the sixteenth chime. Four of the guard escorted them as usual and they took their normal positions just outside the door. They didn't hear anything from inside the room and nobody else went in until two servants arrived to serve the Duke his evening meal at the usual time. They found the Duke dead in his chair with blood everywhere. He had been stabbed. This was lying on his chest."

The commander handed a piece of parchment to the king. "Forgive me, Your Majesty, I could not help reading what it says."

Sulereath looked at it blankly then realised he was holding it the wrong way up. He turned it round and read:

> Your Majesty, it gives me great pleasure to offer the death of Duke Wurauf to you as a delayed birthday present. I can also confirm that another member of the Three, one Jynder, is dead too, although I cannot offer his body as proof. The last of the Three will be dead soon. You are free of their domination. Trust in Huler and rule wisely.

It was unsigned.

"Where's Jynder?" he asked.

"I do not know, Your Majesty. The guardsmen reported that he went in with the Duke but he wasn't in the room when the servants went in. Nor had he left the room through the door. The guardsmen say there were two of them standing outside the door the entire time. I believe them. They wouldn't have risked His Grace's anger by leaving their posts."

"The window. Jynder was thin enough to get through one."

"No, Your Majesty. It's not possible. I tried to open it. The frame is warped and the window is jammed shut. I don't know how Master Jynder could have got out of the room without being seen."

"A Stealther could have."

"Yes, Your Majesty, but Jynder wasn't a Stealther. And I don't see how even a Stealther could have got into and out of the room without bumping into at least one of the guardsmen and giving himself away."

"There must be some other way into the room. A secret passage perhaps."

The commander shook his head. "Secret passages are more common in stories than in real life, Your Majesty. Of course we will sound the walls and search but I would be extremely surprised to find one."

Sulereath read the parchment again, this time noticing and carefully avoiding touching a fresh-looking bloodstain in one corner. He shook his head. "This suggests that Jynder is also dead."

"It does, Your Majesty, but there is no proof."

The king paced around the room thinking furiously. *It can't be some elaborate plot, can it? I've dreamed of being free of Wurauf for years. I've got to assume it's real. Now is my chance to take control of my life.* He stopped in front of the commander to say, "I think I will accept what it says about Jynder and about the third of the Three. That means there is another death to come."

"Your Majesty," said the commander, "I know that Count Graumedel is the other member of the Three…"

"How do you know that? They kept it secret."

"When Duke Wurauf brought the Count to see you recently I overheard them and Jynder say something that made it obvious. They didn't know I could hear them."

"That's potentially valuable information. Haven't you tried to take advantage of your knowledge?"

"Your Majesty, I am aware of the way Duke Wurauf

treated you. I would like to say that I regret my part in that treatment. I had to follow his orders. I swear I am loyal to you and the House of Ereath. May I prove my loyalty by not taking any action that might prevent Count Graumedel's death?"

Sulereath looked at him. *He's humiliated me many times. It was probably at Wurauf's bidding, but I can't trust him. I don't believe in his protestations of loyalty. They're just too – too self-serving. He must think I'm foolish if he expects me to fall for that. He's just looking after himself.* However, he nodded and said, "That seems eminently sensible."

"Then, Your Majesty, may I congratulate you on your escape from the domination of the Three and hope that your reign will be long and peaceful."

"Thank you. Now, please, leave me to think."

The commander bowed himself out of the room.

Sulereath stood in front of the fire gazing into the flames and trying to imagine life without Wurauf. While he stood there a log burned through, the fire slumped into a new configuration with a quiet crackle and released a puff of pine-scented smoke. He nodded as he realised he could now choose his own advisers and restore what had become Wurauf's mansion to its proper function as the royal palace.

I think the first thing to do is to get help from the temple. Then I'm going to dismiss the Duke's Guard and replace them with men I can trust – maybe I can recruit from Graumedel's guard, they've never slighted me.

O

"His Reverence, Rupesc, head of the Brotherhood of Huler."

The guardsman standing at the door, still in the red and black of Duke Wurauf's livery rather than the green and silver of the House of Ereath, stepped aside to allow a middle-aged priest into Sulereath's study.

He could have been any priest except that his tunic was

the finest quality linen and the sun symbol embroidered on it, in gold thread not silk, was more elaborate than most.

He bowed and said, "You requested my presence. How may I serve Your Majesty?"

Sulereath waved everyone but Rupesc out of the room, then stood, walked over to Rupesc and knelt in front of him. "I want to thank you," he said.

"For what, Your Majesty?"

"For ending the rule of the Three."

Rupesc looked puzzled. "I do not understand, Your Majesty."

The king stood again. "When we spoke at the banquet a few weeks ago I asked about the function of the Stealthers in avenging injustices. You told me that the temple sometimes acts through them when the law can't."

"I remember."

"I asked you to have the Stealthers kill the Three. Now that that has happened I want to... You look surprised, Your Reverence. Do you mean that it wasn't a Stealther who killed Duke Wurauf and the others?"

"I am aware of the death of the duke," said Rupesc. "It has been widely reported and has caused quite a stir; the newsmongers are talking of little else. As for the other members of the Three, their secrecy was effective and I do not know who they are, or were if they are indeed dead."

Sulereath started pacing around the room. He avoided the other chairs and the rack of scrolls without noticing them. *I've got to confide in somebody. Who could be more trustworthy than the head of the Brotherhood?* He turned to look at Rupesc and told him, "Count Graumedel was one of the Three."

"I see," said Rupesc. "I have heard that he was found murdered this morning."

"Yes, and in the same way as Wurauf. He was stabbed while apparently alone in a room that no one could enter unobserved. Whoever killed him must have been invisible. That's why I thought Stealthers must be involved."

"That does sound like a reasonable assumption. However, the Brotherhood has not asked the Stealthers to act."

Sulereath stopped in mid-stride. His head jerked round and he stared at Rupesc in surprise. He had been so sure he had solved the mystery. With an effort he cleared his mind. He gestured towards a chair. "Come and sit, Your Reverence. We have a puzzle to solve."

A bell summoned a servant who brought wine for them then left again.

Rupesc looked at the rich ruby red of the wine. He sniffed it and smiled at the complex aroma, full of fruit and wood smoke. When he took a sip he recognised it as one of the best vintages Firten had produced in the last ten years. He paused a moment to savour the wine before asking, "Who was the third of the Three?"

"His name was Jynder. He wasn't a noble. In fact he appeared to be one of Wurauf's employees. Wurauf made some comments about him when he first presented him to me. From what he said I believe Jynder was a powerful magic user, but I never learned what his talent was. He has disappeared. The last time Wurauf was seen alive Jynder was with him but no one has seen him since then. This was found on Wurauf's body," he told Rupesc, handing the piece of parchment to him. "It gives me reason to think Jynder is dead too."

Rupesc's eyebrows rose as he studied the message. "Jynder! I don't know that name. I'll start a search for information about him. If he did hold one of Huler's gifts there will be a record in the archives of the temple and there's bound to be someone who knows of him."

"I need your help, Your Reverence. The rule of the Three is broken. My ancestor signed a document giving away the authority of the House of Ereath to the three dukes who were on his regency council. They, in turn, passed that power down over the years to their children, or whoever they chose to succeed them. Now, with all of them dead and nobody named to follow any of them, there is an opportunity for me to re-establish the rule of the House of Ereath."

"Pardon me, Your Majesty. How do you know they haven't made arrangements for a new Three to take over?"

"Because Wurauf made a mistake. He had no close family and told me Jynder was to be his replacement as leader of the Three. The evening after Wurauf introduced him to me as one of the Three, Jynder celebrated a little too much and spoke a little too freely. I overheard him tell Wurauf that he was only interested in power and didn't care what happened after he died because he wouldn't be around to see it."

"That seems to account for two of them," said Rupesc, "and it's fairly well known that Graumedel wasn't on good terms with any of his family and refused to nominate an heir. With such a gap in the existing power structure of the kingdom you should be able to appear as a legitimate ruler, but you will have to act quickly and decisively."

Sulereath rose from his chair, signalling Rupesc to stay seated. He started pacing around the room again. "That's where I need your help, Your Reverence. The Three kept me isolated from the mechanics of ruling and I am ill prepared for the task. I have met a few priests over the last five years who have encouraged me to discover myself. They have also provided me with books and scrolls about my ancestors, at what must have been great risk to themselves. Wurauf would not have been pleased to know what I was studying. From my reading I have learned a little about politics, but I know I am still woefully ignorant. I am aware that, during the rule of the Three, I have been seen as weak. That must change."

Sulereath hesitated briefly then carried on to say, "The deaths of the Duke and the Count have left large gaps in the hierarchy of the kingdom. I need to decide who fills these gaps and I am going to need advice. I think I should take it slowly but I am afraid that doing so will make me look indecisive. Can you help me? Will you suggest someone from the temple to be one of my advisers?"

"I would be happy to do so," replied Rupesc. "You are in a position of privilege and power. Huler expects such people to have personal integrity and responsibility towards those they lead. For you that is the entire kingdom. It's an awesome task, but one within your capabilities or Huler would not have placed you in such a position. My probable successor as head of the Brotherhood would be a good choice. His name is Grovaen. I will send him to you."

A HOUSE IN GREENBANK IN CARREGIS

The two people standing glowering at each other in the musty atmosphere of a spacious but rather shabby room in Greenbank were cousins. They looked rather like each other – tall and thin with prominent noses and chins, and mud-coloured hair. Harviel's hair was piled up on her head and held in place by a collection of silver and ebony combs while Nurmed's fell to his shoulders in an undisciplined tangle. Both were twenty-seven years old, Harviel being the older by all of six days.

"Didn't really expect you to come," said Nurmed.

"Don't know why I bothered," replied Harviel. "It wasn't exactly a gracious invitation."

"Well, now that you're here we'd better talk. Have a seat. I suppose you'll want tea – or would you rather have avit?"

"Tea will do. Lemon and mint if you can manage that, but I'll drink anything that's not too sweet. You can keep the avit for yourself – from what I hear you're rather fond of it."

A young woman wearing a tight bodice that pushed her breasts up and left them half exposed answered the bell. Harviel sat down on one of the rather threadbare chairs. From her expression it wasn't very comfortable. They sat in silence until the servant returned with a glass of tea and a mugful of avit.

Harviel wrinkled her nose at the smell of the strong spirit. "I suppose she's your current bedfriend," she said as the servant left. "How much are you paying her to put up with you?"

"At least I have one," said Nurmed.

Harviel ignored the jibe, took a sip of her tea and asked, "What have we got to talk about?"

"Which of us succeeds uncle, of course. What else? You must have realised that when you decided to accept my invitation. He's never actually named an heir. It's got to be one of us, unless you think that half-sister of yours has a claim."

"Of course she doesn't. She's only – eight, I think – much too young," said Harviel. "There's really nothing to discuss. My father was older than your mother so he'd have been next in line and me after him. I'm Count of Carregis now."

"You can't be Count. You're a woman."

"Countess, then, don't be pedantic. What I'm called doesn't matter. Uncle always told me I would be his heir."

"Liar!" said Nurmed, "I shared his box at the arena last Birthday and he told me it would be me. He promised he would introduce me to the king."

"But he didn't, did he?"

Nurmed scowled, took a large mouthful of avit then muttered, "The king never came to the arena that day so he couldn't."

"Uncle never liked you. Just look at this – this place he allowed you to live in," said Harviel, pointing at the threadbare rug and the cracks in the wall plaster. "It's not a very impressive residence for a future Count, is it?"

"I suppose yours is better."

"At least it's an estate, not a crumbling ruin in a low-class area that's seen better days."

"An estate! You mean a pigsty."

"You're just jealous that I have land and you don't."

"Why would I want to live like pigs?"

"Quarenna's tits! I don't know why I ever agreed to meet you. We haven't spoken a civilised word to each other for two years, ever since I caught you fucking my maid."

"And you resent that because you wanted her yourself. You never did get her, did you? What a shame, she was good."

"You disgust me. I'm leaving." Harviel stood and

moved towards the door.

"Don't you want a chance to prove you're as good as she was?"

Harviel spun round and practically spat at Nurmed. "That does it. I'll throw you out of here as soon as I can, and that'll be as soon as the ink's dry on my charter as Countess."

"Dear Harviel, you're deceiving yourself. You're not going to be Countess," said Nurmed. "Didn't you wonder why I invited you when the only thing we have to talk about is the inheritance and we both know we'll never agree about which one of us should get it."

Nurmed walked over to the chair Harviel had been sitting in, bent down and picked something up. "I've got what I wanted. You see, I have a friend who's a Daimoner. He's promised me that if I can give him something of yours he'll be able to set a daimon on you. I'll give him this comb you dropped if you don't agree to step down and let me be the next Count of Carregis.

Harviel's face went white under her makeup, the rouge on her cheeks standing out lividly against the pallor. "I don't believe you. You don't have any friends."

"Oh, you believe me all right, or at least you have to behave as if you do. You're not going to risk finding out that I really do have friends. The one you particularly need to know about is called Jynder."

Harviel looked blank for a moment, then she started laughing. She pointed at Nurmed as if he was the butt of a joke, evidently enjoying the mystified expression on his face.

"Huler's beard! A Daimoner is no laughing matter. What's got into you?" asked Nurmed.

Between giggles, Harviel said, "You really don't know? Don't you ever get out and hear the newsmongers, or do you spend so much time drinking and dreaming that you don't know what's going on out there in the real world?"

"What are you talking about?"

"That 'friend' of yours, Jynder. He's too busy looking

after himself to be bothered with a nobody like you. He's suspected of being involved in the death of Duke Wurauf and has gone missing."

"But… "

"That comb isn't going to do you much good, is it? But I've got to say thank you. You've given me an idea. I don't know any Daimoners. However, I do know a couple of Scratchers and I'm sure I can persuade one of them to take care of you for me if I ask nicely enough. Goodbye, Nurmed."

A MANSION ON THE ROCK
IN CARREGIS

"We need to talk, Nasuren. Come with me." Praukel turned and left the room his secretary used for an office. He could hear the faint drag of Nasuren's stiff leg on the carpet as he led him along the corridor to his own study.

He sat down behind his desk, carefully arranged the folds of his long tunic so that the crisp linen wouldn't crease and waited. Nasuren stopped at the door.

"Come in, come in. There's some fresh greenberry tea over there," Praukel said, pointing at a table in one corner of the room. "That is your favourite isn't it? It should be ready. Pour a glass for each of us and have a seat."

Nasuren looked surprised at the invitation. He did as asked, then perched cautiously on the edge of a chair and took a sip of the peppery astringent brew.

"Have you heard the news, Nasuren?"

"I am afraid I do not know what news you mean, master."

"About Duke Wurauf, of course. I would have thought his spymaster would know by now that he's dead."

Nasuren's head jerked up. He slopped some of the hot tea on to his hand, winced and put his hand to his mouth.

"Don't worry. I've known ever since you came to work for me that your allegiance was to Wurauf."

"How?"

"You told me yourself. You won't remember sitting in that chair before, although you have done so at least once a week since you started working here. You've told me everything you told Wurauf and then forgotten doing so thanks to a potion in the tea."

Praukel smiled at the expression on Nasuren's face as he studied the glass in his hand. "I know he gave you a potion supposed to prevent you giving away his secrets. It didn't work. I am a much stronger Chemer than whoever made that potion for him and, in a contest with the one I made, it's quite ineffective. By the way, don't worry about drinking the tea. This time it doesn't have any additions."

"Why are you telling me this?" asked Nasuren.

"Because I want to know who you will serve now that he's dead."

Nasuren sighed and shook his head, "I don't know, master. I am waiting to see what will happen."

"You mean he hadn't planned for his own death. Considering the state of his health that seems improvident. And most unlike him."

Nasuren shook his head. "He did make plans. He told me to offer my services to another of the Three."

"Jynder, I suppose."

Nasuren looked startled. "How do you know Jynder was one of the Three?"

"Wurauf told you, and my potion made sure you told me everything that Wurauf said."

"Yes, master. It was Jynder he suggested that I serve after his death."

"Interesting predicament for you. Jynder has vanished, may well be dead, and is under suspicion of having killed Wurauf. Not somebody it would be safe to serve, even if he lives and you can find him."

Nasuren nodded in agreement and said nothing.

"Do you know why Wurauf wanted you in my household?"

"I think it was because he disliked you and wanted me to spy on you in addition to my other intelligence gathering duties. He did say that planting me in your service would be 'appropriate', although I'm not sure what he meant by that."

"Dislike is far too feeble a description. We hated each other. I'm not going to bother telling you why and it doesn't matter in any case. You were placed in an impossible position by his stupidity. Given the situation you were in you have impressed me. I would like to continue employing you as my secretary and to add spymaster to your duties."

Nasuren looked up and made eye contact with Praukel for the first time. "You would trust me, master?"

"Of course I would. Before you leave this room you will drink one of two potions. Either the one which carries death if you break your oath of obedience and secrecy, or the one which will make you forget this conversation as you have forgotten many others. Which is it to be?"

Nasuren didn't hesitate. "Learning people's secrets is my passion, master. I will use it in your service."

"Good. That's settled. What I want you to do is help me be appointed Duke of Carrh. Becoming Wurauf's successor will give me great satisfaction, and a sort of revenge."

"Forgive me, master. I'm not sure that's possible. I can see two stumbling blocks."

"And they are?"

"For one thing, the talented may not hold political office."

"Let me worry about that. I don't think it's insurmountable. What's the second?"

"I doubt if the other dukes would take kindly to a commoner like yourself inheriting the most important duchy in the kingdom."

"Wurauf must have had plans to deal with that."

"Yes, master, he had two plans. One was to adopt Jynder officially as his heir and let him succeed to the Duchy."

"I don't think the other dukes would be any happier with that. Jynder is, or was, as common as they come."

"No, master. I didn't think so either. That's why I recommended the second plan."

"Which was?"

"To invite Count Graumedel to join the Three with a view to him succeeding to the ducal throne in due course."

"And, of course, that's no longer possible," said Praukel.

"No, master."

"The question of my being a commoner is not an issue. It's not something that's well known, and you're probably not aware of it, but Wurauf and I were related. Admittedly the relationship was distant, but I do have noble blood. We shared an ancestor four generations ago. Part of the reason for our hatred of each other dates all the way back to her. Realistically, there is little to choose between the way she and her children treated each other and I'm not going to try to justify anything that happened.

"I know of only three people who are more closely related to Wurauf than I am. One of the tasks I have for you is to dispose of them, search for others and get rid of any you find."

"I understand, master. I can deal with that."

"I felt sure you would be able to."

"I would like to swear an oath to you now, master. And start the hunt for your lost relatives."

THE ROYAL PALACE

Duke Latisec, a hefty man beginning to develop a paunch, bullied his way into Wurauf's mansion demanding to speak to him. He was passed from guardsman to servant and from one servant to another until he ended up in the south gallery. The servant who had led him there muttered "Please wait here, Your Grace," and quickly vanished leaving the duke looking out across the lake.

Latisec turned away from the view. He wasn't interested in the squabbling waterfowl and was growing angry at being passed from servant to servant and moved from room to room without ever getting to see Wurauf.

A short, rotund woman appeared, ducked her head briefly in Latisec's direction and said, "Your Grace, I am Daersi, mistress of the household."

"About time someone with authority came to meet me. What's going on? I've travelled for days for a meeting with Wurauf. He's expecting me. Why haven't I been taken to see him?"

"I'm surprised you haven't heard, Your Grace," said Daersi. "The news has been all over Carregis. Duke Wurauf can't see anyone – he's dead."

Latisec gasped at the unexpected news. "I suppose his bad chest's caught up with him at last."

"No, Your Grace, he was murdered."

Latisec went pale. "Murdered? When? Who by?"

"Day before yesterday, Your Grace. Who did it is a mystery. He was stabbed but there was nobody else in the room at the time."

"You mean he killed himself! I don't believe it. He wasn't the type."

"I *did* say he was murdered, Your Grace. The only

blade of any description in the room was a penknife and there's no way he could have inflicted those wounds on himself with that."

"Somebody's investigating this I hope."

"Yes, Your Grace."

"Bring whoever it is here."

"He is attending the king, Your Grace. I can't interrupt them."

"Then take me to the king."

"I'm sorry, Your Grace. His Majesty does not wish to be interrupted when meeting his advisers."

"I am one of the dukes of the realm. You cannot keep me from the king."

Daersi shrugged. She had been a servant of Duke Wurauf's for close on thirty years, starting as a scullery maid and rising to her present post. She was used to people attempting to intimidate her. It was a long time since any had succeeded.

"Your Grace, I will ensure that the king is informed of your presence as soon as his meeting is finished. In the meantime, you may ring the bell if you wish for refreshments." She walked out leaving Latisec spluttering behind her.

O

Wurauf's mansion had once been the royal palace and Sulereath was determined to make it serve that function again. At first he wasn't sure in which room he would meet Duke Latisec. He did know it wasn't going to be the ducal throne room. Although it had been once been the throne room of the House of Ereath, it had been altered over the years to display the heraldry of the Dukes of Carrh. He didn't want to look at the red bear any more than absolutely necessary. The room would have to be redecorated before he would use it.

After some thought he chose as his audience chamber an elegantly plain room with colour washed walls, a few painted screens depicting birds and flowers, and a sinuous pattern of green tiles on the floor. An open window admitted the fresh scents of mint, thyme, basil and others from the herb garden. Sulereath looked around the chamber and thought, *This will do nicely.*

Chairs with the pelican emblem of the House of Ereath had been gathered from various other rarely used rooms. They were a bit shabby but at least they showed the correct heraldry. Four chairs stood in a row facing one that was slightly elevated and supplied with a footstool.

Three of the chairs were occupied by the first advisers Sulereath had chosen. He had accepted Rupesc's suggestion and appointed Grovaen from the Brotherhood of Huler. A short, slightly chubby man, he sat there looking comfortable, combing his fingers through his full ginger beard. Sulereath had also asked for a recommendation from the Inner Circle of the Daughters of Quarenna: Jaenis, a frail-looking elderly woman whose sparse white hair peeked out from under the green and gold headscarf of a priestess, had been sent as their representative.

The third adviser was the new commander of the Royal Guard. Sulereath had felt that all of Wurauf's guardsmen had learned to be scornful of him and that he couldn't trust them. He had dismissed all of them. Replacing them had cost him some thought before deciding that Graumedel's guard hadn't had time to learn contempt. One of them, called Fedic, had been spoken of very highly by his colleagues. Sulereath had offered him command of the new Royal Guard and given him free rein to recruit as many men as he thought necessary.

Sulereath was sitting on the substitute for a throne when Latisec was announced. His appearance in Carregis had been an unwelcome surprise to Sulereath. He hadn't known Wurauf expected him. All their previous encounters had been with Wurauf present and treating him as insignificant. He wondered what Latisec would be like knowing that Wurauf was dead.

The duke strode into the audience chamber and inclined his head briefly in Sulereath's direction before heading towards the one vacant chair.

"That is not how you greet your king, my lord," said Sulereath, "and I did not invite you to be seated."

Latisec stopped and looked directly at the king with an air of surprise.

"You should kneel, my lord. It is customary."

"I've never knelt to you before, boy."

"You will from now on, and you will address me with respect if you wish to keep your duchy. Wurauf is dead and so are the other members of the Three. The House of Ereath rules again, and I am king."

Latisec looked blank for a moment then said, "How can you know the Three are dead when their identities are kept secret?"

"You are wrong, my lord. Of course I know who they were. I was forced to deal with them frequently and I assure you they are all very dead."

Latisec scowled, put his hands on his hips and said, "The original Three were your great-grandfather's regents, the Dukes of Alrem, Carrh and Voro. I am a direct descendant of Lurindt, the Duke of Alrem at the time. I inherit his authority as described in the Regency Charter."

Sulereath shook his head. "Again you are wrong, my lord. No Duke of Alrem has been a member of the Three since the death of Lurindt. Apparently the others did not trust his son, your grandfather, and replaced him with the Duke of Geverd who was more amenable to their control. Since then whenever one of the Three died the survivors chose a replacement who suited them, not necessarily the obvious heir. The tradition of secrecy about the membership of the Three started with the appointment of the first non-noble member only nineteen years after the regency council was established. I doubt if you know how many members there have been, dominating my family over four generations. I do. You probably don't even know that Three has at times been a misnomer and they have occasionally numbered as few as two or as many as five. A record naming them all has been found among Wurauf's papers." He paused, smiled and added, "You are not on it, my lord, nor are any of your family since Lurindt."

Sulereath enjoyed the stunned look on Latisec's face for a few moments before adding, "I require you to kneel and swear allegiance to me."

There was a long pause.

"Well, my lord. I am waiting."

At a glance from Sulereath, Fedic rose and took a step towards Latisec with his hand on the hilt of his sword.

Looking sullen, Latisec knelt at Sulereath's feet and muttered, half under his breath, "I am Your Majesty's servant, holding the office of Duke of Alrem by your leave. I swear that I will discharge this office to the best of my ability."

"Then I confirm you in your rank as one of the dukes of the kingdom. Rise, my lord. I appreciate that you must spend most of your time in Alrem but whenever you are in Carregis your rank entitles you to a seat among my advisers."

"I thank Your Majesty," said Latisec through gritted teeth. "I came to Carregis at the behest of Duke Wurauf to discuss issues of trade and tariffs. With his death I am unable to do so but I will stay here for a few days before returning home. I am, of course, at your service."

"Thank you, my lord. I hope you will stay long enough to participate in the next meeting of this council, which will be in three days' time."

"I will do so, Your Majesty."

Sulereath looked around the room and said, "This meeting is at an end. Thank you all for your advice."

Latisec bowed and left before any of the others moved from their seats.

"Your Majesty," said Grovaen, "I would not trust that man. I know he used the correct form of words but it's a weak oath as it does not invoke Huler. I suspect he may try to hide behind the exact words of the oath and ignore its spirit."

Jaenis and Fedic agreed with Grovaen's assessment.

Sulereath nodded. "If he is false then he will pay for it. I will not be merciful."

HOUSE NEYEN

Anarya woke up slowly feeling very comfortable. "Mmmm," she murmured, stretching and turning over, ready to go back to sleep. The movement bunched up the sheets, pushed her face into the pillow and she smelled pine when she inhaled. *Pine?* she thought, *This isn't my bed! Where am I?*

She opened her eyes. Yisul was standing by the bedside smiling down at her. Anarya tried the Oversight, saw a brilliant orange aura surrounding Yisul and relaxed.

She tried to sit up, but Yisul pushed her firmly back down again and said, "You must rest. Give yourself more time to recover."

Anarya tried to recall what had happened. Something of the events in the temple came back to her. *How can I be here? I collapsed, wondering if I'd ever wake up – or if I'd be burnt-out. What happened after I stole The God's talent?*

She couldn't remember.

Yisul said, "I will forgive you for exhausting your talent again, Anra my love, but this has to be the last time."

This doesn't really feel like talent exhaustion, Anarya thought. She reached up, pulled Yisul down on top of her and held her tight. "What happened, Yisa?" she asked between kisses. "I thought I was dead."

"No, my love, don't say that. I was afraid you might be dying. You have been unconscious for three days. I was so worried. I thought I had lost you."

"But..."

"I do not know what you did to defeat The God. One moment he was throwing thunderbolts, the next he was crumpled in a sobbing heap on the floor. You said, 'Kill him', then you collapsed too. I couldn't reach your knife. I tried, but it was trapped under you and I was in chains. It was my father who took it and cut The God's throat."

"I don't understand," said Anarya. "Your father worshipped The God, didn't he? Why would he kill him?"

"Best if you wait until my father comes before asking questions like that. It's a complicated story."

"But…"

"I have questions too," said Yisul. "For one thing, are you fully recovered?"

"I think so. I pushed myself farther than I ever have before. So far in fact that I thought I might be burnt out, if I survived at all."

Yisul frowned and asked, in a quavering voice, "You are not. Are you?"

"No. I feel slightly strange but I can see your aura, like always."

Yisul hugged Anarya tighter. "I am so relieved. You took such a risk coming to save me. That young man, Baram, who came with you. He's nice. Good-looking too. It is difficult to imagine him as the assassin who killed Caseir. He told me all about it – how you made a bargain with a daimon."

"Baram! I haven't even thought about him since I woke up. I remember him trying to tell me something during the fight. Where is he?"

"He left about a tenth ago to stretch his legs. At least one of us has been sitting with you all the time, waiting and hoping for you to recover. I am sure he will be back soon. Do you want something to eat?"

"That sounds like a wonderful idea. I'm starving."

Yisul stood and struck a gong standing beside the bed. Anarya took the opportunity to sit up and look around. The bedclothes were fine silk with decorative lace edgings. The bed itself was three or four times larger than her bed at home. Open windows let in a cool breeze and through them she could see the tops of trees. *Must be on an upper floor.*

A servant answered the summons. He was accompanied by two guardsmen in dark green tabards with scarlet piping. They were carrying drawn swords.

"Bring food," Yisul told the servant, "and tell my father that Lady Anarya is awake."

"Lady?" said Anarya after the servant left.

"Hush," replied Yisul. "That's how you are known here. Do not argue about it."

"Why the guard?" asked Anarya.

Before Yisul could answer a slim man with a thin moustache and long brown hair worn in a loose braid entered.

Anarya said, "Baram," and held out her arms to him.

He responded to the invitation tentatively and was enveloped in a hug. Blushing furiously, he detached himself and backed away. *He's embarrassed! Well, I suppose I can understand that. I'm not wearing much, and what I have got on is almost transparent.*

"Are you well?" asked Anarya at the same moment as Baram said, "How are you feeling?"

"Why the guard?" Anarya asked again after they assured each other of their well-being.

"To make sure you're safe," said Baram. "There have been two attempts on your life already, one before you even got here and the other yesterday by a servant who tried to get past the guards screaming that you're a traitor and blasphemer. Lord Neyen is taking no chances."

"You should not have told her that," said Yisul. "Now she will worry."

"She needs to know," said Baram. He turned to Anarya, "A lot of people are happy that The God is dead but there are some who hate you for what happened."

"What did happen? I can't remember much."

Baram told her about the final few moments in the throne room. His description helped to clarify the events after her collapse.

"I thought I'd have to protect you from the man who took your knife, but I was wrong. Just as well, I wasn't too steady. I think that's because I wasn't touching you all the time when we came through the portal. I had dropped my own knife when I stabbed The God. I looked but I couldn't find it and I couldn't see another blade anywhere in the room…"

"You wouldn't," said Yisul. "Even though he believed he was adored The God would not permit the representatives of the Families to carry edged weapons into the Presence Chamber."

"That doesn't make sense. Many of the talents are usable as weapons."

"True, my love," said Yisul, "but he does not seem to have considered that to be a problem."

"I suppose he wouldn't, he could always steal any talent used against him," said Anarya.

"Anyway," commented Baram, "I was wrong. Yisul's father used your knife on The God, not on you. It took me completely by surprise."

"Then I arranged for you to be conveyed here," said a new, rumbling, bass voice.

Anarya turned to see a richly-dressed man enter the room and bow to her. He was a little shorter than her but slightly taller than Yisul. Like Yisul he had pale, almost white, hair contrasting with very dark skin. *I remember him. He was in the temple. The God asked him if he had anything to say before he passed sentence on Yisa.*

"I am Muhan cra Neyen. I understand you are known as Anarya or Anra. Would you give me the favour of your full name?"

My full name? I never use it but I suppose he wants something more formal.

"In Katelish a woman's full name is her own followed by her mother's. So, as my mother's name is Kirsya, I am properly Anarya d'Kirsya. Although I prefer just Anarya."

Muhan bowed deeply. "Lady Anarya d'Kirsya, I am pleased at your recovery. I wish to thank you for two gifts. Firstly, for the life of my daughter, and secondly, for freeing us of the tyranny of that false god."

I don't understand, thought Anarya, *Didn't he believe*

in the god he worshipped? She dipped her head towards him and said, "Thank you, Lord Neyen. I hope you will pardon me if I seem somewhat confused."

"It is not surprising," said Muhan. "It is a complicated story." He looked around, moved a light wooden chair carved with flowers on the back and legs across to the bedside and sat down on its scarlet cushion. "It starts about thirty-five years ago when my uncle was Head of the House. He became sceptical about The God's claim that the people who were killed when he took their talents lived on in him."

"Much as I did," said Yisul.

"Indeed, Yisul. Without going into details of how it happened, my uncle discovered that the Heads of Shuth and Hivarn had similar misgivings. Together they started a conspiracy against The God and began recruiting other members of the Families into it. If I had realised how Yisul felt about The God I would have involved her in the plot. However, she concealed her true feelings so well that I did not know until she ran away."

"If I had known I would not have run."

"Then we would never have met," said Anarya.

"True," said Yisul. "Strange as it may seem, I do have something to thank The God for."

Muhan sighed. "Yisul, I can see your relationship with Lady Anarya d'Kirsya being a problem for some of the more conservative members of the Families." He shook his head and shrugged. "We will have to deal with that when it happens." He turned to look at Anarya again. "The conspiracy has spread slowly. It now numbers more than a hundred from nineteen of the Families."

"Recruiting must have been dangerous," said Baram. "Approaching the wrong person could have been disastrous."

"There was at least one occasion I am certain of, and I suspect there were others, when a member of the conspiracy killed someone she had approached and then herself rather than have the plot exposed."

"Surely, over all this time, some of the conspirators

must have been called to join The God," said Anarya.

Muhan nodded. "It has happened seven or eight times in the last five years. My daughter Gilearh was one of them. They all stayed true to their promise to submit rather than expose the conspiracy. The biggest risk was whenever The God took a Feeler into himself. If he had used that talent to investigate the emotions of a conspirator he would have realised how much they hated him. Fortunately, the loyalty of the Families was something he never seemed to think of querying."

"That seems odd."

"I suppose that hundreds of years of acceptance produced complacency."

Two servants, with an escort of guardsmen, brought a bowl of thick soup giving off a rich, meaty, garlicky aroma and a platter holding two pieces of flatbread wrapped around a mixture of spiced fish, cheese and olives.

"My daughter told me that you were likely to be hungry when you recovered," said Muhan. "I will leave you to eat in peace. We will talk again later. Yisul will tell you more." With that he bowed himself out of the room.

"This soup is good," remarked Anarya between spoonfuls, "Carry on. Tell me more while I eat."

"When it was obvious that The God was dead, my father took charge," said Yisul. "He had us moved here, to the Neyen mansion, and sent for healers to look after you and Baram."

"I didn't understand what he wanted at first," said Baram. "I don't speak Sitru but Caseir translated for me."

"Caseir! I can't hear him. I've lost my piece of wood. Have you got one?"

"Yes, here," said Baram, producing a fragment of wood strung on a leather cord from around his neck.

Anarya took it and asked, "Caseir, are you there?"

"Where else would I be?"

"Holy Quarenna be praised. It's good to hear you. I don't know what's happened to the piece of wood I had."

"It got thrown out with the rest of your clothes when

the healers tucked you up in bed," said Caseir. "I don't know where it is now. I can't feel it. It's too far away from this piece. Your old clothes were shared out among the servants almost as soon as they left the room. They seemed happy to get them, even if they were torn and scorched."

When Anarya told the others what Caseir had said, Yisul remarked, "They would be very happy. Cast-off clothing is wealth for any of the servants whatever its condition."

"Tell me more, Yisa. What's happened in the last three days?"

"I do not know much as I have stayed by your bedside. However, I understand that there is confusion among the Families. Naturally the members of the conspiracy are delighted. Of the others, most are stunned and are trying to come to terms with what happened. And, of course, there are some who still worship The God and expect him to return."

"I don't understand," said Anarya, "How can anybody still believe in the divinity of The God? Don't they realise his death proves he was just a man?"

"Several Families, most prominently the Guesyr, Pridhar and Widhis, were favoured by The God and given positions of authority and importance. They are the ones who are most reluctant to believe in his death."

They carried on talking until, about two chimes later, a servant arrived to deliver a folded and sealed sheet of parchment. Anarya read it aloud.

'To the Lady Anarya d'Kirsya, Muhan cra Neyen begs your forgiveness for not returning to your side. Much has happened since your recovery. A meeting of the Twenty-three has been arranged for the eighth chime tomorrow. You are invited to attend and I trust you will be able to do so. I will be very busy with preliminary discussions with some of the other Heads of Family and will be unable to meet with you again before then. My daughter will conduct you to the great hall of the Shuth Family where the meeting will be held. Your companion, Baram, is also invited.'

Anarya raised her eyebrows and looked at Yisul.

"Father must be very busy with arranging this meeting. He would not ignore you if this was not the case."

"Why can't the meeting be here?" said Baram. "There have already been attempts to kill Anarya, why go somewhere where she'll be exposed?"

"Oh," said Yisul. "You would not know. The great hall of Shuth is the traditional meeting place of the Families. The Shuth are mostly Scratchers and they have infused the walls of their great hall with spells for many generations. The spells do not stop people with passive talents, such as Voyanters and Feelers, from using their abilities, but they do prevent anyone using an active talent to injure anyone else in the room. The spells have proved their worth many times."

"Then I suppose we had better go," said Anarya.

"Indeed we must," said Yisul.

O

Yisul and Anarya were sitting quietly at ease in the reception room of Anarya's suite: a large well-appointed room decorated in pink and dove-grey, with four deep armchairs and a sofa. Doors led from it to two bedrooms, a balcony overlooking a garden, a private dining room and a room with a sunken bath.

A servant brought them a message. "Lady Lias cra Branidh begs the favour of a meeting with the Lady Anarya d'Kirsya."

"Good," said Yisul. "I asked my mother if she would come. You are about the same size as her and you are going to need clothes for the meeting tomorrow, unless you choose to use body paint."

"No! Absolutely not."

"It would not be inappropriate for a formal meeting."

"It would be as bad as being naked. I'd be so embarrassed. Awful enough if there's somebody there in body paint. I couldn't possibly do it myself."

Yisul's mother was as tall as Anarya and very similar

in build. Her skin was several shades lighter than Yisul's and her hair a tightly braided cap of light bronze. Anarya stood to greet her and they bowed to each other.

In a pleasant soprano, Lias cra Branidh said, "Thank you for all you have done for us. When I visited earlier you were unconscious and we were worried about you – I am pleased to see you on your feet. Yisul has asked me to find suitable clothing for you. Will you come with me?"

Anarya was awed by the splendid garments on display in Lias' wardrobe. She spent most of two chimes there examining them, exclaiming over their style, sophistication and quality, and trying some on.

"It is not essential that you wear Neyen colours," said Lias, "however Muhan and I would be pleased if you are willing to show your association with this House."

Eventually they settled on a sleeveless jacket made of the softest of white suede worn over a silk blouse dyed in the Neyen colours of green and scarlet. The soft wool of the charcoal-coloured, floor-length skirt was heavily embroidered with elaborately plumaged birds. Anarya recognised them as tree-dancers, the Neyen Family symbol, but she was surprised at the shimmering green and blue metallic colours. She had only seen the birds carved on a vurlo tile previously and hadn't realised they were so colourful.

HOUSE SHUTH IN JOTUK

Anarya followed Yisul through the main doors of the Neyen residence, held open for them by servants in the House's green and scarlet livery who were directed by a tall, slightly stooped man with sparse white hair and a bushy moustache.

"Are we going far?" she asked, seeing the carriage and pair standing at the bottom of the broad steps leading down from the door.

"No. It will only take about a sixth, maybe less. Shuth is one of the nearer Houses."

"If it's not that far we could walk."

Baram nodded in agreement.

"Certainly not!" Yisul sounded horrified. "Arriving on foot would give entirely the wrong impression. We have to uphold the dignity and prestige of Neyen."

"I suppose so," said Anarya. "It's just that I've seen nothing of Jotuk and I'm curious. Can't we at least use an open carriage?"

"There are none. You'll be able to get a good view through the window. I will tell the driver to take a roundabout route so you can see something of the city."

"I'd like that if it won't make us late."

"We have enough time to spare for a short detour."

They climbed into the carriage and settled into well-upholstered seats. It lurched into motion and followed the gravelled sweep of the drive in an arc away from the house.

Anarya caught her first sight of the outside of the building. Built of, or at least faced with, red granite, it was far larger than she had realised. It stood three storeys high with towers at the corners and a frontage of seven bays separated by marble pillars carved with the

Neyen tree-dancer.

Anarya and Baram looked around, fascinated by the architecture of Jotuk. The roofs of the buildings they passed were decorated with frequent spires and domes, all covered in brightly coloured tiles. Yisul pointed out the temple of The God, its dome adorned with concentric bands of gold and purple. Many of the tiles were dislodged around a hole punched through the wall on the south side, the only external evidence of the damage caused by the battle four days ago.

"I remember you saying the streets of Jotuk are crowded and can be dangerous," said Anarya, "but they don't look it. There aren't all that many people here."

Yisul looked surprised. "I was speaking of the outer city where most of the people live. This is the inner city. Only the Families live here, and the guardsmen, who have their own barracks. Everyone else lives outside the wall."

"Even the servants?" asked Baram.

"Yes, of course. They work for the Families but aren't members of them."

"I've seen a lot of servants. Must be eight or nine for every Family member."

"More," said Yisul. "You won't have seen the cleaners, cooks, scullery staff, gardeners and so on, only those who come into direct contact with Family members."

"The servants have to come and go every day?"

"Yes, except for the guard and a few of the senior servants. There are seven, or eight, in Neyen who are permitted to live in the House."

"What's the outer city like then?" asked Anarya. "Have we got time to take a look?"

"I suppose we could go that way," replied Yisul. She rapped on the roof. When the driver opened the hatch, she told him to take them to Derchler's Gate.

"We can't stop for long or we will be late," commented Yisul, "but you'll be able to see through the gate and get some idea of the outer city."

The driver changed direction, turned a corner and they

were soon running parallel to a stone wall about three men high.

"There are five gates through the wall. This is the largest one and gets most of the wagon traffic," Yisul told them when they came in sight of Derchler's Gate. "Only servants and suppliers bearing a token from one of the Houses are allowed through."

She rapped on the roof again and told the driver to pull off to one side.

Anarya and Baram looked out at an archway partially blocked by a cart. Several guardsmen in blue and black livery were inspecting its contents.

"The Houses take it in turn to provide gate guards. Those are the colours of House Monost," said Yisul in reply to Anarya's question.

People squeezed past the cart in both directions, those entering the inner city showing tokens, usually strung around their necks, to the guardsmen.

Beyond the gate they could see a crowded open space and a couple of fairly narrow streets leading from it.

"I see what you mean by crowded," said Anarya. "It's as bad as the Great Square in Carregis at Arenafest."

"The whole of the outer city is like that," said Yisul. "In some parts of it a family of six or eight would consider themselves fortunate to live in a room the size of the one you have in Carregis, and at least as many would be living on the roof and in the gutters around the building. Those are the dangerous areas where the *houln* are dominant."

"What are *houln?*" asked Baram, looking puzzled.

"In Katelish you would call them gangs, but they are more than that. Each one, and there are at least forty of them in the outer city, is a community, almost a separate domain. They all have their own rules, territory and power structure. There are often fights between rival *houln*. They can be very dangerous and members of the Families rarely go into the outer city. When we do it is with an armed escort, and usually with a Scratcher to provide a magic shield if necessary."

"Is everyone in the outer city a member of one of these *houln*?" asked Anarya.

"No, but many are. Some *houln* are reputed to have as many as five hundred members."

"Aren't there health problems with the sort of crowding you described?" asked Baram.

"Yes. There is often sickness and every few years there is a *purtirn* – a cleansing."

"A cleansing?" said Anarya. "What do you mean?"

"I am sorry, my love. Is that not the right word in Katelish? What do you call it when many become ill at once?"

"Ill? You mean an epidemic?"

"Yes. That is the word, I should have remembered. Many perish from bad water or lack of food. The last time it happened was a little more than seven years ago. There was a scare about a year and a half ago. Nothing came of it but it cannot be long now until there is another."

"Can't the Twenty-three Families do anything to help them?" asked Baram.

"What could we do? There are many more of them than there are of us. We do not grow food on our estates. In fact, we go hungry during a *purtirn*. The farmers stop sending food to the city because it would be stolen before getting here. We have to live on stored food. Each Family maintains a stockpile ready for such an event. Fortunately, the worst effects last only a few weeks and then things return to normal."

The driver opened the hatch to say, "Your pardon, Lady. I think we should move on. We are causing an obstruction."

"Very well."

As the carriage started moving again Anarya caught a glimpse of a fight at the gate. "What's happening over there?"

"There are always outers without tokens trying to break through the inspection cordon."

"What do they want?"

"Who knows?"

"Aren't you interested?"

"Why? They're outers, not important."

Anarya shook her head. Most of the time Yisa was kind and easy to get along with. Sometimes, she was *cranil* through and through; arrogant and apparently uncaring. It was the way she had been brought up.

O

Anarya was stunned by the size and opulence of the Shuth Family residence. It was almost as wide as the Neyen mansion and, to her amazement, even taller. Five storeys high, it had a central spire covered in yellow tiles soaring up another two. It occupied one side of a grassy open space, with elaborate flower beds defined by low hedges. A herd of about thirty small deer retreated into the cover of the surrounding woods as the carriage approached. Gilded carvings of roses and horseshoes framed the many windows. *I suppose they must be the Family emblems*, Anarya thought.

The motifs were repeated on the beaten bronze doors. Servants in brown and yellow livery opened the carriage doors. They bowed as Yisul, Anarya and Baram descended and escorted them into an atrium where the emblems were repeated on the gleaming parquet floor and on the magnificently carved blackwood staircase leading up to the great hall.

Anarya was expecting there to be twenty-three people at the meeting. She was surprised to find at least ten times that number. It wasn't just the Heads of Family who were present. The room was full of richly-dressed men and women wearing every colour imaginable. She noticed several floral perfumes, the scent of roses being the strongest.

She looked with her Oversight and saw auras around all of them; every talent except Sponger and Thiever was represented. She had never seen, or imagined, as many talented in one place. Some of them were very strong. Her skin tingled and she felt that she wanted to reach out and borrow some of the available talents. *I could pick any talent I want!* The combined brightness of all the auras was enough to make her stop using the Oversight.

She quickly noticed there were at least three distinct groupings of people in the room and, if the colours of their clothing were anything to go by, the groupings weren't always along Family lines. The hubbub of conversation gradually fell into silence when her arrival was noticed. People shifted around and sat down. The groupings changed and became more Family orientated, although there was still a considerable mixture.

Muhan cra Neyen met them and ushered Anarya to a row of three seats facing the audience. An old woman, with her thinning hair threaded with yellow sapphires and wearing a gown of cloth-of-gold, was sitting in the seat to the right. She stood and said, "Lady Anarya d'Kirsya, I am Cuhes cra Shuth, Head of this House. I am pleased to welcome you. Fear nothing while you are here as our guest."

Muhan indicated that Anarya should take the centre seat and he stood in front of the leftmost.

Yisul led Baram off to one side and they sat down away from the others.

Muhan started the meeting by saying, "As all of you know, the rule of The God is over. Some of you were present in the temple when he died..."

"When you killed him," a man's voice shouted out.

"Yes, Pevus. I killed him. I claim no special status or privilege for that. There were others present who would have done the same but the opportunity came my way and I took it."

A burly man in blue and white stood up from the middle of a large group mainly composed of three Families. He was red-faced and spluttering with fury as he shouted, "Godkiller! How dare you boast of your actions. Our God has cared for us for hundreds of years. I can't begin to imagine any punishment severe enough to fit your crime."

"Pevus cra Glinin. How can you be so stupid?" asked a

thin woman with a pinched face, "The God has been extending his own life for centuries by stealing our powers. He took our children, our friends and our relatives without giving us anything in return."

"He gave us the opportunity to achieve godhood."

"Huh!" snorted the woman. "Some of the people he 'took into himself' were strong personalities. Your uncle Calnus, who he took two years ago, was one such. Have you ever seen any sign in The God's behaviour, speech or expression that Calnus, or any of them, still existed within him? No, because they did not. Only The God persisted."

A young man, dressed in what Anarya thought was an unfortunate combination of yellow and pink, stood and said, "I've thought about this a lot in the last few days, Pevus, and I'm convinced he wasn't a true God. The very fact that he is dead is proof enough – or do you have some sort of explanation for that?"

Pevus cra Glinin blustered his way through an argument claiming it was only his body that was killed and that The God still existed and was worthy of their veneration. The speech was greeted by a mixture of jeers and cheers from the various factions.

Muhan waved his arms trying to silence the crowd. Slowly they stopped hurling abuse at each other and settled down again. He said, "We have one among us who can hardly be impressed by the behaviour of the ruling Families of Sitrelk. Our release from the tyranny of The God would not have been possible but for the efforts of this woman seated here beside me. Lady Anarya d'Kirsya is the true hero of the day."

The majority of the audience cheered loudly.

Voices mixed in with the cheers shouting "Hero! Hero!"

"Villain!"

"Murderer."

"Saviour."

"Heretic!"

"Hero! Hero!"

The noise level built and, gradually those shouting praise for Anarya drowned out those abusing her.

Muhan had trouble quieting the crowd again but, eventually, most people resumed their seats and the shouts and cheers died down.

A tall man dressed in black and silver stayed on his feet and waited until Muhan invited him to speak. "I was not present in the temple when The God was killed. It was my nephew Hessilt who was standing for Jerut. I understand he was taken into The God, but I know no more than that. All I have heard so far are second- or third-hand rumours and I would like to hear some details of what happened."

Muhan nodded. "Lord Carilt cra Jerut, I do not think we want to spend time now with a detailed description of the events in the Presence Chamber. I will give you a short version of events now, but will expand it for you in private later in as much detail as you wish. Essentially what happened is that this woman by my side, for her own reasons, came to Jotuk to save the life of my daughter Yisul."

Another voice, this time a strident, penetrating female one, broke in, "Your daughter has been heard to address this foreign whore as 'my love'. This relationship is an abomination and cannot be tolerated."

"The behaviour of my daughter is not an issue here. It can be discussed later if it is needful. All that is relevant at present is that Lady Anarya d'Kirsya fought a duel with The God. During it several members of the Families were either taken by The God or killed by the talents he used. Some of us survived only because Lady Anarya d'Kirsya shielded us."

"Carilt, your nephew was not the only one who died," called a shrill soprano voice. "Four other members of the Families did too."

"I know one of them was your father, Lady Frenuj cra Vilost," Muhan commented. "I am aware of all our losses and I grieve with you and the other Families who have lost members."

"That's easy for you to say, Muhan. Neyen lost nobody, in fact you regained a stray."

"Whose behaviour requires investigation and punishment," called another voice from the back of the room.

"Oh, do be quiet, Lord Guesyr," said Frenuj cra Vilost. "This meeting has something more important to discuss than the romantic foibles of one woman. We need to consider how the death of The God affects the Twenty-three Families."

Everyone tried to speak at once and the noise level soon made it impossible to hear what anyone was saying.

A scream silenced the hubbub. Pevus cra Glinin and everyone else in one of the groups moved quickly away from a woman in purple and white in their midst. She was lying on the floor thrashing about in convulsions. When she stopped twitching two men wearing the same colours picked her up and carried her from the room.

Cuhes cra Shuth stood and said, "I should not have to remind anyone that House Shuth does not permit any talent to be used for violence in this room. I hope no-one else will be foolish enough to try it. That member of the Leynik Family has suffered for her attempt to do so when her attack rebounded on her. I do not know if she will live or not, nor do I care."

Gradually people sat down again. Cuhes cra Shuth said, into the silence, "Many of the Heads, heirs and other members of the Families have been preparing for the overthrow of The God for a long time. We knew that open rebellion would be dangerous and that some of us would probably die. Nevertheless, it was a risk we were prepared to take to free ourselves from the dominance of that monster. Instead our freedom has come in a way we did not anticipate and I, for one, rejoice in it.

"Our plans have always included selecting a council that would rule Sitrelk in much the same way as we have always done, but without the domination of The God and the demands he placed on us. Family rivalries, and not knowing who would survive the wrath of The God when we rebelled, have prevented us deciding in advance who would sit on this council and who would lead it. We must make those decisions now."

"I suppose Neyen wants to rule," said Pevus cra Glinin, jumping to his feet again, "since it was his hand that killed The God."

"What about that woman, Anarya whatever her name is," called another voice from the back of the room. "Neyen says her actions made it possible. Should we select her on that basis?"

"No!" a deep bass voice rumbled. "I was there and I heard The God say to her 'You're just like me'. I don't intend to surrender our new freedom to someone who will duplicate what he did to us for generations."

Cuhes cra Shuth looked at Anarya. "Can you explain what The God meant?"

Anarya stood up. She looked around the hall and waited for silence. "The God thought I was like him because my talent permits me to borrow anyone else's. During the battle I used talents borrowed from a Stealther, a Terromancer, a Pyromancer and a Scratcher. All except the Stealther's skill I obtained from members of the Families."

A mutter started and she continued over it. "You will say that that was his talent too and you are almost right, but there is a difference and that difference is crucial. When I borrow a talent the person I copy it from still has it. He, on the other hand, stole talents, depriving people of them, and had the people he stole from killed so that he could hold on to them for longer. The talents would have returned to their original holders if they had lived. That actually happened during the battle when he took an Aeromancer's skill. In the confusion he failed to have the man killed and the talent reverted. That Aeromancer was brave enough to speak out, and suffered for it."

"That was my father," said Frenuj cra Vilost.

"I thought it might be. I see you have the same talent he did," said Anarya.

"How do you know that?"

"Because I can see everyone's magical abilities. They appear to me as differently coloured auras. It's part of my talent. For example, you are a Lifter," she pointed at the middle-aged woman next to Frenuj cra Vilost. Then she indicated the young man in yellow and pink, "you are a Pyromancer and you, Lord Glinin are a Seeker. I can identify all of your talents."

Anarya looked over to where Yisul was sitting and said, "Ask Yisul cra Neyen. I have used her skills many times without her losing their use or even being aware that I had borrowed them."

"It is true," Yisul confirmed. "I confess I was frightened by her ability when I first encountered it but now I am not, and I trust her completely."

The angry, strident, female voice shouted out, "She is lying to protect her lover! The forbidden relationship between Anarya d'Kirsya and Yisul cra Neyen makes their testimony untrustworthy."

"You have many Feelers amongst you," Anarya said, pointing out some of them. "Ask them if we are telling the truth about what happened when I borrowed Yisul's skills."

Anarya felt the tension in her neck relax a little when the Feelers agreed she wasn't lying.

"Before you ask any more questions I will say this. Someone suggested that I rule over you. I will not. I am of Carrhen and do not know your country, culture, problems or needs. I would make a very poor ruler. Unless you wish to ask me any more questions I think I should leave now and let you get on with choosing a leader."

When there was no dissent she bowed to Cuhes cra Shuth and left with Baram at her side.

HOUSE NEYEN

Anarya was very quiet on the journey back to the Neyen mansion. She answered Baram's comments about what he could see from the carriage with grunts and monosyllables, if she responded at all.

Servants escorted them to the reception room of her suite. One of them asked, "Do you require anything, Lady?"

She shook her head and the servants withdrew.

As soon as the door closed behind them Anarya let herself slump on to the sofa and curled up into a ball.

"You look upset. What's wrong?" asked Baram. "That meeting was pretty intimidating but I think you handled it really well."

"Quarenna's mercy! Of course I'm upset. I lied to them."

"What do you mean? The Feelers vouched for you. There's no way to lie to them."

"Yes, there is! Haven't you realised that? All you need to do is misdirect them with the wrong question."

"There's no need to snap at me. Just tell me what's the matter."

Anarya snorted. "I fooled them into confirming everything I had said about my talent when I actually only asked if Yisa and I were telling the truth about what happened when I borrowed from her."

"I get that, I think, but I don't understand why it's significant."

"It's important because things have changed. Don't you see?"

"See what?"

Anarya uncurled herself and sat up straight. Her voice rose to a shout. "I *am* like The God now."

"Calm down," said Baram. "You're not making sense. You're upset over something but you haven't explained what it is."

Anarya took a deep breath. "Sorry, Baram. You're right, I haven't. I'm too caught up in feeling sorry for myself. Give me a glass of wine and I'll try to make sense."

Baram went into the dining room then stuck his head back around the door to ask, "Wine? Or would you rather have some of that pomegranate liqueur you like?"

"Wine, please."

Baram came back carrying two glasses of deep red wine. He gave one of them to Anarya and sat down beside her.

She sniffed the wine. Its aroma was deeply layered with hints of blackberries, grass, lemon and burnt oak. She inhaled deeply, enjoying the complexity of the bouquet before taking a sip. It helped to settle her mind. "Thank you, Baram. I'll try to explain.

"There was more animosity in that room than I expected. I didn't need to be a Feeler to know that some of them, like that Pevus cra Glinin, really hate me. I was getting nervous when describing why my talent was different from The God's. I was going to borrow Yisa's talent because I feel her love for me when I do and I needed her support. I started to reach out to her and had to stop."

Baram said, "I'm sure Yisul wouldn't have minded."

"She would have noticed something wrong and her reaction would have caused all sorts of problems." Anarya paused and gulped some wine. "I thought I had got over talent exhaustion without being burnt out because I can still see auras, but I was wrong."

"You mean you are burnt out?"

"Yes – No," she said, with a quaver in her voice, "It's worse than that."

"How can it be worse?"

"My own aura is like a rainbow but I'm not usually aware of it. Unless I specifically look for it, and that's quite difficult, I only see it when I borrow. I haven't tried to absorb another talent since I recovered so I hadn't seen my aura until I reached out to Yisul. Now I have – and it's black!"

"What does that mean? I don't understand the significance of a black aura," said Baram.

"That's what The God's aura was like. The last thing I did in the fight was borrow his talent and use it to steal it from him so he had nothing left. Now it's all I've got because it stayed with me after his death. If I take a talent now I'll be stealing it not borrowing it and I don't want to do that. I want to be a Sponger, not a Thiever. Not like him. Holy Quarenna, please, not like him!"

"You can't be sure, can you?" asked Baram. "This is a new situation. You've got to try it. You might be wrong. Try it on me. See if I notice anything."

"You mean that?"

"Yes."

"Baram, I hated you for killing Caseir but you've turned out to be a really good friend. I'm not sure I would have the courage to offer my talent the way you have just to see what happens. I've no idea how long I'll keep it for."

"Then it's about time you found out, isn't it?"

Anarya used the Oversight to see Baram's aura then reached out to touch it with her mind. She saw a black tendril extending from her aura to his brown one. She shuddered because black looked so wrong. When the thread made contact she had the usual sensation of being in two bodies at once and felt the confidence, dedication and ruthlessness she associated with a Stealther's talent. A brown stain travelled back along the tendril towards her. When it reached her Baram's aura disappeared. The second body feeling disappeared too but the other sensations persisted instead of lasting only a few moments.

"It's gone," gasped Baram. "You're right, my talent's gone. It vanished. I've just tried and I can't go into Stealth. I feel so – so empty, so strange."

"Now we have to wait to find out how long it stays with me."

They sat quietly drinking their wine, unable to sustain any conversation for more than a few words. After about a third, Baram's talent returned.

He was about to tell her when Anarya stood up, whispered, "Lost it," and drained the remnants of her wine.

"That didn't last long," said Baram.

"No, it didn't."

"Any idea why?"

"Not really. Whenever I've borrowed your talent before it was a good fit, if that makes sense. I felt comfortable with it and it would last chimes. It wasn't as nice, as well-fitting, this time and it didn't slip gradually away from me. It just went out like a snuffed candle. Give me some more wine, please."

Baram refilled her glass. She gulped it down paying no attention to its quality.

"You told me you felt empty when I had your talent," she said. "Well that's the way I feel right now. I hate it. Now that I've used it once I want to do it again so that I have a talent of some sort. Being a Thiever is very different from being a Sponger. I can almost understand why The God had his sources of talent killed so that he could keep whatever he stole for longer. It's frightening. It's as if stealing a talent gives meaning to being a Thiever in the first place."

Baram shook his head, "I don't like the sound of that. I've heard ganj users saying the same sort of thing about the drug. You could get addicted to that."

"You're right," said Anarya. She dropped the wine glass, careless of the possibility of breakage, and threw herself at him, sobbing. His arms closed around her.

O

Yisul walked into the room, stared at them standing there with their arms wrapped around each other. She said,

"Oh!" and turned to walk away.

Anarya disengaged herself from Baram. She took a couple of tentative steps across the room towards Yisul, who carried on moving away.

"What's wrong, Yisa?"

"I am sorry to have disturbed you. I will go."

Anarya and Baram spoke together.

"No, Yisa, don't go. I need you."

"No," said Baram, "it's not like that."

"It did not look as if you needed my presence," said Yisul, scowling at them.

"I've just realised what that might have looked like but it isn't. Really it isn't. Please believe me. Baram was just comforting me."

"If that is what you wish to call it. Your lips were but a fingerbreadth from his. Your dress is dishevelled and Quarenna only knows where his hands were. What am I to think? I had thought we belonged together."

"We do, Yisa. We do. *Gal-mussen-hu ven galis.* Don't you remember? 'Your soul sits within mine'."

Yisul's face fell. "I did say that to you, didn't I?"

"Yisa, what's wrong?"

"I have not regretted saying that until now. It was presumptuous of me as you could not know its full meaning. It is part of the marriage bond here in Sitrelk, and I did not tell you that."

"Oh!"

"I told myself that it did not have the same meaning between us since you did not fully understand it, but I find I was wrong. I am jealous of seeing you and Baram together."

"Yisa! There is nothing to be jealous of. I discovered something that frightened me and he was the nearest person I could go to for support."

"What is it?"

Anarya's explanation shocked Yisul.

"I did not know," she whispered. "How awful. I cannot begin to imagine what you must feel like. I am so sorry. I misunderstood when I saw you in Baram's arms. I reached a wrong conclusion. Can you forgive me?"

"Of course I can. I love you. *Heru-ven ti lusegri-gal.* Clean air lies between us."

"Thank you, my love," said Yisul. She kissed Anarya then added, "This discovery about your talent is most important. We must keep it a secret."

Anarya agreed. "We won't even tell your father."

Yisul frowned. "I think you are right. That knowledge might disrupt his plans."

"What plans? What happened at the meeting after we left?" asked Baram, pouring wine for all of them.

Yisul sat down on the sofa, patted it to indicate that Anarya should sit beside her and said, "A Sovereign Council of five has been appointed to rule for one year in the first instance. What happens after that is uncertain. The council will consider various options and make recommendations for the future."

"It didn't take them very long to decide that," commented Baram. "I thought the meeting was set to go on for chimes."

"I confess I was surprised how easy it was. The Families are used to taking instructions from The God and doing whatever he wanted done without argument. I think that allowed one strong man, my father, to take control of the meeting. I am sure there will be much more debate in the future, particularly since Pevus cra Glinin and Dunel cra Guesyr managed to get themselves on the council."

"That's your father, one, or is it two, opposed to him. And who else?" asked Baram.

"Two, definitely two. Dunel cra Guesyr has disliked my father for a long time and is almost certain to oppose him. In the opposite seat, Cuhes cra Shuth will support him. It was largely due to her influence that my father will lead the council."

"And the fifth member?" asked Anarya.

"Jemol cra Fimigh. She is quite influential but you won't know her, she didn't speak while you were still at the meeting. I'm sure she will support my father but I fear she might side with the Guesyr and cause problems if your new talent becomes known."

"Why?"

"I think I told you the Pridhar, the Guesyr and the Widhis were treated by The God as first among the Families. Because of that everyone thought it likely that they would support The God during a rebellion. They deny it now, of course. The conspiracy included plans to kill or capture their leaders. Now Guesyr, with some support from Glinin, is suggesting that my father should be executed as a deicide. They propose searching for someone with the powers of The God and turning over the governance of Sitrelk to him or her."

"You mean a Thiever?"

"Yes."

"Are they crazy? Why, in Quarenna's name, would they want to become victims of another Thiever?"

Baram gave a short laugh. "That's easy. They think a new god would be grateful for their support and keep them in a pre-eminent position among the Families. Isn't that right Yisul?"

"I think you are correct. Jemol cra Fimigh will oppose that strongly. If she does realise that you now have The God's talent it would bias her against you, and possibly against my father because he supports you."

"Is there any risk that these three Families will conspire to kill your father, or you?" asked Anarya. "What skills do they have that would put you in danger?"

"All of the Widhis are Feelers. One of those who you pointed out at the meeting was a Widhis and so was one of the people taken by The God before the battle in the temple. Almost all the Glinin are Seekers, except for a few Aquamancers and Chemers, all of whom are now denying belief in The God. There is more variation among the Guesyr. They are mostly Voyanters and Whisperers, with an occasional Chemer and Lifter among them. None of them have skills that can be used directly against you, me or my father."

"Lifters can be dangerous," said Baram.

"That is true," agreed Yisul. "However, Guesyr Lifters are usually fairly weak and need to be touching whatever it is they are attempting to Lift."

"That doesn't mean they're harmless," said Anarya, "and there are other, more dangerous, talents. I think we should go home."

"Home?"

"Sorry, Yisa. I didn't think. This is your home. I meant back to Carregis. I don't like this empty feeling I've got. It's dragging at me, wanting to be filled. Doing what The God did is very tempting and I'd hate myself if I gave in to it. I think I should leave. Will you come with me?"

Yisul frowned. "It is difficult, my love. I do want to stay with you. However, going with you may make things more difficult for my father. Some of the conservatives among the Families are intolerant of our relationship. It gives people like Dunel cra Guesyr another way to cause trouble – you heard him going on about it at the meeting."

"He, and a few others, sounded quite vehement about it. I don't understand how something that does no harm to anyone and shouldn't matter to any but those involved can get people so excited."

"I do not know but I suspect this attitude was encouraged by The God. We know he was against same sex partnerships because he wanted the Families to have as many children as possible to maintain his supply of talents."

"Of course!" said Anarya. "That would explain it."

"Guesyr and his like can argue that parents are supposed to educate their children and if my father has not brought me up properly then how can he be trusted to rule. Going with you would emphasise our togetherness and give them something to use against my father. In the opposite seat, staying here would keep them constantly reminded of me, and my 'foible'. I do not know which would be better."

Anarya started pacing around the room. "I have to go back to Carregis. I need to discuss my situation with

Tilua. I hope you will come with me but I can understand why it might be better if you didn't. I will miss you if you stay."

"Why don't you ask your father which would be better from his point of view?" asked Baram.

O

"I don't think there is a good answer," said Muhan on his return from the Shuth mansion when Yisul asked him what she should do. "It's like many things, there are advantages and disadvantages both ways."

Settling down into one of the chairs, he sighed and shook his head. "I can see many problems ahead, Yisul, and an argument about you and your association with Lady Anarya is only one of them."

"I spoke to some of my friends after the meeting," said Yisul. "None of them seems to mind and there are a couple who hinted they might be tempted to copy Anra and me."

"It's not surprising, you've always been a leader among your contemporaries," said Muhan. "I just hope none of them are too blatant about it. The old reactionaries are going to give me enough trouble without giving them any more causes for complaint."

"Should I go, or stay?"

"I suspect the better option is probably to have you out of sight, Yisul, although that would mean I would lose the advantage of your influence among the younger and more flexible members of the Families."

"I could always come back if you need me."

"It wouldn't work. Getting a message to Carregis and then having you take a ship back here would take too long."

"It takes no time at all to get here," said Anarya. "I have access to a portal made by a daimon. It lets me travel anywhere instantly. How do you think I managed to get into the temple at the right moment to save Yisul?"

A look of blank astonishment appeared on Muhan's

face. "So much has happened that I did not wonder how you came to be in the temple."

"That was where my portal opened. It should still be there waiting for me to return. Take me to the temple and I can be back in Carregis about a twelfth later. From the other end I can reposition the portal to open in this room and we can move freely between Carregis and here. I can bring Yisul back any time you need her."

"Lady Anarya d'Kirsya, you are a most remarkable woman." Muhan got up, bowed to Anarya and left the room saying he would arrange a carriage and escort to take them to the temple.

"Are you sure, Anarya?" asked Baram. "Will you still be able to use the portal?"

"I hadn't thought about that, I just assumed I could. I hope so. It doesn't depend on any talent of mine – at least I don't think it does."

Yisul tried to reassure her, saying, "If it does not work, there is still the option of a ship and I am certain my father will provide a rather more salubrious vessel than the one I used before."

"You've got me worried now. Will the portal still be there for me?" She thumbed her forehead and prayed silently. *Bless me, Holy Quarenna. Let it be that the portal is still mine to use.*

THE SHRINE OF QUARENNA IN CARREGIS

Just after dawn, Tilua and two of the other members of the Inner Circle knelt to sing the morning prayer before the altar dedicated to Quarenna in her aspect as The Guardian.

"I've had that dream again," she said, as the echoes of the chant died away.

Jaenis, nodded, "So have I."

"What can it mean?" asked Nuasi, the oldest and most frail looking of the three as she wriggled a bit and winced.

"You should sit, Nuasi. There's no need for you to be uncomfortable," said Jaenis.

"And Holy Quarenna will forgive you," added Tilua. "You know she doesn't insist on you being uncomfortable when it's not necessary."

"True," admitted Nuasi, "but irrelevant. I will carry on showing her my respect for as long as I can."

Tilua shrugged. "I can't force you to think of yourself, you're too stubborn for that. Just remember, it is an option."

Nuasi snorted. "Never mind me. We need to think about what these dreams mean. We've been having them for five nights now. They have to be significant."

"Were there any words in your dream last night?" Tilua asked.

"No words," said Nuasi. "Just a threatening feeling and a sense of – I guess I'd have to say pressure, isolation and impending doom."

"There *was* a voice in mine this time."

"What did it say, Jaenis?"

"Mostly it was what we have heard before. It wasn't coherent, or very loud, and it repeated itself a lot saying,

'Loosening', 'Retribution' and 'Progress'.

Tilua shook her head, "Those words, as well as 'Alone' and 'Hate', have been the commonest ones we've heard."

"But there was something new," said Jaenis. "One bit that almost made sense. It was 'loose prayer – nobody – take – available – prayer no focus – no focus – can get – power.'"

"Huh! Those fragments don't help much," commented Nuasi. "You could make almost anything out of them."

Tilua bent forward to touch her forehead to the ground and implored, "Holy Quarenna we beg for your guidance. Help us to understand this riddle."

Jaenis repeated the prayer.

Nuasi did too, adding a plea for forgiveness because she couldn't bend far enough to show proper respect.

Then Tilua assisted Nuasi to her feet and the three of them made their way to breakfast.

THE TEMPLE OF THE GOD

Anarya's only previous view of the outside of the temple had been from the carriage taking her to the meeting at the Shuth residence. It had impressed her then. Now, getting closer to it, it was overwhelming. She found herself getting a crick in her neck looking up at the layer upon layer of domes and half domes, trying to take it all in. It was, by far, the largest building she had ever seen; so big that it was almost impossible to appreciate as a single structure.

The carriage rolled into a courtyard and came to a stop. "This is the Family's entrance," said Yisul, waving at a massive pair of carved oak doors. Anarya saw tree-dancers among the carvings and guessed that the doors showed the symbols of all the Families. A close look confirmed this when she found the garlanded horseshoes of Shuth too.

"The great doors are only opened on Revelation Day, that's the anniversary of The God's arrival in Jotuk. They are so heavy that each takes two men to move it. Fortunately for us there is another door which is easier to open." She led them across another courtyard, along a colonnade, through the Court of Statues and round a corner into a small herb garden where a fountain was playing. The scents of thyme and verbena were overlaid with a faint smell of burning. This became stronger as they penetrated deeper into the building. Its source became obvious when they turned a corner and found a hole in a wall next to a pile of scorched rubble.

"The Presence Chamber is through the next door," Yisul told them. She led them through it, pausing at the threshold to cross her arms over her chest and incline her head slightly.

"What are you doing?" asked Anarya.

"Oh!" said Yisul, looking startled. "It is a gesture to indicate submission to The God. I have done it so often on entering the Chamber I simply did it without thinking." She uncrossed her arms and touched her right thumb to her forehead. "Holy Quarenna forgive me."

Anarya recognised the room where she had fought The God. She was shocked to see how much damage had been done by the battle. Debris from the throne littered the floor, the marble dais was fragmented and, in places, looked as if it had turned to sand. Scorch marks from the fire and the thunderbolts scarred the stonework. The silk hangings were tattered and charred, some had fallen into heaps on the floor. The burnt smell was very strong. Pieces were missing from some of the pillars, and glass fragments were strewn around where windows had been blown out. She could see the sky through a hole high in one of the walls. Under it was a scattering of gold and purple roof tiles. Despite all the damage, it was still possible to see how magnificent the room had been.

"The bodies have been removed," said Yisul, "and the fires extinguished. Nothing else has been done because nobody knows what will happen to the temple. Most people are staying away from it, although I hear that some servants are still going into the Hall of Supplication. That's as far as they are allowed to go when they come to worship."

Anarya suggested, "Let's try to find the portal. It should be over there somewhere." She pointed towards the other end of a side aisle and started walking in that direction.

"Assassin! Heretic! Murderer!"

The shouts came from a man who burst through a door at the opposite end of the room. He was dressed in green and black.

"Vilost colours," commented Yisul, "but I don't recognise him."

Baram vanished, saying, "I'll try to get close to him."

Anarya invoked the Oversight and saw the man had a

strong white aura. It flared and she felt her breath catch in her throat. *Aeromancer. He's cutting off my air.* She saw Yisul's hands go to her throat. *He's got Yisa too!*

Her vision started to close in. *Got to do something.*

She reached out, seeing a tendril of her black aura bridge the gap to the Aeromancer. Then his aura snuffed out and when he lost his talent she could breathe again. Now she was an Aeromancer. It was different from previous times she had borrowed that skill. Then it had lasted only a few breaths and she had never been able to do anything useful with it. Now she could see the air currents in the room and the ebb and flow of the attacker's breathing. She sucked the air from the Aeromancer's lungs, saw his hands scrabbling at his throat and held a bubble of no air around his head until he fell and stopped twitching.

Baram reappeared, close to the body. "Are you all right," he asked.

"Yes, I'm fine. What about you, Yisa?"

"I feel a little dizzy but otherwise I am well."

"He's dead," said Baram, bending over the body. "What did you do to him?"

"Cut off his air, as he tried to do to us."

"How?" asked Yisul. "You told me Aeromancy was not a good skill for you."

"It never was in the past, but things are different now that I'm holding it as a Thiever. When I took his talent he lost it and couldn't carry on strangling us but I could choke him, deny him air. I've still got his talent, just like The God kept the skills of the people he had killed. Now I know why he did that. Having another talent I feel more – complete."

Anarya wrapped her arms around herself. "Stealing his talent was the only way to stop him killing us. Then I had to kill him, don't you see? If I'd let him live he'd have told everyone I'm a Thiever. You do see that, don't you? I had no choice."

Yisul moved to comfort Anarya, hugging her and making quiet consoling noises.

"Do you know him, Yisul?" asked Baram.

They joined Baram at the body and bent over it.

Yisul's hand went to her mouth. "Oh! Quarenna's grace! I have met him. His branch of the Family lives mostly in and around Edhisam. He's some sort of cousin of Frenuj cra Vilost. His name is Gerfit, or Geruft, something like that."

"Frenuj cra Vilost didn't seem antagonistic at the meeting," said Anarya.

"She was not. However, the same isn't true for others of the Vilost Family. In the debate after you left it seemed to be one of the most divided. Some of them were happy about the new situation and others very resentful about the killing of The God."

"I wonder if he was acting on his own."

Yisul shrugged. "I do not know how to find out. We must tell my father about this. He is at risk."

"Let's check on the portal before we go back," suggested Baram. "That's what we came for."

"We don't need to check," said Anarya. She could see the weather-beaten green plank door with the seven footprints scratched into it. It looked incongruous in the temple, but she was pleased to see it. "It's there, just behind that pillar with the bite taken out of it. We know nobody else but me can see it. Since I can I'm sure it will work for me."

"Good," said Yisul. "Let us go back to Neyen. I am anxious to warn my father of possible danger."

INTO THE DARKWORLD

"Make sure you're touching me," said Anarya. "I don't want you to end up somewhere else."

Yisul took a firm grip of her left hand saying, "No more do I."

"I don't either," agreed Baram, putting one hand on her shoulder. "It was bad enough losing contact in mid transit when we first came here. It felt as if I wasn't all here for a few chimes. Don't want that, or worse, to happen again."

They'd hurried back to House Neyen to let Muhan know about the Aeromancer's attack.

He hadn't been surprised. In the time they'd been away from Neyen he had received reports of four skirmishes between members of other Houses with different views about the death of The God. They had resulted in two other fatalities.

"I'm sure there will be more clashes," he said. "I was hoping you would be well away by now and out of danger. You are going, aren't you?"

"Yes."

"Then this time you get an escort."

The inner city was quiet but there were more guards than usual at the gates of two of the Houses they passed on their return to the temple. Yisul led them back to the Presence Chamber where they now stood, slightly apprehensively, in front of the portal.

"Ready?" Anarya looked at Yisul, who nodded, then at Baram who did likewise, albeit with a slight hesitation.

"Here we go." Anarya reached out with her right hand, grasped the door handle only she could see, pulled the door open and stepped forward. There was a blur of movement, then she was by herself in complete, utter darkness unable to feel the touch of either of the others.

"No!" she screamed into the total silence around her. *I'm in the Darkworld. Why? What did I do wrong?*

Nothing to see; nothing to hear, not even her scream; just nothingness. It wasn't hot or cold. She couldn't even feel a surface under her feet. Her throat tightened. She felt sick, tasted bile and was almost relieved to experience some sensation, however unpleasant. It was every bit as bad as the first time she had been taken into the Darkworld, totally unexpected, disorientating and frightening. At least this time she knew that, sooner or later, a daimon would confront her. She just had to wait. *It will come, won't it. It can't leave me here forever – can it? Holy Quarenna aid me! What's happened to Yisa and Baram?*

She remembered the first daimon she had encountered, and what it had threatened her with, and shuddered.

I should have tried the portal on my own to make sure it was safe. I shouldn't have risked Yisa.

After a wait that dragged on and on until she wondered if it would ever end, she felt a presence, a wrongness, and a hollow sighing voice she knew spoke to her.

{You altered. Why?}

It was with some sense of relief that she recognised the voice of the daimon she had bargained with for control of the portal. *At least it's not the one who threatened me. I can talk to this one.*

"What do you mean, altered?"

{Feel difference when portal opened. You here more strong than before. Why change?}

"Where are my friends? Have you captured them too?"

{Irrelevant. Answer. Why you more now?}

"I don't understand."

{Before you Borrower. Here once. Now not same. Here twice, Gatherer and Breather. How possible?}

Surprised, she guessed that the daimon must be able to recognise the difference between her as a Sponger and as a Thiever, and could tell that she still had the Aeromancer's ability as well. She did her best to explain what had happened to her. As on her previous visits to the

Darkworld she couldn't hear her own voice but the daimon seemed to be able to.

{*Comprehension. Here twice because taking power from two conduits. Will understand if feel change again.*}

"You mean you'll be able to tell when I take another talent."

{*Only if come here. Then feel flow of power. Otherwise not.*}

"Feel the flow of power? I thought it was only Daimoners, those who can compel you, who have power in your world."

{*Not so. Power for all talents from here.*}

"Really? All of them?"

{*All.*}

Anarya shook her head in amazement. *Can I trust what it says?* She frowned to herself. *Well, it did keep the bargain we made. Maybe I can.*

{*You twice, also one Hider, one Seer. Too many for easy hold. Go now. Want talk again when alone.*}

Anarya had just enough time to realise the daimon was talking about Yisa and Baram before there was another blur of movement and she found herself stepping through the door of the tavern called *The Seventh Step*. She gasped in relief, not least because she was holding Yisa's hand again and she could feel Baram's hand on her shoulder.

Holy Quarenna be praised. We're safe.

"What happened?" asked Baram. "There was something felt a bit different about that. A sort of – hesitation? As if we stopped for a moment during transit."

"Only for a moment? It took a lot longer than that. I was in the Darkworld and talking to a daimon for what seemed like at least three chimes."

"Surely not," said Baram. "There was just a momentary pause, nothing more than that."

"A daimon!" gasped Yisul. "What did it want?"

Anarya looked around as she led them to their table, saying that she would tell them all about it once they were seated.

O

The common room of *The Seventh Step* was quiet. It held only nine people, including two magic users. One was the Whisperer who was always there, sitting in her corner under the stairs. The other was a middle-aged woman with the pale blue aura of an Aquamancer.

Anarya shuddered. After sixteen or seventeen chimes she still held the Aeromancer's ability. Given how fleeting that talent was for her as a Sponger she was amazed, and grateful, that it was still available to her. It helped to blunt her awareness of Yisul's and Baram's talents and let her fight the desire to steal them. However, the presence of two more talents in her vicinity increased the pressure on her. Having a talent meant the empty feeling wasn't as strong but she still had to struggle a bit to keep control.

She was so involved in her mental battle that she didn't even notice when Caseir's voice said, "You've been gone a long time. I was getting lonely."

"What do you mean?' asked Baram. "This is a tavern. There are people in and out of here all the time. How can you be lonely?"

"Because nobody talks to me. They're all frightened because they think this table is haunted."

"They are correct, in a way," said Yisul.

"I suppose they are," admitted Caseir. "I'm dead but, because the daimon trapped me in the bloodstain, I'm not. Now that you're here with one bit of the tabletop you carried to Jotuk I've got some idea of what happened, but I want to know more. You had another piece, what happened to that?"

"We don't know." Baram shrugged. "It got lost somewhere in the confusion."

When the server brought them wine she said, "Limabur told me he wanted to talk to you next time you came in. I've sent somebody to fetch him. He'll be here soon."

"I can guess what he wants," said Caseir. "He's been grumbling about this table again and its effect on trade. I bet you he wants to cancel your deal. Any takers?”

“You must think me foolish,” snorted Yisul. “Do you seriously think I would take a wager like that when we’ve been away and you’ve been around to listen to him?”

“It was worth a try.” Caseir laughed. “So, who’s going to tell me everything that happened?”

“Later, I think,” said Yisul. “We must deal with Limabur first; he has just come in.”

The landlord came across to the table and inclined his head towards Yisul. “Lady, it’s good to see you back. That table has been kept for you and you’ve been away for weeks. It’s not good for business having it standing empty all the time. It’s even empty when we’re busy, just because of the bloodstain. I want rid of it. You gave me enough to rent it for another two months but I’ll give you three month’s rent back if you’ll give up the table and let me get rid of it. That’s sixty bits in your pouch.”

“No,” said Yisul. “I like the arrangement we have.”

“Seventy bits?”

“No.”

“Seventy-five?

Yisul shook her head.

“Eighty?”

“You seem very anxious, master Limabur. Let me think about it. We might be able to come to some agreement.”

Limabur wandered off muttering and shaking his head.

“You’re not going to let him have the table!” said Caseir.

“No, of course not. I simply wanted to get rid of him while we talk.”

“You’ve got to do something. All he needs to do is wait until the present rent runs out then refuse to renew it. You remember he was going to burn the table. I don’t know what that would have done to me, and I don’t want to find out.”

“We’ll have to think about what to do.”

“I hope you do think of something. Just don’t take too long about it.”

“Don’t you want to know what happened in Jotuk?”

asked Yisul. "And what the daimon told Anra."

"A daimon! You've met a daimon again," said Caseir.

"I have. I was taken into the Darkworld on our way here."

Anarya's account of her encounter with the daimon produced gasps of horror from Yisul and Baram and incredulity from Caseir.

She finished her wine and announced, "Yisa and I are going back to Carregis. Do you want to come too, Baram?"

"Yes," he replied, "I'm not keen on another trip through the Darkworld if there's a risk of meeting daimons, but I ought to go to the temple. The priests like to know what Stealthers get up to and they'll be wondering what's happened to me. It's getting on for two months since I reported."

A VILLAGE NEAR CARREGIS

The way he doesn't fall the bastard must have a daimon's own luck, Nasuren grumbled to himself. *Would make my job a lot easier if he fell.*

He had located one of Praukel's relatives working as a builder in a village about half a day from Carregis.

The tavern opposite the three-storey building his quarry was re-roofing was a convenient place to watch him from. The ale wasn't very good – too sweet in Nasuren's opinion, sweet enough to attract wasps – but it gave him an excuse for sitting there.

The builder, who Nasuren reckoned must be about sixty, looked frail but he was active. He clambered rapidly up and down a framework of narrow, rough-looking planks and poles without even getting a splinter in his hand as far as Nasuren could tell.

There were a couple of times when he apparently slipped on his way down, but it didn't seem to bother him. He just stuck his foot out, without looking, and it landed safe and secure on a lower plank.

I'd like to organise an accident for him. I could try to weaken one of the planks overnight so it broke under his weight. But I don't know if that would be enough. He must be part cat the way he balances.

I think I'll have to be more direct.

When it started getting dark, Nasuren's target bundled up his tools and carried them into the tavern. He settled down with a mutton pie and a mug of ale. Nasuren watched him from a dark corner and waited patiently until the man picked up his tools again and left with a muttered "Good Night" to the tavern-keeper.

Nasuren didn't want anybody to think he was following the builder so he went out the back of the tavern as if he was going to the privy. Moving quickly he hopped over the wall in time to see his target turn down a side street.

He followed, taking a blow-pipe from his pack. His bad leg dragging on the ground made enough noise for the builder to turn to see who was behind him. Halfway through the turn he slapped the side of his neck cursing 'them Huler-be-damned wasps'. Then he staggered and fell. Nasuren was satisfied. The slap had forced more of the poison from the dart into the man's neck. He wasn't quite dead, but he soon would be. Nasuren carefully retrieved the dart, wrapped it up safely and put it in his pack. He left the man in the dust, apparently dead of a heart attack.

Nasuren hurried back to the tavern, over the wall and back to his corner with another mug of ale where he sat drinking for about a half. Nobody was likely to associate him with the unexpected death of the roofer even if there was an investigation – after all, everyone in the tavern would swear he had been there all the time.

That's the first of the master's relatives disposed of.

A SQUARE IN JOTUK

Richak, with an escort of eight of the biggest and roughest members of his *houln*, looked around cautiously as he entered the open space just outside Derchler's Gate. The irregular area, rather inaccurately described as a square, didn't belong to his *houln*, or to any of the others. Five narrow streets converged on it, each of them from the territory of a different *houln*. Many fights over the last thirty-odd years had established the square as a free marketplace where people of many different loyalties could mix in relative safety.

The hubbub of voices diminished as people around Richak recognised his presence, and that of the rulers of two other *houln* with their escorts arriving from other streets. The space started to empty as the unaffiliated realised something was going on and decided they didn't want any part of it. Members of the Three Flowers, Stone Grasshoppers and Dark Fountain *houln*, thinking there was a threat of some sort, congregated around their own ruler and waited to see what would happen. Those associated with other *houln* moved away, clearing a space in the middle of the square.

Richak took a knife from his belt and laid it on the ground with the point towards him. It wasn't the only weapon he had, not even the only visible one, but the action indicated he was there to talk, not fight. A sigh from the people gathered around him was echoed by the other groups as the two other rulers did likewise. The tension eased.

One of the other rulers, a little taller than Richak, with half of his right ear missing and a patch covering his right eye, straightened up after laying down his knife. He scowled and asked, "What's this all about, Richak?

You've got some nerve calling a truce after that trouble we had at the south bridge last week. What do you want?" He pointed at the third ruler. "And what is he doing here? Wasn't expecting anybody else."

"Stay calm, Hentro, and you'll learn something."

"It'd better be good," said Jemak. He was the shortest of the three leaders and he limped badly because his legs had healed bent after being broken. "There's been too much trouble lately and I'm in no mood to listen to you. But you made it sound urgent."

Richak nodded. "It's important. I asked the two of you to come because you're the only other priests I know who rule a *houln*. I know you're both dedicated to the Confined Gods."

Hentro and Jemak both lifted clenched fists to shoulder level. "That's something we can agree on," said Hentro.

"We need to talk privately," said Richak. "I swear by the Confined Ones that I intend no harm to you or members of your *houln* at this time. I would offer you hospitality but you might feel safer if one of you chooses a meeting place."

Jemak chewed his lip, then he pointed to one of the streets leading from the square. "Two buildings down that street there's a tavern. The landlord is part of my *houln*. He will empty it at my request. I offer it, in the names of the Confined Gods, as a place we can meet in safety."

"That will do," agreed Richak.

"Very well," said Hentro. "But my *houln* secures the door and nobody else comes within ten paces of it."

"That's an insult." Jemak's hand went to one of the other knives at his belt. "How dare you suggest that I wouldn't abide by my promise of safety in the names of the Confined Ones."

Hentro snorted. "I trust *your* promise to the gods. You won't start anything, but I don't trust your followers not to do something on their own initiative. Particularly that Ivarros. He's too fond of making trouble, always trying to raise his status by appearing to be strong. If he doesn't speak the promise himself, I don't think he'll consider himself bound by whatever you say."

"I know Ivarros fancies himself as my successor but I don't believe he's ready to make a move against me yet," said Jemak.

Hentro shrugged. "Your funeral!"

Jemak scowled, "Ivarros, come here."

There was a short delay during which Jemak, irritated at the slow reaction from Ivarros, repeated his command. A powerfully built man slowly stepped forward from the crowd. He towered over Jemak and had to bend down to look him in the eye.

"I'm here. What do you want?"

"I've promised Richak and Hentro that this meeting is safe. They've agreed. You're not going to start anything, are you?" asked Jemak. "I need you to promise me, in the names of the Confined Gods, that there'll be no trouble."

Ivarros looked at the other rulers, spat and growled, "I don't trust them. Easy to promise and not mean it."

"Even a promise to the Confined Ones?"

Ivarros licked his lips. "Yesss…"

Jemak moved quickly, and suddenly there was a stiletto sticking out of Ivarros' left eye.

He slumped to the ground as Jemak snarled, "That's not an acceptable answer."

The tension was back and everyone around the three rulers had knives in their hands.

"He's not going to cause any more trouble," said Jemak. "I repeat my promise of safety. Will you accept it?"

Hentro nodded, "Yes. Now I'll agree to this meeting place."

O

The only window of the tavern was too small to adequately illuminate the single room. Candles provided what light there was and the acrid smell of burning tallow permeated the room. A communal table occupied most of the space except for one corner where the landlord presided behind a row of barrels.

Any occupants had been distracted by the happenings in the square and the tavern was empty, apart from the landlord, when the three rulers entered.

"Give them whatever they want," Jemak told the landlord, "then get out and leave us alone."

Richak waved the landlord away saying he didn't want anything. Both Hentro and Jemak accepted a mug of ale.

"So, Richak, you've got your meeting," commented Jemak. "I suppose I should thank you for setting this up. It's given me a good reason to get rid of Ivarros."

"Wasn't part of the plan, but you're welcome."

Richak was sitting across the table from Hentro with Jemak on his left at the end of the table. He looked at them, raised a clenched fist to shoulder level and said, "I swear by the true names of the Confined Gods; by Lohkrah, Mueliss, Pronathu, Yvernis, Abrenli and Kehsieh that I am telling the truth."

Hentro and Jemak nodded, copied his gesture and accepted his oath.

"What's all this about?" demanded Hentro.

"I have spoken with Kehsieh."

"What!"

"Four days ago, I was trying to find out what had happened at the temple when Kehsieh came to me. He is present in this token." Richak removed the necklace and placed it on the table in front of him, being careful to keep a finger on it.

"Touch it," he told them. "Touch it and Kehsieh will speak to you too."

Hentro scowled and hesitated while Jemak eagerly stretched out to make contact with the piece of wood. Jemak's face lit up with awe when he heard Caseir greet him by name. Hentro quickly reached out too and clenched his fist again when he heard Caseir introduce himself.

"Great One! How may I serve?" asked Hentro.

"You can start by making sure all three of you are

touching the token and can hear me."

There was a bit of jostling as they struggled to get comfortable while maintaining contact with the small piece of wood.

Richak lifted a clenched fist again, "Greatness, will you tell these others what you told me."

"I am still partially confined," said Caseir. "I can touch the world through this piece of wood but in no other way at present. The wood also lets me hear everything people say in its presence, however quietly."

"What of the others, Great One. Are your brothers and sisters free too?"

"No, Hentro. I do not think so. I have never been aware of their presence at any time during my imprisonment. It may be that each of us was confined in a different place or in a different way."

"But you are free. Will you lead us to victory over the Families?"

"My power is restricted, but I will do what I can," said Caseir.

"What must we do?" asked Hentro.

"First of all, know that I have chosen Richak to speak for me at present. However, there may be times when I designate another to do this."

Richak frowned and shuffled a bit causing Hentro to lose contact. He pushed back and there was a brief scuffle as they all made sure they were touching the wood.

Caseir snapped, "That is enough! I require an undertaking from each of you that whoever has the token speaks with my voice and is to be obeyed while he holds it. I also want a promise that none of you will seek to take the token from whoever I have chosen to hold it at any time."

"But, Great One, you came to me…"

"Are you arguing with me?"

"No, Greatness," said Richak, shaking his head vigorously, "Never."

All three of them tried to leave loopholes in the wording they used, but Caseir was implacable and insisted on extracting the promises he wanted.

THE SHRINE OF QUARENNA

The scent of the orange blossom incense and the quiet reverberations of low-pitched intermittent gong strokes let Anarya relax to some extent when she walked into the shrine. Every one of the occasional talented people they had passed in the street on their way had been a temptation for her. She had to get help and advice and she was sure Tilua was the person to ask. She led Yisul to the altar of the Friend and Comforter and knelt there, allowing the peace of the shrine to calm her. About a tenth of a chime later she stood up and moved to the altar of the Helper. She stabbed her thumb, allowing blood to drip into the collection bowl at the foot of the statue. The familiar ritual of offering blood to Holy Quarenna was a blessing in itself and she knelt patiently until one of the priestesses came to offer assistance.

"I regret that I am unable to take you to see Blessèd Tilua at the moment. She was summoned to a meeting at the sixth chime this morning and, if it matches other recent meetings, it is likely to last until the tenth or eleventh. Will you wait or return later?"

"We will wait," said Anarya, sitting back on her heels.

"As you wish. Should you desire refreshment during your vigil you may ask an acolyte to bring you water or fruit juice." The priestess offered her blessing, then moved away leaving Anarya and Yisul kneeling at the altar.

"I'm sorry, Yisa. I told her we would wait without consulting you. I'll stay by myself if you want to go." *I hope she'll stay. I need all the support I can get.*

"I am content to stay. I recognise how important this is. I would not abandon you."

Anarya reached out to touch Yisul's cheek, "Thank you

for understanding." She settled back on her heels to wait.

About half a chime later Anarya sighed, "I'm worried and restless and can't settle. I need to do something. I'm going to try the dynamic meditation. Do you know it? Did you get that far in your lessons with Tilua?"

"I did, but I know only about three-quarters of the first sequence."

"That sequence lasts about half a chime. It would be a good use of the waiting time. Will you join me?"

They stood up together and moved to a paved area near the middle of the shrine. Several women were already there moving through the steps, twists and poses of the meditation in motion. It was a popular thing to do.

As soon as she made the first move Anarya found herself completely immersed in the flow. Time passed without awareness and she moved seamlessly on from the end of the first sequence to the longer and more complex forms of the second. At the end of that she drew herself up into the tall pose, arms extended overhead, stretching upwards. Then her arms slowly drifted down, crossing and re-crossing in front of her to end up by her sides. A momentary pause with her head bowed, a final exhalation, and she looked up to see Yisul watching her.

"I am sorry, Yisa. I didn't intend to go beyond the first sequence, but Holy Quarenna was with me today and the flow simply carried me through."

"It was elegant and beautiful. You are very skilled."

Anarya bowed her head in recognition of the praise. "We should return to wait at the altar."

"There is no need," said Yisul. "Tilua has just come out of the building behind you and is coming towards us."

Anarya turned in time to see Tilua wipe a frown from her face as she approached.

"Blessèd Tilua, it is so good to see you."

"Come with me," said Tilua and led them to her study.

The door was no sooner closed behind them than Tilua asked, "What's happened to you? Your aura…"

"Is black. Yes, I know." Anarya, with help from Yisul, told the story of the death of The God while Tilua sat and listened in silence.

"I hardly know what to say. Several of the Inner Circle, myself among them, have had disturbing dreams for the last week. Now they start to make sense. Holy Quarenna, may her name be praised, has been speaking to us through those dreams and we have been too stupid to understand what she has been telling us. I must tell the others about this. Excuse me a moment."

Tilua rang a bell and told the acolyte who came to answer it, "Find Nuasi and as many others of the Inner Circle as you can and ask them to come here as quickly as possible. This is important. Go on. Run."

She turned back to look at Anarya. "What are we going to do about you?"

"Can you heal a burnt-out talent?"

Tilua sat back in her chair, indicated with a wave that the others should sit too and looked down at her lap. "A Sponger is someone who has received the greatest of Holy Quarenna's gifts and as such is of paramount interest to the Inner Circle. Everything known about every Sponger who ever existed is recorded in the archives along with whatever happened to them. Not all of the stories are complete. Some, as I told you before, were killed by jealous untalented. Others simply disappeared and it isn't known if they too were killed or if they successfully hid themselves and lived a peaceful life.

"There are stories there about Spongers who burnt themselves out. Most, I am sorry to say, never recovered. A few did manage a limited recovery, regaining some ability but usually with less scope and retention of borrowed talents than previously. If I recall correctly, the few recoveries which have occurred have taken anywhere from six months to almost seven years."

Anarya had a sour taste in her throat as if she was going to be sick. *I was afraid of that.* She had hoped to hear something different, but it didn't surprise her. *What am I going to do now?*

There was a knock at the door before Anarya could say

anything. An acolyte opened the door and entered, saying, "Your pardon for the interruption, Blessèd Tilua. I have brought Blessèd Nuasi as you wanted and have sent others to find the rest of the Inner Circle. At least two of them were seen leaving the shrine and it's not known where they have gone."

"Thank you. You have done well."

The acolyte helped an old, stooped woman walking with the aid of two sticks into the room, supporting her as she winced with each shuffling step she took, and made sure she was comfortably settled in a chair before leaving.

Nuasi scowled at Anarya. "Who and what are you?"

"This is Anarya," said Tilua. "For the first time all three Spongers known to be alive are present in the same room at the same time."

"She's no Sponger. Not with that sinister looking aura. And what about her?" She pointed one of her sticks at Yisul. "What's a Sitrelker doing here?"

"Peace, Nuasi. I will explain as soon as a few of the others get here."

"Hope they hurry up. I haven't got enough time left to enjoy just waiting for something to happen."

"I'll tell you this much. It has to do with the strange dreams we've been having."

"Does it now? Does it? Hmm. That is interesting. I might as well stay around then."

Tilua laughed. "You are incorrigible. I know you, nothing will drag you away from a mystery."

"Huh!"

Three other members of the Inner Circle arrived within a fifth. Every chair in Tilua's cosy little room was occupied. Anarya rose from her chair to allow the last of the three to sit and settled on the floor, leaning against Yisul's legs. The contact with her lover helped her resist the temptation presented by the strong talents of the Inner Circle, but she couldn't help an occasional shiver and lapse of attention. She kept muttering under her breath, invoking Quarenna's grace to stay calm.

"I think we should start," said Tilua. "It's unlikely anyone else will come now. Allow me to introduce Anarya, who is a Sponger, and Yisul cra Neyen, a Voyanter from Sitrelk. They have a story to tell which I think sheds light on our recent disturbed dreams."

The story of the death of The God was told again, accompanied by gasps and exclamations. When Anarya described using his own talent against him, Nuasi complimented her, "That was quick thinking, girl. Well done." Then she paused. "Now I understand what's happened to your aura. Am I right in thinking Thiever is the only talent you have left?"

"It is."

"Have you used it?"

Anarya nodded and said, in a very quiet voice, "I have."

"And?"

"It's awful. It's like a hunger, an emptiness that's desperate to be filled by some talent, it doesn't matter what. I wasn't really aware of the craving until after I realised what had happened and had used the Thiever skill for the first time. Since then it has been there constantly, waiting to pounce if I relax. The first time I Thieved it was a Stealther friend I stole from. I felt like using his own talent to kill him so that I could keep it. Then I stole from an Aeromancer who was trying to kill me. I killed him instead and his ability stayed with me for most of a day before it vanished. I'm worried I'm going to become what The God was, and the idea terrifies me."

"You poor girl. I'm sorry to say there's nothing to be done except wait and hope," said Nuasi.

Anarya felt herself shivering. *I can't stand this much longer.* "Can't you destroy the talent. I don't want it. I'd rather be truly burnt out than live with this – thing hanging over me."

Nuasi frowned, sighed and said, "Unfortunately, there have been many women who have misused the abilities given them by Holy Quarenna. A few of them have done so to such an extent that the Inner Circle would have removed their talents if we could. However, they have had to be left to Holy Quarenna's judgement. We know of no way to destroy one of her gifts. I am so sorry."

Anarya jumped up and ran for the door saying, "I can't stay. All of you are so strong and the temptation to Thieve one of your talents is almost too much for me. I've got to go before I do something terrible."

The door slammed shut behind her. Yisul started to rise, saying, "I have to go too. I must do whatever I can to support Anarya."

"Wait. Please wait a moment," said Tilua. "We want to know what is happening in Sitrelk now. Nuasi and I, along with the two Feelers in the Inner Circle, have had dreams that started the night The God died. It cannot be coincidence."

Yisul looked longingly at the door, wanting to follow Anarya. She took a deep breath and said, "The Twenty-three Families, including I am sorry to say mine, are squabbling over who rules. A joint council has been appointed and will rule for a year. However, I do not see it lasting beyond that, and I suspect it may not even last that long."

"There is a voice in the dreams we have been having," said Tilua. "It's not very clear or coherent but it seems to speak of unfocussed prayer, whatever that means."

Nuasi remarked, "I wonder if that means the prayers directed to The God fail to find a target since his death."

"It could be," said Yisul. "The Families know about his death but the word can't have spread far yet and he will still be the focus for the worship and prayers of the ordinary people."

"I think you are wrong," Tilua said. "Eight days is more than enough time for rumours to spread. Your servants must know, and they will have relatives elsewhere in the city who will talk to their friends, particularly about something as important as this. I think you might be surprised how well known his death has become."

Nuasi said, "The voice we are hearing is sometimes

aggressive in tone. We don't know what it means, and we are frightened. Now I wonder if it is the voice of some entity wanting to replace The God. Could it threaten Holy Quarenna? What can we do?"

"There is something that has just occurred to me," said Yisul. "As Blessèd Tilua knows, I had a religious crisis last year shortly after I came to Carregis. I had lost faith in The God and the feeling of loss and helplessness without having a god to rely on was overwhelming. People in Sitrelk who know the truth, or have heard rumours, may be starting to feel the same way. Holy Quarenna filled that need for me. Perhaps she could do the same for my countrywomen."

"But there is nobody in Sitrelk who could speak of Quarenna's glory," remarked one of the other priestesses.

"Then some of us must go there," said Tilua. "I am willing; who will join me?"

Nuasi shifted in her chair, "I would go gladly, if I could. Alas I fear my health will not permit it."

"One small problem," said one of the other priestesses. "Holy Quarenna cannot receive the worship of the men of Sitrelk. We need to talk to the Brotherhood of Huler about this."

"It would not surprise me to find that some of their priests have been having similar dreams."

"That is something I can do to assist," said Nuasi. "I am willing to act as liaison between the Inner Circle and the Brotherhood."

"You can't at the moment, Nuasi. You're not mobile enough to leave the shrine for meetings with one of Huler's priests.

"Your pardon, Blessèd Ones. May I leave now?" Yisul asked. "I want to go home and comfort Anarya."

"Yes, you may," Tilua responded after a quick look around the room. "Thank you. Your assistance has been invaluable."

THE TEMPLE OF HULER
IN CARREGIS

Which of Huler's aspects should I approach? The Judge – or the Pardoner? Or perhaps the Grieving Parent or the Good Companion.

Baram walked into the temple uncertain of what to do. He knew he would have to speak to Raifen, his link to the higher echelons of the priesthood. Going directly to see him after such a long interval seemed wrong, even although he had important tidings to relate.

He found himself striding towards the Men's Gate into the sanctuary with his steps loud on the polished slate floor. He hadn't made a conscious decision. *Is Huler guiding my feet?*

He stopped outside the Men's Gate and drew his long knife from its sheath. Lifting it high overhead he stepped through, starting to sing the plea for help from the liturgy of the Judge.

The four priests standing around the altar took up his words and sang with him, their voices, in perfect harmony, drowning his as they reverberated from the dome high above. The glory of the sunlight pouring in through the many colours of the stained glass in the great east window dazzled him. He laid his knife on the altar and prostrated himself in front of it.

The hymn reached its end and the nearest of the four priests bent over him, raised him to his knees and asked, "What is the nature of your troubles, little brother?"

"I come bearing news for the ears of the Brotherhood. I must speak to Raifen, or someone of similar rank."

"Who are you to ask that?"

In answer Baram used his talent to disappear for a few moments. When he became visible again the priest smiled at him and said, "I am honoured to meet one of the hands of the Avenger. I invite you to stand watch with us while we summon someone to take you to Raifen."

Baram stood, picked up his knife and turned away from the altar holding it ready for action in the first guard position. He blinked several times trying to clear tears from his eyes. *I never thought I'd be asked to stand watch, even for a short time. It's such an honour.*

It wasn't long before another man stepped into the sanctuary. He came through the Priest's Gate, his sword cradled in his arms. The sanctuary rang again with a brief chorus in praise of Huler.

"He will take you to Raifen," said the priest who had questioned Baram. Then he raised his sword to touch Baram's weapon and said, "May you walk in the presence of the god at all times."

O

The escorting priest ushered Baram into Raifen's study. It was unchanged since his last visit. The tapestry depicting Huler as the Craftsman still hung on the wall behind the desk, which was as cluttered as ever. He thought Raifen might have a little more grey in his beard but otherwise he looked the same.

"Well, Baram," said Raifen. "I'm glad you're here. It's been almost two months since you last came to see me. Tell me why it's taken so long and why you chose to be guided from the sanctuary. It's not as if you don't know the way here."

"I wanted to show Huler that I need his guidance so I used my journey here from the sanctuary as a symbol of that. I've a complicated story to tell and it leads on to something else that the Brotherhood should know about."

Raifen poured a glass of wine for Baram and said, "First of all you'd better tell me how you managed to kill Graumedel when you were forced by magic to serve him; and why you killed him at all when we had discussed the chaos his death might cause?"

"It wasn't me who killed him."

"It wasn't?"

"It's a long story," said Baram, and carried on to tell Raifen all about the deaths of Wurauf, Graumedel and The God. It took rather more than half a chime, interrupted as it was by exclamations of surprise and questions from Raifen when he wanted clarification of various points.

"Well, Baram. That's quite a tale," said Raifen, sitting back in his chair and stroking his beard. "You and this Anarya woman, who, although you didn't say so, has got to be a Sponger, have managed to disrupt Carrhen and Sitrelk at the same time. I hardly know what to say. One thing is obvious, the Brotherhood need to hear your story. We must go to the temple on the Great Square. The Brotherhood has been meeting there almost constantly since Wurauf's and Graumedel's deaths became known. There's a lot of tension and anxiety in the city right now."

"What's been happening?" asked Baram. "I'm only just back from Jotuk and I haven't heard anything."

"Let's get going and I'll bring you up to date as we go."

Baram had to be content with that.

They set out at a fast walk. Once they were well clear of the congestion on the Oxway, Raifen spoke, "One unexpected consequence of Wurauf's death is the king suddenly thrusting himself into the political consciousness. He's stopped being a figurehead and is establishing himself as a major player in what looks as if it might develop into a serious struggle for power. He seems to have considerable popular support."

"That's not surprising. Wurauf was never popular."

"That's why it isn't everyone who is in favour of Sulereath. If Wurauf was still alive the king could probably represent himself as a saviour, but he's declared himself Duke of Carrh as well as king. Go into any tavern and you'll hear some grumbling about that. Part of Wurauf's legacy is a distrust of anyone calling himself Duke of Carrh. People are afraid Sulereath is going to be as self-serving and as ruthless as Wurauf was in that position."

Raifen stopped talking as they tried to negotiate a corner blocked by two wagons jammed together. The drivers were screaming abuse at each other. The horses tried to pull their way clear but the wheels were interlocked and all they managed to do was jerk the wagons from side to side. People pushed their way past with many of them shouting curses at the drivers. Caged poultry on one of the wagons added to the cacophony with loud clucks and screeches.

Baram saw two men in the red and black tabards of the Duke of Carrh standing in the doorway of a nearby tavern. "Aren't they going to do anything?" he asked Raifen. "Shouldn't they be sorting this out?"

"You'd think so, and normally they would. The problem is their status is a bit uncertain at present and it's going to stay that way until the question of who rules in Carregis is sorted out. Anyway, two men aren't enough in a situation like this. I doubt if they'll do anything unless help arrives."

Two men in the leather vests of porters pushed their way through the crowd with remarkable ease. Gaps opened up for them and people staggered as they went past. Baram realised they were Lifters using their talents to push people aside and create the gaps. They got between the wagons and started pushing them backwards. The horses objected loudly to being forced back. The interlocked wheels separated. One of the porters waved the wagon with the poultry forward. It rattled around the corner away from the bottleneck and disappeared along the road.

The driver of the second wagon started berating the porters for letting the other one go first claiming that it had all been the other driver's fault. He stopped in mid-curse and sat down suddenly when one of the porters glared at him. Baram wasn't sure if he had been pushed by the Lifters or had decided he didn't want to antagonise them.

With the streets clear again Baram and Raifen continued on their way.

"One of the other main players is Latisec, the Duke of Alrem," said Raifen. He was in Carregis for talks with Wurauf when you killed the duke and he's hanging around trying to gather support for the argument that combining the roles of king and duke is too much for one person to cope with."

"You could say the same about combining two duchies."

"He's thought of that and says he will relinquish Alrem to his son if he becomes Duke of Carrh."

"Makes some sort of sense I suppose. I can understand why he wants Carrh. It's by far the richest duchy."

Raifen nodded his agreement.

"Who's going to succeed Graumedel?" asked Baram. "I remember you saying that if I killed him, the simplest solution would be for Wurauf to take over as Count of Carregis as well as Duke of Carrh, but that's obviously not possible."

Raifen snorted. "That's a good question. There are all sorts of rumours going around, some of them very far-fetched. The simple answer is nobody knows and that's why the city is so tense."

O

Baram had been in the main temple only once before. It was at least twice the size of the one on the Oxway he was familiar with, and was even more richly decorated. He paused at the entrance to touch his forehead, left shoulder, right shoulder and navel, making the sign of Huler's lightning bolt.

"Follow me," said Raifen and led Baram through an inconspicuous door and along a short passage to a small room. It held a statue of Huler in his aspect as the Good Companion, and two senior priests sitting at a desk.

One of them looked up as they entered and raised an eyebrow.

"I have urgent tidings for the Brotherhood," said Raifen.

The priest's other eyebrow went up. He gave Raifen parchment, a pen and ink and waited while he wrote a message. Then he took the folded parchment, said, "Wait here," and went through another door.

About a quarter later he returned and said, "The Brotherhood will see you now." Baram followed Raifen through the door and stopped. The murals depicting the eight aspects of Huler caught his attention as soon as he walked into the meeting room. They were stunning works of art and at first distracted Baram's attention from the people in the room.

Six senior priests in their rich red and gold vestments sat in comfortable looking, well-upholstered armchairs. One of them, seated in front of the stern-faced image of the Judge, was Rupesc, the head of the Brotherhood.

Raifen said, "Elder Brothers, it is my privilege to introduce Baram. He is the newest Stealther. He has important news."

Baram made the sign of the lightning bolt and waited to be addressed.

Rupesc echoed the gesture and said, "Stealthers are the hands of the god in his aspect as the Avenger but it is rare indeed for one to appear in front of this assembly. What do you have to say, younger brother?"

At the end of Baram's tale Rupesc sat forward in his chair and said, "We must think on this. Please wait outside while we discuss the news you have brought."

Baram made the sign of the lightning bolt again and left the room. He waited in silence, walking restlessly around while he tried to stay calm, aware of the scrutiny of the two priests at their desk. *Huler bless me, am I in trouble? Will they blame me? What else could I do?* Telling the story to such an exalted audience left him apprehensive and uncertain. He had seen all of them make the sign of Huler at some stage during his tale and knew it had disturbed them. *What will they do if they decide I was wrong to do what I did?*

He waited for the best part of a chime until Raifen appeared and invited him back into the meeting room.

"Little brother," said Rupesc, "Please be seated. We need to talk."

Baram relaxed a little. *It can't be too bad if they're asking me to sit.* He looked around. One of the empty seats was in front of the image of the Avenger, depicted with a bloody sword in one hand and lightning bolts crackling off the other. It seemed appropriate so he chose that seat.

"It seems, Baram, that you are, to some extent at least, responsible for the present situation," said Rupesc.

Baram shivered.

Rupesc continued, "However, there is no blame attached to that statement. You acted in accordance with the will of Huler as far as you could determine it."

Thank Huler, thought Baram, so relieved that he missed the next few words.

"...a task for you," said Rupesc. "Huler will not tolerate a woman entering the temple and you've probably heard that any who do die immediately."

Baram nodded.

"It is true, and it is also true that a man cannot enter a shrine of Quarenna and live. As a result, we must use intermediaries when it is necessary for the Brotherhood to speak to the Inner Circle of the Daughters of Quarenna. You are young for such a task but you are already involved and it would be foolish not to take advantage of that. We want you to be our liaison and suggest that you work with this Anarya to establish lines of communication between the temple and shrine."

"I understand," said Baram.

"Good. We suggest you involve Yisul cra Neyen too as the events in her homeland are also an issue."

Baram nodded.

"You need to know," said Rupesc, "that the Brotherhood is aware of creatures who would prey on people's emotions if given the chance. They are prevented from doing so by Huler and Quarenna. Several of us have experienced disturbing dreams recently. They suggest that Huler – and Quarenna – may be threatened by these creatures in some way. We must protect them as they protect us."

"What can we do against something that can threaten the gods?"

"We don't know, but we think it will involve encouraging Sitrelkers to adopt Huler and Quarenna as replacements for their dead god."

Baram sat in stunned silence for a while. "I will do what I can," he said. "May Huler be with me."

"We will all agree with that sentiment."

ANARYA'S LODGINGS
IN CARREGIS

When Anarya left the shrine and hurried away she had no destination in mind. Without thinking about where she was going she moved through the streets, wincing inwardly whenever she passed someone with a talent. The pressure and temptation weren't as bad as in Jotuk where the talented of the Twenty-three Families had been all around her. She could have helped herself to any talent she wanted at any time. The difficulty had been that they would immediately equate her to The God. That was something she didn't want and couldn't tolerate.

There were many talented in Carregis, perhaps not as many as in Jotuk, but their numbers were diluted by the majority with no talent at all and she met fewer of them. Nevertheless, just walking through the streets was difficult. She was much more aware of the talented she did meet than she had been before.

Her undirected wandering took her home, back to the room above the carpet shop where she had lived since moving to Carregis. *Thank Quarenna I paid three months rental in advance before we set off following Caseir, otherwise we'd have nowhere to stay.*

In the small square at the end of her street there was a tavern called *The Jolly Potboy*. A Whisperer used it as her place of business. Anarya knew the woman and had borrowed her talent several times. Previously she hadn't been aware of the Whisperer's aura unless she went into the tavern and looked directly at her. Discovering that now she could detect it from outside the building came as a shock.

Although it was months since she had been there she remembered the rickety step on the external staircase in time to be very careful about putting weight on it. The familiar surroundings of the small, cosy room made her feel more at ease after spending so much time on the road, in Verenthe and in Jotuk. She knelt in front of her statuette of Quarenna, touched her right thumb to her forehead and prayed for guidance.

She looked into her store cupboard wondering if there was anything there that was still edible after all that time away. Shrivelled fruit, mouldy bread, green bacon, petrified cheese and puddles of slime that had once been vegetables greeted her. The smell was eye-watering. She shut the cupboard door again quickly.

There was nothing there to distract her from the need to fill the emptiness inside her. It was getting stronger. She flung herself on to the bed and huddled in the corner feeling miserable. *What will I do when Yisa comes home? I'm not sure I can stand being so close to such a powerful talent without Thieving it.*

She must have dozed off because the next thing she knew was a gentle touch on her shoulder. She jumped up, instantly aware of Yisa's orange aura filling the room.

"No, I can't. I mustn't," she wailed.

Yisul wrapped her arms around her and said, "I am here, my love. Let me help."

"You can't. Let me go."

"I *can* help. I cannot bear to see you suffering like this. It is not needful. If you need to take my talent, you may have it."

Anarya looked into her partner's tearful face and felt her resolve shatter. The tendril of blackness from her aura zipped across the gap between them faster than she expected. An orange glow returned along it and Yisa's aura was extinguished."

Anarya stretched and took a deep breath. "That's wonderful. I feel alive again. Thank you."

Yisul gasped and shivered. "I did not know it would be like this. Now I understand what you mean by feeling empty."

Anarya closed her eyes, revelling in the sensation of holding a skill even if she wasn't using it.

"How long is this going to last?" asked Yisul.

"I don't know. It used to be I could hold your skills for three to four chimes. Somehow, I don't think it will be as long now. It doesn't feel quite the same. I'm not sure what the difference is. When I took from Baram I could only hold it for a sixth and I used to be able to be a Stealther for much longer than that."

It was less than a quarter later when Anarya slumped on to the bed saying, "It's gone."

"That was very quick, my love. I thought it would be longer."

Anarya tucked herself into the corner again and said, "Get out. Go now before I Thieve it from you again. The emptiness is back and I don't know what would happen if I filled it again. I desperately want to hold a talent, any talent. You're in danger, Yisa. Go!"

"I'm not afraid of you, Anra. I do not believe you would hurt me. Anyway, I have this," she picked up her cane from the table and twirled it. It hadn't been there before. She must have put it down when she came in. "I can protect myself."

"Please go," said Anarya through her tears, "The hunger is worse when you're near, when there's any talent nearby for me to steal. I've got to be by myself."

"If you insist."

O

Anarya was still huddled in the corner when Yisul returned that evening. "What are you doing here?" she snarled when she walked in. "I told you to go."

"I could not bear to see you like this," said Yisul. "I went to see Tilua and told her how you were suffering. She thought it might be possible to suppress your hunger or at least minimise it somehow. There are two possibilities. I have a potion here concocted by one of the Inner Circle which she thinks might help. It is based on one used when someone with an elemental affinity is fevered. Pyromancers, Aquamancers and the like can be dangerous if they lose control and don't realise what they are doing."

"I suppose it's worth a try." Anarya took the vial and drank its contents. She made a face. "Why does it have to be aniseed flavoured? I hate that."

"You do? You've never told me that before. It is a favourite ingredient in Sitrelk cooking. I often use it."

"That doesn't matter. How long will it take to work?"

"Probably about a quarter," said Yisul. "Do you really not like my cooking?"

"Only the stuff with aniseed in it. The rest's fine. We can talk about it later if you want. Just leave me alone until this concoction has a chance to work."

"I will come back in about a third," said Yisul as she left the room. "I am sure you haven't eaten, so I will bring some food back."

O

When Yisa returned Anarya looked warily at her. Then she relaxed a bit. "It's done something," she said. "The hunger's still there but it's not quite as bad. I can cope with this. How long will it last?"

"Who knows? This is as new to the Chemer who prepared the potion as it is to you."

"You said there were two possibilities. What's the other?"

"There's a Scratcher among the Inner Circle who thinks she can block the hunger. 'Put it in a cage' was the way she described it."

"I think I know what she means. I'd like to try that."

"Then we need to go to the shrine. The Scratcher can't leave it. But you must eat before we go, I have fried lentil cakes with bean curd."

LADRYSIDE IN JOTUK

A horse-drawn wagon carrying two men clattered across the cobbles on the approach to the tannery and pulled up at the entrance. The driver tossed the reins to his companion and jumped down from the box. "Stay there," he grunted. "Don' even think 'bout moving."

A man in a leather apron looked out from a shack and asked, "Whatdya got?"

"Eight hides."

"Where from?"

"Gronish, an' a couple o' farms round about."

"Got some from there only last week. What's they doin' sendin' more?

The driver shrugged. "Just bring what I can get," he said.

"Them animals healthy?"

"How would I know? Never see the beasts, do I, just their hides."

The tanner snorted. "Don' need them, got plenty right now. Can't give you more than three for each."

"Three! That's robbery! Worth six."

"They're worth what I'll give you for them, an' that's three."

"Look, two o' them is calfs, ye'll get good leather from them."

"Calfs? At this time o' year! What'ye tryin' to pull?"

The driver argued that the farmer had kept too many bull calves then changed his mind and decided to get rid of them. The tanner wasn't sympathetic, but he did examine the calf hides.

"They'll do," he admitted. "Five each for the calfs. Give you thirty for the lot, and I'm bein' generous."

"Cost me more than that," complained the driver.

"More fool you! Awright, I'll make it thirty-six."

"Forty."

"Thirty-eight, an' that's top."

The driver opened his mouth to try to push the price up some more.

"That's it," the tanner said. "I mean it. I don't do no higher. I gotta make a living too."

The driver grumbled but accepted he wasn't going to get any more. Actually, despite his continued complaints, he was satisfied with the outcome; he had made a profit.

"Second stack on left," said the tanner withdrawing into his shack after pouring tokens into the driver's hands.

"Get down," the driver told his assistant. "Gotta shift this lot."

"Don' feel too good."

"Tough! Didn't otta guzzled so much last night. Get down here an' do some work for a change."

The two of them manhandled the bundled hides into the indicated stack amid continual complaints from the assistant. Then they turned the wagon round and left.

They got as far as the bridge over the Ladry before the assistant groaned, doubled over and almost fell off the wagon.

"What's wrong with you?"

"Musta ate somethin' bad."

He clambered down from the wagon, vomited violently into the grass by the side of the road and collapsed.

The driver looked down at the puddle of vomit. It was a green liquid, with some streaks of blood in it. Nothing solid. He went pale and got the horse moving, leaving his companion face down in the ditch. "May The God protect me," he muttered over and over again as he whipped up the horse and rushed away from Jotuk as fast as he could.

THE SHRINE OF QUARENNA

"Ah'm Belari," said the priestess, in a thick East Illic accent. "Can't get up, sorry." She pointed at her right leg which was propped up on a cushion. "Broke my ankle. Hope ah'll be able to help you. Sit yourself down. Need to wait until potion wears off or we won't know if glyph ah'm planning to use works." Belari picked up an embroidery frame and settled back in her chair with a grunt.

Anarya waited, getting more and more impatient as time went by and the potion still seemed to be working. It took almost two chimes before she was tempted by Belari's talent to an extent that she could say the potion was no longer effective.

She reported that to Belari who said, "Since you're a Sponger ah suppose you've tried being a Scratcher."

When Anarya agreed that she had, Belari continued, "Be you familiar with basket glyphs?"

"I think I know what you mean," replied Anarya. "I have seen glyphs that could be described that way but I only know how to construct two of them. One of the ones I know causes sleep and the other produces pain."

Belari raised an eyebrow. "Them are advanced constructions. How did you learn them and no any easier ones?"

Anarya started to answer then Belari interrupted. "Don't matter. Ah'm going to try something that'll isolate a craving. Ah've used it to treat addictions. Works most times. That feeling you have and call a 'hunger' might be same sort of thing. Might be ah can isolate and mask it. Sit yourself there and don't move unless ah tell you."

Anarya took the indicated seat. She squirmed a bit,

trying to get more comfortable.

"Sit still, girl," snapped Belari. "Be difficult enough without distractions."

Hardly daring to breathe, Anarya sat as quietly as she could. A tenth of a chime passed, then she felt that something was closing in on her from behind. She was tempted to turn and look over her shoulder but managed to stay still except for one small twitch which elicited an annoyed tongue click from Belari.

Moments later Belari said "Got it," in a pleased tone. "How d'you feel?"

"Better. Yes, much better! I can still see auras, but they're not so clear, and there isn't the same feeling of need. I could live like this, I think."

"Good!" Belari looked and sounded contented. "Now we need to know how long effect'll last. Do you play vurlo?"

Anarya blinked in surprise at the change of subject. "I know the game but I'm not very good."

"Pity. Still, we can play for a bit until glyph wears off. Set's on table over there."

As Anarya expected, Belari was an expert player and beat her easily in six straight games without Anarya making a single scoring combination in the last of them. Then Belari got fed up with easy victories and said, "Anarya, bring me scroll from top of pile over there, to left of door. One with silver spiral on end o' rod." Anarya was surprised to find it was a copy of *The Lives of Jurtey*, a famous erotic novel. Belari read for a bit, then put the scroll down, shuffled down her chair and went to sleep.

Anarya managed to fall asleep in her chair, waking up with a crick in her neck just after the fourth chime. She stood and moved through the first sequence of the dynamic meditation, stretching the kinks out of her back and neck.

"You still here?" asked Belari. "Help me sit up."

Acolytes came in at the fifth chime with breakfast for both of them. Yisul and Tilua appeared soon after, wanting to know how Anarya was feeling and seeming satisfied with her response. They were followed by two more of the Inner Circle, an Aquamancer and a Seeker who wanted to ask Yisul questions about Sitrelker society.

They were deep into discussion when the Seeker suddenly jumped up saying, in a shocked voice, "What's happened? I'm lost! My talent's gone!"

"I'm sorry, Your Reverence," said Anarya. "I couldn't help it. Suddenly everybody's aura flared up and I couldn't stop myself grabbing one of them."

Belari looked at the waterclock. "Eleven chimes. Glyph lasted eleven chimes. That's good. Sit still and ah'll renew it."

Once the glyph was re-established Anarya knelt in front of the Seeker and said, "Forgive me, Your Reverence. My Thieving of your talent was involuntary. It will return to you."

"When? It was quite a shock when it vanished, and it's a very strange and uncomfortable sensation being without it."

"It should come back to you soon. I've never been able to be a Seeker for very long," replied Anarya.

"My love, you have already held that talent for three quarters of a chime. That is much, much longer than you usually can."

"Holy Quarenna, you're right, Yisa. The timings are all mixed up." She shook her head. "I'm afraid I don't know the answer, Your Reverence."

It was three chimes later when Anarya lost the Seeker's ability. The glyph was still effective, so she didn't immediately grab another talent from someone.

"Thank you, Belari, thank you. I think you have saved me. I was beginning to think I might go mad from the need."

Tilua said, "I'm afraid this is only a temporary solution. The glyph lasts about eleven chimes before needing to be renewed. That's good, but not good enough. To be safe it would have to be remade twice a day and that would put a great strain on Belari."

"One of my students is nigh as strong as me," stated Belari after a moment's thought. "Might be she could give you her talent and let you cast glyph on yourself."

"Is that possible?" asked Tilua. "I've never heard of Scratchers using their talent on themselves."

"Done it a few times," said Belari. "Not easy but worth a try. Might help. Course it's not a permanent answer."

The student, Kemeneah by name, was a waif-like girl of eighteen with big brown eyes in a heart-shaped face framed by long chestnut hair tumbling out from under her green and gold headscarf. Belari told her what was needed and she agreed to take part in the experiment.

Anarya took Kemeneah's talent. That meant she could see the thin yellow threads of the Scratcher's magic as Belari drew them in the air. She concentrated on remembering the twists and turns of the basket weave and what Belari told her about each part of the structure as she demonstrated how to put it together. It was much easier learning from an expert than trying to do it all herself from watching it happen without any guidance.

Belari dismissed the glyph once it was formed. She made it once more with Anarya again watching carefully. Then she dismissed the second one too and told Anarya to try it herself.

She made two false starts and hesitated several times before Belari was satisfied that she had got it right.

"Now aim it at yourself and let it go."

Anarya watched the glyph float up from the space in front of her until it surrounded her head. Then it shrank inwards and was gone.

"Well done, girl. You got it."

Anarya lost Kemeneah's talent in a little over two chimes. The glyph she had cast worked. She was aware of the hunger, but it was controllable.

"Thank you for your assistance, daughter," Tilua said to Kemeneah, "What I am about to ask is not something you have to do. It is entirely voluntary. Anarya has a serious problem and needs to have a glyph cast on her every ten chimes. We have just proved she can cast it on herself. However, she has to have a Scratcher's skill to do so. Would you be willing to let her steal your talent often enough over the next few weeks to keep herself from running amok?"

Kemeneah thumbed her forehead, "It is my duty to help."

"No," Tilua disagreed. "It is not a duty. It will be difficult for you being without your talent and we cannot ask you to make such a sacrifice for more than a short time. We are looking for a permanent solution to her problem. Even if we fail we will not ask you to do more."

Anarya got up from her seat and walked over to stand in front of Kemeneah. She went down on her knees to say, "I can't thank you enough for what you have done today. I didn't know that Blessèd Tilua was going to suggest what she has. I wouldn't have dreamt of doing so myself, because I know what it feels like to become talentless. It's not something I would wish on anyone."

Kemeneah lifted her head and said, "Blessèd Tilua, I hear what you say about this not being a duty. One of the things you have taught me since I became a novice is the importance of personal integrity. There is something I can do to help a needy daughter, so I must do it." She turned towards Anarya. "I will help you. All I ask is that you continue to trust in Holy Quarenna."

"I will do that gladly," replied Anarya. "I will also make a promise to her that I will not accept your sacrifice for more than – let's say two months. If we don't have an answer by then I will find an alternative solution somehow. After all, the potion isn't as effective as the glyph but it does work and I could use that."

Tilua shook her head. "I trust that isn't a rash promise. I think you are a potential danger, to yourself as well as the talented. We must take precautions. I believe it would be best if you stay here in the shrine while we try to find a permanent answer."

"Your pardon, Blessèd Tilua," said Yisul, "do you mean Anarya will not be able to take me back to Jotuk through the portal?"

"I don't know," shrugged Tilua. "Give us two days to make sure she can deal with her craving for a talent. If she can cope with using the glyph, then I see no reason why she couldn't make a short trip."

A VILLAGE IN THE DUCHY OF ALREM

Nasuren sat in one corner of the tavern with a mug of ale in front of him waiting for his new friend, Jaric the miller, to arrive. They had met the previous day when Nasuren walked into the tavern looking for somewhere to stay for a couple of nights. *The Ploughman's Rest* was too small to have a guest room so when Jaric had offered him a room at the mill for one bit a night he had accepted gratefully. It was a better arrangement than he could have hoped for.

The tavern's one room was small, but then it didn't have any reason to be bigger. The village had only fifteen houses, clustered round a crossroads. One of the roads was in a better state of repair than the others. It was the one that led to the mill, then across the border into the duchy of Carrh and, eventually, to the market town of Bouren. The other roads were little more than rutted tracks leading to nearby farms.

Properly speaking the village was in Alrem, but nobody cared about that except when Duke Latisec's tax collectors arrived on their twice a year circuit. Then the villagers and farmers gathered in *The Ploughman's Rest* and grumbled about the benefits they didn't get in return for their taxes.

The tavern-keeper, who was also the nearest thing the village had to a blacksmith, remarked, "You did well to get out of the mill today if Jaric is grinding. It gets terrible noisy and dusty when he does."

Nasuren agreed. "I'd have been out and about anyway. Can't check the maps without looking around." He had told the villagers he worked for a map maker. It had provoked comments about the accuracy, or lack of it, of the existing maps and he had been accepted by the tavern customers. "Did well today. I'll finish my survey tomorrow and move on the day after."

"Jaric'll be here soon," said the tavern-keeper. "He usually finishes milling about the fourteenth chime and comes straight here to wash the dust from his throat. But he might be earlier if you're going to take him on at 'shoes again."

Nasuren nodded. "Yes, I told him I'd have another game with him today. Can't do any worse than yesterday."

"You'd better get some practice in then. Jaric's been tossing 'shoes all his life, and you told us you'd never seen the game before. Not surprising he thrashed you."

"You're right," said Nasuren. He finished his ale and walked out the back door to the horseshoes pitch. He was hefting some of the 'shoes trying to find the lightest when Jaric arrived.

"Ready?" asked Jaric.

"I guess so."

"You can toss first. Loser buys, right?"

Nasuren wasn't sure if being first was an advantage or not but he nodded to Jaric, stepped up to one of the metal rods embedded in the ground and took aim at the other one ten paces away. His first horseshoe hit the ground well short and the second toss was only slightly better.

Jaric laughed. Both his 'shoes clanged against the target post and fell encircling it.

"I'll get the ale," said Nasuren, stepping back into the tavern and emerging with two full mugs.

Jaric downed half a mugful in one gulp and stepped up to throw again. He tossed another two ringers. Nasuren's efforts were little better than his first pair. It wasn't until the fourth attempt that he managed to hit the post with one of his 'shoes. Even then, it spun away and didn't score.

Half a chime later two of the tavern's regular customers, a shepherd and a pig farmer who Nasuren had met the previous day, walked into the tavern. They saw there was a game in progress and settled down to watch.

Their comments on Nasuren's lack of skill annoyed Jaric who told them, "At least he tries. If you think you can do better, prove it."

The shepherd took up the challenge. He played well, scoring several times, but it wasn't enough for him to win. The pig farmer then refused to face Jaric, saying, "I know you're too good for me." He pointed at Nasuren saying, "But I reckon I can beat him."

"What about the two of you against Jaric and me," asked Nasuren. "Loser buys."

"I'll go for that," said the pig farmer.

Jaric looked sceptical but agreed when Nasuren said, "Won't cost you if we lose. I'll pay."

The contest was watched with interest by the three other villagers who had turned up. It was close but, on the last end Nasuren threw two bad 'shoes and lost the game.

"First time he's been beat in, what is it – three years, or four?" commented the tavern-keeper, filling their mugs. "Do him good to be took down a peg."

Nasuren passed the mugs around, making sure Jaric got the one he had added a potion to.

It was getting too dark to throw again, so they moved inside and chatted for about half a chime. Jaric said he didn't bear Nasuren any ill will for the loss, drank the ale off in a couple of swallows and got some more. A quarter later he started slurring his words and blinking uncertainly.

Jaric pulled himself to his feet and staggered his way to the door with Nasuren following him amid comments that they couldn't hold their ale.

"'Bout time we was going too," said the pig farmer. The shepherd agreed and both of them left *The Ploughman's Rest* and turned along a different road from the one Jaric and Nasuren took.

The Bouren road ran alongside the river. Jaric came to a stop where a bridge carried it across. He peered at the amount of water running into the mill stream, muttered something incoherent and reached out unsteadily to make an adjustment to the sluice gate.

The potion Nasuren had put in Jaric's ale wasn't enough to kill him but it exaggerated the effects of the alcohol and Jaric was, by now, very, very drunk. Nasuren had taken another potion that had the opposite effect and was quite sober. He bumped into Jaric hard enough to send him into the stream then flopped on top of him to hold him under.

Soaking wet, Nasuren went back to the tavern to report that both of them had fallen in the stream and ask for help getting Jaric out. Of course, it was much too late for his victim.

Another relative taken care of.

A VILLAGE WEST OF JOTUK

"Go away!"

The voice came from behind a barricade of overturned wagons, fence posts, barrels and hay bales

"Go back where ye came from. Ye're no welcome here an' ye're no comin' through."

"We aye come this way," called a melodious voice from the wagon stopped on the road outside the barricade.

"No this time. Leave!" The message was emphasised by the twang of a crossbow and the thud as the bolt struck the wagon only a foot or so from the driver.

"Hey! What's wrong? You know us! We come this way every year and fix your broken pots and pans, sell you needles, thread and yarn and that sort of thing; and we'll play, sing and dance for you!"

"We know ye. But we don' want ye here this year. Go back to Gronish."

"Came from Ferchett, not Gronish."

"Go back there then. Ye're no bringin' the Sickness here."

"Sickness? What Sickness?"

"Don' pretend ye don' know. Seventeen people died in Gronish in last week, pukin' their guts up wi' the Greenwater. Half the village tried to run here but we kept them out. Ain't had any die on us and we're makin' sure it stays that way."

"Greenwater! That's bad. Anybody passed the word eastward? A lot of people will die if it gets to Jotuk."

"No. We're no goin' anywhere t' tell anybody anythin'. Let Jotuk look after itself."

"But…"

"But, nothin'. You turn ye'selves round right now or the crossbows'll be aimed at flesh."

CARREGIS

"Can I go out today?" asked Anarya over breakfast. "Please say yes. I love it here in the shrine, it's so calm and peaceful. But it's been three days and we know the glyph works. I can't stay here forever."

Tilua frowned. "Are you sure you can cope with the 'hunger'?"

"Yes, I am. Holy Quarenna be my witness, when I have a glyph protecting me I do notice talents more than I used to, but there isn't the compulsion to Thieve one unless the glyph wears out. Then it's sudden and irresistible. On the two occasions it's happened I've grabbed a Seeker's talent and an Aquamancer's just like that." She tried to snap her fingers and failed to produce any sound. She laughed. "I've never been very good at doing that, but you know what I mean."

"I do," said Tilua. "And I'm relieved you've managed to hold on to a sense of humour. I think we can risk letting you go out. Take a walk when you've finished eating but come back at least a chime before you need to renew the glyph."

Anarya folded the last fragment of a pancake, used it to wipe the remains of a smear of winterberry jam from her plate, stuffed it into her mouth, gulped down the dregs of her redleaf tea and said, "I'm ready."

"Very well," said Tilua, smiling at her haste. "Take care."

O

The warden stopped Anarya on her way back into the shrine and said, "There's a message for you. First for a long time, but I suppose you get most of your business through your contract with the newsmongers these days." She reached back into her cubbyhole and produced a folded parchment. "Here it is."

Anarya accepted it and paid the warden a quarter-bit. *What is it? Hope it's something I can ignore. I don't really need a quaestor's contract at the moment. Not on top of everything else.* She walked into the peace of the shrine. Although the glyph she had cast on herself had kept her from feeling the need to Thieve, she was relieved to be back in its calm atmosphere.

She found a quiet corner of the garden and settled herself on a bench under an oak tree laden with acorns before opening the parchment.

It was from Baram. 'Can we meet tomorrow? Got something we need to talk about. How about lunch at the *Halfway Point*? I'll pay.'

I wonder what he wants. No harm in finding out – at least I'll get a good meal out of it.

O

The weather was cool for mid-autumn so Anarya went to meet Baram wearing a knitted shawl over a cream linen blouse and a full skirt of pale green felt. He was waiting for her, looking smart in a grey and black velveteen doublet and tight breeches. He was standing on the terrace looking out over the river when she came up behind him. *He's got a nice bum*, she thought, *never noticed that before.*

"It's good to see you, Anarya. Thanks for coming."

"Your message was intriguing. What's on your mind?"

"Let's have lunch first."

"That sounds ominous. Are you trying to soften me up for something?"

"Not really, it's just that I'm hungry and I've watched several platters of good looking food being served while I've been waiting.

"All right. Food first, business later."

"Have you heard about the fire in Trevemb?" asked

Baram after they had ordered their meal.

"Did hear the newsmongers say something about it, but I didn't pay it any attention. I don't even know where Trevemb is."

"It's a little place up in the mountains of Simand, hardly big enough to be called a town."

"So why is this backwater interesting enough to get the newsmongers talking?"

"They're saying the fire was started deliberately. Not only that, somebody stabbed the only Pyromancer in the area when he went to put it out. He survived, but two buildings were destroyed, and everybody who lived in them, including five children, died."

"That's terrible. Why would anybody do that?"

"That's where it gets a bit speculative. One of the women who died was distantly related to Wurauf…"

"Poor woman. Not something anyone would want to boast about."

"No, but I suppose he had to have relatives of some sort. Anyway, two other people with similarly distant relationships to Wurauf have died recently, one of them in a brawl and the other in what seemed to be an accident."

"So?"

"It's being suggested that somebody with a grudge against Wurauf is going around killing his relatives."

Anarya snorted. "Funny sort of revenge when the person it's aimed at is dead. More likely it's another distant relative eliminating people who might have a better claim to his estate."

"That's very cynical."

"But you've got to admit it's more likely than somebody exacting revenge."

"I suppose. Right now I'm more interested in food."

A server brought them bowls of a thick, spicy seafood casserole, small loaves of freshly baked bread and mugs of apple cider.

"Looks good," said Baram, sniffing the casserole

"Is good," replied Anarya around her first mouthful.

A quarter later they were using the last of the bread to mop up the remains of the casserole. Anarya took a deep draught of cider, sat back and asked, "What is it you wanted to talk about?"

"Because of what I've told the Brotherhood about the death of The God I've been asked to act as liaison between the Brotherhood and the Inner Circle. They suggested you would be a good point of contact since you already know about the events in Jotuk."

"But I'm not… I mean…"

"I know what you're thinking – that you're not important enough for this sort of thing. I feel the same. But I've got to try. The Brotherhood told me about strange dreams they've been having."

Anarya interrupted him, saying, "Blessèd Tilua told me some of the Inner Circle are having disturbing dreams too."

"Dreams which seem to be threatening the gods?"

"What! No, she didn't say anything like that, just dreams that worried them."

"Will you help me set up a meeting with Tilua, or somebody else from the Inner Circle?"

"Yes, of course I will. The problem is where. You live in the temple, don't you? Tilua couldn't go there. And I wouldn't want to entertain her in my room, it's not good enough."

"How about Graumedel's mansion?" said Baram, after a moment's thought. "It's grand enough and nobody's using it at present. Both of us are known to the guards and they're not going to refuse access to important people from the temple and shrine."

"Good idea, Baram. Let's go and set it up.

"When for?

"Soon, I think. Shall we try for tomorrow?"

O

Anarya led Tilua along the upper corridor on the southern side of Graumedel's mansion, opened the door to a room close to the south-west corner, indicated that Tilua should enter, and followed her. *Hope I got it right and this is the room Baram meant.*

The room was both library and picture gallery. Several desks were dotted around the room with a lightweight wooden chair at each of them, their woollen cushions decorated with the beehive emblem of the Counts of Carregis. A blue deep pile carpet covered the floor and muffled any footsteps. Black and gold embroidery bordered the linen curtains at the windows overlooking the central courtyard.

A portrait of the late Count Graumedel occupied a prominent position above a fireplace. Tilua studied it and commented, "I don't know the artist but, if that's a typical example of his work, he certainly knows how to flatter his clients."

Baram arrived a few moments later and ushered a short, slightly chubby man with a full ginger beard into the room. He bowed towards Tilua saying, "May I introduce Grovaen, a senior member of the Brotherhood of Huler."

Grovaen also bowed, saying, "Thank you for agreeing to meet me. We have a lot to discuss."

"Indeed we do. I am Tilua. Jaenis has mentioned your name so I know you are one of the king's advisers."

"I have that honour," said Grovaen. "I don't know if she also told you about my talent. I am sure our discussions will be open and honest but politeness requires me to tell you I am a Feeler."

"I knew that," replied Tilua. "I am a Sponger, and I have just copied your talent."

Grovaen looked surprised, "Really? I felt nothing."

"No reason why you should. Now that we know about each other perhaps we should sit and start our meeting."

Baram moved two of the chairs closer together. With a gesture he invited Tilua and Grovaen to sit, then he stepped back and started towards the door.

"Don't go, Baram," said Grovaen. "I think you will have some information to contribute. Although I wasn't at the meeting when you told the Brotherhood about the events in Jotuk, I have been briefed on what you said. I think this discussion might bring up some points that need clarification."

"You stay too, Anarya. Get chairs for yourselves." Tilua turned to Grovaen and waved towards Anarya and Baram. "These two are already deeply involved. I think they should be told more, if only for their own protection."

Grovaen sighed and signed himself with Huler's lightning bolt. "It goes against the grain to tell this to anyone not in the highest rank of the priesthood, but I suppose you're right."

"I know what you mean," said Tilua. "To the best of my knowledge only the other eight members of the Inner Circle know anything of what we are going to discuss. I'm reluctant to increase that number but I think we must tell these two."

She looked at Anarya and Baram and added, "We will require promises from you that what you hear goes no farther than your ears."

Grovaen nodded his agreement, listened while Anarya and Baram swore oaths of secrecy, then commented, "I think it will be interesting to hear if what the Inner Circle knows is the same as what the Brotherhood knows."

"I hadn't thought about that. There might be some differences," said Tilua, nodding. "Shall I start?"

"Not quite yet. We're sitting in the shade. Let's move the chairs into the sunlight. I think I would feel more comfortable being in Huler's gaze for this discussion," said Grovaen.

When the chairs were rearranged to his satisfaction, Tilua started by saying, "Anarya, I know you come from Hemeark because that's where I first met you. You had friends among the expatriate Sitrelker community there, didn't you?"

"Yes."

"Did they ever speak of their gods?"

"No," replied Anarya, in a puzzled tone after a moment's thought, "Now that you mention it, the ones who didn't revere Quarenna never said anything I can remember about who they did worship."

"It's unusual for someone untalented to become a member of the Inner Circle but it has happened twice in the last hundred years. Both times the women were refugees from Sitrelk. They have told us about what they believed prior to becoming worshippers of Holy Quarenna."

"Interesting," said Grovaen. "The same sort of thing has happened in the temple. Thirty-odd years ago a Sitrelker convert became a member of the Brotherhood and told us what he knew about the gods of Sitrelk. He would have been a good person to ask. Unfortunately, he's been dead for four years."

"It's difficult to believe," said Tilua, "considering how well Quarenna and Huler complement each other, but at one time they were enemies."

"It's true." Grovaen confirmed Tilua's statement over the incredulous gasps from Anarya and Baram. "There were once many gods who fought among themselves. Gradually the weaker were defeated by the stronger until only Huler, Quarenna and a few others were left."

"How many does the Brotherhood think 'a few' is?" asked Tilua.

"I believe there were six others."

"That's what the Inner Circle has been told too. It was only after Quarenna and Huler agreed to a partnership that they managed to defeat and imprison these other gods."

"The six who were imprisoned are known to Sitrelkers as the Confined Ones."

"Pardon me, Your Reverences," said Anarya into a pause, "I didn't hear anybody in Jotuk mention these Confined Ones'"

"You have only been among the Twenty-three Families, the elite of Sitrelk, and they don't recognise the Confined Gods," remarked Tilua.

"However," said Grovaen, "they *are* worshipped by many in Sitrelk."

Anarya saw Baram frowning and knew she was too. "I'm confused. I don't see how this relates to The God and the current situation in Sitrelk."

"The Brotherhood keeps a record of the talented. I imagine the Inner Circle does too."

"We do."

"The archive of the temple goes back almost nine hundred years. Some of the oldest documents are fragmentary but there is a good record for at least eight hundred. The rarest talent of all, Thiever, has only been listed twice in that time. On both occasions the talent was associated with multiple murders when the Thiever learned how to keep the abilities he took."

"I've nothing to add," said Tilua. "We know the talent exists but there are no Thievers listed in the annals of the Inner Circle."

Grovaen got up and started pacing around the room. "There was one occasion, nearly three hundred and fifty years ago in the reign of Fereathlin II, when one of the Thiever's victims was his own sister. He was so horrified at what he had done that he surrendered to the Brotherhood and confessed his crimes. Before being executed he claimed that a god had forced him to do what he did.

"Needless to say, that claim wasn't given much credence at the time. Now, knowing about the Confined Gods, and the blood-thirsty nature of some of them, we wonder if there might be something to it after all. Perhaps The God was influenced in the same way."

Tilua blanched. "You're suggesting that one, or more, of the Confined Gods is free."

"Perhaps not totally free," replied Grovaen, "but able to reach out from prison to touch the world and influence susceptible people."

"Holy Quarenna aid us!" said Tilua. "They must hate her and Huler for imprisoning them. That could explain the threatening dreams we have been having."

"What can we do?" asked Anarya and Baram almost simultaneously.

There was silence in the room for about a tenth except for the quiet scuff of Grovaen's feet on the carpet as he paced around. He stopped near Anarya's chair and said to her, "You say most of the Families have stopped worshipping The God and some of them are finding the lack of a god troublesome. What about their servants?"

"And what about the segment of the population who worship the Confined Ones?" added Tilua.

"I don't know." Anarya shook her head, "As I told you, I've never heard of the Confined Gods before today. But I can think of one thing that might help."

"What?"

"I've been asked by some of the leaders of the Families to invite volunteers to go to Jotuk and tell people about Quarenna and Huler. If the Families start worshipping our gods then their servants are likely to do the same, as they did when The God was the focus of their devotions."

"And that will weaken these Confined Gods," said Tilua. "The Inner Circle has already considered this and we agree it's the right thing to do. We have started recruiting potential teachers to go to Jotuk."

"I feel sure that the Brotherhood will do likewise, although I must admit that your planning is ahead of ours," said Grovaen. "However, we will have to restrict our teachings to those who are willing to learn and not fill the ears of those who don't want to hear. The last thing we want to do is antagonise people and harden their attitudes towards the volunteers."

"I think we are finished now," commented Tilua after the discussion had gone on for another half and they were starting to repeat themselves.

Grovaen agreed and left with Baram escorting him.

"I noticed you didn't tell him you're now a Thiever," said Tilua when they were alone.

"You didn't mention it either."

"It's your secret, not mine to give away."

"Do you think there's a possibility that this thing Grovaen talked about might try to take control of me?"

"I don't know, Anarya. I really don't. All I can say is trust in Holy Quarenna."

Anarya thumbed her forehead and said a silent prayer, but it didn't settle the hollow feeling in her stomach.

HOUSE NEYEN

"We can go to Jotuk today, Yisa. Everyone is satisfied that the glyph can cage my hunger and I have a couple of vials of the potion as well, just in case. Tilua has given me permission to go as soon as I construct a new glyph so that I have the maximum protection while we're away."

"Good."

When Anarya was ready they set out to find the portal. She berated herself again for not moving the Carregis end to somewhere more convenient than the alley near the Sailmaker's Guildhouse. She had just accepted that as the default destination in Carregis, though she could have moved it at any time since she bargained with the daimon for control. *I'll do it this trip. Where will I put it? Home is the obvious place, and it would be best, wouldn't it?*

"Keep watch, Yisa, we don't want anyone to notice us going down the alley and not coming out again."

Yisul used her talent to check that nobody was in position to see them as they manoeuvred themselves past the bales of canvas stacked along one side.

"It's still here," said Anarya, spotting the portal near the end of the alley.

"Where else would it be?"

"I don't know. It's just that I have to trust the daimon, and I worry about that. I can't do anything if it's changed its mind about our bargain and moved or closed the portal for some reason. I'm always relieved to find it where I expect it to be."

She took a firm grip of Yisul's hand, grasped the doorknob and, with a muttered prayer to Holy Quarenna, pulled the door open.

The hubbub of the midday crowd in *The Seventh Step* greeted them. It was as busy as they had ever seen it.

Busy enough to keep three servers occupied as they bustled around the room dispensing mugs of ale and platters of food, trying to keep the customers satisfied.

Anarya noticed that despite the crowd nobody was sitting at, or even standing close to, the table with the bloodstained top. She nudged Yisul and said, "I can see why Limabur wants the table back."

They turned around, avoiding more people entering the tavern, and Anarya opened the door again. This time it led to the reception room of the suite she had occupied in House Neyen.

O

Yisa struck a gong and asked the servant who answered, "Is my father in his study?"

"No, Lady Yisul. He has gone to a meeting at House Shuth."

"Has my mother gone too?"

"Lady Lias is at home."

"Would you tell her we are here and ask her to join us."

"Certainly, Lady Yisul."

After a short wait, Lias cra Branidh entered the room. She was wearing a sheer watered-silk dress with a deep V-neckline which showed off a silver and emerald pendant in the shape of a tree-dancer.

Anarya responded to her bow with one of her own. *I wish I could look as elegant as she does.* She watched as Lias hugged Yisul. The close bond between mother and daughter was obvious and made Anarya regret the rather turbulent relationship she had with her own mother.

"It is good to see you both again," said Lias. "Have you come to stay for a while?"

"I can stay a day or two," answered Yisul, "but Anarya has to go in four or five chimes at the latest. We have come to find out what is happening."

Lias sank gracefully on to the sofa, making Anarya feel clumsy by comparison when she sat on one of the chairs.

"Is the Sovereign Council a success?" asked Yisul.

Lias made a derisive noise. "If what you want is endless arguments then I suppose it can be considered a success. I'm getting worried about Muhan. He's wearing himself out trying so hard to reconcile the different factions. Not just those on the Sovereign Council but all the other splinter groups that are forming, breaking apart and re-aligning themselves. A surprising number, maybe as many as sixty, still revere The God. Most of the others are prepared to wait and see what happens. There are some who want their status enhanced but aren't prepared to participate in decision making and others who are willing to involve themselves, but only on their own terms."

"At least they're still talking and not fighting," said Anarya.

"I wish it were so," sighed Lias. "There have been many skirmishes and a few major confrontations between different factions. At least seven people have been killed."

"Who?" asked Yisul, "Anybody I know? Anybody important?"

"Mianil cra Hivarn was badly burnt when a Pyromancer attacked her. She was saved by an Aquamancer from the Colnis Family who filled the Pyromancer's lungs with water and drowned him. Apart from her, the Heads of Family haven't been attacked. Most of those killed have been relatively obscure and I doubt if you'd know them." She looked thoughtful and then said, "Except, that is for Ionek cra Fimigh. I remember you were quite friendly with him at one time."

"Ionek's dead! How?"

"He was distracted by a Terromancer destabilising the ground under his feet at just the wrong moment."

"Oh! Poor Ionek." She shuddered. "Don't tell me the details. I don't want to know what happened to him." Yisul turned to Anarya. "I liked Ionek. We sang in the same choir. He was a Daimoner but he hated his talent and rarely used it. He was always afraid he would make a mistake summoning a daimon and…"

"And the Terromancer made him lose concentration while calling one" said Anarya. "I understand. I don't want to know the details either."

"Are you safe, mother?"

"I think so. The more progressive Families, mostly those involved in the conspiracy, have banded together to protect each other. Lodesh has made sure everyone involved is trustworthy."

"Good."

"Excuse me," said Anarya, "who is Lodesh?"

"She's mother's sister," answered Yisul. "She's a very strong Feeler. I'm glad to know she's vetting the people around my parents."

The conversation stopped when a servant arrived with a trolley carrying a stack of pastries, a selection of teas and a jug of hot water. She quickly made and served chamil to Anarya and greenberry tea to Lias and Yisul before passing round the pastries. Anarya sniffed one and was relieved to find it didn't smell of aniseed. She took a cautious bite and discovered they were filled with a delicious honey and nut paste.

Anarya caught an expression on Lias' face that made her say, "Something is bothering you," after the servant had left with the remnants of the snack.

"Yes," admitted Lias, with a sigh. "It's all quite worrying but there's one thing in particular. Some members of the Families, particularly the younger ones like Rinil cra Monost, are becoming – I suppose dispirited is the best way to describe it, maybe even apathetic. Those of us who have lived for years with the idea that The God wasn't divine seem to be coping pretty well. However, many now seem to feel there is something missing in their lives."

"I understand, mother," said Yisul. "I felt the same at one point. Anarya was a great help to me. She introduced me to the worship of Holy Quarenna and I have found that fulfilling and rewarding. Perhaps it would be the same for others."

Lias looked at Anarya and told her, "I have heard the

names of the gods you worship in Carrhen but I know nothing more of them than that. Can you enlighten me?"

"Are you also affected, mother? Is that why you're asking?"

"No – well, yes, to some extent, I suppose. I can understand why some are troubled without feeling it greatly myself. I am fortunate to have Muhan's support, although he has enough to worry about without me adding to his problems." Lias turned to Anarya. "Will you tell me about Quarenna and Huler."

"I – I don't know where to start," said Anarya. "Quarenna just *is*. She is the god of women. She has always been part of my life, even before she blessed me with a talent. I don't have to think about my bond with her. I can answer your questions but I don't know how to teach you in any organised way. And I can't tell you anything about Huler. Women don't relate to him." Anarya stood and started pacing around the room. "Yisul would be a better teacher for you because she has come late to Quarenna's worship and you must have the same questions she did."

"A priestess would be even better," commented Yisul.

"But there are none in Jotuk," said Lias. "Just imagine how The God would have reacted to someone speaking of other gods. He wouldn't have tolerated it."

"There are none now, but there could be. Anra could bring someone through the portal quite easily."

"Would it be safe?" asked Anarya. "There are still those who revere The God. Could someone teaching about Quarenna be kept safe from them?"

"I will talk to Muhan when he gets home. We have been wondering what to do about the disinterest that seems to be afflicting some of the Families. Inviting people from Carrhen to speak to us of their gods might be the answer."

"I believe Tilua has started recruiting teachers for you. I'll ask her how it's going when I get back to Carregis," said Anarya. "Speaking of which I think I should leave soon."

"You know you are welcome to stay here as long as you wish," said Lias.

"Thank you," said Anarya. *I wish I could tell Lias about being a Thiever. I'm sure she'd be sympathetic. But I'd better not.* "I would like to stay but I have things to do and I must leave. I will return in a couple of days."

IN THE DARKWORLD

Anarya opened the portal to take her back to Carregis and once more found herself stepping into darkness.

Oh, not again! What does it want this time?

She waited for the daimon to appear, remembering that it had said *'want talk again when alone'* the last time she had been in the Darkworld.

I'm almost getting used to this. Then she shivered. *It's not actually something I want to get used to.*

{*You one. Gatherer only. Why shrouded?*} asked the hollow, sighing voice of the daimon.

"Shrouded? What do you mean?"

{*Enclosed, held away from others.*}

"Oh, I understand. I don't want to take other talents from their owners so my awareness of them has been reduced."

{*Not want Gather? Incomprehension.*}

"Never mind me. What do you want?"

{*Bargain for portal.*}

"We've done that."

{*Alter bargain.*}

"You can't do that," objected Anarya. *I've got used to having the portal available. I don't want to lose it.*

{*Agreement. Cannot change promise alone. Make new pact. Needful.*}

"You want me to agree to changing the way I can use the portal."

{*Yes. Agree.*}

"Why?"

{*Irrelevant.*}

"Oh no it's not. If you want me to agree to a change I need to know why."

{*Portal waste strength. Want. Need.*}

"You need the power that's being used to keep the portal open."

{*Yes. Agree.*}

"When we were bargaining before you asked 'What benefits me?' Now I'm asking the same."

{*What want?*}

"I want to be able to keep access to the portal. It's useful to me."

{*Need constant?*}

"Are you asking if I need it all the time?"

{*Yes.*}

"No, not all the time but I do want to be able to use it when I do need it."

{*Portal anchor same place?*}

"Does it have to be?"

{*No.*}

"Can you arrange it so that I can open a portal from anywhere to anywhere?"

{*Yes.*}

"That would be good. And I'll be able to see where it will open before it does?"

{*Yes.*}

"What would you want in return?"

{*Limitation. Use once in cycle. Not more.*}

"How long is a cycle?"

{*You call twenty chimes.*}

"A day? Once a day isn't enough!"

{*Twice in cycle.*}

"More."

{*No. Twice enough.*}

"You get the power you want back if I agree."

{*You get portal ability anywhere. Twice enough. Not agree more.*}

"If I don't use it one day can I save that use to the next day?"

{*No.*}

"Why not? You'll still save power. After all I don't use the portal every day. How about – six uses every two days?"

{*Four.*}

"Four, but only if I can save unused times for later use."

{*Save two. Never more.*}

Anarya did some quick thinking and decided that was as good as she was likely to get. "I agree. Four every two days with the ability to carry two forward if unused."

{*Acceptable.*}

"What if I need it more often? Can I use one a day early?"

{*No! Extra use bring retribution.*}

Anarya realised that she couldn't push the daimon too far or it might take rather than negotiate. Four times in two days sounded pretty good and not having to go to the *Seventh Step* each time was really good. It would mean having to do something about Caseir's table, but that was a minor problem.

"Bargain," she said.

{*Bargain,*} echoed the daimon.

Why did the daimon bother negotiating? It's strong enough to do as it likes and there's nothing I could do if it just closed the portal. She asked it why and thought the daimon sounded shocked when it replied, {*Not possible. Deal is deal.*}

Before she could ask anything else she was out of the Darkworld and stepping into the alley at the Sailmaker's Guild. *That step started before the new agreement. I wonder if it counts as one of the four. Better not risk any more today.*

A SAFE-HOUSE IN JOTUK

"Boss! Boss!"

Richak looked up from his abacus when one of his lieutenants clattered up the stairs shouting to get his attention.

"What's up?" he asked.

Gasping for breath, the man told Richak that a fight had broken out in the Three Flowers territory on the other side of the south bridge.

"Damn Hentro and the rest of the Stone Grasshoppers," said Richak. "I thought we had sorted that out."

"Not the 'hoppers, not this time," the man managed to gasp.

"Who?"

The man gulped several mouthfuls of water before he got his breath back. Then he told Richak it seemed to be a conflict between two of the smaller *houln* in the area, the Bronze Leopards and the Victorious Owls.

"Why are they fighting? No, never mind that for the moment. Let's get people there to protect our interests in the area."

Thirty of the Three Flowers' enforcers got together and set out for the south bridge. Richak followed them with a bodyguard of six of the biggest men in the *houln*.

The disputed area beyond the south bridge had always been a problem for the Three Flowers. It consisted of seven streets, and parts of three others, isolated from the rest of their territory by a major road on one side and a tributary of the Ladry on the other. It had belonged to both the Flowers and the Stone Grasshoppers at various times in the last ten years.

Richak knew those streets were difficult to defend, but he couldn't admit that holding on to them didn't make sense.

"We've got to make sure our people are safe," he told his lieutenants. "This doesn't turn into a land grab by the Grasshoppers, or anybody else. Understand me?"

"Yes, boss."

"Catch me somebody from the Bronze Leopards or the Victorious Owls if you can. I want to find out what this is about."

The Three Flowers men forced their way into the heart of the disputed territory and started pushing the combatants apart. They got hold of one man with an owl's face tattooed on his forehead and brought him to Richak.

"Why are you fighting in Three Flowers territory?" he demanded.

"You're not the target. The fight just came this way. It's them damned Leopards we're fighting. They won't believe The God is dead. We've got people in Leynik, Branidh and Shuth who say the Families are convinced he is and they're in shock. That gives us the chance to attack the Families now, while they're in disarray."

"So why are you fighting the Bronze Leopards instead of the Families?"

"Because they won't join us."

"The Three Flowers will help you against the Leopards if you promise to be guided by the priests of the Confined Gods in a rebellion against the Families."

"Yes! We will join you. We'll even split the Bronze Leopard's territory with you."

O

Richak felt very satisfied with the day's work when the fighting was over. He had new allies and the Three Flowers had more territory.

What a wonderful day! I'm sure Kehsieh will be pleased.

HOUSE NEYEN

"You look worried," Anarya said, as she stepped into the pink and grey of the reception room two days later. "Why? What's happened while I was away?"

Yisul jumped up from the sofa and wrapped her arms around Anarya. Between kisses she said, "Anra! I've been hoping you would come back. I'm so glad you have. I'm so happy to see you."

"Why wouldn't I come? There's something wrong, isn't there? Tell me. What is it? Sit down and tell me."

"Everything's wrong." Yisul's voice caught in her throat even when she was seated again and Anarya's arms were around her. "My father has been attacked and injured. The Sovereign Council has fallen apart and there's fighting in the streets."

"Is your father badly hurt?"

"His injuries aren't too serious, but it's the fact that he was attacked that's so worrying."

"What happened?"

"There have been arguments about what should happen to the temple. Some want to tear it down, some to convert it for any one of a number of different uses. Yesterday morning the Sovereign Council, and about twenty others, went there to assess the damage, to see what needed repairing and discuss possibilities.

"They were in the Presence Chamber looking at the broken pillars when somebody from the Leynik Family Lifted a piece of masonry and hurled it at my father. A Feeler gave enough warning of murderous intent to let my father partially shield himself. Oddly enough, it was Julnaw cra Widhis who gave the warning and she is a fervent believer in the survival of the spirit of The God. You wouldn't expect her to protect father, but she did."

"It sounds as if there's dissent among the opposition."

"If there is I'm glad of it. Father's shield was incomplete when the piece of rock hit it. His wrist took most of the impact. It's broken, as are several ribs. He has been coughing up some blood but the healers say he'll recover."

"Go on," said Anarya when Yisul paused.

"What happened after that is a bit confusing. I wasn't there but I was told that somebody, I don't know who, pulled a knife and stabbed the Lifter. Then the meeting degenerated into violence. Almost everyone was injured to some extent and six people died, including Dunel cra Guesyr."

"He was one of the Council, wasn't he?"

"He was. And now the believers among the Families are claiming that it was all a plot to subvert the Council by weakening their representation on it."

"But it was a believer who started it."

"I know. It doesn't make sense but that doesn't seem to matter to them," said Yisul. She sighed. "My father told me he would like to see you whenever you arrived. I'll take you to him."

She led Anarya down a flight of stairs and along the main corridor on the first floor to her father's rooms.

Anarya wasn't surprised to see they were decorated in the house colours of green and scarlet with frequent images of tree-dancers. She couldn't help thinking that, however attractive the images were, she would soon get tired of seeing them everywhere. Lady Lias was sitting by Muhan's bed and stood to greet them. Anarya was surprised to see that she was wearing blue and grey instead of her usual green and scarlet. Then she remembered that blue and grey were the colours of Branidh, her birth house.

Muhan was sitting propped up in bed. His eyes lit up when Anarya and Yisul entered and he pushed himself more upright, provoking a bout of coughing. Through it he managed to wheeze a welcome. Then he picked up a porcelain bowl, held it to his nose and inhaled the steam rising from it. Anarya caught a whiff of cinnamon, cardamom and something else she wasn't sure about. *Is that marjoram?* Whatever it was it seemed to be soothing and he gradually stopped coughing.

"Yisul told me what happened," said Anarya. "I'm happy to hear it's not worse."

"Couldn't get much worse," replied Muhan. "Oh, you mean me. I thought you meant the overall situation. I'll be fine in a day or two but the city is in chaos."

"What are you going to do?"

"I'm going to have to call a meeting of the Families and hope the violence has been enough to make people think about the safety of the city. Inter-house skirmishes have distracted the gate guards. Some of them have been drawn into the fighting and left the way open for incursions of outers into the inner city. It's happened three times already at different gates. They've been pushed back each time but there have been deaths on both sides and some damage to properties near the gates. The last was the worst and it needed a Pyromancer to end it."

Muhan winced as he changed position and Lias told him, in a tone that wouldn't tolerate argument, "You're not going to go to any meeting until you can walk and talk without discomfort."

"But I have to try to calm everybody down."

"Then have small meetings here if you must. Invite them to come a few at a time."

"And ask aunt Lodesh to come to all of them," suggested Yisul. "Particularly any attended by the devout."

"Good idea," said Anarya.

"Can you stay, Lady Anarya?" asked Muhan. "I think it might be useful if you could talk to some members of the Families on a personal level. Several have expressed an interest in meeting you."

"I would like to help," replied Anarya, "but I must get back to Carregis." *I suppose I've got to give them some sort of excuse.* "You see, I need special treatment from a priestess of Holy Quarenna twice a day because my battle with The God has left me weakened."

"Oh, no," said Lias. "After what you've done for us. It's so unfair."

"You didn't say anything about this before, Lady Anarya," said Muhan.

"Please, I'd rather you call me just Anarya. I didn't know about it before. It crept up on me and it took some time to realise what had happened. There is a treatment that works, but it only lasts about ten chimes. We are still looking for a longer-term cure. I need to go back today but I'll come again the day after tomorrow and then I'll talk to anybody you want me to." *I just hope they're not too antagonistic.*

"That's kind of you," said Muhan. Then he looked at Yisul and added, "You go with her. Look after her and give her what help you can. She deserves it. Don't worry about me."

"Yes, father."

"There's one more thing," said Anarya. "Hearing about your injury almost made me forget. I've met with members of the Inner Circle of the Daughters of Quarenna and with a senior priest from the temple of Huler. They've agreed to send teachers, if you are sure you want them. They are most insistent that you must agree to being taught. They don't want to force our beliefs on the unwilling."

Both Muhan and Lias said, "Good."

Lias added, "We will welcome them."

A SAFE-HOUSE IN JOTUK

"Look at this, boss," called the man watching the square outside Derchler's Gate from an upper floor window. The Three Flowers had taken over the building, despite the protests of the occupants, so that Richak would have a good view of the planned attack.

"What is it?" demanded Richak without looking up. He carried on rattling the abacus beads around.

"It's them cursed 'hoppers. Wasn't they supposed to wait a couple o' days before starting anything."

"They were."

"Well, they ain't. There's a right old rammy starting up."

"Let me see," said Richak, getting up and pushing past the man to reach the window.

His view of the Gate itself was limited but he could see a sizable group of men making their way through the crowd towards it. Seen from above it was obvious they were staying together and moving with purpose. Hentro himself wasn't there but Richak recognised several prominent members of his *houln*, the Stone Grasshoppers, in the throng. Many people were being carried along with them and others were struggling against the flow. Richak leaned out to get a better view. Voices were raised, adding to the noise in the square. Steel flashed, blood spurted and the sound changed from the usual hubbub of a busy crowd to screams of pain, anger and fear.

"What does that fool think he's doing?" demanded Richak. "He knows the plan."

The gate guards set up a cordon anchored on a cart stopped partway through the Gate, but there were too many people pushing, or being pushed, towards the inner city and they were shoved back. Two fell, opening a gap in their line, and the mob surged through trampling the fallen.

"That's done it," said Richak. "Looks promising, but that breakthrough isn't going to last long. It's not well enough organised. Are any of our people out there?"

"Saw one or two, boss. Might be more. Don't know."

"Take a few men out and have a look. If you find any give them refuge downstairs but don't take too long about it. I'd say you've only got a tenth or so before that lot get pushed back."

Richak waited, sure that many of those who had broken through into the inner city would soon be coming back through the Gate as a panicked mob driven by magic.

Not everyone in the square had gone through the Gate. Of those who hadn't some decided to leave the square as quickly as they could; some spent time picking up merchandise from the stalls and handcarts that had been overturned in the confusion; others helped themselves to the contents of the baskets and packs people had dropped.

People started coming back through the Gate, just a few at first then more and more until there was a pushing, screaming, frightened mob fighting their way across the square and into one or other of the streets. Among the throng were some who huddled together and helped each other to walk or limp. One group of twenty or so backed slowly into the square staying together, shouting abuse back towards the Gate and throwing anything throwable. Richak spotted several among this disciplined group that he knew to be 'hoppers. He cursed Hentro for arranging this debacle. *How many has he got killed? What will Kehsieh think? I wish I had the necklace so I could ask him.*

A curtain of fire swept through the Gate and bulged into the square. It caught up with four people trying to help each other along. They fell screaming. The fiery barrier stopped expanding. The frightened crowd dispersed down the side streets and the sounds of panic gradually faded. The square emptied except for a brave, or foolish, few who paused at some of the street junctions to see what happened next.

"Fire again!" said Richak. "That's twice recently they've used it to drive people back after they got through the gate." He shook his head, thinking, *We'll need to stop Pyromancers when we make the major attack, and I don't know how to do it.*

The fire burned for about a quarter then went out leaving a semicircle of glowing cobbles where it had been. A middle-aged man in the pink and yellow of House Dunish walked through the Gate to stand on the hot stones without apparent discomfort. He looked around the empty square and announced, "Between the eighth and tenth chimes tomorrow you may enter to recover the bodies of your dead. Use of this Gate for other purposes is prohibited for the next five days."

HOUSE NEYEN

Anarya, Yisul and her parents were relaxing in Muhan's sitting room. He was propped up on a stack of pillows watching his wife and daughter play vurlo. Anarya wasn't paying attention to the game.

Yisul frowned at the arrangement of vurlo tiles on the low table in front of her. She could see three possible moves. One looked promising, but she suspected Lias wouldn't give her the chance to profit from it. If she was right about the orientation of one of the opposing tiles, then her mother could be able to follow her move with a simple shift that could have devastating consequences. *She could sweep a third of my pieces from the board. I'm five down already, I can't afford that sort of loss.* She paused, looking over the array hoping to find a better alternative. *In the opposite seat, if I'm wrong about it and it is in my favour I lose the chance to take the lead by two, maybe three, tiles.* She hesitated. *Is it worth the risk? No, I don't think so.* She shifted her attention to the other side of the board and turned over a tile which Lias promptly removed with a move she hadn't seen coming.

"You are out of practice, Yisul," said Muhan. "You'd never have let your mother get away with that before you ran off to Carregis. Don't they play vurlo there?"

"Yes, they do. It's quite popular. But I haven't had the chance to play."

Anarya looked up from the thread wrapped around her fingers in an early stage of a cat's cradle, "I'm afraid you can blame me for that. I really don't care for the game. I rarely play and I'm not very good."

"You'll never get better if you don't play," said Lias.

"I can never remember how more than a few of the

revealed tiles are orientated, or work out anything about the concealed ones."

Muhan turned away from the gameboard to look at Anarya. "They say playing develops memory and deductive skills. I'd have thought that would be useful to you in your business. Perhaps you should practice more."

"It just doesn't seem worth the effort."

"It's a shame you feel that way. Your move, Yisul."

"I know." Yisul scanned the gameboard again. She saw her mother's smile and thought, *I'm afraid she's got something in mind that I haven't seen.*

After another examination of the board Yisul couldn't see any better move than the one she'd already dismissed as risky.

She reached for a tile but she never found out if her contemplated move would have been a good one or not because Baram came into the room, looking excited.

Yisul paused before lifting the tile when Baram announced, "There's been trouble at the gate."

Muhan sat up, asking "What trouble?" As he did so he dislodged one of his pillows. It fell on to the gameboard and knocked most of the array to the floor.

He apologised for his clumsiness and asked again, "What trouble?"

"Something like eighty people forced their way through Derchler's Gate. They've been pushed back, but there have been deaths on both sides."

"How many?" asked Muhan.

"Four of the gate guard and seven or eight servants."

"Which House?"

"I don't know. I couldn't understand much of what was being said."

"You said the outers were pushed back. How? And how many of them died?"

"I think a dozen or so were burned down by a Pyromancer."

Anarya said, "That's awful." She dropped the yarn she was playing with, saying, "I've got to go back to

Carregis. Are you coming with me Yisa?"
  "Yes, I will."
  "And you, Baram?"
  "Yes"

A TAVERN IN JOTUK

Richak, Hentro and Jemak met again in the same tavern. They settled themselves around the table, this time with Hentro at the end. Richak accepted the beer that was offered. He took one mouthful then set the mug aside with a grimace. He had hoped for something drinkable but it was musty and sour.

As before the landlord left after serving them.

Jemak took the necklace off and placed it on the table. They jostled for position making sure each of them could touch it.

"What news do you have?" asked Caseir.

"Nothing of note," said Hentro.

"Haven't you even got something to say about that mess at Derchler's Gate yesterday?" asked Richak.

Caseir wanted to know what happened and Richak described what he had seen.

"That didn't go well, Hentro," said Caseir.

"No, Greatness. It didn't."

"It was a disaster," growled Richak.

"Who was at fault?"

The three of them all looked at each other, then Richak said, "Greatness, I am ashamed to admit that I was, to some extent. I beg your forgiveness. I shouldn't have relied on Hentro doing what he was told."

Hentro shouted, "Don't try to blame me."

"Tell me, Hentro," said Caseir, "what instructions did Richak give you?"

"To arrange a mass attack on the Gate…"

Richak interrupted to snarl, "Six days from now! I told you to keep things as quiet as possible at all the gates to keep the Families unworried."

"But…"

"Is that what he told you, Hentro?"

"Greatness…"

"Is it?"

"He told me to attack the Gate with as many men as I could muster."

"And when did I tell you to attack, Hentro? When?"

"I…"

"Be quiet, Hentro," said Caseir. "It's obvious you didn't obey. I suppose you were trying to inflate your own importance by taking independent action."

"Greatness, he's not worthy of your trust," commented Jemak.

"I agree," said Caseir.

Hentro started to rise but was pushed back down into his seat.

"Richak, you must take more care with who you trust in future." Caseir paused.

Richak felt his heartbeat quicken and his hands start sweating. He held his breath wondering if it would be his last.

"You asked for forgiveness. I grant it."

Richak released the breath he was holding, bowed his head and said, "Thank you, Greatness."

"However, I cannot forgive you, Hentro. Nor can I trust you. Kill him!"

Hentro started to rise but hadn't even pushed his chair back when Richak's and Jemak's knives slid between his ribs. He coughed a spray of blood, slumped forward over the table, slid back and fell to the floor tangled up in his chair.

"Who will succeed him?" asked Caseir.

Jemak and Richak looked at each other.

"Your territory overlaps the Grasshoppers' more than mine does, Jemak," said Richak. "You must have a better idea about that than me."

"There are at least three who are ambitious enough to try to take over the *houln*," replied Jemak, "but I don't know which of them will come out on top."

"Are any of them followers of the Confined Gods?"

asked Caseir.

"All of them, Greatness. I believe all of them are devout, but there is one who has been considered a candidate for the priesthood. His name is Yarelk."

"Excellent. Do what you can to make sure he becomes the next ruler of the Stone Grasshoppers, then bring him to meet me."

"Yes, Greatness," agreed Jemak. "It will take two or three days to arrange that."

"It is possible the Families will feel complacent after suppressing yesterday's attack," said Caseir, "We might take them by surprise if we could organise another assault tomorrow but until the Grasshoppers have a new leader that *houln* will be in disarray and it won't be possible to coordinate another assault. So I want the Families to think we have been cowed by the suppression of the last attack. There must be no trouble at any of the gates for at least three weeks. Allow them time to forget, then we will assault all five gates at the same time."

"Your pardon, Greatness," said Richak. "I fear there is one, possibly two, of the other gates where we can't prevent attacks. They are far from here and we have little influence with the adjacent *houln*."

"Not even as priests?"

"I fear not, Greatness. Two of the *houln* based at the docks near the east gate have rejected the Confined Ones."

"Who do they worship?"

Richak swallowed. "I mean no blasphemy, Greatness. They have been corrupted by tales told by the fishermen who sometimes sail to another country where they revere those we do not name."

"I see," said Caseir. "I did ask, so I will forgive you. I am disappointed to hear this and I must think about it. Meanwhile, use what influence you do have to minimise violence at the gates until I tell you otherwise."

ANARYA'S LODGINGS
AND *THE SEVENTH STEP*

Anarya finished her morning prayer to Quarenna and touched her thumb to her forehead. She stood up and said, "There's nothing for breakfast. We have to go shopping."

"How did we let the stores get so low?"

"It's jumping back and forth to Jotuk and staying there as long and as often as we do. That what does it."

"But..."

"Don't get me wrong, I don't begrudge the time we're spending there," said Anarya, "and we get well fed by your Family. But we need to remember to keep the cupboard here stocked. Let's go to the market."

"We need to go to the shrine for you to take Kemeneah's talent."

"Not until later. The glyph I cast on myself yesterday evening is still active. There's a chime or so before I need to renew it."

"Are you sure? You did it about the eighteenth chime last night..."

"And it's now the sixth chime, more or less. We know the glyph lasts about eleven. That gives me plenty time – at least two, maybe three chimes."

"As long as I have known you, you have had a tendency to stretch your talent to the limit. You must not get into the habit of doing the same with the protective glyph."

"I only ever risked talent exhaustion when it was necessary and there was no other alternative."

Yisul gave a sceptical grunt.

"It's true!" said Anarya.

"Well, risking your sanity with exposure to the empty, hungry feeling isn't necessary. You must make sure you have the protection of the glyph at all times."

"All right! Don't nag. We'll go to the shrine first. Does that suit you?"

"Yes. I'm glad you're being sensible," responded Yisul. "We can go shopping after going to the shrine."

"And then we need to meet Baram."

"Where will we find him?

"At that little shop on Gatt Street, just off the Great Square. The one that does that delicious orange and nut cake. We've arranged that as a place to be every day from the fourteenth to fifteenth chimes if we need to meet."

"You'll need the glyph renewed again before then."

"Yes, I know!"

O

The tenth of the fourteen chimes rang out from the tower of the temple of Huler as Anarya and Yisul turned into Gatt Street, the deep boom of the gong carrying a long way and being echoed from other temples across the city.

Yisul spotted Baram sitting at a cane table under one of the four green parasols outside the shop. From the evidence of the crumbs on his plate he had been there for a while.

The remaining four chimes masked the sound of their approach. Baram didn't see them coming and almost choked on a mouthful of tea when they came up behind him and sat down.

"Give me some warning," he spluttered.

"Starting without us you don't deserve one," said Anarya.

Baram raised a questioning eyebrow. "I suppose that means you want cake."

"Of course," replied Anarya, "and two mugs of tea. Stargrass for me, I think. What about you, Yisa?"

"Peppermint, please."

"Your wishes will be fulfilled," said Baram waving to a server.

When the tea arrived Anarya took a deep breath of the

sweet peppery steam rising from the mug, nibbled a corner of the cake, licked the sticky syrup from her fingers and settled back in her chair. "I would like to go to Verenthe and bring Caseir's table back here to Carregis. Will you come and help me?"

"Why?" asked Baram. "With your control of the portal we can go to *The Seventh Step* anytime if we need to talk to Caseir,"

Anarya told them about the new restriction on her use of the portal and added, "I don't want to have to use up some of my quota whenever I want to talk to Caseir. All three of us have fragments of table top and we know they let us talk to each other using Caseir as an intermediary as long as we're not too far apart. But they have limited range and Verenthe is too far away for Caseir to communicate with these other bits of him. Bringing him to Carregis will minimise that problem."

"That makes sense," agreed Baram. "I'll come with you."

"Thank you."

"I will come, of course," added Yisul. "I will enjoy haggling with that innkeeper again."

O

The common room of *The Seventh Step* was fairly quiet for early evening. Most of the customers, fifteen or sixteen of them, were clustered around one of the tables, laughing and jostling each other for position. Some of them were spilling ale as they waved their arms around.

"What's happening over there?" asked Yisul as they took seats around Caseir's table.

Caseir dismissed it, saying, "It's only a game of bones."

"I have heard of this game," said Yisul, "but it's not known among the Families and I have never seen it."

A voice called out an invocation of Huler in his aspect as the Good Companion, the bones rattled in the horn and it was slammed down on the table. Bets were shouted out, denied or accepted. When no more were offered the man with the horn lifted it to reveal the five bones. Four of them were standing on end and the fifth concave side up. One man yelled in delight, most groaned and two cursed their bad luck.

"Am I right in thinking they are betting on the patterns made by the bones?" asked Yisul.

"Yes."

"It looks simple enough."

Caseir advised her, "Don't even think about it. You don't know these bones. No two sets are ever quite the same and whoever owns them has an advantage over everyone else because he knows how likely a particular fall is with his bones."

"But that's cheating."

"No, it's not, it's just the way the game works. The only way to cheat is for a good Lifter to tweak the bones to get the fall he wants. And he has to be very good to be able to manipulate the bones while they're in the horn and he can't see them. Anyway, serious gamblers usually make sure there's a Feeler nearby to detect the tension and anxiety that goes with cheating. I'm pretty sure there must be one in that group."

"There is," said Anarya, "the tall one with the droopy moustache. But never mind them. Where's Limabur?"

"Why do you want him," asked Caseir. "He'll just pester you about the table again."

"That's why we want to see him."

"You're not going to let him have the table," said Caseir.

"No, we're going to take you to Carregis. It will be more convenient than coming here."

"Surely coming here isn't a problem. You've got the portal to come through."

Anarya had to explain the new restrictions on her use of the portal before Caseir grudgingly admitted she had a point.

Limabur lumbered his way across the room from the vicinity of the bones table and bent over to glower at

Yisul. "What do you want?"

"You offered to buy out our contract for the use of this table. Do you still want to do that?"

"Yes, Lady," he agreed, standing up straighter.

"I have thought about it," said Yisul, "and I may be prepared to relinquish the contract…"

A smile spread across Limabur's face, "Yes, Lady."

"…for the right price."

"I offered you sixty bits and I'll stand by that."

"Actually, master Limabur, that was your starting offer and you raised it to seventy, then seventy-five, then eighty. Don't you remember?"

His face fell and he admitted he had offered eighty bits.

"I will remove the table and you may have the space for another one…"

"Thank you, Lady."

"…for two dukals."

"What! That's robbery!"

"You tried to cheat me with a lower offer and I caught you out. Think of it as retribution."

Limabur was speechless, his mouth moving but no words coming out.

"Consider this," said Yisul. "You will not have the bother of disposing of the table. We will take it away with us."

Limabur muttered and argued but Yisul was implacable and he finally gave up. With ill grace he dumped coins on the table saying, "There. It's yours. Now get it out of here."

Baram and Yisul picked up the table and manoeuvred it to the door. It was awkward but Anarya made sure both of them were touching her when she opened the portal into her room in Carregis.

They set the table down in the middle of the room. It took up a lot of the available floor space, making the room rather cramped for three people.

Anarya waved for Baram to take one of the chairs and Yisul took the other. "Well, Caseir. Here we are. Welcome to my home."

Silence.

"Caseir?"

Silence.

"He must be there," said Yisul. "He must."

Silence.

Anarya slumped down on the bed with her head in her hands. "I never thought that bringing him through the portal would injure him."

Baram looked everywhere except at the table.

Yisul sniffed and seemed ready to burst into tears.

"Of course I'm here. Where else would I be?"

"Caseir!" cried Yisul. "That was cruel, making us think something had gone wrong."

"So was making decisions about me without even asking. You didn't know what effect passage through the portal would have on me. Remember the reason the daimon set it up in the first place was for revenge."

"You're right," said Anarya. "I didn't think about that. I'm sorry."

"Never mind. It didn't hurt me."

"Good."

"But it did have a curious effect on me."

"What?"

"Did you know that distance means nothing to daimons because the Darkworld is everywhere?"

"Yes," said Anarya, thinking about the only time she had borrowed a Daimoner's talent and what he had told her in that awful little tavern by the fish dock. "I remember being told that. What about it?"

"Well, when you go through the portal you go through the Darkworld."

"You do?"

"Yes, I'm certain of it. A daimon took me through the Darkworld once before, when I was still alive, and I recognised the feeling when we went through the portal just now. For a moment there was no distance at all between all the pieces of me. Now I know what happened to the bit you lost in Jotuk."

"Something interesting?"

"You could say that. It seems I'm a god in Jotuk."

"What!"

"Ridiculous!" exclaimed Yisul.

"Have you ever heard of the Confined Gods?" asked Caseir.

Anarya and Baram looked at each other wondering if they should say anything.

Before they had time to decide Yisul snorted and said, "Bogeymen! Scare stories told to children by nurses and other servants to keep them quiet and well behaved. Nobody believes in them."

"Maybe the Families don't but a lot of people in the outer city do. The piece of wood you lost is in the possession of a priest of the Confined Gods. Because my name sounds similar he believes I'm one of them, called Kehsieh."

"That doesn't sound much like Caseir," commented Baram.

"I've got to admit it's not too different," said Yisul, "if you say Caseir with an outer's accent it could easily be confused with Kehsieh."

"The me in that bit of wood is as much a survivor as the whole of me. It had to pretend to be Kehsieh in case Richak burned the wood."

"I suppose Richak is the priest," said Anarya.

"Yes. He's a powerful man. He rules the *houln* called the Three Flowers as well as being a priest.

Baram smiled. "I hope you're a benign god."

"Well, no, I'm afraid I'm not. You see, what Richak really wants is to overthrow the rule of the Families and I'm helping him plan a revolt."

"What! You can't do that," exclaimed Yisul.

"It's not me that's doing it, it's the other me that's been separated from most of me for too long."

"You're confusing me," complained Anarya.

"I understand, I think," said Yisul. "The important question is whether the other you is still going to help this – what did you call him – Richak? – to rebel against the Families?"

"He probably will," said Caseir.

"Why? Surely it won't happen now that you're together again."

"But we're not. It was only when going through the Darkworld that we were together. We're too far apart again now."

"I don't understand," said Anarya. "I've carried a bit of wood through the portal several times since I lost the bit that's in Richak's possession. Why didn't it happen before?"

"I guess it's because there's more of me in the table top itself and that dominates the other pieces when it's in the Darkworld and in contact with the other fragments."

"Makes sense," agreed Baram. "It's only when the table top itself is in the Darkworld that the other you – Oh, let's call him Kehsieh, it's easier than 'other you' or 'other me' – is part of you."

"That's right. When we're together Kehsieh is part of me and thinks the same as I do. The problem is when we're apart. He'll start thinking about survival again. I know I would."

"And that means assisting Richak with his rebellion?" asked Yisul.

"I think so."

"I've got to warn my father. As if he didn't have enough to worry about."

"You've got plenty time to warn him. Nothing's going to happen for about three weeks. Kehsieh wants to lull the Families into a false sense of security after the fight a couple of days ago."

"What fight? Anra, my love, we've got to go to Jotuk."

"First thing tomorrow. As soon as I've got protection in place."

THE ROYAL PALACE

Sulereath glanced around the newly chosen council chamber making sure everything was the way he wanted it. He nodded in satisfaction. *The other one was acceptable, but this is much better.* A massive blackwood table dominated the room, its top inlaid with decorative woods forming a map of Carrhen. A series of cupboards along the sides held more detailed maps that could be displayed as needed on the main table or an easel. The chair at the end of the table farthest from the door was new. It wasn't quite a throne, but it was a touch more elaborately carved and upholstered than the others. Crystal glasses and carafes of water and wine engraved with the pelican of Ereath stood on side tables at each of the places. Another table off to one side had seats for the three scribes who would record the proceedings of the council.

Am I doing the right thing making them come to me? Or should I be keeping them waiting for my entrance? Oh well, it's too late to change my mind about it now. Hope I did the right thing.

He settled into his chair, told the guardsman to open the door and watched the councillors enter, acknowledging their bows with a nod and a gesture inviting them to be seated.

Huler's beard, he thought, when Latisec stalked the length of the table and claimed the chair to his right. *Trust him to assume that was his place. Should I have specified who was to sit where? Can't do anything about it now.*

Latisec had stayed in Carregis much longer than expected and Sulereath was sure that it was because he was still hoping to be appointed Duke of Carrh. *Perhaps he'll be upset enough to leave when I don't make an appointment today – no, don't be silly, he'll stay until I do decide who will be the next Duke.*

Fedic, the guard commander, took the seat at the far end of the table while Grovaen and Jaenis sat opposite each other next to him.

The king switched his attention to the three newcomers on the council. The first, who took the chair to his left, was Yertis Pirrosha. She had been suggested by both the Inner Circle of the Daughters of Quarenna and the Brotherhood of Huler when he asked them to nominate someone to advise him on legal matters. A rather short woman with a calm demeanour, she had chosen to wear her judge's robes and the red facings and fastenings stood out prominently against the white cambric of the loosely draped gown. Her nondescript brown hair was pulled back in a tight bun under the traditional judge's skullcap.

Sulereath had also asked for suggestions for someone to advise on business matters. Several names had been mentioned and he had chosen Kieret Beghroth, a ship owner who he had met a few times at the Arena and at formal dinners. Although one of the richest men in Carregis, Beghroth had dressed simply in a brown jacket and sand-coloured trousers. The only sign of his wealth was a gold chain with an enamelled pendant showing a silver kraken on green, his company's badge.

In complete contrast, the third of the new councillors was wearing yellow satin and green velvet with multiple gold chains round his neck, rings on every finger and gold embroidery in decorative panels on his sleeves. Aness Debengis had acted as Duke Wurauf's master of coin and Sulereath had met him many times in Wurauf's company. His dismissive attitude during those meetings had made the king rather doubtful about appointing him to the council but he had been assured by everyone that he was the best financier around.

Sulereath took a deep breath. He was nervous because this was the first formal meeting of his council since his restoration. *Whatever I do today will set a precedent. I have to get it right.*

He looked down the table and said, "Reverend Grovaen, please ask for Huler's blessing on our deliberations."

Grovaen stood, signed himself with the lightning bolt and prayed, "Great Huler, Lord of the Sky and Illuminator of the World, we beseech you to watch over us and lend us the wisdom of the Judge that the decisions we make will be just and in the best interests of the people of Carrhen."

Sulereath turned to Jaenis who thumbed her forehead and begged, "We ask the blessing of Holy Quarenna on this meeting. May we be guided by the compassion of the Helper in all that we do."

"Thank you," said Sulereath. "Councillors, I ask for your advice."

"We are at your disposal, Your Majesty," replied Fedic, exactly as the king had asked him to do in a private meeting the previous day.

Latisec's head jerked around to glare at Fedic. Obviously surprised, he was slower than the others to echo Fedic's words.

"Our first task," said Sulereath, "is to consider filling the gaps left by the deaths of Duke Wurauf and Count Graumedel. This is complicated by neither of them having nominated successors. Although I have, for the moment, assumed the role of Duke of Carrh, I don't think that is a viable long-term solution." From the corner of his eye he saw Latisec nodding agreement as he continued, "Nor can Graumedel's seneschal continue to run Carregis for long without authority from the Duke of Carrh. Have you any suggestions?"

Yertis Pirrosha surprised Sulereath when she spoke first. He had been expecting Latisec to jump in and advance his case to become Duke of Carrh.

"Your Majesty, although Count Graumedel never specified who would inherit his rank and holdings he did have blood relatives who must be considered potential successors. The legal grapevine is full of gossip about it and I know of at least one lawyer who is hoping to be retained by one of these possible heirs and is preparing a case on their behalf."

"A moment, Your Majesty," said Latisec. "Should we not consider the higher-ranking position first?"

I knew he'd butt in. I can't let him take over the meeting.

"Both are important, Your Grace, and your suggestion would make sense if I was sure of making any appointments at this meeting. I think this unlikely, although I am prepared to be surprised. What I hope to achieve is some understanding of the people who might fill these posts and what further information I will need about them before making decisions." Sulereath paused briefly before saying, "We will carry on as we have started, by considering Graumedel's possible successors."

Sulereath turned to Yertis and invited her to continue.

"Your Majesty," she said, "Count Graumedel had a brother and a sister. Both of them are dead, as are two of their five children. There's a nephew called Nurmed..." She paused at a derisory snort from Fedic.

"Sorry," he said, putting down the glass of wine he had picked up. "It's just that there's a Nurmed who has a rather unsavoury reputation. I don't know if it's the same man."

"Do you think it might be?" asked Grovaen.

"It's possible," replied Fedic. "It's not a very common name. The one I'm thinking about is rather arrogant. He's generally disliked because of his I'm-better-than-you attitude but he's tolerated at the pits and in gaming houses across the city because he's a poor gambler who loses regularly yet always seems to have money in his pouch."

"He doesn't sound as if he would make a satisfactory Count," commented Sulereath.

"No, Your Majesty, I don't think he would. But in fairness I have to repeat that I don't know if it's the same man."

"We need to know," said Sulereath. "Commander

Fedic, will you find out more about him."

"Yes, Your Majesty."

"Judge Yertis, please carry on."

"Graumedel's brother married twice and both wives bore him a daughter. I believe the older one, Harviel, is about the same age as Nurmed, somewhere in the mid-twenties. The younger, Dartiel, is only seven or eight."

"Well, Dartiel is obviously too young," said Sulereath. "What do we know about Harviel?"

"Not a great deal, Your Majesty," remarked Yertis. "I believe the lawyer is planning on arguing that she should inherit on two counts. First, that her father was older than Nurmed's mother and also that she is older than Nurmed."

"That doesn't matter, does it?" asked Sulereath.

"No, Your Majesty," she replied. "If the case came before me I would have to remind the lawyer that primogeniture is not, of itself, a criterion for inheritance."

"What are the other criteria?" asked Jaenis.

"A stated preference witnessed by others not directly involved, whether verbally or in writing. Or an implied preference expressed by known interactions between the parties."

"The latter sounds delightfully vague," said Grovaen, "and must result in a lot of arguments."

"It keeps lawyers in business," agreed Yertis, with a smile.

"Anything else?"

"Harviel has a small farm just outside the city, off the Voro road. It once belonged to Graumedel. I'm not sure how it ended up in Harviel's hands. It seems to be fairly successful, which could be a point in her favour. However, it could be just that she has a capable estate manager."

"Does anyone have any comments about Graumedel's heirs?"

"Yes, Your Majesty," said Kieret Beghroth. "I have several competent subordinates some of whom deal with providing fresh food for my ships. They may already know Harviel's farm. Even if they don't it would be easy for them to investigate and find out who actually runs it."

"And," suggested Yertis, "I will have the records of the Office of Deeds and Contracts searched to find out how ownership was transferred from Graumedel to Harviel."

Sulereath looked around the table. Everyone, except Latisec, was nodding approvingly at these suggestions. Latisec was slumped down in his chair, scowling into the dregs of a glass of wine and not paying attention.

"Very well," said Sulereath. "Commander Fedic, please arrange for all the possible heirs to appear before us at the next council meeting. That will be at the dark of the moon. I hope I will be able to make a decision then and I expect that meeting them will help me do so." He paused for a mouthful of wine then turned to his right and said to Latisec, "We will now consider the Duchy of Carrh. Your Grace, I know you have an interest in this subject. Please start our deliberations."

Latisec sat up straighter. "Thank you, Your Majesty. The Duchy of Carrh is not only the largest of the five but it also holds as many people as the other four combined. For the good of the country it is essential that Carrh is well governed. The late Duke Wurauf was an effective ruler, although it must be admitted that he was not popular. In the absence of any nominated heir it would seem reasonable for Carrh to pass into the hands of someone, such as myself, who has experience of governance. Alrem prospers under my care. I see no reason why Carrh shouldn't do the same. I realise I couldn't govern both at the same time, so I would pass the rule of Alrem to my son Laerten, who is twenty-two and has been watching me rule for several years. I am sure he will be a suitable and capable replacement for me."

Latisec looked around, smiled, refilled his wine glass and raised it towards his lips.

Before he had a chance to do more than sniff the bouquet, Jaenis spoke up. "Your Grace, would you tell us what happened in Gospind two years ago."

"I don't understand your question," said Latisec.

"I would have thought it an easy question for a good ruler," commented Jaenis, provoking a scowl from Latisec. "Your Majesty, Councillors, I suspect that some of you will never have heard of Gospind, so those who have please forgive me if I tell you something you already know. It is a rather small town in Alrem, only a couple of chimes' travel from the capital, Merlsen. It's a weaving town with particular expertise in working with silk, gossamer and other fine fabrics. It's also where I was born. A little over two years ago there was a catastrophic fire. With no Pyromancer or Aquamancer resident in the town the fire quickly became uncontrollable. One of the weaver cooperatives was burnt to the ground. Three people died in the blaze and six looms were destroyed."

"I remember the incident," said Latisec. "There was a riot afterwards and soldiers had to be sent to quell it."

"Which they did, by killing almost every member of that cooperative; three men, fourteen women and two girls, one of them only eleven years old. And there wasn't really a riot."

"Oh, what would you call it if not a riot? Two men were lynched."

"Two arsonists who were responsible for three deaths!" Jaenis turned to Sulereath saying, "One of them was a weaver taking revenge for being ejected from the cooperative for poor quality work. The other was his wife's brother. Your Majesty, I'm not attempting to justify their deaths. There is no doubt that they were guilty, but they should have been brought to trial instead of being hanged by a mob incensed by their actions."

"We are discussing the Duchy of Carrh," said Latisec. "I fail to see the relevance of this incident in Alrem."

"It's relevant," said Jaenis, "because it was your son who commanded the soldiers who suppressed this non-existent riot. And it was his orders that caused the deaths. By the time he and his men reached Gospind the crowd had largely dispersed. Witnesses who survived the 'suppression' reported that the members of the cooperative were still gathered around the gallows when the soldiers arrived, and they were ridden down without mercy. Your son attacked the largest group of people he could see without stopping to find out what had happened."

"That would seem to show a lack of judgement," said Yertis. "A serious fault in someone who might become a Duke."

Everybody around the table nodded in agreement with Yertis.

Latisec scowled. He licked his lips and said, "Your Majesty, I was not pleased with my son's actions and I reprimanded him. I should point out that it was two years ago and he was only twenty at the time. He has learned how to conduct himself more responsibly since then."

"What do you think, Your Reverence?" asked Sulereath looking towards Grovaen.

"Your Majesty, I can't say what, if anything, Laerten has learned. However, I can Feel that Duke Latisec believes what he has just told us."

Sulereath looked to Jaenis who, with obvious reluctance, nodded, "I agree. He does."

"Very well. We will move on and consider other possible Dukes of Carrh. Who has any suggestions to offer?"

"Your Majesty?" Aness Debengis raised a hand sending multicoloured gleams from the gems in his rings flashing across the table. "There is considerable interest in the banking community about Wurauf's successor."

"Doesn't surprise me," commented Kieret Beghroth. "There's similar interest among the merchants."

"Indeed. I would expect as much," said Aness. "One of my staff has, on her own initiative, started a search for Wurauf's relatives."

"Good for her. Has she found any?" asked Grovaen.

"It's well known that his parents are dead and that he had no surviving siblings, so her search took her farther back. She has had some success in tracing his lineage but, so far, all the relatives she's been able to identify and investigate are dead, many of them quite recently. The family seems to have had a run of bad luck."

"Is there a pattern to the deaths?" asked Yertis.

"No," said Aness. "Some have died as the result of illness, some by accident or getting caught up in a fight. Oh, and there was one killed in a duel."

"But duels are illegal," Jaenis objected.

"That prohibition is ignored in quite a lot of places." Yertis shrugged, "Duke Wurauf didn't care about enforcing it."

"Unfortunately," said Aness, "tracking Wurauf's relatives is confused because the family was, for about forty years, based in the Duchy of Geverd. You might remember there was a major flood there a couple of years ago when the Gevve burst its banks. Many records were damaged. From the few clues my researcher has been able to find, the family seems to have scattered through all five duchies since then. Not only that, but there have been at least three intermarriages between various branches of the family. She hasn't had time to investigate all of them."

"It sounds as if she's lucky she's got as much information as she has," commented Kieret.

"Could we give her some help?" asked Sulereath. "Any relatives, however distant, are potential heirs."

"Not if their noble blood has been diluted by too much common blood, Your Majesty," said Latisec.

Aness grunted at this comment and, before Latisec had time to react to the disparaging sound, said, "Anticipating that this search would be important I have taken the liberty of engaging two more researchers and paying them from the ducal purse."

"Good, Master Aness. That's well done."

"We cannot keep searching forever," said Latisec. "Sooner or later a new Duke must be appointed. I remain convinced that my experience makes me a suitable candidate."

Sulereath nodded to Latisec, "You are right, Your

Grace, it is something that cannot be delayed for too long. However, we must examine all possibilities. I have sent messages to the Dukes of Geverd and Voro and the Duchess of Simand instructing them to come to the next meeting. I intend to fill these vacancies then, if necessary by ennobling a commoner."

Sulereath saw Latisec look horrified and carried on before he had a chance to speak, "I am aware that such a thing hasn't been done for a very long time but that's how noble houses became noble in the first place." He looked directly at Latisec and added, "including your own, my lord Duke. There is precedent and I will resort to that if necessary. If anyone finds a suitable candidate please produce them in time for that meeting." He paused, "Are there any other matters you wish to bring before the Council today?"

He looked around the table but nobody had anything to offer.

He stood, signed himself with the lightning bolt and said, "Thank you all for your contributions to this discussion. I am grateful for your advice. In token of this you have my permission to style yourselves Lord Adviser to the Crown. This meeting is at an end."

A MANSION ON THE ROCK

The door opened. Praukel looked up from his workbench ready to reprimand whichever servant dared to disturb him. The potion he was brewing was a difficult one and he was at a critical stage, carefully stirring the mixture over a flame with a thin glass rod while waiting for it to change colour. He couldn't afford distractions. Missing the change meant the mixture would spoil and that would ruin more than two chimes' work. *I'll make the intruder drink it to see what effect it has if it is spoiled.*

His anger melted away when he saw the person standing in the doorway was a short man with thinning hair pulled back in a pigtail. Nasuren was back from his latest trip and was obeying his instructions to come to him immediately on arrival whatever time it was. Praukel held up a hand, palm towards Nasuren, then pushed him away while continuing to stir the mixture. He turned back to concentrate again on the potion.

A sixth later he sighed. The interruption had been enough to curdle the mixture. It smelled like rotten eggs and burnt-out candles. You never knew what you would get if a recipe as complex as that went wrong. Occasionally the outcome turned out to be useful but most of the time the resulting concoction was poisonous, or neutral at best.

The thick, sticky blue-green mess in the bowl should be a clear, sparkling, fragrant violet. It was useless, unless it could be used to stick things together. He snorted at the idea – it would be a very expensive glue.

He quenched the burner and tossed the bowl and its contents into a box of assorted rubbish. Removing his apron, he ran his eye over the bench and shelves making sure all the jars and bottles were closed. Satisfied that everything was in order he left the workroom, locking the door behind him.

Halfway along the corridor he stopped when there was a muffled bang from behind him. He hurried back to the workroom, opened the door cautiously and looked inside. The rubbish box was in pieces, its contents scattered across the floor. A large fragment of the bowl he had thrown away was embedded in one leg of the bench and another had been thrown across the room to smash a jar of oil standing in the opposite corner.

Several servants gathered outside the room in response to the strange noise. After them Nasuren came limping around the corner asking, "What was that?"

"Something I'm going to have to investigate," answered Praukel. He told the only servant allowed into his workroom to get on with clearing up the mess and turned away.

"Interesting," he said as he led Nasuren to his study. "The potion I was working on went wrong. I threw it away and left the room. I'm glad I did. It would have been unpleasant if I had still been there when it exploded."

"Do you know what caused it, master?"

"That's none of your business."

"Sorry, master. It's just that I think I could find a use for a controllable explosion."

"Indeed? Does this have something to do with your task?"

"Yes, master."

Praukel unlocked the study door, sat down behind his desk and waved Nasuren to a deep, leather upholstered chair. As always, Nasuren didn't sit back into the comfort of the chair but stayed perched on the edge.

"Tell me," said Praukel.

"Yes, master. I have managed to find another of your relatives. It has been an interesting assignment. Some of them have been quite difficult to locate."

"That's not surprising."

"So far I have disposed of five of them and another was

kind enough to die of spotted fever quite recently."

"I didn't know there were as many as that!"

Nasuren waggled a hand from side to side. "I must admit I was uncertain about one of them."

"Better to be safe and get rid of them. You're doing well. Are there any more?"

"As far as I can tell, there is only one left who may be more closely related to Wurauf than you are. "

"Well done. I presume you have plans for him…her?"

"Her, master. Yes, I have. However, I fear there is one problem. I used different methods for all five killings so that there isn't a pattern but that hasn't stopped someone who is investigating Wurauf's relatives on behalf of the king's council noticing the recent high death rate among them. The newsmongers mentioned it for a couple of days but it hasn't held their interest and it's been dropped again. That interest could revive if another one dies and perhaps even stimulate an investigation. Something unusual and apparently unrelated might divert their attention. That's why I was curious about your explosion."

"I see," said Praukel. "Unfortunately, I don't know if I can reproduce the effect. It took me by surprise." He paused. "There might be something in one of those recipe books in my library. One of those you acquired for me. I couldn't make sense of it at the time but, thinking about it, it might have been describing a mixture which was stable while hot but reacted violently and spontaneously when it cooled. I will have to read it again and experiment before I can provide you with anything safe to use, if indeed that's what happened."

"Pity," commented Nasuren. "It would be useful. I will have to find an alternative distraction. With your permission, master, I will be away from Carregis for a few days."

"Where are you going this time?"

"Hemeark, master."

"I know one branch of the family settled around there but I thought it had died out long ago. I had no idea it still exists."

"There is only one person, master. Her name is Melauthua."

"I've met her! Just once, when I was passing through Hemeark. Must be eight or nine years ago. I rather liked her. She's a no-nonsense sort of business woman. It's quite a surprise to find out we're related."

"I think she is a third cousin several times removed, but the genealogy is confusing. Your great-great-grandfather was married three times and one of his wives had previously been married to his brother. The same name crops up four times in two generations and I'm not quite sure which one of them is which. Not that it really matters, Melauthua is the only living descendent of any of them."

"Isn't it a shame that that lineage will soon be extinct."

HOUSE NEYEN

"Be welcome to Jotuk," said Yisul, making a sweeping gesture with the arm that had been wrapped around Anarya's waist.

Tilua released her grip on Anarya's right hand and slowly turned around, eyes widening as she took in the elegant, restful decoration of the room. It was so different from the fussy, over-decorated room in Graumedel's mansion where Anarya had opened the portal. She thumbed her forehead and commented, "It's difficult to believe. Jotuk is one of those places you think of as far away and exotic. Being able to get here so easily is – astonishing."

Baram removed his hand from Anarya's right shoulder. "You get used to it, to some extent at least."

The last of the group, a short, balding man wearing the red and gold tunic of a priest of Huler, let go of Anarya's left shoulder and stroked his neatly pointed beard. "That was remarkable, a truly awesome experience."

"Please, be seated," said Yisul. "I will be back in a moment." She opened the door into the corridor, spoke to someone outside and returned to say, "My parents are in a meeting. They will be told we are here when the meeting is finished."

Tilua sat on the sofa next to the priest of Huler, whose name was Desern, and said, "I agree the experience was remarkable but I wouldn't have called it awesome. What did you see, or feel?"

"I had a momentary glimpse of a vast network of threads that apparently connected everything to everything else," replied Desern. "It was as if I had invoked my talent to Seek without defining what I was looking for."

"That is different from what happened to me," said Tilua. "I saw a brief flash of light and there was a sensation of rapid movement. I felt as if I was about to fall on my face – I wonder…"

She called Anarya over and asked her to describe what she felt when she went through the portal.

"Nothing that I haven't felt every time."

"No, I didn't mean this time. Is it always the same?"

"Yes, there's a flash of light, and then it feels as if I'm falling forwards. The first few times I had a tendency to stumble but I've got used to it. Why?"

"That would describe the sensations I had," agreed Tilua, "but it's quite different from what Desern says he felt. Tell me, has what you feel changed since your battle with The God?"

"No – not really – well – maybe a little bit, now that I think about it"

"What's the difference?"

"There are colours in the flash of light. They're duller than they used to be and aren't everywhere I can see but start at the edges of vision and move in on me, like a net being drawn in."

"Interesting. What does Yisul feel going through the portal?"

"I don't know. I've never asked her."

"You haven't!"

"No, I've just assumed she feels what I do."

Tilua shook her head and clucked her tongue. "Really Anarya! I'm surprised at your lack of imagination. Yisul, Baram, come here a moment, please. I think we may have discovered that passing through the portal feels different to people with different talents. I'd like to find out if this is right. Tell me, what sensations do you get in transit?"

Baram looked at Yisul who gestured for him to speak first. "I'm not sure how to explain it. When I'm in Stealth I feel – it's difficult to describe. I suppose safe, secure and protected is as close as I can get. I get the same sensations going through the portal, only they're much more intense. But they only last a moment."

"Yisul?"

"I see a brilliant blur of light and hear a loud noise along with a feeling that I'm moving very fast. It's as if I was seeing everything and hearing everybody between the starting point and the destination, all at once."

"Well," said Tilua, "that seems to settle it. Going through the portal produces a momentary enhancement of individual talents. I wonder why."

"I might have an answer for that," offered Anarya.

"Well, what is it?" asked Tilua into the expectant hush that followed Anarya's comment. "You can't say something like that and not explain what you mean."

"Sorry," said Anarya, shaking her head. "I was thinking of what the daimon told me that time it took me into the Darkworld and left Yisa and Baram nowhere while it talked to me."

"Please explain," asked Tilua.

Anarya apologised again and told them about the incident when she had been separated from the others during transit. "About the last thing the daimon said before reuniting us was 'power for all the talents comes from the Darkworld'."

Tilua asked, "Are those its exact words?"

"Maybe not exact, but I'm sure that's what it meant."

"Fascinating!" said Tilua. "It definitely used the word 'power'?"

"Yes. And it used it again when we renegotiated the terms of use of the portal. It wanted to restrict my use of it because it needed the power."

"I can sort of see what it means," mused Tilua. "Think about it – a Scratcher's glyphs might be made of bits of the Darkworld she's pulled into the real world."

"Or," said Desern, "the Darkworld might act as a map for Seekers like me allowing us to see the way everything is interconnected. I'm sure the Brotherhood will spend a lot of time talking about the implications of this and how each of the talents draws on power from the Darkworld. However, it doesn't seem particularly relevant at the moment."

"No," agreed Yisul, "it's more important to know what's happening about the planned rebellion. Did you get anything, Caseir? Were you in contact with the other bit of wood during transit?"

"Yes. Giving some of the wood to Tilua and Desern was a good idea. As I thought, the five pieces of wood you are carrying were enough to dominate the one Richak has."

Yisul said happily, "So Kehsieh won't help Richak. Quarenna be thanked."

Caseir contradicted her, "It's not as easy as that. We outnumbered Kehsieh, but only for the moment of transit. We're still in the same position, I felt Kehsieh as we came through the portal but I can't feel him now. We're still too far away."

"But he's got to be in Jotuk somewhere."

"I'm sure he is, but Jotuk's big and wherever he is in the city it's not close enough."

"Oh!

THE DUCAL MANSION
IN SIMAND

Aesol, Duchess of Simand read the summons from Sulereath and passed it to her seneschal, saying, "What do you think of that?"

"Interesting, Your Grace."

"The king's about twenty-three now, isn't he?"

"I think that's right."

"I've met him twice," said Aesol, running her hands through her copper coloured hair.

"Your Grace, take care of your appearance."

Aesol ran her hands through her hair again. "There's no court today so I can look tousled if I want to."

"But you do have an audience with the Navigators Guild."

"That's not until the fourteenth chime. I can get tidied up again by then."

"Yes, Your Grace."

"Don't be a stick-in-the-mud, Hegris. You like the dishevelled look."

"Yes, I do. But I prefer to get it that way myself."

Aesol laughed. Hegris was not only her seneschal, he had been her lover for six years. He could be rather formal and aware of her dignity but, in the right circumstances, he could be quite relaxed and even a bit wild.

She stood up and moved behind his chair to nibble his ear.

"Aesol!"

"You sound shocked. There's nobody else here."

"No, but we are dealing with business, not being… "

"Frivolous."

"Exactly."

"Oh, well. Let's get the boring stuff out of the way,

then we can frivol."

"You will be going to Carregis, won't you," asked Hegris when the duchess sat down again and picked up the message from the king.

"Yes, I wouldn't miss it. I'm sorry you'll have to stay behind."

"I'm not. I've never liked Kuranesh… "

"The man's an idiot."

"… or Latisec and I'm glad I won't have to put up with them."

"You know, I think this might be interesting. That summons wasn't written by the spineless rabbit I met on my last trip to Carregis – of course that was nine years ago. It reads as if the rabbit has grown a backbone."

"Could be just that he has good advisers."

"You think? I rather hope he's doing it on his own initiative. I felt sorry for him being so much under Wurauf's thumb. Perhaps I can help save him from Latisec's."

Aesol stood up and added, "I'm going to have to take ship tomorrow if I'm to get to Carregis in time, so I want you in my bed tonight."

"Yes, Your Grace. As you command, Your Grace."

HOUSE NEYEN

"We need to get closer to Richak," said Anarya. "I've carried a bit of wood through the Darkworld often enough since we took the table there that Caseir can confirm Richak is still planning an assault on the inner city. But, except for the moment of transit we can't overwhelm Kehsieh. I think the best thing to do is open a portal to wherever he is…"

"No! You can't go into *houln* territory, that's much too dangerous," said Yisul. "There's got to be an easier way."

"An easier way to do what?" asked Muhan as he and Lias entered the room.

The question was forgotten for a while as servants brought more chairs and arranged them round a low table. On it they placed an engraved silver salver with matching jugs of hot water, tea glasses, an assortment of teas, a plate of candied fruit biscuits and a bowl of roasted mixed nuts.

Lias waved the servants away saying, "We will serve ourselves," and asking Yisul to help her.

"Meanwhile," said Muhan, "perhaps someone will tell me what you want an easier way of doing."

Anarya and Baram started talking at the same time. Yisul paused with a full hot water jug in one hand to expand on something Anarya said; she turned around quickly to appeal to Tilua for confirmation and almost spilled it. Muhan and Lias were looking more and more confused until Muhan said, "Stop! Please, just stop. I'm not following this at all. Just one of you at a time, if it's not too much to ask. Otherwise it's like a meeting of the Council with everybody speaking at once."

He, and Lias, had to experience talking directly to Caseir before they understood what he was and how he could hear whatever was said in the vicinity of one of the pieces of wood, even if whispered.

"So you think you could – dominate, outvote? – the piece of Caseir that this Richak has if you can get close enough."

"Yes. We believe so," agreed Anarya.

"I'm certain," said Caseir, and Yisul echoed his comment to Baram who had relinquished his piece of wood to Muhan.

"You should know if anybody does," replied Muhan. "That leaves us with the question of how to get within range of Richak."

"Yes. But he's an important person among the *houln*. There are bound to be other people around if Anarya opens a portal to get near him," grumbled Yisul. "That's why I said there has to be an easier way."

"Pardon me, Lord Muhan. Do you know where in the city this Richak is based?" asked Desern.

"No, I don't. But I may be able to find out. Why?"

"I was wondering, if he's close enough to the wall and we are safe on this side of it, will we be close enough for our five pieces of Caseir to overpower his one?"

"Nice idea," remarked Caseir, "but I don't think it will work. I can feel the other bits of me if we're close enough. Unfortunately, we're not likely to get that close if we're on opposite sides of the wall."

"But it's worth a try, isn't it," asked Lias.

"I can try finding out more about Richak," said Muhan. He opened the door and told the servant waiting outside to find and bring someone called Trusef.

"Do you think he will know anything about Richak?" asked Yisul.

"If he doesn't he will know someone who does," replied Muhan.

"Who is he?" asked Anarya.

"He's the Master of the Keys," said Yisul. "That's the title given to the senior servant in a House. You'll like him. When I was little he would play with me and let me ride on his shoulders."

"He is also one of the longest serving members of our staff," Muhan told them. "One of his functions is recruitment. He will know if we employ anybody associated with the Three Flowers."

Anarya recognised Trusef when he answered the summons. A slightly stooped figure, a little taller than her, with sparse white hair and a bushy moustache, he had been organising the servants present when she got into the carriage for her visit to House Shuth.

"No," said Trusef in response to Muhan's question. "Nobody in the House is a member of the Three Flowers. However, two of the grooms and one of the footmen have reported being interrogated by the ruler of that *houln*."

"Can any of them put me in touch with him? I believe his name is Richak."

"I'm told there was a truce recently between the Three Flowers, the Stone Grasshoppers and the Dark Fountain *houln* and we do have two members of the Dark Fountain working in the laundry. I will try to find out more from them. They may provide a way of contacting the Three Flowers."

"Good," said Muhan. "Do what you can, and as fast as possible."

HEMEARK IN THE DUCHY OF SIMAND

Nasuren finished a very enjoyable meal in the dining area of the House of Silken Delights, leaned back in his chair with a glass of apple brandy and sipped appreciatively while he watched people entering and leaving. His table was well positioned to see activity in the atrium and, after spending most of a chime watching, he was sure he had identified all of the House staff. A rotund middle-aged man sitting in one corner next to a stout brass-bound oak door was, almost certainly, the Scratcher who maintained the privacy spells. *That door probably leads to Melauthua's office and rooms.* Two big, tough-looking men were continually wandering back and forth through the various doors leading from the atrium. They were clearly hired muscle. He wondered a bit about a third, much smaller, man. *He's behaving the same way as the bouncers, but he can't be one of them – unless he's a Lifter.*

Four men pushed their way through the main door. They were swaying a bit, as if they were at least partially drunk. One of them staggered over to the scantily-clad women standing by the bead curtain that gave access to the whorehouse section of the building.

"You'll do," he said, snatching at one of the women. He got hold of her halter top and pulled it down to expose her breasts.

"Yeah, she'll do for all of us," laughed one of his companions, leering and reaching down to rub his crotch.

Another woman grabbed a hand bell and rang it vigorously. One of the bouncers went to help the woman who was trying to pull away from her assailant. His companion stepped up to guard his back.

Nasuren was pleased when the men he had tentatively identified as magic users proved him right. The Scratcher stood up and started drawing symbols in the air but, before he finished his spell, he was knocked to the floor by a punch from one of the newcomers. The Lifter crouched, extended his arms as if gripping someone around the waist and straightened up again. One of the attackers started screaming as he found himself suspended head-down over the tiled floor.

The noises attracted the attention of people in the dining area. Several of them stood up and craned their necks to see what was going on.

The other troublemakers looked at their companion hovering in mid-air his own height above the ground. They turned to run for the door. One of them made it, the other two were taken down by the bouncers. The Scratcher picked himself off the floor, shook his head, spat out some blood, gestured quickly and immobilised the attackers.

"What's this all about, eh?" asked the statuesque woman in silk and feathers who came through the oak door. "You should know better than to bother my girls. What do you think you're playing at?"

There was no response.

"All right. If you won't talk now you can tell it to the Baron's court in the morning. Get them out of here."

Melauthua turned to the diners to say, "Please return to your meals. We are sorry about the disturbance. To compensate for any annoyance that little incident caused there will be no charge for your after-dinner drinks – as long as you don't want Miros that is."

The offer of a free drink and the joking reference to the extremely expensive liqueur relaxed the crowd, who started to drift back to their tables.

Nasuren settled back in his seat. *They handled that fracas rather well. No chance to get to her. I'll need to think of another distraction.*

He finished his brandy then left the House of Silken Delights, thinking hard about how he could get close enough to Melauthua and how he could arrange for an accident.

○

When he stepped out of his inn the next morning he was facing into the sun and was dazzled.

"That's him!"

Shading his eyes, Nasuren looked around to see three men in the black and apple-green tabards of the Baron of Hemeark surrounding another man who was pointing at him.

"You sure? Won't go well for you if you're lying."

"I'm sure. See the way he limps. It *is* him."

One of the Baron's Proctors walked up to Nasuren and said, "Your pardon, sir. I must ask you to accompany us to the Baron's court. He wants to see you."

Still dazzled, Nasuren asked, "Why?"

The man put his hand to the hilt of his short sword and said, "I dare say you'll find out when we get there. Shall we go?"

Nasuren had no choice. He couldn't fight even one of the Baron's men, far less three of them. They turned a corner into shade and at last he could see the fourth man's features clearly. It was his principal agent in Hemeark and he was the one who had found the men to create the disturbance at the House. *Huler's balls! How did they get hold of him? They shouldn't have been able to trace it back to him – unless he was greedy and didn't arrange a cut-out because he wanted to keep most of the money for himself. Now he's trying to get out of trouble by turning on me.*

○

The Baron's court was housed in a big, two-storey building occupying one side of the market square. Apart from a pair of solid, square columns on either side of the entrance the facade was undecorated and its appearance said, quite clearly, that this was a no-nonsense town.

Somewhat to Nasuren's surprise he was taken to a comfortable sitting room, not a courtroom. Two men and two women stood just inside the door. Melauthua, dressed conservatively in a dark blue jacket and skirt with a small frill of lace at collar and cuffs, sat in one of the armchairs and a portly man sat in the other. Nasuren recognised him as Ghendul, the Baron of Hemeark. *He's got a reputation of not being too bright. If it was just him I'm sure I could confuse him enough to let me walk away. Trouble is she's not stupid and she's the power in this town, not him.*

"I want to know why this man organised a disturbance at the House last night," said Melauthua.

"Well," Ghendul commanded, "answer her."

"Whatever it was had nothing to do with me," said Nasuren.

"He's lying, my Lady" commented one of the women standing by the door.

"There's no point in trying to lie to a Feeler," said Melauthua, pointing at the woman who spoke. "My staff captured three of the four you hired to start that fracas. The leader of the group described you well enough for a Seeker to find you. I know you had dinner at the House yesterday but, as far as I know, our paths have never crossed before. Have you got something against me, or are you working for someone else?"

"It's someone else, my Lady," said the Feeler. "He's been slightly anxious since he was brought here but the level jumped when you asked that question."

"I want to know who's behind it. Your Grace, would you allow the use of a truth potion?" asked Melauthua.

"Certainly."

The Feeler produced a vial of clear liquid and offered it to Nasuren, "Drink this."

Nasuren turned his head away.

The two men took a firm grip of him and forced his mouth open while one of the women poured the liquid into his mouth.

Nasuren tried to spit it out but was forced to swallow some of it. *Now what? I can't betray the master but the potion won't let me lie.*

His throat tightened.

Melauthua asked, "Who are you working for?"

Nasuren gasped for breath, mumbled, "Pr…" and collapsed.

The Feeler bent over him. "He's dead! Somebody didn't want to be identified."

"Somebody with access to quite sophisticated potions," said Melauthua. "I wonder who, and why."

THE ROYAL PALACE

Sulereath had already welcomed the Duke of Voro and the Duchess of Simand to Carregis but did so again formally at the opening of the meeting of the King's Council once the blessings of Huler and Quarenna had been invoked.

"My Lords, I am pleased you have been able to come to this meeting. It is my hope that you will contribute to the deliberations of this council and assist me in making the decisions that must be made. It is unfortunate that the Duke of Geverd was unable to make the journey and join us. However, it is not surprising. He is, after all, nearly ninety, and very frail."

He looked along the length of the table. The seat to his right was occupied by Duke Latisec, then there was a gap and the remaining seats on that side were filled by Aness Debengis, Kieret Beghroth, Grovaen and Commander Fedic. On his left sat Yertis Pirrosha, Jaenis and the two newcomers.

Interesting that both of them have stayed as far away from Latisec as possible. I wonder if that's deliberate.

"I am honoured to be here, Your Majesty," said Kuranesh of Voro. "The journey was fatiguing but to be of assistance to you makes it worthwhile." He waved a hand dismissively then had to rearrange the flamboyant lace cuff to show it off to best advantage.

Sulereath winced inwardly and hoped his reaction wasn't visible. *He hasn't changed, still an overdressed fop taken with his own importance. I don't like agreeing with Wurauf, but I think I must as far as Kuranesh is concerned. He's a quarter shy of a bit.*

The other new face on the council belonged to Aesol of Simand who smiled at Sulereath from under her ornately-arranged hairstyle and the rope of pearls threaded through it. "Thank you for your welcome, Your Majesty. I shall assist you to the best of my ability."

Sulereath smiled back. She'd struck him as sensible on the two occasions she had visited Carregis to see Wurauf. *Even he admitted she's got a reputation for pragmatism.*

"Well my Lords, shall we begin with considering the vacant Duchy of Carrh?"

Heads nodded all around the table.

"Duke Latisec has expressed an interest in taking over Carrh, and that is something we should consider. However, I would prefer to look at the possibility of keeping the position in the family." When Sulereath said this, he saw nods around the table except from the seat to his right where he was aware of Duke Latisec shifting in his chair. *Hope he's going to keep quiet.* "I understand from Lord Adviser Aness that his staff's search for the late Duke Wurauf's relatives has been successful." Sulereath looked at Aness Debengis. "Please tell us what they have found."

Aness was about to pour himself some wine, his many rings clinking against the carafe, when the king spoke. He stopped, dipped his head and said, "Certainly, Your Majesty. I'm told it was a difficult search, but I'm happy to say it was productive. My staff have produced three possible candidates."

From the corner of his eye Sulereath saw Latisec scowl at this news.

"One of them," continued Aness, "I feel we can dismiss immediately as he has spent the last four years as an oarsman on one of the naval galleys. He is serving a five year sentence for theft and assault."

"Not at all suitable," said Latisec quickly, and everyone else agreed with him.

"In any case, his relationship is the most distant of the three. The other two are much more interesting. Both have become rich through their own efforts, an accomplishment which shows competence and ability which might be to the benefit of the Duchy."

"Sounds good," commented Kieret Beghroth. "Who are they?"

"Their names are Praukel Vecsin and Melauthua Minobis."

"What! Melauthua Minobis? You can't seriously be considering her," said Latisec.

"Why not?" asked Sulereath.

"She runs a whorehouse!"

"And apparently does it very well," observed Yertis Pirrosha. "The House of Silken Delights is quite famous." She smiled and added, "While it might be a somewhat unusual occupation for a prospective Duchess it is not illegal, and I don't see that it excludes her."

"I know of her," said Kieret reaching for a glass of water, "I don't know how she got started but now she owns about half of Hemeark and the surrounding orchards. My company deals with her a lot although I haven't met her myself. I'm told she's a shrewd negotiator."

"She's one possibility," said Sulereath. "Who's the other?"

"Praukel Vecsin. He's a merchant here in Carregis. He's grown a small legacy from his mother into a fortune over the last twenty-five years."

"Yes," agreed Kieret, "Praukel Vecsin must now be one of the wealthiest men in the Duchy, if not the whole country. I have to deal with him on a regular basis."

"Pardon the interruption," said Duchess Aesol, "but the way you said 'have to' makes me wonder if you trust him."

"I have nothing specific against him, but he makes me uncomfortable. Probably because he frequently gets the better of me in our negotiations."

"Your Majesty," Fedic interrupted to say, "there is something you should know about him which rules him out of consideration. He's a Chemer."

"How do you know?"

"I haven't had any dealings with him myself but it's well known among the guardsmen that he is the best person to go to if you want a love potion, or need something to make people forget."

"We can't have that," said Latisec.

"No, we can't," agreed the king. "There's a law against the talented holding civil power." He saw Yertis Pirrosha shake her head and added, "Isn't there? Judge Yertis, please tell us the legal position."

"Your Majesty, it is commonly believed that the talented are prohibited from holding a position of authority whether inherited or elected. However, this is custom rather than law. It dates from the end of Fereathlin II's reign. His daughter had a relatively minor talent, she was a rather weak Seeker I believe. She chose to pass the succession to her brother, who became Gelereath I, because she felt it inappropriate for someone gifted with a talent to rule those not as fortunate."

"That's a belief encouraged by the Brotherhood," admitted Grovaen, "and, I think, by the Inner Circle." He looked across the table at Jaenis who nodded her agreement.

Sulereath frowned and asked Yertis, "So being a Chemer wouldn't actually be a bar to Praukel inheriting the Duchy."

"No, Your Majesty," said Yertis. "Not legally, but you should consider the effect on the populace of appointing someone believed to be ineligible. Custom can sometimes be stronger than law. The reaction could influence how you are perceived."

"I think the separation of talent and authority is a good one," stated Latisec flatly. "Praukel should be removed from consideration."

It's one less rival for him to worry about, thought Sulereath. *That's why he's so strongly against Praukel. But he's probably right.*

"We seem to be left with only one candidate from among Wurauf's relatives," said the king. "Does anyone wish to say more in her favour or against her?"

Nobody answered, although Latisec fidgeted and Sulereath thought he was trying to find something detrimental to say.

"In that case, I think we should meet Melauthua. I assume she was invited to attend today."

"Yes, Your Majesty, she was," said Aness.

"Then bring her in."

While he was waiting Sulereath sat back in his chair and wriggled a bit, trying to find a more comfortable position. The seat cushion was a bit too thin. *Must remember to mention that to somebody and get it fixed.*

A guardsman ushered Melauthua into the council chamber. She was wearing a simple blue-and-green full-length skirt and a lace-trimmed silk blouse with a necklace of amethysts; simple and elegant but not too formal.

"You are Melauthua Minobis," said Sulereath.

"I am, Your Majesty," she said, bowing low.

"Are you aware of why you are here?"

"Yes, Your Majesty."

"What do you think about the possibility of becoming Duchess of Carrh?"

Melauthua looked the length of the table and met the king's gaze without seeming overawed or anxious.

She looks calm in what must be a trying situation. I like that.

"Your Majesty, I knew that I was related in some roundabout way to Duke Wurauf but it never occurred to me that I might succeed him."

"And what is your reaction to the idea?"

"Quite frankly, Your Majesty, I rejected the idea at first. However, the more I thought about it the more attractive it sounded. My businesses and estates more or less run themselves now and don't need tight control so I have time to do other things. Recently, one of these has been answering appeals for help from Baron Ghendul of Hemeark. Many of the problems he's brought to me have been stimulating and I would expect running a duchy to throw up more such."

"So you would accept the position if I offered it to you."

"Yes, Your Majesty. I believe I would," said Melauthua, inclining her head towards Sulereath.

The king looked up and down the table and asked if anyone had questions for her.

Latisec sat up straighter and almost snarled, "What makes you think a career running a whorehouse makes you fit to run a duchy?"

"I did not say it did, Your Grace. I answered His Majesty's question about how I feel about the possibility of becoming a Duchess."

Sulereath listened to Melauthua's answers to questions posed by several of the council members. The inquisition went on for about another half chime. He was annoyed by Latisec's constant harping on about her lowly status and brought the questioning to an end, asking Melauthua to wait outside.

"Well, my lords. The decision is mine but I would like to hear your opinions. What do you think?"

"Totally unsuitable," said Latisec. "Her occupation is incompatible with the dignity of the position."

"I disagree," said Duchess Aesol. "I thought she presented herself well. The fact that she's advising Ghendul is a point in her favour. The man is barely competent but, thanks to the advice she's been giving him, there have been few issues that have required my attention."

The rest of the King's Advisers nodded or made brief comments in favour of Melauthua.

"Bring her back," instructed Sulereath, and waited until she was standing at the end of the table again.

"Melauthua Minobis, I offer you the rank and status of Duchess of Carrh in succession to your distant relative Wurauf, along with the privileges and obligations of that position. How say you?"

"I accept, Your Majesty."

"Then I require you to swear allegiance to me. Lady Adviser Jaenis, will you administer the oath."

Sulereath had remembered that Grovaen was sceptical about the oath Latisec had sworn and had spent some time with him and Jaenis discussing how to make it stronger. Now Melauthua knelt at the king's feet while Jaenis led her through the new version, invoking Quarenna in her aspect as the Guardian to give it the force they felt it needed.

"Rise, My Lady Duchess," said the king. He leaned forward to give her a ring engraved with the seal of Carrh. "Take your rightful place on this council. We have another matter to discuss which affects your Duchy."

Melauthua made her way to the empty seat between Latisec and Aness. She settled into it with a quiet sigh. Sulereath saw Latisec scowl and twitch his garments away from her as if avoiding contamination.

Aness leaned over and pointed out who was who among the people she didn't know. Jaenis, Duchess Aesol and Commander Fedic lifted their glasses in salute to her and she reached for the wine to respond in kind.

"Now we need to consider a replacement for Count Graumedel," said Sulereath when Melauthua seemed settled. "Lord Adviser Fedic, you were going to bring the possible heirs here today. Have you done so?"

"Yes. Your Majesty. Do you wish to see them now?"

"I think we will discuss them first, then bring them in one at a time – or all together if that seems appropriate."

"Together could be quite interesting," said Fedic. "From what I hear Nurmed and Harviel really don't like each other."

"You had doubts about Nurmed. Is he the same man?"

"Yes, Your Majesty, without doubt. I had a couple of men at the pits two nights ago and they confirmed my suspicions."

"He's out then." Aness, the chains around his neck jingling as he shook his head and gave his opinion in a firm voice. "Makes things a bit simpler."

"Lord Adviser Kieret, you offered to investigate Harviel and her farm. What have you found?"

"It has little to recommend it. Harviel occupies two rooms in one wing of the farmhouse. They are reasonably sound but the rest of the buildings are in poor repair. The farm servants are scruffy and surly, except for the estate manager. He seems to be the organiser. Harviel, as far as I can judge, leaves the running of the farm entirely to him. I've been unable to discover what she does with her time. The one advantage it does have, and the reason why my people buy from it, is that it breeds a miniature variety of pigs."

"Miniature! How is that an advantage?" asked Grovaen.

"Because they can be shipped live and butchered on board ship as required. One animal is the right size to feed the crew for a day. Bigger pigs not only take up more space, reducing that available for cargo, but they provide more meat than needed for one day when slaughtered and the excess needs to be stored and that's another demand on cargo space."

"I'd never have guessed that the size of a pig would be important aboard ship," said Sulereath.

Yertis announced, "I looked into how Harviel came to own the farm. The answer seems to be that she was given it by Graumedel. Now that sounds as if it might be expressing a preference for her over Nurmed because he was given a rundown house of lower value in Greenbank at the same time. Look into it a bit deeper and you find that Nurmed was also given two hundred and fifty dukals. A friend of mine who deals in property estimates that, at the time of this transaction, Harviel's farm was worth about two hundred and fifty dukals more than the house. So both gifts had the same value."

"But land has to be worth more, doesn't it?" asked Fedic. "It doesn't have to stay a farm; it could be built on and become much more valuable."

"True," said Yertis, "but I found a document tucked away in the Office of Deeds and Contracts which is relevant. It's signed by both Nurmed and Harviel and dated eight years ago. According to it they acknowledge that gifts of equal value, and of their own choosing, have been made to them as Graumedel's nearest relatives on the understanding that they relinquish any farther claim on Graumedel's estate."

"I wonder," remarked Melauthua, "if that stipulation is relevant to the donor's rank as well as his wealth."

"That is a reasonable question, Your Grace," said Yertis, "and it could provide the opportunity for years of debate in the courts." She inclined her head towards Sulereath and continued, "Of course, the rank is in the king's gift and doesn't have to follow any other bequest."

"I remember someone saying that there is another niece who is about eight years old," said Jaenis. "Dartiel, or something like that."

"Yes."

"Might it be significant that the document you described is also eight years old? Dartiel is as close a relative as the others but did not receive a gift from Graumedel nor did she agree not to make a claim on his estate."

"She must have been less than a year old at the time of that agreement," remarked Aesol, "so she couldn't."

"True, but her guardian could have done so on her behalf. Does the lack of any prior agreement make her a potential claimant now?"

"It is possible," agreed Yertis, "but I would hate to give a ruling on the matter without considerable research."

"I would like to make a suggestion, Your Majesty," said Fedic. "I have been impressed with the way Graumedel's seneschal, Corvek, has managed to maintain order in the city in the absence of delegated authority. He is obviously competent and he has the advantage of experience. Might I suggest that Dartiel is appointed Countess of Carregis with Corvek as her regent."

"Won't work," Grovaen stated, "for the same reason Praukel can't be Duke. Corvek's also a Chemer."

"I don't see why that should be a problem," said Yertis. "Nobody is objecting at present and, as regent, he wouldn't actually be a noble."

Grovaen smiled, "That sounds like a good bit of legalistic wriggling. I think it could work."

I don't want to appoint a regent, thought Sulereath,

that's how the Three started. On the other hand, the council is supposed to give me advice and I should listen to them. I don't have to like what they say, or accept it, but I should at least consider it.

Sulereath sat quietly thinking while still paying some attention to the continuing discussion. He realised that Fedic's idea was a viable solution when Melauthua said, "Corvek has experience in that role and his support would help me settle in to my new position. I would be happy with that arrangement."

"My Lords, I thank you for your advice. Duchess Melauthua, I will leave it to you to inform Corvek of his appointment as regent for Dartiel. I don't believe we need to see Nurmed and Harviel after all. Lord Adviser Fedic, would you let them know that their presence is not needed and apologise for disrupting their day."

He stood, made the sign of Huler's thunderbolt and said, "This meeting is at an end."

A MANSION ON THE ROCK

Praukel was trying again to make sense of an old Chemer's recipe book. About a hundred and thirty years old, it was battered, torn, stained, and in some places quite illegible. Even where he could read the handwriting, the author had often used abbreviations and what appeared to be a private shorthand. Praukel felt he was making progress in understanding the explosive nature of some of the described potions, but many passages remained opaque. He looked at the book again and frowned at one sentence. *Can it really mean that?*

Looking at the book made him think of Nasuren, who had acquired it for him. He found himself wondering what had happened to him. He had obviously failed in his task to kill Melauthua. *What went wrong? He was usually quite competent. He must be dead, but even if he still lives the loyalty potion will make sure he can't compromise me.*

He looked up when somebody tapped on his study door and frowned. He wasn't expecting anyone. It was probably just someone wanting a potion of some sort. Sometimes being available to whoever wanted a bit of magic was a nuisance. With a sigh, he said, "Come."

"Your pardon, master," said the servant who opened the door. She entered, placed a small sealed scroll in front of Praukel and stepped back.

The image on the pale-blue wax of the seal was a stag's head, the emblem of Alrem. Praukel wondered why Duke Latisec was writing to him. He looked up at the servant, who hadn't left the room, and asked, "Is the courier waiting for a reply?"

"Yes, master."

"I'll ring when I have an answer."

The servant bowed and left.

He carefully laid his book aside. A quick twist broke the seal on the scroll and scattered fragments of wax on the desk.

'To Praukel Vecsin, greetings.

In the light of the events of yesterday His Grace, Duke Latisec of Alrem, invites you to attend him at his residence at a convenient time as soon as possible after the twelfth chime tomorrow in order to discuss matters of mutual interest.

This by the hand of His Grace's principal secretary.'

It's got to be about the ennobling of that slut Melauthua. I can't imagine why she was preferred to me, unless it was that nonsense about my talent. Rumour has it that Latisec wanted the Duchy for himself, so why does he want to talk to a rival? He re-read the letter and decided it wasn't quite a command, although it was close to one. *I'd better accept the 'invitation'.*

O

The town house of the Duke of Alrem, high on the east side of the Rock, was built almost two hundred years ago, in the reign of Jenereath II, the last ruling queen of Carrhen. Typical of the period, the elaborate patterns formed by the multicoloured bricks and tiles of its walls were visible from afar and were a landmark eagerly looked for by the pilots of ships making their way upriver.

His carriage deposited Praukel at the main door a carefully calculated third after the twelfth chime. Not so early that he seemed overeager, nor so late that he was rude. After all, the message had said 'as soon as convenient.'

Admitted to the building by two guardsmen in the Duke's pale-blue and yellow livery, he was ushered along a corridor lined with watercolours and oil paintings of scenes from Alrem.

A door into a corner room was opened for him. With

books and scrolls stacked to the ceiling on two walls, this was evidently Latisec's library.

The Duke stood to welcome his visitor, a courtesy Praukel hadn't expected.

"Thank you for coming," said Latisec. "Please, sit and take some wine with me."

Praukel bowed. "Your Grace is kind." He sat and accepted a glass of pale-yellow wine from a servant who then left the room.

Praukel examined the wine carefully. He had given someone a potion disguised in wine so many times that he looked at every glass he was offered with suspicion. He was confident in his own strength as a Chemer and was sure that nobody could conceal a potion from him. This wine was free of any taint. He sniffed, sipped, and raised his eyebrows at its delicate bouquet and taste.

"From my own vineyard near Merlsen," said Latisec. "I trust it meets with your approval."

"Indeed it does, Your Grace. It is very fine."

"I expect you have some idea of why I invited you here."

Praukel nodded.

"It's simple enough. I imagine you are – shall we say – disappointed with the outcome of the council meeting two days ago."

Praukel nodded again.

"So am I. You would have been, in my opinion, a far better choice than Melauthua, despite the problem of your being talented."

"But you also think you would be an even better choice," said Praukel.

"I do. I'm sorry to say I think His Majesty's decision was poorly thought out."

"However, there's nothing to be done about it."

"Melauthua has no obvious heir. If anything happened to her the country would be in the same position as it was before," remarked Latisec. "Who do you suppose the king would select to replace her?"

Praukel didn't answer immediately. He swirled his

wine glass, held it to his nose and sniffed before saying, "Given the prejudice against someone like me holding political office, I think he would have to choose you, Your Grace."

"I am somewhat less certain. I admit I would like to think so, but the way he has behaved towards me since Wurauf's death has been insulting, and it is clear he dislikes me. The one thing I am confident about is that the two of us are the only realistic candidates in the event of Melauthua's demise. It would be sensible for us to agree about what would happen if that unfortunate event occurred."

"Is there any indication she's in poor health?"

"Who knows? I understand she has enemies who might resent her sudden elevation to the peerage."

Praukel sat forward in his chair. "Your Grace, don't you think it's time we stopped prevaricating and started speaking plainly. The state of Duchess Melauthua's health is not an issue, there are many ways in which it can suddenly deteriorate, particularly if someone wants that to happen."

Latisec grunted and Praukel continued, "There are many ways in which I could ensure the worsening of her health, but only one of us can replace her. I believe the king would choose you over me, so why should I help you? What can you offer in return?"

"How about the Duchy of Carrh?"

Praukel blinked in surprise. That was the last thing he had expected to be offered. "But…" He paused. "There is only one way you would be in a position to offer me that."

"Yes. His Majesty has denigrated and insulted me to an extent I find intolerable. Assist me in removing him and you will be the next Duke of Carrh."

"While you sit on the throne."

"Precisely."

Praukel sat back, lifted his glass in a salute and said, "I believe we can work together, Your Grace."

HOUSE NEYEN

When Anarya opened the portal and stepped through into her rooms in Neyen she brought two people with her.

"Any news?" she asked Yisul, after wrapping her arms around her for a big hug.

"No, for once there isn't." She looked at the people with Anarya, "I wasn't expecting anyone to come with you." She bowed and added, "Blessèd Tilua, I'm very pleased to welcome you to my home again."

"I want to talk to your parents, and discuss housing for the teachers Anarya will start bringing soon," said Tilua.

Anarya beckoned the other priestess, who was looking around awestruck, to join her and Yisul. "Yisa, you remember Kemeneah, don't you? Tilua thought that since I was spending a lot of time jumping around between here and Carregis it would make sense for her to travel with me. That way I won't have to travel so much and waste transits simply to get to wherever she is and get her talent."

Yisul smiled, saying, "Kemeneah, you are very welcome. I hope we will get to know each other well."

"Holy Quarenna make it so," agreed Kemeneah.

"My parents have been in a meeting with Cuhes cra Shuth all morning, concerned about finding a replacement for Dunel cra Guesyr on the Sovereign Council. They are trying to find someone who is acceptable to the Families and to the Faithful – that's what those who persist in believing in The God have started calling themselves. I don't know how much longer they will be. Allow me to show you the rooms that mother is allocating to you."

"I would like that," said Tilua. "But before we go, I have two questions."

Tilua sat down on the sofa and indicated that Kemeneah should sit beside her. "People Anarya brings through the portal seem to have a range of experiences and I find the differences are fascinating. So, every time someone new passes through it I want to find out what happened to them. You're the first Scratcher I know of to come. So, please, tell me what you saw or felt?"

"Glyphs," Kemeneah replied. "For a moment I was surrounded by hundreds of glyphs, most of which I didn't recognise. Some I knew and they shone a little brighter than the ones I didn't."

"You see," Tilua said to Anarya, "that fits with the Darkworld being involved with the talents."

"It does, and it's interesting, but I don't see the knowledge having much in the way of practical use."

"Really, Anarya! Aren't you curious? Don't you want to know as much as possible about Quarenna's gifts?"

"Is it going to help me with the hunger?"

Tilua's shoulders slumped. "I suppose that's a reasonable concern. The answer is, I just don't know."

"You did say two questions," Yisul reminded her.

"Yes," said Tilua, sitting up straighter again. "The other one is for you. What do your servants think of people appearing and disappearing from these rooms? Are they frightened, or alarmed?"

"Nobody has commented on it in my hearing. Once or twice I have seen looks of surprise when I open the door into the corridor from what they must have thought was an empty room. But there's been no more reaction than that. They're used to the Families having magical talents and probably believe one of us is a Traveller. Anyway, what does it matter what they think? They're just servants."

Tilua looked at Yisul in surprise. "They're people. I thought you recognised that Holy Quarenna regards all women as equals and you should too."

Yisul looked abashed, bowed her head and apologised in a small voice, "I am sorry, Blessèd One. I have learned this, but sometimes I forget and revert to what I learned as a child."

"Try to remember," replied Tilua.

"I will try."

"One more question," said Tilua. "I've never heard of a Traveller. What's that?"

"Oh, you know, people who could jump from place to place. Rather like going through Anarya's portal. There are stories about them, at least there are here, don't you have them in Carrhen?" asked Yisul. "Travellers appear in children's tales and few people believe in them. If they ever existed the talent was lost two or three hundred years ago."

Tilua shook her head. "I've never heard of such a talent. If there was one we'd know about it. The talents don't change."

"Blessèd Tilua, I'm sorry to contradict you but they do. Seeker was a new talent not that long ago."

"What do you mean? It's not new. There have always been Seekers."

"Not in Sitrelk, Blessèd Tilua," said Yisul. "Seekers first appeared sixty-odd years ago in the Glinin Family and that's still where most of them are found."

Tilua blinked. "I'm astounded," she announced. "I've always known there were differences in the way talents occur in Sitrelk and Carrhen but I thought the talents themselves were the same. Do you know any others that aren't?"

"No, I don't think so," replied Yisul.

"Wait – there is something," said Anarya. "When I first told you I was a Sponger you didn't know what that was."

"That's right! I was so frightened when you told me about it because I thought you were describing The God's talent."

"You mean there are no Spongers in Sitrelk?" asked Tilua.

"None. It's a completely unknown talent here," said Yisul.

"I wonder if that is a real difference, or did The God kill any woman who showed a talent similar to his."

"Blessèd Tilua, it wouldn't surprise me if he had," said Yisul, "but why would he stop at women? He'd also want to stop any men from challenging him."

"Don't you know that there's never been a male Sponger; they're always women."

"You never told me that," said Yisul, frowning at Anarya.

Anarya shrugged. "I wasn't trying to hide it. It's just never come up."

"While we're talking about differences, are you aware that there are no women Stealthers?" asked Tilua.

"Yes, there are," said Yisul. "About one in five of the talented in House Jerut are Stealthers and half of them are women."

Tilua looked startled again. "Now that *is* unexpected. I'm so used to thinking of Stealther as a male-only skill. You know, I am beginning to think we don't understand nearly as much about the talents as we thought we did."

"We could probably spend chimes talking about them and being surprised," said Yisul. "Let me offer you refreshments while we wait for my parents to finish their meeting, and we can carry on."

THE TEMPLE OF HULER

Raifen tugged at his beard as he strode through Priest's Gate into the sanctuary, wondering why he had been summoned to meet Rupesc.

I suppose it must have something to do with Baram.

He knelt in front of the altar while he sang appropriate verses from the liturgy of the Pardoner – it always felt right to beg forgiveness before meeting the Head of the Brotherhood.

A sixth later he stood, walked back through the Priest's Gate and entered one of the passageways built into the walls of the temple. He reached Rupesc's study, tapped on the door and waited for the command to enter.

When it came he opened the door, stepped inside and bowed to Rupesc who was seated behind his desk with a pen in his hand and a stack of paper on the desk in front of him.

"Thank you for coming, Raifen."

"It is my pleasure and privilege to attend you, Your Reverence.

"You are a Feeler, are you not?" said Rupesc.

Raifen recognised this as a rhetorical question and didn't reply – the Head of the Brotherhood knew very well what he was.

"You have been at the Oxway temple for four years now?"

Raifen nodded.

"And you found Baram, didn't you?"

"Yes, Your Reverence, although it might be more accurate to say Huler's grace brought him to me."

"Of course!" agreed Rupesc. Then he sat back in his chair and studied Raifen for about a twelfth before saying, "Tell me, Raifen, have you had any dreams of late?"

"Yes, Your Reverence

"Troubling dreams?"

"Yes."

Another pause during which Raifen felt he was being studied very carefully.

"Do you know Musceln?"

"Of course, Your Reverence."

"Yes, you would, wouldn't you? He is, after all, the oldest of the Brotherhood."

What is this about?

"Are you aware that he has decided to retire from the Brotherhood?

"No, Your Reverence."

"He feels he has become too frail to fully participate in the more strenuous of the rituals of Huler. We regret his decision but understand it. His wisdom will be missed."

Why is he telling me this?

"I can see you are puzzled, Raifen. Please forgive me for keeping you in suspense. The Brotherhood met yesterday and selected you to replace Musceln."

"Me!"

"Yes! You. You will be admitted to your new rank in two days' time. Just long enough for you to learn the liturgy of the Greatest and get ready to lead the progression of all stages, degrees and ranks at the noon service. Now pick your jaw off the floor and join me in a glass of wine to welcome you to the Brotherhood."

Rupesc poured a glass of the richest wine Raifen had ever tasted.

"There is one thing I must ask of you.

"Yes, Your Reverence?"

"Sorry, two things. Firstly, you have the rank to call me by name, so please do. And, secondly, are you prepared to go to Jotuk to educate people there in the ways and worship of Huler?

"Yes, Your Rev... Sorry, I mean, Rupesc. I will be happy to go."

HOUSE NEYEN

Trusef tapped gently at the open door to Muhan's study and announced, "I have news, Lord Muhan, please pardon the interruption."

Muhan looked up from the document he was examining. "Good news, I hope. I could do with some. Come in. Come in."

"I am uncertain whether it is good or not. It concerns the information I have obtained from the members of the Dark Fountain we employ."

"If it's about the *houln* Lady Anarya needs to hear it too. Please send for her, and for my wife and daughter."

"Certainly, Lord Muhan." Trusef went off to find them.

Muhan sighed as he looked at the stack of papers on his desk. Almost any news would be worth having if it would take him away from worrying about the Sovereign Council for a while. He picked up another document. It was a report from House Guesyr saying they still hadn't decided on a replacement for Dunel. *You'd think they'd want to get on with it. They've got to be unhappy about not having anyone on the Council to represent their point of view.*

He was still thinking about how the absence of one of the Faithful changed the balance of power in the Council when Lias and Yisul arrived with Anarya and Baram.

"Sit down," he said. "Trusef has something to tell us."

Muhan saw Anarya looking around the room. He realised it was the first time she had been in it and tried to imagine her reaction. The light, creamy, wood panelling gave it a warm look; the desk and the chair behind it occupied about a quarter of the space and opposite it was a low table with four ladderback chairs.

He saw Anarya take one of the chairs and sit gazing

through the window. It overlooked a calm, peaceful garden. A small stream gurgled over pebbles before falling a finger length into a pool partially bordered by rushes. They provided shelter for some waterfowl and were overhung by a willow. *She spent a lot of time in that garden when she was recovering. She must like it.*

"What have you to tell me?" asked Muhan when Trusef led two men in House livery into the room.

Anarya stopped looking out the window, shifted her chair to a better angle, and sat down again.

"Lord Muhan," said Trusef. "These are the men I told you about."

"I understand you are members of the Dark Fountain."

The two men looked at each other, then the taller one nodded, "That's right. Wh'dya want?'

Muhan tried to reassure them, "Don't worry. I have nothing against you or your *houln*. What I want is some information, but nothing which is, as far as I know, to the disadvantage of the Dark Fountain. I need to speak to the ruler of the Three Flowers. Can you help me reach him?"

"Don't know nuthin' 'bout Richak."

"I'm sure that, at least, you must know where the Three Flowers is based."

The shorter of the two men nodded. "Know that."

"Where?"

"Down hill from Derchler's Gate. Most of them streets on left from Gate t' Listern Market."

"'Cept round south bridge, that's Stone Grasshopper territory."

"Could you pass a message through the Dark Fountain to the Three Flowers saying I want to meet Richak?" asked Muhan. "I will provide a token to let him into the inner city and I will guarantee his safety."

"Can try, but can't promise."

"That's all I can ask. Trusef will add something to your pay as thanks for your help."

"Just one thing before you go," said Anarya. "Do you know this Richak? Can you describe him?"

"Seen him," admitted the taller laundryman. "Ugly so-

and-so." He described Richak in unflattering terms before Trusef ushered them from the room.

Muhan looked at Anarya and asked, "Too far away?"

"I'm afraid so. He would have to be very close for our wood to overwhelm his and it doesn't sound as if he is, or is likely to be. If he doesn't respond to your invitation and come to the Inner City the only thing left to try is using the portal to go to him."

"Or we prepare for an assault we know is coming and station strongly talented people at every gate ready to repel it."

"But that will get many people killed," said Anarya.

"I know," sighed Muhan, "but if they start trouble we've got to defend ourselves, and I'd prefer do that on our terms rather than theirs."

"We know roughly when the attack is supposed to happen, so let's wait and see if Richak responds," said Anarya. "If we haven't heard after – shall we say two days? – I'm prepared to try the portal."

A Safe-House in Jotuk and House Neyen

"What are you up to?" Jemak demanded when he and Richak met again, this time at a place of Richak's choosing. It was in a grocer's shop near the south bridge, full of the smell of garlic, aniseed, pork sausage, ripe cheese and pickles.

"Up to?" asked Richak, in a puzzled voice.

"Getting messages from Neyen."

"What are you talking about?"

"You really don't know?"

"I swear by the Confined Ones that I don't," promised Richak, lifting a clenched fist to shoulder height.

Jemak was still looking sceptical when he said, "There are two of my *houln* working at Neyen and they tell me Muhan himself has been questioning them about you. Seems he wants to meet you inside and has offered safe passage."

"You're joking!"

"Why would I do that?"

"But why would he want to meet me? None of mine work at Neyen and I've never set eyes on him. Tell me more."

"There's nothing more to tell," said Jemak. "You can ask them yourself, but they don't know any more than that. They'll take a message back to Neyen if you want to meet Muhan."

"Certainly not. He's the enemy. Apart from anything else, nobody would trust me if I went to see him. I'd be lucky to survive to see the next sunrise if I did that, and you know it. Is this some sort of ploy to get rid of me?"

"If it is, it's not of my doing," said Jemak, raising a clenched fist. "I swear it."

"We must ask Kehsieh about this. It's a pity Yarelk has the necklace at the moment."

"That's one thing that's going well. Yarelk is a lot easier to work with than Hentro ever was."

"Maybe that mess at the gate he was responsible for has actually done us a favour."

"It'd be the first time Hentro ever did that for anyone."

Richak snorted and agreed, "True enough."

○

"No reply?" asked Anarya.

"Nothing. Not even an acknowledgement," replied Muhan.

Anarya gazed at the peaceful garden visible through the window in Muhan's study, sighed and sat down.

"That leaves us with no alternative. At least two of us have to use the portal to get close enough to Richak for our bits of Caseir to overwhelm the one he has. Baram tells me he's willing to go with me."

"I am too," said Yisul. "I think going unasked among the Three Flowers is likely to be dangerous but I will not allow you to take a risk like that without me."

"Lady Anarya, you have already done a lot for us and I cannot ask you to do more," said Muhan. "Anyway, the *houln* are often at odds with each other and Richak probably has a permanent bodyguard. I don't think you will be able to get to him."

"You're wrong," Anarya stated calmly. "I've used the description of Richak we got from the laundrymen to see if I could open a portal near him. They gave me enough to get a good picture of him and I've been able to view him and his surroundings. There are normally others around him, but at dusk I've usually found him by himself. We could get to him then."

"The first thing he'll do is call for help," Muhan objected, "and you'll be outnumbered."

"Anarya, I have an idea," said Baram. "You remember how you dealt with Jynder by snatching him through the portal before he knew you were there. Could you do the same to Richak and bring him here?"

"I don't see why not," replied Anarya after a moment's thought, "although it might depend on how quickly he reacts."

"If you've taken my talent and are in Stealth when you go to him he'll never know you're there until he finds himself here."

"Yes, that should work," agreed Anarya.

Yisul started to object and Anarya cut her off. "Don't worry. It's a better plan than all of us turning up in the middle of the Three Flowers territory."

"I can have a spell ready to immobilise him on arrival," offered Muhan.

"Good idea," said Anarya. "Shall we try this at dusk today?"

They agreed to meet in the reception room of Anarya's suite at the sixteenth chime and left Muhan to his stack of documents.

O

Anarya's view of where the portal would open stabilised quickly and easily as she concentrated on visualising Richak and his surroundings. He was alone, as she had hoped. She Thieved Baram's Stealther ability and experienced the usual feeling of confidence that came with it. As always when in Stealth, her vision dimmed as if she was looking through a muslin curtain. She opened the portal and found herself behind Richak who was standing with head bowed and both fists lifted to shoulder level. She reached out, grasped his right shoulder and wrenched him backwards through the portal.

Richak's reaction was fast. He spun around with a knife in his left hand that hadn't been there earlier. Then he was caught by Muhan's spell and frozen in an awkward twisted pose, like an insect in amber, his knife only a couple of fingerbreadths from Anarya's neck. She jumped backwards away from the knife before becoming visible again.

"I am Muhan cra Neyen, Richak, and you have been

brought to House Neyen so that I can speak to you. I will relax the restraint enough to allow you to find a more comfortable position but I can re-establish it quickly if you attempt to attack any of us."

Richak straightened up, still with knife in hand, and growled, "What do you want?"

"I swear we're not going to harm you; we only want to talk. We know you are planning a mass attack on the city gates. I want to persuade you to cancel it."

"How do you know about that? Who's the traitor?"

"Nobody," said Anarya. "Tell Kehsieh we are forewarned and many of his followers will die if the assault goes ahead. See what his answer is."

"How do you know about Kehsieh? The Families have never believed in the Confined Ones."

Caseir interrupted, saying, "Anarya, there's a problem. He doesn't have a piece of the wood on him. I still can't influence Kehsieh, we're too far apart."

"Richak, what have you done with the necklace?" asked Anarya.

"How do you know about that?"

"Because it's mine. I brought it to Jotuk and somebody took it away from me. I know you ended up with it, so where is it?"

"Are you Anarya?"

"I am."

"The Blessings of the Confined Gods be upon you. Kehsieh told me about you. By freeing the Families from their bondage to that false god you have given us hope that our bonds may be broken too."

"Bonds! You're not enslaved," said Muhan.

"Aren't we? The Families have all the talents, and all the power. You look down on us and treat us with contempt. You despise those of us who give up hope and go to work for you. They can see what you have but they have no chance of getting similar things for themselves; no chance of improving their lot. Just look around this room and compare it to the conditions in the outer city. And this is a small, plain room compared with some I've heard described. Are you surprised you're hated?"

"My Family doesn't mistreat the outers."

"Oh no? Even what you call us says what you really think – 'outers' is a derogatory term. It's just another way of showing how inferior we are in your eyes. Try coming to live for a day in the outer city. Then you'll see the reality of our position and the treatment we get."

"I can't do that. I wouldn't survive a tenth, and you know it."

"I do. I also know that Neyen is one of the more 'enlightened' Houses, but that makes no real difference. It's only better by comparison with Houses like Glinin or Pridhar. The Families' behaviour towards us, particularly during a *purtirn*, deserves our hatred."

Muhan's shoulders slumped. He looked around at the others and said, "He has got a point, but what can we do? Open the gates and the violence outside the wall floods into the inner city and puts all of us at risk."

Anarya said, "Richak, if you go ahead with your plan a lot of your people will die for no reason. You can't hope to win against all the talented in the inner city."

"But we *can* kill some of them!"

"Isn't there anything that would persuade you to cancel the attack?" asked Anarya after a pause while everyone absorbed the implacable hatred in Richak's statement.

Richak snorted. "It would take Kehsieh changing his mind to do that."

"But Kehsieh isn't real," said Anarya.

"Of course he is. You brought the token he inhabits to Jotuk. How can you not believe in him?"

"I brought a piece of wood containing the spirit of Caseir, not Kehsieh. You don't speak Katelish, do you? You've misheard his name."

"I don't believe you."

"Here," said Anarya, removing her necklace and making sure she was touching Yisul's before passing her own to Richak. "Hold this."

"Hello, Richak," said Caseir. "Do you recognise my voice?"

"You sound like Kehsieh, but you can't be. Yarelk has the token he speaks from. I don't trust this other voice." Richak threw the necklace back to Anarya.

"Who is Yarelk?" asked Muhan.

"None of your business," replied Richak.

Anarya looked at the others and sighed, "We're not getting anywhere. Any ideas?"

There was no reply.

"I'll take him back to where I found him," said Anarya.

"Yes," agreed Muhan. "We did swear not to harm him."

Richak looked surprised. "I didn't think you would keep your promise. Very few of you would consider a promise to one of us as binding. Not that it matters – you've probably already killed me by bringing me here."

"What do you mean?"

"If anybody discovers I've been talking to you I'll be considered a traitor. I wouldn't live long enough to persuade anybody it wasn't by choice. I would feel the same about anybody else if they were standing here."

"You were alone when I found you," said Anarya, "and I'll take you back to the same place. Won't that be good enough?"

"Perhaps," said Richak. "I'm left undisturbed during the evening prayer to the Confined Ones. Unless something urgent that needs my attention comes up." He shrugged. "If that's happened, I'm dead."

"Holy Quarenna, I hope it's not so," said Anarya.

"Don't use that name!"

"What?"

"I know it and despise it. We never name the two who imprisoned the Confined Ones."

Anarya frowned and said, "I will try to remember that but I often invoke her name. It wasn't my intention to be insulting – I was merely hoping nobody has interrupted your devotions today. It's not as if you had any say in coming here."

"I find myself believing you, but having no choice will not spare me if someone discovers we have been talking."

"Anarya, you'd better take me with you when you return Richak so that I can maintain the restraint on him until you can get back here," said Muhan.

"I will not harm her," promised Richak, "In the names of the Confined Ones, I swear it." He raised a clenched fist and repeated, "I swear it."

"I trust his oath," said Anarya. "There is no need for anyone to come with me."

Muhan frowned. He took a deep breath, "I have to show trust in you if we are ever to be able to negotiate anything. Very well, I will release you when Anarya says so."

"Now would be good," said Anarya. "The room he was in is still empty."

Muhan nodded. "It's done."

There were audible cracks from his spine as Richak stretched.

Anarya offered him a hand. He took it, stepped forward with her and vanished.

Moments later she reappeared. When she stepped back into the room she had just enough time to say, "We were right to trust him," before Yisul flung herself into her arms.

O

"You look like I feel," said Anarya to Yisul. The two of them, and Baram, were having breakfast together in Anarya's suite the next day. Anarya had her elbows on the table, chin on clasped hands. Yisul was picking apart a pastry and showing little interest in eating any of it. She ignored the crumbs that fell on to her skirt and was letting her mug of redleaf tea get cold.

"It's so stupid!" said Yisul. "A battle isn't going to benefit anyone, particularly the outers."

Baram commented, "You shouldn't call them that. Richak really didn't like it, and I can sort of see his point."

"What do you suggest we call them instead?"

Baram shrugged. "How about 'people of Jotuk'?"

"Jotukil," muttered Yisul, looking thoughtful. "Yes, that would work. It also applies to the Families so it puts everybody on an equal footing."

"That's quite a good idea, Baram," said Anarya. "Now we need you to have another one. Tell us how to persuade Richak that Kehsieh is Caseir and not his god."

"I have an idea about that," Caseir offered. "I can't say I like it much but it should work."

"What should work?" asked Anarya when Caseir didn't elaborate on his plan.

"When you moved the table through the portal the amount of me in it dominated the small part that's been calling itself Kehsieh. I'm wondering if there's any way to keep the table in the Darkworld for longer than a transit takes? That would…"

"Let you convince Richak that the voice he called Kehsieh has changed its mind. Yes! That's a great idea," said Anarya.

"It's not too great from my point of view. I don't want to live in the Darkworld forever but I think I could stand it for long enough to convince Richak."

"We can try it, but we'll have to wait until tomorrow. I can't use the portal again today."

Yisul sat up straighter, looked at the crumbs scattered on her dress and the floor, called for a servant and asked her to bring more food and hot drinks.

Anarya was relieved to see Yisul acting more herself, and hid a quiet smile.

IN THE DARKWORLD

Yisul kissed Anarya and said, "Take care, my love and come back to me."

Anarya returned the kiss, reached out to open the portal and stepped through into darkness. As always there was a complete lack of sensation in the Darkworld; no sound, no smell, nothing; just blackness so complete that her eyes responded by inventing little flashes of colour as she strained to see anything.

She sighed, and couldn't even hear that. *Being here is sort of boring and frightening at the same time. Hope the daimon doesn't take too long to notice I'm here.* She sighed again. She knew from experience there was little correspondence between duration in the Darkworld and real time and settled down to wait.

{*Why here?*} The daimon's hollow voice came after she had been waiting for what seemed to be about three-quarters of a chime. {*What want?*}

"I need your help."

{*Why Gatherer need help?*}

Gatherer? It's called me that before. Must be its name for Thiever. "I want to bring something here and leave it."

{*What thing?*}

"The object where you trapped one who compelled you."

{*Incomprehension. Already have here.*}

"Only a small part," she said, assuming the daimon meant the piece of wood around her neck.

{*One piece same as all.*}

"Not in my world. Distance between pieces there means they're not connected to each other."

{*Incomprehension. What means 'distance'?*}

Holy Quarenna aid me! I've been told often enough that distance doesn't mean anything to daimons. How do I explain it?

"When I open a portal to go from here to there what lies between these places?"

{Question unreal.}

"For you, perhaps, but it's important to people like me."

{Irrelevant.}

Anarya sighed. "I don't know how to let you understand what it means. Since it doesn't matter to you, just tell me if can I bring something here and leave it."

{Possible.}

"Good."

{What benefits me?}

I should have expected that. "What would you want in return?"

{Less transits.}

"How many less?"

{Half number.}

"Reduce the number or lengthen the time allowed for the same number? Do you mean four every four days, or two every two days? Either way that's a big reduction."

{Important for you.}

It is important. I've got to give it that. "I will agree, but only while the object I bring is here in your world. I will take it away again soon. When I do the transit agreement reverts to the present one."

{Agreement, but now four in four cycles.}

Anarya sighed. *I've no choice really.*

{Bargain.}

"Bargain," agreed Anarya, and found herself back in House Neyen. She slumped on to the sofa and was joined by Yisul who snuggled up to her asking what had happened. Baram handed her a glass of wine.

"That place scares me," she said after telling them the details of the new terms. "It will take one transit to get to my home in Carregis to pick up the table, one to carry it into the Darkworld, one to get out again and another to get back here. Caseir, that means you'll be in the Darkworld for at least four days. I hope you'll be able to cope."

"I'm sure I can. Scary doesn't bother me, never has. Anyway, if it goes right then I'll still be in contact with the pieces of wood all of you are carrying and get some input from them."

"I'll come with you," offered Baram. "You'll need help carrying the table while opening the portal."

"You're right. I hadn't thought of that."

O

"Here we go," said Anarya four days later. She took Baram's hand, opened the portal and stepped through to Carregis.

They experimented a bit to find the best way to carry the table. It was awkward and they ended up with Baram bent over, taking most of the weight on his left shoulder while holding on to Anarya with his right hand. She had one hand free for the doorknob and the other wrapped around a table leg trying to take some of the weight.

Anarya thumbed her forehead and prayed, "Holy Quarenna aid me," before opening the door and guiding them into darkness.

In the Darkworld she wasn't aware of Baram or the table. She tried to talk to Caseir but there was no reply. Time passed and nothing happened until the daimon's voice suddenly said {Go.} and she stumbled forward. She landed on the floor of her room with Baram on top of her and with his arms wrapped around her.

"Are you all right?" she asked.

"Fine," he mumbled. He let go of her and rolled off to one side. She turned her head to see him blushing.

"I'm sorry," he said. "I didn't mean…"

"Don't worry about it," she made him blush even more by kissing him gently on the cheek before rising to her feet. "Thank you for going with me. I couldn't have managed to carry the table myself. What happened to you?"

"Nothing. As soon as I went through I lost my grip on the table and found myself holding you when we came back again. It seemed to take no time at all."

"I thought it lasted about a half," said Anarya.

"Actually," Caseir remarked, "it was more like two chimes."

"Caseir! Are all of your bits together? Did it work?"

"Yes. I'm everywhere there's a piece of wood, including the piece you lost. Somebody called Yarelk, who's the ruler of the Stone Grasshoppers *houln*, has that at the moment. I can choose which piece to pay attention to and which one to speak to. I haven't tried pretending to be Kehsieh yet. I thought I'd wait until you're all together before doing that."

"Right. We'll be back in Jotuk in no time."

"No, wait Anarya," said Baram. "Can I stay here? I need to report to my superiors at the temple. Keep them up to date."

"If that's what you want, but it'll be four days before I can come here again."

"I understand. Unless the Brotherhood has a task for me, I'll be at the shop in Gatt Street from the fourteenth to fifteenth chime every day after that. Look after yourself."

"And you do the same. By the way, watch out for the second bottom step as you go. It's a bit rickety."

Once Baram had gone, Anarya opened the portal again and took herself back to House Neyen.

Yisul was waiting for her and greeted her with hugs and kisses. "It worked! It really worked. Caseir told me."

"Let's go and tell your parents. I'm sure they'll want to know what we've accomplished. Then we can try to change Kehsieh's mind."

HOUSE NEYEN
AND A SHOP IN JOTUK

"Richak hasn't got the wood," Caseir told them when they were all together. "It's still with Yarelk."

"I've done a bit of investigation," Muhan reported. "This Yarelk has recently become the ruler of the Stone Grasshoppers. I think Richak must be gathering allies from the other *houln*."

"And we know why," said Anarya with a shudder.

"Dare we try influencing Yarelk?" asked Yisul.

Caseir remarked, "I don't think so. It was Richak who accepted that part of me as Kehsieh in the first place. He's the one we need to convince."

"Are you sure that Kehsieh can't convince Richak to carry on with the planned attack?" asked Muhan."

"Quite sure," said Caseir, "I've absorbed that part of me. Kehsieh doesn't exist as a separate entity anymore."

Caseir promised to let them all know when Richak and Yarelk got together and they all went off sighing, muttering to each other and speculating about what might happen. Everyone was concerned about the wait.

It was two days later that Caseir announced there was going to be a meeting of the *houln* leaders and everyone with a piece of Caseir's wood gathered in Muhan's study to eavesdrop on the meeting and see what would happen.

O

The meeting took place in a combined bakery and butcher's shop owned by the Stone Grasshoppers. The morning rush was over and the staff were sitting in a back room enjoying a quiet period before starting to make the pies, savoury pasties and soups for their evening customers. About a dozen loaves and a few buns were left on the shelves and the warm, comforting smell of fresh bread greeted Richak when he walked in leaving his bodyguards outside. He sniffed appreciatively and smiled, knowing the scar on his face would turn the smile into a grimace. At times it was a useful way to frighten people. However, he knew Yarelk was used to his distorted features and the smile wouldn't intimidate him.

Yarelk said, "If you want something, take your pick from the shelves. If you choose for yourself, you'll know I haven't had it poisoned for you."

Richak's scowl distorted his face even more as he said, "Don't think you'd do that when we're meeting in the name of the Confined Ones." He selected a bun half the size of his fist and sticky with honey, flicked away a couple of wasps that were interested in it and took a seat next to the bakery counter.

Jemak arrived about a twelfth later and perched on a stool next to Richak. "I'm here. Let's get on with it."

Yarelk put the piece of wood on the counter between them and the other two reached out to touch it.

"Greatness, we are all here."

"Good," said Caseir. "Yarelk, I want you to confirm to the others that this wood has not been out of your possession since you were given it at the last meeting."

"I swear it, Greatness. In your name and those of the other Confined Ones, I swear it."

"Why did you want this promise?" asked Jemak.

"I need to make sure you know who I am."

"I don't understand, Greatness." Richak sounded puzzled. "You are Kehsieh the Great, last to be confined."

"You are mistaken," said Caseir.

"What!"

"My real name is Caseir."

"But that's what I said. I don't understand."

"Listen carefully and I will explain. Caseir is a Katelish name that sounds similar to Kehsieh. When I first introduced myself to you, you misheard. I am afraid I took advantage of your error because I was feeling lost and your belief in Kehsieh gave me some security. The bit of wood you have is only a small part of a larger piece which contains me. I am the ghost of a man trapped by a daimon. The piece you have and the larger one were too far apart and my consciousness was split between the two. Now we are connected again and I don't need to pretend any more. I am not your god."

"I don't understand," said Yarelk. "You claimed to be Kehsieh and led us in planning the attack on the inner city. Are you still going to help us with that?"

"I can't. I only agreed because I didn't know what had happened to the rest of me and I thought I was on my own."

"Traitor!" yelled Richak, losing contact with the wood as he jumped up shaking his fist.

"You're the traitor," shouted Jemak, pulling a knife from his belt and lunging at Richak. "You've betrayed the Confined Ones by letting this imposter fool you."

Richak ducked out of the way and drew a knife of his own to block Jemak's attack. Then Yarelk attacked him too. He was forced into the corner between the wall and the counter where he could keep both of them in front of him. He shouted, "Flowers! Treachery!"

Yarelk over-reached himself and Richak's knife sliced into his forearm.

The door burst open. Two of Richak's escort came through it in response to his shout, one of them already bleeding from a scalp wound. The rest of his bodyguard tried to fend off Yarelk's and Jemak's escorts; some fell and members of all three *houln* forced their way into the shop. Crammed into a small space, not knowing what had happened and finding their leaders involved in a knife fight, each one of them immediately attacked any member of the other two *houln* within reach. The situation quickly degenerated into a vicious three-way fight.

Yarelk vaulted across the counter and threw open the door to the back room where the butchers were resting. They joined in the fight.

The last thing Richak saw was the edge of a butcher's cleaver as it chopped at his face.

When the fighting stopped Jemak and Richak were dead, along with every member of their bodyguards. The only survivors were Stone Grasshoppers, and all of them were injured to some extent.

Yarelk had his left hand clamped around his right forearm. Blood was dripping from it and from a scalp wound. He couldn't use his right hand. One of the butchers treated his wounds, binding up his forearm. He commented that the tendons were cut and he was going to have to live with a hand that didn't work properly. Yarelk looked at the carnage and shook his head. There would be no coordinated attack on the inner city after this. Nobody would trust anybody else long enough to work with them, even for that goal.

He saw the piece of wood lying on the counter and scooped it up. "Are you still there?" he asked.

"I am," replied Caseir.

Yarelk snarled and said, "I have to believe you. You are not Kehsieh and have no loyalty to the followers of the Confined Ones. You've managed to destroy our hopes and plans. For that, and your blasphemy in pretending to be Kehsieh, you must be punished."

He walked to the back of the bakery, opened the firebox of the oven and threw the wood into the flames.

O

Anarya and everyone else with a piece of wood had been listening to the events. They heard Richak's shout of 'Treachery', but nothing after that.

"What's happening?" asked Muhan.

"Nobody's touching the wood," said Anarya. "I hope somebody picks it up soon."

They waited – and waited. Almost a half passed before they heard anything. Then they heard Yarelk talking to Caseir about punishment. Then Caseir shouted, "No!"

And there was silence again.

"What's wrong? asked Anarya, "Caseir, what is it?"

There was no reply. They looked at each other wondering why he wasn't answering and with no idea what had gone wrong.

What 'punishment' did Yarelk have in mind?

A quarter later, Caseir said, in a weak, shaken voice, "Huler's beard, that was awful."

"What was?"

"Yarelk threw the wood into the fire. It's all burnt up and I felt it, every moment of it. It was – was like being the fuel in a forge. Imagine picking a burning coal from the fire and not being able to let go. It was like that. I could feel every bit of the wood charring and crumbling in the flames. It was worse than any injury I ever experienced in the arena. I thought I was going to die. I'm so glad you stopped Limabur burning the table. That would have been hundreds of times worse and I'm certain it would have ended me."

"Are you all right now?"

"I will be. It'll take me a bit of time to get over the shock but I'll be fine. Anyway, you can be sure the planned attack won't happen. The *houln* aren't going to trust each other for quite a long time after today."

THE TEMPLE OF HULER
AND THE ROYAL PALACE

Where should I go? Baram wondered. *Will Raifen be at the main temple or at the one on the Oxway? Should I report to him or to the Brotherhood?*

The Oxway was closer to Anarya's room than the Great Square so he decided to go there first. It felt more comfortable too. The main temple was magnificent and imposing but, somehow, a bit impersonal.

Raifen wasn't there. One of his colleagues told Baram that he had been summoned to a meeting of the Brotherhood so, after kneeling to the image of the Avenger in one of the side-chapels, he set off for the Great Square.

As he went he overheard fragments of conversations and discovered that, while he had been away in Jotuk, the king had appointed replacements for both Count Graumedel and Duke Wurauf.

He signed himself with Huler's lightning bolt as he entered the temple. Just inside the main door he saw a senior priest and asked him if he knew Raifen.

"I do," replied the priest. "However, he is not available today. May I assist you?"

"I was given a task by the Brotherhood. Raifen is my contact and I must report to him."

The priest raised an eyebrow and asked, "Is your name Baram?"

"It is."

"Your name has been made known to everyone with instructions to take you to see Rupesc should you appear. Follow me."

Rupesc wants to see me! Why?

Baram followed his guide through an inconspicuous door and into a corridor built into the wall of the temple.

It bypassed the sanctuary and opened into the area of the temple where the priests had private rooms. His guide knocked gently on one of the doors and waited until a voice from inside told him, "Enter."

The priest ushered him into the room saying, "Baram is here."

"Welcome, younger brother," said Rupesc from behind the desk that occupied most of the room. "I am happy to see you. Please, sit down."

Baram made the sign of the lightning bolt, sat on the chair Rupesc indicated and looked around. The desk held an abacus, an inkwell and pens as well as a stack of scrolls. Standing on a side table was the only sign of luxury in the room, an exquisite set of miniature paintings of the aspects of Huler. This was clearly a room for working in.

"I am very pleased to see you, Baram," repeated Rupesc. "There is something I must ask you to do. It may not seem a suitable task for one of the hands of the Avenger but I assure you it is important. What I am about to tell you is in the strictest confidence."

Rupesc paused until Baram indicated with a nod that he understood.

"We are worried about the king's safety," he continued. "Grovaen, who is one of the king's advisers, and a Feeler, says that he doesn't think Duke Latisec of Alrem is trustworthy. He was hoping to become Duke of Carrh and it's reasonable enough for him to be upset when the king chose Melauthua over him. However, Grovaen says he felt more than just disappointment from him. He describes 'a surge of murderous rage' directed at the king. Combined with the disdain he tells me Latisec has shown towards His Majesty in the past, during the rule of the Three, I think we have cause for concern."

"You want me to be an invisible bodyguard."

"Exactly. I doubt if a physical attack on the king is likely but, as long as Duke Latisec is here in Carregis, I'd rather not take any chances."

"I do have some experience in the role," said Baram.

"It's what I did when I was forced to work for Graumedel."

"I have an appointment to see the king tomorrow. Come here at the eighth chime and I will take you to meet him."

○

"Your Majesty, I would like to present Baram," said Rupesc when they were admitted to the presence of Sulereath III in the room he favoured as a study.

Baram bowed deeply.

The king looked puzzled at the introduction.

"I hope he will be a valuable addition to your household."

"There must be something special about him," said Sulereath. "You have other concerns than suggesting new members of my staff."

Rupesc nodded to Baram who promptly became invisible.

The king gasped.

"You did want to meet a Stealther."

"I did, but that was when I wanted to get rid of Wurauf," answered Sulereath. His head swivelled from side to side trying to spot a clue to where Baram was. "Why are you bringing him to me now?"

"The Brotherhood has received information that suggests your life may be in danger, Your Majesty. We want to avoid this if at all possible and Baram's presence by your side will be a precaution against physical attack."

Sulereath stopped trying to find Baram and faced Rupesc. "Who is threatening me?"

"Forgive me for not answering that, Your Majesty. It is only a suspicion and I would not like to accuse someone unjustly."

"And you would ignore me if I demanded an answer, wouldn't you?"

Rupesc said nothing.

"Very well, I won't insist."

"Thank you, Your Majesty. I suggest that you talk to Baram and get to know his ability and limitations. You should have him by your side whenever you give an audience. It would be a good idea to have a Feeler present as well."

From just behind the king, Baram said, "A Feeler should be able to give me warning of intent in time to let me act."

Sulereath jumped and spun round to find Baram on one knee facing him.

"I am at your command, Your Majesty."

"I promise, in the name of Huler, that you may trust him unreservedly," said Rupesc. "He will do whatever you ask, except that he will not obey a command to leave you alone with anyone, no matter how trustworthy that person appears to be."

Sulereath looked back and forth between Rupesc and Baram several times before saying, "Rise, Baram. I accept your service."

Still kneeling, Baram said, "Thank you, Your Majesty. Be assured that, in the light of Huler and in the hope of his beneficent regard, I vow to protect you to the best of my ability whatever the risk to my own life."

Sulereath blinked. The words Baram had used were those of the oath taken by the king's bodyguard at the time his ancestor Sulereath I, had consolidated the five duchies into the kingdom of Carrhen.

"Don't look so surprised, Your Majesty. Baram found those words himself and thought them appropriate."

"Did you find them in Dezzian's *The History of the Unification*?

"Yes, Your Majesty."

"Are you interested in history?"

"I am."

"Good. There's quite a lot of things I'd like to discuss about that book but I've never met anyone else I could talk to who's read it."

"I'd be honoured, Your Majesty."

"Take a seat, Baram. There's no need for you to stand

while Rupesc and I have our weekly chat."

Baram stood, bowed, walked across the room to a chair near the door, waited until the king was seated then sat down himself. He didn't pay attention to the discussion between Rupesc and the king, being more interested in getting to know a room where he was likely to spend a lot of his time.

He had been in the room before briefly, in Stealth, when acting as bodyguard to Count Graumedel. That was when he had realised how much the Three had dominated the king and he had witnessed his defiance when they were trying to force him to marry. Already with some feeling of affinity for the king because they shared a birthday, his resistance to their bullying tactics had consolidated his liking for the man. He was glad to have been given the task of protecting him.

"One more thing, Baram," said Rupesc. "I presume you have some means of contacting Anarya."

"I do. We have made arrangements to meet."

"Good. Please keep in contact with her. We are interested in whatever is happening in Jotuk."

THE MANSION OF THE
COUNT OF CARREGIS

Melauthua stood at the foot of the staircase leading up to the entrance of the battlemented slab of a building that had been the home of the Counts of Carregis for almost a hundred years. She shook her head.

"You'd be welcome to keep this – this pile," she remarked to Corvek, "if it wasn't that I need it now that the king has taken back the ducal mansion to serve as his palace."

"I understand, Your Grace. It *is* an exceptionally ugly building. However, it is well appointed inside. The late Count had excellent taste and many of his possessions are quite remarkable. Your offer to share it until one of us can find a suitable new residence is very generous." Corvek paused briefly, "You do realise it might take a long time to find somewhere. There aren't all that many buildings big enough to be converted into the seat from which a city or a duchy can be governed."

"We can worry about that later," said Melauthua. "For the moment I want to get us working in harmony and I want the benefit of your advice. My experience of governing is limited to telling Ghendul what to do when he was out of his depth in Hemeark – between the two of us, that wasn't an uncommon situation."

"I've heard rumours to that effect, Your Grace."

"Never mind him. Please show me around."

They climbed the stairs to the main door on the upper floor. As they went Melauthua noted the bees and beehive motifs on the balustrade. *They'll have to go and be replaced by the bears of Carrh if I end up staying here, but there's no hurry about it.*

"The Count's rooms are on the other side of the building," said Corvek. "My office is only a few doors away from them but I can move elsewhere quite easily. In fact, if you take over the main suite I will have to move because my office won't be big enough."

"Let's worry about who gets which rooms later. For the moment just show me round."

"With pleasure, Your Grace. We'll start on this floor and go down later." Dark oak panelling with goldenwood inserts gave the corridor an opulent look, enhanced by some very fine tapestries and glass-fronted cabinets displaying delicate porcelain vases and enamelled jugs. Melauthua had noticed the absence of exterior windows as they had stood looking at the building and was surprised by seeing doors in the outer walls of the corridors. She commented that those rooms must be dark and Corvek told her that supplying them with candles and lamp oil was one of the biggest items in the budget. *I wonder if windows can be installed. It would be difficult, and probably expensive, but it might be worth it in the long term.*

She was impressed with the rooms on the eastern side of the building where windows in the inner walls of the Count's suite overlooked a garden with a lily pond. Where the windows were open, they let in a fresh green smell. One room attracted her attention because the furnishings, including a large goldenwood and ebony desk, were particularly impressive. The only sour note was that the door looked as if it had been forced.

"Am I right in thinking this was Graumedel's study?" she asked Corvek.

"Yes, Your Grace. His body was found in that corner when they managed to get the door open."

"I think this is the best room I've seen so far. I'll take it, once the door has been repaired."

"Certainly, Your Grace."

"You sound disappointed."

"I am. I agree it's a beautiful room, and I was hoping you'd reject it because this is where Graumedel died."

"That doesn't bother me at all. Everybody's got to die somewhere."

With a shrug and a sigh Corvek showed Melauthua around the rest of the mansion. They ended up in the garden sitting under the shade of a palm tree.

"I instructed one of the servants to bring wine once we stopped wandering around," said Corvek. "It should be here soon. Have you decided what you want to do with the rooms?"

"Yes. I will take Graumedel's study for my own. I'll let you pick next. Do you want to keep your present room?"

"No, I don't think so. There's a suite on the south corridor that's big enough. I think I'll take that."

They were still dividing the rooms up when a servant arrived with a carafe of yellow wine and two glasses.

Melauthua lifted her glass in a toast, saying, "I hope we can work together amicably." She took a sip of the wine.

Corvek also raised his glass but he didn't drink. Instead his eyes widened and he jumped to his feet saying, "Stop! That wine is poisoned! Don't drink it."

She let her glass drop and it shattered on the paving stones. A couple of fragments stung her foot between the straps of her sandals and she winced. Her hand went to her mouth, "Why did you..."

"It's not my doing, I swear," said Corvek. "Don't worry, I don't think you drank enough to be dangerous. I'm sorry I didn't catch it earlier. It wasn't until I was about to drink it myself that I looked at it properly, with a Chemer's eye. Someone has added a potion to it, quite a subtle one too. The taste you had won't do any damage of itself but, if you had drunk enough it would have settled in your brain until you drank a second, different, potion. Then the two would combine and you'd suffer a fatal stroke."

"That's the second sophisticated potion I've met recently. Where did that wine come from?" she asked.

"No idea." Corvek summoned a servant and asked her to find out who had chosen that wine and why.

It took a sixth before the reply came. The bottle, and another seven like it, had been delivered two days earlier. The message accompanying it said it was a token of respect for the new Duchess and asked that it should be given to her to celebrate her elevation to the peerage. The butler had tasted it and confirmed that it was good enough to be served.

"So it *was* aimed at me," said Melauthua. "Who by?"

"I'd better have a look at the other bottles," suggested Corvek.

They made their way to the kitchens where he examined the untouched bottles and reported, "No doubt about it. Three of the bottles are the same as the one that was opened, the other four contain the second potion."

"That means chance would dictate when I took a fatal drink. Who is responsible?"

"There aren't many Chemers around who are capable of making such a potion," said Corvek. "I'm one of them and you should get me to swear in front of a Feeler that it wasn't me."

"Who else is there?"

"There's one in Simand but she's too far away to have got the adulterated wine here two days ago and I can't think of a reason why she would want you dead. The only one I know of who is both strong enough and close enough is Praukel."

"That makes sense. It could have been him sitting here instead of me if the king had chosen differently. He's got to resent me, but I'm surprised he'd resort to murder."

"It gives him a motive," agreed Corvek, "but it's not proof. I think you should tell the king. He's going to want to know about an attempt on your life."

O

"Your Majesty," said Latisec, bowing as the king entered the audience chamber, "Thank you for seeing me."

Sulereath sat down. "You did ask for an urgent meeting, Your Grace. What is it you want?"

"I must leave soon and return to Merlsen. Thanks to the presence of a Whisperer among my staff I have been able to deal with most of the business of my duchy while here.

However, there are some things that require my presence and cannot be dealt with from Carregis. With your permission, I will leave in four days' time."

"Very well," said the king. "You have leave to depart."

"I will be happy to entertain you in Merlsen if at any time you wish to visit Alrem, Your Majesty. Until then the best I can do is invite you to an Alremer banquet at my town house. Would the evening before my departure be suitable?"

Sulereath was taken by surprise. He hadn't expected Latisec to be so cordial. "Thank you for the invitation, Your Grace. I am happy to accept."

"In that case I will look forward to welcoming you." Latisec bowed and left the room, followed by an escort of two of the King's Guard.

The king jumped when Baram's voice said, "Your Majesty, I will have to find a way to be present at this dinner."

"Baram. You startled me. I had forgotten you were here."

"Good, I'm glad to hear it. It's best if you do or you might inadvertently give my presence away simply by looking for me."

"I expect I'll get used to it. Are you sure you need to come to this dinner? Surely I'm not in danger. Latisec invited me to a banquet. I'm not sure I trust him but he's not going do anything in front of his other guests."

"I hope you're right, Your Majesty, but Rupesc did tell me to be with you at all times."

"So he did. I suppose you'd better be. Will you be able to stay with me at the meal?"

"Yes, I'll find a way. I'll talk it over with Fedic. We have some experience of working together with me in Stealth."

"How?"

Baram let himself become visible again and gave Sulereath a brief description of his time as a spell-bound bodyguard for Graumedel.

Afterwards he said to the king, "There is one thing I

must emphasise before we go. You won't know I'm there unless something goes wrong. Should that happen I will give you instructions. If I tell you to get down or hide or run, you *must* obey immediately and without argument."

"Is that really necessary?"

"I hope not, but I would rather be prepared unnecessarily than not be ready for trouble. If you won't agree to that then it's best you refuse the invitation."

IN THE DARKWORLD

Caseir had nothing to do but listen to, and talk to, the daimons. He knew that some people, probably most, would find his situation frightening. That was an emotion he had never been familiar with – an arena fighter couldn't afford emotional weaknesses.

He had to admit that what happened when Yarelk threw the piece of wood into the oven had terrified him, but it was over, and he had survived.

A moving shadow attracted his attention. *How can I see anything? Anarya sees nothing but darkness when she's here. Is it because I was a Daimoner before I was killed? Or is it that the bits of wood let some light into the Darkworld?*

He concentrated on the various bits of wood in turn to find out what their holders were doing. The most interesting thing happening anywhere was Baram agreeing to be a bodyguard for the king.

The shadow shifted again and seemed to settle around him. A hollow, sighing voice he had become familiar with whispered, {*Tell more.*}

It was the daimon he had forced to obey him when he was alive. It seemed to be the strongest, or at least one of the strongest. It was no longer as antagonistic as it had been when he was alive and they had reached an agreement to explain things to each other.

"What do you want to know about this time?"

{*Distance. Explain meaning.*}

Caseir sighed, *Not again!*

The whole concept of distance and movement was alien to the daimons. They were fascinated by it and had asked him to explain it on several occasions. He had tried, but without success.

"The object that forms my prison. It's in several pieces."

(*Irrelevant. One thing only.*}

"Not in my world. Try to imagine one of the pieces separated from the others."

{*Try.*}

"Distance is the space between the pieces."

{*Not space. Time separates.*}

"What?"

{*Touch piece, change time, touch all.*}

"You mean you can manipulate time?"

{*Stretch, squeeze, whatever needful.*}

"So the last time we spoke is the same as the time before?"

{*Affirmation.*}

Caseir was silent for a while as he tried to absorb what the daimon had told him, then he asked, "Does that help you understand?"

{*Possible. Think.*}

Caseir sighed again. *Is that progress? Might be, I'm not sure.*

"It must be my turn for a question."

{*Ask.*}

"Why do you allow people like me to command you?"

{*Gods agree, not we.*}

"Do you have to obey the gods?"

{*We, gods, same. They stronger.*}

"You're the same as the gods?"

{*Almost. Strength difference. Chase we here.*}

The shadow lifted from around Caseir before he could ask anything else and he was alone again. *At least I've got things to think about while I wait.*

DUKE LATISEC'S TOWN HOUSE IN CARREGIS

As they stepped out of the carriage Baram slipped his hand into Fedic's belt to let him know where he was. He took care to avoid contact with any of the Duke's men as he followed the king into Duke Latisec's town house. It was a narrow building, with no more than three rooms on any of its six floors. They climbed two flights of steps and turned left into the dining room which extended the full width of the house. A large window provided a magnificent view downriver as far as the Ferrahn islands. The other walls held a display of weapons; swords, halberds and axes among them. The table was set for two with a wealth of silverware and fine porcelain.

Sulereath was surprised by that and asked, "Am I your only guest tonight?"

"Yes, Your Majesty. I wanted to take this opportunity for us to become better acquainted and others would get in the way."

I don't like this, thought Baram as he found a corner to stand in. *I'd be happier if there were more people here, although that would make it more difficult for me.* Knowing what Rupesc had told him of Latisec's feelings towards the king, he was worried that one of the dishes might be poisoned. If it was there was nothing he could do about it, although he did know that Corvek had provided the king with an all-purpose antidote. He hoped that would do, but he didn't like having to rely on hope.

Baram regretted not being able to taste the food. He was certain he would enjoy it. The meal was served as a classical Alremer banquet with twenty or more small courses, including soups, salads, eggs, fish, roast meats, grilled cheese and sweet cakes. Many of the items were rolled in spicy rice or cornmeal balls or wrapped in pastry, and some were fried. Each was accompanied by a different wine. A mixture of fruit poached in brandy and honey finished it off. The aromas were enticing and Baram was salivating well before the end of the second course.

The conversation during the meal was dominated by Latisec who talked in detail about the architecture of Merlsen and the latest performances of the Alrem Players Guild. Then he described his hunting preserve, including the various animals to be found in it. He repeated his invitation to Merlsen with an offer to take Sulereath on a hunt there.

It was all very friendly and relaxed. Baram was beginning to wonder if there was any substance to Rupesc's worries.

Finally, the servants produced thimble-sized glasses of a thick golden liquid and Latisec said, "Allow me to offer you a taste of Miros."

Sulereath smiled. "Thank you, Your Grace. I will be most interested in tasting it. I know it by reputation only."

"I'm surprised, Your Majesty. I know Duke Wurauf was a connoisseur. There should be some in his cellar."

"If so, he never shared it with me. I must investigate."

"I have managed to purchase some of the distillate from three separate casks. This one is eleven years old and is, I think, the best of them. I hope you enjoy it."

Something about the way Latisec spoke, with an air of anticipation, made hairs stand up on Baram's neck. *Is this where the danger lies? Should I reveal myself?*

Sulereath was lifting the glass to his lips when there was a loud bang and the room shook. He jumped to his feet, letting the glass fall and turned to stare at the door leading to the stairs where the sound had come from.

Latisec ran to the door, moving quickly for someone of his bulk and threw the door open. Smoke billowed up the stairs and into the dining room. Several voices screamed for help from the floor above.

"Take care, Your Majesty," shouted Latisec. "The staircase is damaged, don't go too close."

Baram wasn't surprised when Sulereath ignored Latisec and moved to where he could peer through the door. He was about to pull the king back into the room when he saw Latisec lift a mace down from the wall, move to a position behind the king and raise the weapon.

"Down, Your Majesty," he shouted as he drew his short sword and stabbed at Latisec. His aim was good and the blade sank into the Duke's left arm.

Latisec screamed, dropped the mace and grabbed another weapon from the wall. It was a longsword and he swung it at Baram, blood running freely from his wounded arm.

Baram stepped inside the swing and put his shoulder into Latisec's paunch. The Duke dropped, gasping for breath. Baram slammed the hilt of his sword into Latisec's jaw knocking him out.

"This way, Your Majesty," he said after helping the king to his feet. "There's a servant's stair over here."

"What about Latisec?" asked Sulereath.

"What about him?"

"I want him to stand trial."

"We've got to get out of here ourselves before worrying about that. Come on." He grabbed the king's arm and pulled him towards the other door.

They hurried out, meeting nobody until they were nearly at the bottom of the last flight of stairs.

Baram heard running footsteps, stepped in front of the king, raised his sword and waited to see who appeared at the bottom. *At least I've got the advantage of position.*

It was Fedic and another of the King's Guard. Baram exhaled, let his point drop and asked, "Is it safe?"

"Yes," Fedic replied, "thank Huler."

"Good. I will use the carriage to take His Majesty back to the palace. You take some men, go up to the second floor and arrest Duke Latisec. Have his wound treated and find somewhere secure to keep him until a trial can be arranged."

Fedic looked at Sulereath who answered the unspoken question with a nod. "Do as he says."

THE ROYAL PALACE

Sulereath III walked into the audience chamber, which had been converted into a courtroom, and took his seat on the throne. He wore judges' robes, embroidered with the pelican emblem of the House of Ereath. On his head was a silver circlet set with emeralds and moonstones. He carried a naked sword which he laid across his knees.

He looked at his advisers who were seated to either side of the throne, nodded and said, "Bring in the prisoner."

Latisec was dressed in simple, unadorned clothing. His left arm was in a sling and his face was bruised.

Judge Yertis Pirrosha stood up and said, "Latisec of Alrem, you have been questioned under the influence of a truth potion and in the presence of three Feelers who vouch for the accuracy of your testimony. At present, the details are not known to any of the council. They will hear the particulars of your actions and motives for the first time here. What say you?"

"I did what I did," snarled Latisec, glowering at the king. "My only regret is that I failed in my attempt to provide a competent ruler for Carrhen."

"Why did..."

"Does it matter? I did it and that's that. I'm not going to beg for mercy. Just get on with it."

"With your permission, Your Majesty, I will have the record of the accused's questioning read."

Sulereath said, "Proceed," and sat back to listen.

Most of Latisec's answers had been justification of his actions. According to him he had acted in the interests of the kingdom. He claimed Sulereath was incompetent, as exemplified by his failure to recognise the best option for the vacant duchy of Carrh.

It was when the actual mechanics of the assassination

attempt were described that Sulereath realised what had happened and how close the attempt had come to succeeding.

The explosion that partly demolished the main staircase had been due to a special mixture provided by Praukel and had been timed to occur towards the end of the meal when Sulereath would be most relaxed. The choice of a mace as the murder weapon was so that, when he was pitched down the broken stairs, people would assume he had received the head injury on landing.

"A clever, nefarious plan," said Grovaen. "Fortunately, and thanks to Baram, it failed."

Sulereath stood and raised his sword. "Duke Latisec of Alrem, you are guilty of treason. Your rank is forfeit and your title will not pass to your son. You will die as a common criminal, executed in the dark of this night so that you will not see Huler's dawn again."

"My son has done nothing!" Latisec shouted. "He should inherit."

"You should have thought of that before plotting against the king," said Yertis. "It's not that long ago that your family would be condemned with you and suffer the same fate. Consider yourself fortunate that His Majesty is being merciful."

He was led away still protesting that his son should become the next Duke of Alrem.

Sulereath sighed, "Now we have another empty ducal throne to fill."

"Your Majesty," said Melauthua, "Praukel Vecsin is implicated in this attempt on your life and there is also a suspicion that he may have tried to kill me."

"He will be arrested and brought to trial."

"Actually, Your Majesty, I fear that will not be possible," reported Fedic. "One of the Feelers who questioned Latisec told me there was evidence against Praukel, although he gave me no details. I sent men to arrest him, but he took poison rather than surrender to them."

"A guilty conscience," remarked Grovaen, making the

sign of the thunderbolt.

"Lord Adviser Grovaen, please tell me what you think would be a suitable reward for Baram?"

"Nothing," said Baram, appearing from Stealth next to the throne. "I want nothing."

"I didn't know you were here or I would have asked Grovaen in private. You deserve something. This is the second time your actions have benefitted me."

"The second time?" asked Grovaen.

"Yes. Baram and I have discovered a common interest in history. We have been discussing various texts and passing written comments to each other. I recognised his handwriting the first time I saw it. It's the same as on the message found with Wurauf's body." Sulereath looked at Baram and added, "It was you who killed him, wasn't it?"

Baram went to one knee, laid his sword at the king's feet and admitted, "Yes, Your Majesty, it was. I surrender to your justice."

"Considering what has happened as a result and how earnestly I had wished for Wurauf's death, I cannot blame you. You are pardoned. Pick up your sword and continue to use it on my behalf."

A SAFE-HOUSE IN JOTUK

Yarelk twisted and turned in his bed, unable to sleep. He'd had a room to himself ever since he succeeded Hentro, but he couldn't get used to the absence of snores. *The silence keeps me awake; isn't that silly!*

He sat up, despite telling himself getting up in the middle of the night wasn't a good idea. He was supposed to be meeting with the ruler of the Bronze Leopard *houln* the next day. Some problems had cropped up where the two ran together. *I'll be in no condition to negotiate if I can't sleep.*

He punched his pillow, unwrapped himself from the bundled up blanket and lay down again, pulling the blanket over himself.

Don't think, he told himself as he slid towards sleep, *let the Confined Ones guide you.* It was enough to take him to the edge and almost over it. Then he heard Kehsieh's voice telling him to prepare.

"Prepare for what, Greatness?" he asked, sitting up again. There was no response and he decided it had been his imagination wakening him up again.

The voice didn't sound quite like the one from the token. *But that wasn't really Kehsieh. Curse that traitor Richak, may he freeze his balls off in the coldest hell. Because of him, if Kehsieh really does speak to me I won't be sure it's not an imposter.*

Yarelk clenched his fist in prayer, "Greatness, I beg you, let me know the truth."

He heard a faint whisper. "Prepare. Stronger. Soon."

The voice *was* different. Yarelk jumped out of bed to stand with head bowed and both fists raised. "Greatness? Is it really you?"

"Soon free," the voice sighed, "soon… "

HOUSE NEYEN

Anarya shuffled awkwardly through the portal with two priests and two priestesses holding on to her.

"You can let go now," she said.

The awed looks on their faces amused her. This was the second group of teachers she had brought to House Neyen and she had seen the same expression on the faces of the first group.

They had started from a room in Graumedel's mansion full of rich hangings and gilded pillars. The sight they saw now was much less ornate. They were looking through an arch at a long corridor with woven bamboo matting laid over green, scarlet and white tiles. A series of doors, painted white with gold trim, stretched along both sides of the hallway. Chairs and small tables stood against the wall between each of them. There was a window at the end, next to a staircase, overlooking an orchard.

"How many more are you going to bring?" asked Lias after she welcomed them and directed them to the rooms she had set aside for their use.

"Another group the same size in four days' time," said Anarya. "That will make twelve in all. It's not very many, but Blessèd Tilua thinks that will be enough to start the process of introducing our gods to the Families. I can always bring more later if all goes well and more are needed."

"Is it a strain for you? Transporting people from Carregis to here?"

"No. I'm not exactly carrying them you know. It's no more difficult than opening a door. I could move more in a trip if I could work out some way of making sure everyone stays in contact with me as we step forward through the door.

"What would happen if somebody lost contact?"

"I don't know, but I'm pretty sure it wouldn't be good. It almost happened to Baram when we first came here. He ended up a dozen or so paces away from me and he says he was dizzy and shaky for chimes afterwards.

One of the newly arrived priestesses hesitated. Instead of going to her room, she approached Lias and said, "Please forgive me for interrupting. Can you tell me where to find Blessèd Tilua? I have a message for her."

"She's talking to a group of young women from Houses Branidh and Hivarn," replied Lias. "Their meeting started more than a chime ago so they should be finished soon. She told me she would come here to meet the new arrivals when she's done with the meeting. You're a little earlier than we expected which is why she's not here. Why don't you get yourself settled in your room and come back in a tenth?"

They watched the priestess leave before Lias spoke, "We can house these four, and the next group easily. However, I don't think twelve newcomers, plus Tilua and Desern, are going to be nearly enough to teach everyone. Many from the Families want to learn about Quarenna and Huler. I've even heard of some servants who are interested.

"I've been wondering about spreading people to other Houses," said Anarya. "It will make it easier if Neyen isn't the only place to learn."

Lias frowned. "True," she admitted, "but we will have to take care. Houses Guesyr and Widhis aren't going to like what your people are doing and could attack, or at least, threaten them."

"Everyone I bring is a volunteer and has accepted there may be a risk. It hasn't stopped them being willing to come. I'm told there are at least another forty wanting to help."

They walked away from the archway where Anarya had created the portal, heading towards the staircase at the end of the hall.

"Are all of your people talented?" asked Lias.

"So far everyone who has come is."

"Good."

"It was a deliberate choice on our part," said Anarya. "Although a priestess of Quarenna doesn't have to have a talent most of them do. And I believe the same is true of the priests of Huler. But I remembered what Yisul told me about how the Families hold the untalented in low esteem and I thought it better to avoid that complication."

"Very sensible of you. Unfortunately, it is true that we don't pay much attention to the untalented, even those born into the Twenty-three."

"You seem to regret that."

"I do," said Lias. "You see, just as occasional untalented are born in the Families sometimes talents show up among people outside the walls. They get adopted into the Families."

"I remember Yisul saying that. She told me it was rare for someone born in the outer city to develop a talent. If I remember correctly, she said it had only happened once in the last twenty-five years."

Lias frowned. "I suspect it's not as rare as we think. We sometimes hear rumours of talented who don't survive to get the chance to be adopted. I fear it's often their parents who kill them when they develop a talent."

Anarya stopped and turned to Lias in surprise. "How awful!"

"It almost happened to my great-grandmother. If her mother hadn't worked for House Shuth, and taken her there pretending she was being considered for a maid's position, she'd have been killed. As it was, she was lucky it was Shuth her mother worked for and not a House like Pridhar that's never adopted anyone."

"You mean Pridhar won't take in a threatened talented?"

"No. They have refused on at least two occasions I know of."

"That's outrageous!"

"I agree," Lias said. "Every other Family, except Guesyr and Widhis, is recorded as adopting some. Their disdain for Shuth, Branidh and Neyen, who have adopted the most and 'diluted the pure bloodlines' is one of many reasons why there is enmity among the Families."

"I hadn't realised there were such divisions among the Twenty-three. I thought it was only the attitudes to the death of The God that separated them."

"No, there are other causes. Some are quite stupid, for example some Seekers and Feelers think their talents are somehow superior to others because they are more cerebral. They look down on those who can manipulate earth, air, fire and water as having 'mechanical' skills, barely worth considering as talents."

Anarya snorted. "How ridiculous."

As they started walking along the corridor again Tilua joined them with the news that she had spoken to a Terromancer about what she had felt during transit. "Her usual awareness of the earth's structure was enhanced. She could feel all the way down to the centre of the world and, for a moment, she felt she could move mountains."

"That suggests your idea about the significance of the Darkworld is right," commented Anarya.

"I've just realised I interrupted you, Lady Lias," said Tilua. "I'm sorry. What were you saying?"

Lias replied, "We were talking about the attitudes of the Families towards the untalented. I feel strongly that change is necessary but I am probably being stupidly optimistic when I hope the influence of those you bring as teachers will change them. We should be thinking of all Jotukil as people, but we don't and are hated as a result. Unfortunately, the hatred spills over to any child who develops a talent outside the walls. I am very blessed, my ancestor survived to be adopted, and I would like all others to have the same opportunity."

"It's something I'm sure Holy Quarenna in her aspect as the Mother must want too," said Tilua. "You are fortunate to have the support of Muhan; he seems to have similar beliefs."

"That's one of the reasons I fell in love with him."

HOUSE SHUTH

An escort of six Neyen guardsmen accompanied the coach-and-four on its way to House Shuth. It carried Yisul, Tilua, Desern, two other priestesses of Quarenna and two more priests of Huler. The occupants craned their necks trying to see out as Yisul pointed out the temple of The God. It was just visible beyond House Neyen as the carriage turned away from it into an avenue shaded by a double row of tall popanash trees. The next buildings she drew attention to were the mansions of Houses Pridhar on the left and Monost on the right. They drew gasps of astonishment from the passengers seeing Jotuk for the first time.

"Shuth is even more impressive," said Yisul. "I think it is probably the grandest of the Twenty-three mansions, although as a member of House Neyen I'm not sure I should admit that."

The tall central spire of House Shuth appeared through the trees before the rest of the building, its yellow tiles gleaming in the afternoon sun and echoing the colour of the autumn foliage.

"Magnificent," said Tilua when she climbed out of the coach and could see more of the frontage.

Cuhes cra Shuth was waiting for them in the atrium. She welcomed them saying, "I am grateful to you for agreeing to teach here as well as at Neyen. I expected interest, but the number wanting to attend has surprised me. Forty-seven women and thirty-three men have come here today from six different Houses to hear what you have to say. I trust that is not too many."

"It is rather a lot," said Tilua. "Although most of our teaching is normally done in small groups, and often one-to-one, I am sure we can cope with larger numbers. It may be necessary to limit the class size later, but we can make a start. The Daughters of Quarenna are happy to do whatever we can to help."

Desern nodded his agreement, "Much the same applies to us. We will do what we can."

"I have been warned that men and women must be taught separately so I have had two rooms prepared for you. The servants will show you where they are. They will also provide whatever you wish in the way of refreshments. I hope you will accept an invitation to dine with us this evening."

"Thank you Lady Cuhes," said Tilua. "We will accept your hospitality."

The teaching sessions lasted about two chimes and everyone involved agreed they had been worthwhile. However, they also agreed that the numbers involved were excessive.

"I think, Lady Cuhes," said Tilua, after enjoying a sumptuous meal, "that we must reduce the classes to no more than three, or at the very most four, students per teacher. That will mean increasing the frequency of the classes if we are to deal adequately with all those interested in learning."

Desern agreed. "And there is one more thing to be considered. I haven't heard anyone mention it yet, but we will need buildings to become a temple of Huler and a shrine of Quarenna."

Tilua nodded. "A building would be desirable, however the rites of Quarenna do not require one. Any enclosed area consecrated in her name will suffice."

"A building *is* needed to glorify Huler. Several elements of the liturgy are processional. His devotees go through a well-defined sequence of instruction. They pass through various stages, degrees and ranks each of which gives them access to different areas of the temple."

"How about the temple of The God?" asked Yisul, who was sitting in on the discussion. "The Sovereign Council has yet to find a use for it. Would it be suitable?"

"Probably," said Desern. "I would want to take a close

look at it before deciding but I can think of no reason why converting it shouldn't be possible. In fact, from the little I saw of the exterior on our way here, it is certainly impressive enough to be an appropriate place in which to worship Huler."

"Would it also be acceptable to Quarenna?" asked Cuhes.

"I suspect not," replied Tilua, "unless there is a garden, or an area that can be become one. In any case the shrine and temple can't be side by side. There would be too big a risk of someone accidentally intruding into the wrong one, with fatal consequences."

"Fatal?" asked Cuhes, sounding surprised. "Surely you wouldn't kill someone just because they happen to wander into the wrong place."

"It's not a case of *us* killing them," said Tilua. "Trespassers die as soon as they set foot in ground consecrated to the god of the other sex."

"Oh!"

"Do you know Voro?" Desern asked Tilua.

"No, I've never been there," she replied. "All I know about it is the smoking mountain. Why do you ask?"

"That is its best known feature," said Desern. "It's also the only place I know of where the shrine and temple back on to each other. I've never heard of that causing any problems. Of course, they are surrounded and separated by high walls."

"I didn't know it was a possibility," Tilua said. "I suppose it could happen here too. We must take a look at the temple."

Cuhes remarked, "It's not going to be possible to take you there tonight. "Talk to Muhan when you get back to Neyen and I'm sure he will arrange a visit."

O

One or two of the passengers weren't feeling well as the coach carried them back towards Neyen through the twilight. They had eaten a bit too much and the swaying of the coach made them queasy.

They were about halfway along the popanash avenue when Desern suddenly sat up straight and said, "Somebody out there hates us."

He turned to lean out the window, made a harsh gurgling noise and fell backwards into the carriage with an arrow in his neck.

Other arrows thudded into the side of the coach. The commander of the escort shouted, "Go! Get out of here!"

The occupants bounced around and tumbled into each other as the driver whipped up the horses.

Tilua found herself face-to-face with Desern, looking into his blank eyes. She used the Oversight and saw no aura surrounding him. She could see Yisul's Voyanter talent and those of a Scratcher, a Whisperer, a Seeker and a Terromancer. She started to borrow the Scratcher's talent, hoping to use it to cushion the bumps. A flailing foot caught her in the face, she lost concentration and had to start again.

A horse screamed.

The coach lurched sideways and fell over.

The Scratcher had the same idea as Tilua and managed to soften the impact as the coach came to a grinding halt.

They untangled themselves from each other with groans and hisses of pain.

Tilua shook her head to clear it. "Who's the Scratcher?" she asked.

"Me, Kesren," one of the priests replied.

"Good work cushioning us. Can you manage to hold a shield over all of us while we find out what's happening? Is everyone else all right?"

"I'm not injured," said Kesren. "I can maintain the shield."

"Good. What about the rest of you?"

"Broken finger. That's all."

"Nothing but bruises. Ouch! … and maybe a broken rib or two."

"Just bumps and scrapes," said Yisul.

There was no answer from Jilesi. Tilua couldn't see the

Seeker's aura. *Oh, no. Not Jilesi too.*

She had more urgent things to do than discover what had killed Jilesi, so she pushed it firmly to the back of her mind. *How do we get out of this?*

"Yisul, see if you can tell me how many are out there and where they are."

"I make it twelve in all," replied Yisul after a moment's thought. "One of them is Hulser Pridhar and there are two more from that Family I don't recognise. They're probably Scratchers too, most of the Pridhar are."

"Who else?"

"There's also two Leynik," said Yisul. "One of them is Esayn, and I know he's a Lifter. I'm not sure about the other."

"That's five. What about the others?"

"Pridhar Guardsmen."

"Where are they?"

"All of them are together over there," Yisul pointed to the right. "Over towards House Pridhar."

"Any ideas, anyone?" asked Tilua. "How do we survive this?"

"Just keep us shielded until help comes," said the other priest. "I'm a Whisperer and I've spent a lot of time exploring the Whispermesh and making friends on it since I got here. I've just spoken to one of them who says he can get a message to Lord Muhan in about a quarter."

"And it will take at least another to get anybody here from Neyen to rescue us," added Yisul. "Can we hold on that long?

"We have to."

"We'd better decide what to do quickly," said Yisul. "Esayn cra Leynik is talking about dropping trees on us to crush the coach."

"What about our escort. Can they do anything?"

"I can't sense them any more," Yisul reported. "They tried to charge the attackers. I think they're all dead."

"How far away are the Pridhar?" asked the other priestess.

"Twenty, twenty-five paces. Why?"

"I have an idea but I will need help to make it work."

"What is it, Trenyas? What sort of help?" asked Tilua.

"First I have to be able to touch the ground. Then I'm going to soften the soil under their feet until it's like quicksand. When I harden it again they'll be trapped. It might even kill them if they sink far enough."

"It's worth a try," Tilua agreed, "but you won't be able to see what you're doing."

"That's where Yisul comes in. I'll do something that will let her see where my focus is and she can direct me to the right place. I'll start now. Just keep the coach shielded so that I'm not distracted."

Trenyas wriggled her way to the bottom of the coach. She knocked out most of the broken glass and reached through the window, having to lie across Jilesi's body to do so. Her talent softened the soil so that she could sink her hands into it, wincing as she cut herself on bits of glass. She took a deep breath and closed her eyes.

"Was that you?" asked Yisul about a tenth later. "Something happened. It was like a fountain of soil some five paces to the left of where the Pridhar are standing and at about the right distance. I don't think they saw it."

"I'll do it again, closer."

"That's it, right in the middle of them," said Yisul. "That made them jump."

Tilua borrowed Yisul's talent and the two of them watched in amazement as Trenyas exerted her talent to the utmost. The process was much faster than they had anticipated. The men were neck deep before they had a chance to move and were trapped as the ground resumed its normal consistency.

"That's all I can do." Trenyas sounded exhausted.

"That's enough," said Tilua. "Kesren, can you hold the shield around the coach while we get out of it?"

"Yes, of course."

"Let's not get complacent. There are still enemies out there with talents. We can't give them the chance to kill more of us. Once I'm out I'll put a shield over them and you'll be able to relax yours."

They clambered from the ruins of the coach, stretched and moved away from it.

After half a chime, which they spent doing what they could for each other's injuries, the sound of galloping horses attracted their attention. It was coming from the right direction but they weren't taking chances; they stepped back into the shadow of the trees. It was Muhan and another dozen from House Neyen including Anarya, who had firmly refused to be left behind. Anarya threw herself into Yisul's arms sobbing with relief as soon as she dismounted.

Shortly afterwards more riders appeared, this time from House Shuth. The message on the Whispermesh had spread like a *purtirn* and Cuhes had sent help in force.

With the aid of a Shuth Terromancer, Hulser Pridhar and his companions were released from the grip of the ground and promptly restrained with manacles spelled to prevent the use of any talent.

"What do we do with them?" asked Muhan.

"Kill them, of course," replied Cuhes. "Oh, I suppose we'll have to give them a trial first. But House Shuth isn't going to tolerate an attack that cost the lives of two of our guests."

"It's not going to be popular with the Sovereign Council."

"Quite frankly, Muhan. I don't care about the Sovereign Council. It's a failure, and we might as well admit it."

Muhan sighed. "You're right. I wish you weren't, but I can't deny it any longer."

"We've got to do something about it."

"Yes, but what?"

○

Muhan cra Neyen walked into the great hall of House Shuth. Eighteen other Heads of Family were there and all were looking subdued. What little conversation there was quickly died as he stopped in front of the frail-looking figure of Cuhes cra Shuth and bowed to her before turning to face the assembly.

"Look around you," he said. "Four of our number are not present. One of them, Mianil cra Hivarn, is too badly injured to attend. House Guesyr has still not selected a new Head since Dunel was killed and so are unrepresented. That accounts for two of the missing four. Why are the Heads of Houses Pridhar and Leynik not here?"

He paused.

Nobody answered.

"I can't believe you don't know already, but I will tell you, just in case by some miracle you haven't heard about it. They are in chains in a secure room of this House because they are responsible for the deaths of two visitors who have come to help us."

"Help you, you mean!" grumbled Pevus cra Glinin. "I don't need their help. The spirit of The God is still alive and I will continue to worship him."

"As will I," added Julnaw cra Widhis. "I don't wish to have other beliefs stuffed down my throat. Having said that, I too find the behaviour of Pridhar and Leynik unacceptable. All they needed to do was refuse to listen to these visitors and deny them access to the susceptible members of their Families."

Muhan nodded. "You're right, Julnaw. I haven't agreed with you very often over the years but on this occasion I do. Nobody is being forced to listen to what my guests have to say. I find their willingness to teach only at the request of their pupils very acceptable. I would not have invited them here otherwise."

Cuhes cra Shuth levered herself out of her chair with the aid of a stick and stood leaning on it. "Some of you know what I'm going to say as I have discussed it with you. However, I think I am going to surprise many of you when I say I believe the Sovereign Council is a failure and we need something to replace it." She paused, looked around and tried to make eye-contact with as many as possible before continuing. "Julnaw, you're the only

Feeler here, did I mean what I just said?"

Julnaw cra Widhis looked surprised at being asked but she said, "Yes, you did."

"Thank you. I think the problem is that we are used to obeying one voice, that of The God, and the Council doesn't provide the same clear, unequivocal instructions. That's why I have come to believe that we need to abandon the Council and select a monarch."

"You?" bellowed Pevus cra Glinin.

"No, not me. I'm too old."

"Who, then? Neyen?"

"Possibly. Or you. That has yet to be determined. What I suggest is that each House chooses a candidate from another one and we select the person with the most support. How you choose who to nominate is up to you. Keep the choice in your own hands if you wish; let everyone in your House participate in the selection; or use any other system you can come up with. Of course, we also have to ask those Families not represented here today to join in. When the suggestions have been tallied we will all swear allegiance to the elected monarch."

"Utter nonsense," said Pevus.

"Anyone who finds it unacceptable and doesn't want to live under the elected monarch is at liberty to go elsewhere. Jotuk is not all of Sitrelk. For example, Pevus, Glinin has lands around Embrett, you could go there. House Shuth could go to West Hesth, or House Vilost to Edhisam. All the Families have out-of-the-way places they could go to and live free from the rule of the monarch. Any who chose to live in exile would, of course, be excluded from whatever decision making process the monarch sets up."

"But…"

"No!"

"What an idea."

"Makes some weird sort of sense."

"She's right about the Sovereign Council."

"I think it could work."

Everyone present wanted a say. Most agreed that the

Sovereign Council should be abolished but they debated what, or who, was to replace it for most of two chimes. It soon became evident that Cuhes had put a lot of thought into her suggestion, because nobody else could offer a viable alternative. A few, like Pevus cra Glinin, were opposed to the idea, particularly that part of it which would have the Families nominating a monarch from a different Family. Others found that element of her proposal the most attractive part.

"From what I have heard," said Cuhes, as the debate started to wind down, "Most of you are in favour of this, admittedly radical, change. Let me urge those who aren't to reconsider. The majority want it to happen so do not disenfranchise your Family by failing to nominate someone. Your candidate, I should remind you, does not need to be a current Head of House. Nor, I suggest, will the role be hereditary. In the event of the death or abdication of the incumbent another election will be held. We will meet again in three days to tally the results after you have had a chance to discuss this within your Families."

IN THE DARKWORLD

"I'm sorry I've left you in the Darkworld for so long, Caseir," said Anarya. "I can't use the portal again until tomorrow but I'll come to collect the table and get you out of there as soon as I can."

"How long has it been in the real world?"

"Three days. How long has it felt like to you?"

"Five or six, I'd say."

"Oh, Caseir. I know time is different there but I didn't expect that much of a disparity."

"Don't worry about it. Being here has been a more interesting experience than I expected."

"Interesting? I'd have thought you'd be bored, unless you get enough information through the little bits of wood we're carrying around to know what's going on."

"I've got some that way," admitted Caseir, "although it's rather like peering through keyholes, a bit limited. It has helped but mainly it's been talking to the daimons that's kept me sane."

"They talk to you!"

"Huler's beard, don't they just. I've met four of them so far and they all seem to be fascinated by the chance to talk to somebody who isn't a Daimoner."

"But, you are… Oh, that's right. I remember, you lost your talent when you were killed. So, you mean the daimons have forgiven you for compelling them."

"I can't compel them now, I've been punished for it and apparently they're satisfied with their revenge."

"So now they treat you as a friend and talk to you. That's difficult to believe."

"Friend might be overstating it a bit, but they want to hear about our world. Although they can do all sorts of things there they don't really understand it. It's as strange to them as the Darkworld is to us."

"And what are they giving you in return?" asked Anarya.

"I'm learning about the Darkworld."

"Can you make sense of what they say? I've always had problems understanding what it means when I've been talking to one about the portal."

"It's not easy, but most of the time I can make sense of it. And repetition helps."

"You can tell me all about it when I get the table back here."

O

"You can't manage the table on your own," said Yisul. "You needed Baram to help you when you took it to the Darkworld and he's in Carregis. You don't want to waste transits on going there just to collect him, so I'm coming with you."

"But you're hurt."

"Just bruises. Nothing serious."

"We got separated going through the portal before. I don't want to risk it again. I almost lost you in that ambush and I'm not going to take any chances with your safety."

"Anra, my love…"

"No!"

"Then you're going to have to leave Caseir in the Darkworld until you can bring Baram back here. You can't do that to him."

Anarya stopped pacing around the room, dropped into a chair and put her head in her hands. "Do you think I want to?"

"It seems like it," said Yisul. "I am perfectly capable of helping you carry the table."

"Didn't say you weren't. I'm just afraid of losing you in the Darkworld. You've no idea what it's like there."

"I have been there before, as you reminded me. And it seemed to me it was for no time at all. Why should it not be the same this time?"

"Because I don't understand the daimons." She was desperate to convince Yisa to stay and felt her voice catch in her throat. "They might do nothing. On the other hand, if they think about it, they could hold you hostage to force me to use the portal even less, maybe even give it up entirely. They want the power it uses. And even if I agreed there's no guarantee they'd let you go."

"They could do the same if it was Baram with you. You wouldn't abandon him any more than you would me."

Anarya hesitated.

"You wouldn't, would you?" asked Yisul.

"No, of course I wouldn't," said Anarya, shaking her head vigorously.

"Good."

"You sound as if you don't believe me. Holy Quarenna be my witness, I would never leave someone in the Darkworld if I could avoid it. I swear it."

"In that case, why shouldn't I be the one to go with you?"

"Because I love you and I'm frightened of what the daimons might do. They control the Darkworld, there's nothing I can do there." She felt her throat tighten and her eyes fill with tears. "I couldn't stand it if anything happened to you."

"And I love you. We will do this together. Give me your hand and open the portal."

I'm not going to win this. Anarya sniffled, wiped the tears from her eyes and did as Yisul wanted.

Then she stood alone in silent darkness. The only thing she could feel was the tears running down her face. There was nothing else, no heartbeat, no sounds, just nothing. She shivered. *Please let Yisa be safe.*

"Caseir, can you hear me?"

"Yes, I'm here."

"Can you speak to Yisul? She came with me but we're not together."

"I can," said Caseir. "Don't worry, she's safe."

"Where is she?"

"You know that question doesn't make sense here where distance is irrelevant."

"Yes, but…"

{*What want?*}

Anarya was relieved to hear the daimon's voice after such a short wait. "I've come to get the object I brought," she said.

{*Why?*}

"I want to take it away again as we agreed."

{*Not needful. Good here.*}

"We made a bargain to reduce portal transits while it's here. I've kept to that. Now I want to revert to the previous arrangement."

{*Good here. Much interest. Much help. Stay here.*}

"Our bargain said it would be here for a short time only. I want it back."

{*Want keep. Good power. Help.*}

"Help? I don't understand. What do you want help with?"

{*Imprisoned one give assistance… strength… firmness… resistance. Stay.*}

"Do you understand what it's talking about, Caseir?"

"I think it wants me to do something for it, but I don't know what."

{*With help stop threat. We grateful.*}

"Are you saying there's some sort of danger?" asked Caseir.

{*Yes. You help stop.*}

"Danger to who?"

{*All.*}

"I don't like the sound of that," said Caseir. "Look, Anarya, I think I should find out more about this. You go and leave me here for another few days. Give me time to learn more."

"But…"

{*Need power. Imprisoned one stay. Others go. Portal use still same.*}

"I don't understand. Why do you want Caseir to stay?"

{*Imprisoned one strong. Need power.*}

"Have I got this right, Caseir? Is it saying it can use you as a source of power?"

"I think so."

"What will that do to you?"

"I don't know. I'll find out if you leave me here, and I'll ask them about this danger. You can stay in touch with me through the wood."

"Are you sure?"

"I'm a survivor, remember. I was always too stubborn to be daunted by the daimons when I was alive. I might be dead now, but that side of me is still the same. I'll be fine."

{*Bargain?*}

"I can't stop you keeping Caseir here. You're breaking our agreement.

{*Not!*}

"Yes, you are. I can't take the object I brought unless you give it to me. By refusing you're forcing me to keep to a bargain that was supposed to be temporary. You're cheating."

{*Need. Imperative.*}

"Are you sure you're happy staying here for a bit longer, Caseir?"

"Yes. I'll be fine."

"I'll make a new bargain with you. You can keep Caseir here and the portal use at the present level until the next time I come. Then I will take him away unless you can explain to him why you want him to stay."

{*Bargain.*}

"Bargain."

Anarya stumbled out of the portal into her suite in Neyen and bumped into Yisul.

"Holy Quarenna's grace. You're all right."

"Yes, my love. Nothing happened except Caseir told me at one point, 'you're safe' and I was back here almost immediately. There didn't seem to be any time between me stepping into and out of the portal. That was about half a chime ago. What happened to you? Where's the table?"

"Still in the Darkworld."

Yisul glared at Anarya. "You've left Caseir there! I can't believe you'd do that."

"He wanted to stay. There's a good reason – at least I think there is. You've got a bit of the wood, you can ask him yourself. He'll explain."

Yisul walked across the room, out on to the balcony and stood there muttering to Caseir for a while.

She came back to Anarya, knelt and said, "Please forgive me. I didn't understand."

Anarya lifted her to her feet telling Yisul she was forgiven. "*Heru-ven ti lusegri-gal.*"

"Thank you, my love," said Yisul, wrapping her arms around Anarya. "I must stop jumping to conclusions like that."

A SAFE-HOUSE IN JOTUK

Yarelk sat close to the fire in the room that had belonged to Hentro, tossing a dagger from hand to hand while he waited. He was satisfied with the way the Stone Grasshoppers had recovered from the fight that killed Richak and Jemak. His *houln* was stronger now than it had been for a long time. The Three Flowers had been devastated, more than sixty of its members so affected by Richak's treachery that they had changed allegiances.

Two of his people came into the room escorting a big, swarthy man who had had his nose broken at least twice. "We've searched him, boss. Got all his weapons."

"Good," replied Yarelk, slipping his dagger into its sheath. He studied the big man for a few moments before asking, "Well, what have you decided?"

The big man licked his lips and said, "The Dark Fountain's one of the oldest *houln* in Jotuk…"

Yarelk interrupted him. "Don't tell me things I know."

"It matters."

Yarelk leaned forward, scowling, "Not to me it doesn't. Get on with it."

The big man pulled back slightly, licked his lips again and said, "Yeah, well. There's some as don't want to see it die an' they're staying with it."

"How many?"

"There's about hundred 'n' fifty'll stay. Rest of us want to change."

"How many is that?"

"Ninety-three."

"Who are they?"

"Two smiths, twenty-one other craftsmen, fifteen shopkeepers, two brewers, a scribe an' seventeen Family servants. Rest of us are like me, enforcers."

"A nice mixture. Which Houses do the servants work at?"

"There's two in Neyen, six in Hivarn an' three each in Vilost, Dunish an' Monost."

"The Stone Grasshoppers will accept all of you who want to join us. Swear allegiance and we'll look after you, same as we do for everyone in the *houln*."

The big man raised a clenched fist and said, "In the names of the Confined Gods, I promise I will obey the ruler of the Stone Grasshoppers and put my skills at his disposal."

Yarelk nodded, "I accept your oath. Are any more of you here?"

"Yes, boss. There's eighteen more of us waitin' outside."

"I'll take their oaths now. Bring the rest who want to join here soon as you can and I'll welcome them too. You can have your weapons back now."

A short sword, four knives, and a set of knuckledusters were handed over. The newest recruit to the Stone Grasshoppers accepted them gratefully, distributed them about his person, and started to leave.

"One more thing." Yarelk pointed at a tattoo showing a stylised fountain on the man's left arm. "You'll need to get rid of that before you come back here."

"Yes, boss. I'll take care of it."

When he had accepted the oaths of the other men changing *houln*, Yarelk got up from his chair feeling very satisfied. With ninety-three new members, plus the sixty from the Three Flowers, his *houln* had just become one of the biggest. He had more influence than he could ever have imagined when he joined the Stone Grasshoppers on his eleventh birthday all those years ago.

He tossed another log on the fire, turned around and asked, "Anybody waiting?"

A skinny boy came in, stopped just inside the door and, rather tentatively, said, "Need help, we do."

"What sort of help?"

"Mam runs grocery at Kedba Corner."

"I know it."

"Man came in yesterday, threatened her. Says she needs protection since she ain't got a man now. Accident could happen and shop get damaged less'n she pays him t' protect her."

"What about your father?"

"Got killed in fight with Three Flowers at south bridge."

"Don't you have an uncle, or an older brother to look after your mother?"

"No. There's just me. Mam don't want me to join *houln*. Says she don't want t' lose me too. But I will join if you help us."

"No need. We look after the families of our people, especially those killed on *houln* business. I'll send somebody to take care of this man. He won't be bothering you again."

The boy smiled, ducked his head and left.

"Anybody else?"

"No, boss. That's all," said a voice from the next room.

"Good. Get me some ale, will you." Yarelk sat down again and waited until one of his men arrived with a mug of ale. *This has been a good day.*

He took a couple of mouthfuls of ale and started to relax.

About a quarter later, running footsteps disturbed him. He looked up as one of his men burst through the door.

"Boss, we might got troubles."

"What?"

"Hearing stories from Ladryside. You know that bit where the stream from the tanneries runs into the Ladry? They're saying supplies of hides haven't been arriving and there's rumours of illness out west where they come from. There's people round there took ill too and there's been some as died."

Yarelk jumped up. "That's the way the last two Sicknesses started!"

"Yeah, boss."

"Right. Could be we're in for another one. We're not

taking chances. You know what to do. Start getting everyone to a safe-house with as much food and water as possible. Do it quietly, we don't want a panic."

"Yeah, boss."

"I'm going down to Ladryside to take a look. Get me an escort."

LADRYSIDE

Yarelk took a piece of cloth soaked in lavender oil from his pouch. He held it to his nose in a vain attempt to avoid the stink. Stepping carefully around piles of dung, he turned the last corner on to the tongue of land between the river and the stream carrying the effluent from the tanning vats, and stopped. He expected to see a busy scene with men working in the pools trampling hides underfoot and others scraping hair off the dripping skins. Instead there was little activity.

A cluster of men were watching the outflow from one of the pools, pointing into it and shaking their heads. Two of them held hooked poles, normally used to lift soaked hides from the vats. They used them to drag a body to the side of a partially drained pool and draped it over the walkway separating two of the ponds. Murky greenish liquid drained from the bloated body. The stench became much worse.

Yarelk turned away. "I've seen enough. Let's get out of here."

He led his escort away, saying as they went, "I've seen bodies looking like that before, during the last Sickness. Could be it's the Greenwater flux, same as last time. Get your families to safe-houses as quick as you can. And tell them not to drink water from the Ladry. They were running contaminated water from that vat into the stream and it'll poison the whole river. Make sure the safe-houses have water from upstream."

"What do we do about them as want to switch from the Dark Fountain?"

"If they can bring food we'll let them swear. Once sworn they're ours and we look after them."

"And if they ain't got nothing to offer?"

"Then they're still with the Fountain. Can't be helped. We've got to look after our own first."

"Hear that, boss?" said one of Yarelk's escort.

"Hear what?"

"It's all gone quiet. They know something's wrong."

Yarelk listened and realised the man was right. There was a hush in the city. People were moving quickly and purposefully. The streets were emptying.

"News travels fast."

"And panic even faster."

HOUSE NEYEN

Guards from House Neyen stood at Derchler's Gate. The ebb and flow of people through the square outside the gate diminished. That was so unusual that the guards looked at each other speculatively, wondering what was happening.

One of the guardsmen recognised a servant in Neyen livery walking briskly up to the gate. "What's going on?" he asked as he examined the token the servant offered. "Out there," he nodded in the direction of the square, "It's too quiet."

"Not sure," was the reply. "Some deaths down Ladryside this morning."

"Nothing unusual about that."

"No, but there's rumours some are ill. That's why everybody's walking cautious."

"A Sickness?" asked the guard.

"Too early to tell. Remember there was a scare not so long ago that turned out to be nothing."

"Better tell Trusef, just in case."

"I will."

The guardsman told his colleagues what the servant had said. The story reached his sergeant who told them all to keep quiet and stay alert. That didn't stop the rumour spreading to the next squad when they came on duty, then to the rest of the Neyen guard and from them to the servants. With the rumour coming both from the guards and from those who had been near Trusef when he was told, it quickly assumed the status of news rather than speculation.

O

Muhan found Lias, Anarya and Tilua in the garden, sitting near the stream listening to its peaceful gurgling.

"I have bad news," he said. "There is reason to believe we may be about to experience a *purtirn.*"

Anarya saw the blank look on Tilua's face and explained what the unfamiliar word meant.

Muhan waved towards the outer city and told them, "It's not certain but the gate guards report increased tension out there."

"Could it be more riots?"

"It could, but I'm told the feel of the city is different. It's more like it's waiting for something. Just like the last Sickness seven years ago."

"I must tell Trusef," said Lias.

"He knows," Muhan told her. "He's already given orders to start rationing food and open the emergency accommodation."

"I remember you telling me the Families go hungry during a *purtirn,*" said Anarya, "so rationing makes sense but what do you mean by emergency accommodation?"

"We can't have the servants moving back and forth through the gates and risk bringing the Sickness into the inner city," said Yisul, "so, during a – what did you call it – an epidemic, the gates are closed and the servants already in the House have the chance to stay in rooms kept for the purpose."

"Not all of them take it," Lias added. "Some prefer to be with their families beyond the wall and accept the risk. That cost us almost a hundred of our staff the last time there was a *purtirn.*"

"A hundred! Holy Quarenna! That's awful."

"It could have been worse. Thousands died in the outer city. Nobody knows how many."

"Is there any danger I could take it back to Carregis with me?"

"Don't worry, Lady Anarya. The disease is usually the Greenwater flux and that spreads through contaminated water. We boil every drop used in the House and make sure it's clean."

"If you know how to prevent the spread why does it kill so many?"

"Because many out there are so ignorant that they don't believe boiling the water does any good," Muhan commented. "And some of them distrust us so much they think we're lying about it."

"Also," added Lias, "many are so poor they don't have the fuel to burn."

"I can't believe you are helpless," said Anarya. "Not with all the talents available. How about Aquamancers? They could purify water. And Pyromancers don't need fuel to burn if they're strong enough, so they could boil water."

"That would work," said Muhan, "if we could get people into the outer city without them being attacked."

"Then use other talents, like Scratchers and Lifters, to protect them."

"All the Families would have to work together. It's not possible. I can't see Glinin, or Pridhar, being willing to help."

"They'd rather let thousands die!"

"I fear so."

HOUSE SHUTH

"We are all here now," said Muhan as he nodded to the last of the Heads of House making their way into the great hall. He watched the swirl of colour as they greeted each other, trying to work out who was talking to, and who was ignoring, whom.

Cuhes cra Shuth was already seated. She started proceedings by saying, "Be welcome to House Shuth. Fear nothing while you are here as our guests. Please, make yourselves comfortable. Forgive me for not rising, I am afraid that age is catching up on me. Once seated I prefer to stay that way." She paused briefly to give everyone time to find a seat. "There are some new faces among us. We should greet them first before proceeding to the main business of the meeting."

She looked at the tall, blond man in orange and green who had taken one of the front row seats, and said, "I am pleased to see House Guesyr has finally nominated a new Head of House. You are welcome here, Therem cra Guesyr."

He stood and bowed to her, then said, "This is a momentous occasion. I regret the time it has taken to fill the vacancy left by the death of my cousin Dunel. The House has been divided, but the invitation to participate in the selection of a monarch has unified us. Although the majority of us in House Guesyr still worship The God, we do recognise that he is no longer physically present in the world. A single figure of authority is needed in his place."

"Thank you," responded Cuhes. She looked along to the other end of the front row where a short, dumpy woman wearing dark-blue and silver was sitting.

This woman stood to say, "Some of you will not know

me, as I live two days' travel from Jotuk and rarely come to the city. I am Febay cra Hivarn and I have been asked by Mianil to substitute for her until she has recovered from her injuries. I can report she is making good progress, but it will be several weeks before she can resume her duties as Head of House."

A thin-faced woman in the colours of House Pridhar stood from a seat in the back row and spoke in a shrill, carping voice. "I am here in the place of my uncle Hulser who is being illegally detained in this House. I demand his release. If he cannot participate in these proceedings then House Pridhar will withdraw and refuse to take any farther part in this farce."

"You realise that will put you at a disadvantage," said Cuhes.

"The House will not tolerate the imprisonment of its chosen Head. Release him now, or I leave."

"Go ahead, leave," called Sahnes cra Colnis, "We can do without you and your bigoted Family. Hulser was properly arrested for participating in the murder of guests of House Neyen."

"They are blasphemers and intruders with no status here."

"They are guests and deserve to be treated as such."

"Bah!" shouted the Pridhar representative and stalked from the room.

Cuhes looked at the last of the four newcomers and raised an eyebrow.

"Lady Cuhes, I, and the majority of House Leynik, do not condone the actions of the previous Head of House. He has been deposed and I have been elected to replace him. The House accepts the idea of replacing the Sovereign Council. The suggested method of selection of a monarch is very similar to the procedure used within House Leynik to elect a Head and we approve of it."

"Thank you. We should get on with the main business."

"Before we do," said Pevus cra Glinin, "I wish to make a statement."

"Yes, Pevus. What is it?"

"Initially I was shocked by the suggestion of electing a supreme ruler. It seemed to me quite unnecessary. However, the rest of the council of Glinin disagreed with me and have overruled me. I am still not persuaded that it's actually a good idea, but I must respect the decision of my council. Accordingly, I wish to announce that I will work with whoever is elected, despite a personal dislike of the person I strongly suspect will be chosen, unless there is an attempt to force us to abandon the worship of The God."

Cuhes cra Shuth broke the silence that followed this statement saying, "Thank you, Pevus. You make a good point. I suggest that, before we proceed with the election, we should declare that everyone's religious beliefs are their own business and cannot be forced."

"I agree," said Therem cra Guesyr. "If the elected monarch cannot accept this stipulation then he or she must abdicate immediately and the person second in the voting will replace them."

There was silence for a moment, then everyone wanted to speak and the consensus was clearly in favour of Therem's suggestion.

Cuhes looked around, "Has any House, apart from Pridhar, chosen not to make a nomination?"

People shuffled in their seats, craning their necks and turning to look along the rows of chairs. Nobody said anything.

"Lady Julnaw cra Widhis, you are the only Feeler among us. Meaning no disrespect to you, or insult to anyone else here, I have taken the liberty of asking three Feelers from other Houses to join us as witnesses. Statements will be made here today and we will need to be sure of their truth."

Julnaw frowned. "I would prefer to be trusted. However, there are several here who I haven't seen eye-to-eye with over the years. I must accept that my unconfirmed word is probably not sufficient for this important meeting. You'd better bring them in."

At a sign from Cuhes, Muhan went to a door and

admitted the three Feelers Cuhes had invited, all three from different Houses.

Cuhes struggled to her feet, saying, "Each of us will place a piece of paper with the name of our House's candidate into a bowl and say, for the benefit of the Feelers, that the nominee is someone from another House."

She hobbled across the room to drop a folded piece of paper into a large bronze and alabaster bowl on one of the side tables and said, "The person named on this paper is not a member of House Shuth."

The Feelers agreed she was telling the truth and she went back to her seat.

One-by-one the other Heads of House did likewise and the Feelers confirmed that they were telling the truth, each of the Feelers remaining silent when their own Head of House spoke.

"Thank you for your assistance," said Cuhes to the Feelers as they left, "it has been valuable."

Silence fell in the great hall as everyone cast speculative looks at the bowl.

"Let's get on with it," said Pevus when nobody made a move towards it. "Who's going to do the counting?"

"Go ahead, Pevus," said Sahnes cra Colnis, "since you're eager to know the result. Pick an assistant and get started."

"You'll do, Sahnes. You read the names, I'll sort and stack them."

Pevus cra Glinin was the first name read out. The next two names surprised many. One of them rarely got involved in politics; the other wasn't a Head of House. After them the voting went much as most had anticipated with Pevus cra Glinin and Muhan cra Neyen being named frequently and one other occasionally. With three still to read, Muhan was four votes ahead.

"That's it," said Pevus. "That's what I expected. I concede."

"Wait," called Therem cra Guesyr. "I agree Muhan has won but I would like to know by how much."

"If you insist," said Pevus. He riffled through the remaining papers. "All three are for Muhan."

"That's convincing enough for me," observed Therem. He turned to look at Muhan saying, "House Guesyr acknowledges you as the elected ruler. Do you wish to be known as 'Your Majesty' or do you prefer another title?"

"I hadn't thought about the ruler's title," said Muhan. "I don't like 'Your Majesty'." He looked at Cuhes and asked, "This was your idea. Do you have a title in mind?"

"I thought perhaps 'Leader' would do."

That suggestion produced a murmur of agreement. The other Heads of House followed Guesyr's example in acclaiming Leader Muhan, promising him their support and swearing to obey his decrees.

"I'm not sure if I should thank you or not," said Muhan as everyone settled back in their seats. "This is not going to be easy. I will need your assistance if I am to rule well. I confess the idea worries me. There is a difference between ruling a House and ruling a country. It's not just a matter of scale."

"Leader," asked the Leynik representative, "what do you propose we do about House Pridhar?"

"I haven't given the matter any serious thought because it never occurred to me that they would isolate themselves from the rest of the Families."

"House Leynik wishes to dissociate itself from the actions of the previous Head of House and his connection with Hulser cra Pridhar. The actions of House Pridhar are unacceptable. Accordingly, we would like to suggest that House Pridhar is disbanded. Any individual members who wish to swear allegiance to the Leader may do so and be adopted into any House that will accept them. Those who won't take an oath should be banished from the city. They hold enough land elsewhere they can go to."

Muhan looked around to see a majority of the Heads of House nodding in agreement with the Leynik proposal. "So be it," he said. "Now there is something else we have to discuss. There is a *purtirn* to deal with and I have an idea which will make many of you uncomfortable."

"We have sworn to be guided by you," said Pevus.

"This morning, before the meeting, I went to the top of the wall and looked over. I saw very few people and most of those I did see appeared to be ill and some were unmoving – probably dead. We must do something."

"There's nothing we can do except wait it out," Julnaw commented. "You know that. A *purtirn* happens every seven years or so. You must have lived through several of them."

"You're wrong, Julnaw, there *is* something we can do." Muhan went on to describe Anarya's idea of using talents to make the water safe.

A man in the black and silver of House Jerrut stood to say, "What's the point? They're just outers."

"They're people!" Muhan said. "Or don't you think of your servants as people? All of them come from the outer city. We should look after them, not ignore them and wait for them to die."

"But…"

"No buts, no equivocation. You agreed to be ruled by me. Well, this is the first thing I'm telling you to do. Disobey and you can join House Pridhar in exile."

Silence.

"Are you with me? Or was the election a farce after all?"

"House Colnis stands with you, Leader," said Sahnes. "There are many Aquamancers among us. We can purify the water if we can get to the source of contamination."

"Neyen can supply Scratchers to protect the Aquamancers," said Muhan.

"As can Shuth."

Once the first offer of assistance was made every House joined in, suggesting how different talents could be useful. Even Pevus admitted his Family's Whisperers would be able to help by keeping different groups in touch with each other.

"This is not going to be easy," said Muhan. "There are relatively few of us and the outer city is big. It will be tiring and will take time. But I feel it must be done."

JOTUK – THE OUTER CITY

Twelve people stepped through Derchler's Gate early the next morning followed by another six pulling a cart. They turned left and, rather cautiously, made their way along the street running parallel to the wall. It was deserted. At the first corner they found two bodies slumped in a doorway. A Lifter moved them on to the cart. A putrid smell accompanied the movement and many grimaced.

A Voyanter told them there were two more bodies on the next floor and another Lifter climbed the stairs to bring them down. They were a young woman and a child of about four. That discovery made the second Lifter, a Guesyr, feel ill. The child reminded him of his own daughter, who was about the same age. It became harder to argue against helping to cleanse the city. He realised that Muhan was right; these were people.

It was slow progress. The cart filled up many times and was taken back to the square at Derchler's Gate, the largest open space anywhere nearby. The bodies were stacked there and a Pyromancer burnt them to ashes.

It was mid-morning and a couple of hundred bodies had been disposed of before they discovered anybody alive. When they did, the three men they found were weak and barely able to move. Despite their condition they threatened the Feeler who had located them. It wasn't until they were given fresh water and bread that their attitude changed. Even then they were abusive and reluctant to accept that the working party were trying to help.

Other groups spread out in other directions into the outer city. Muhan accompanied one of them. That group found nobody alive until noon. Then a Feeler pointed out a doorway and told him there were a lot of people crammed into the building – and that they were healthy, although tired, hungry and thirsty.

"They know we're here and they're feeling aggressive," the Feeler noted. "I think they're getting ready to attack us."

Muhan used his talent to erect a shield around the door then pulled it open. Three knives bounced off the barrier.

"We want to help," said Muhan.

"Yeah, right!" called a loud voice from an upper floor window. "As if you ever helped before."

"Really, we do. We've started cleaning up the city but it'll take time. We want to keep as many of you alive as possible. We're surprised to find so many of you here. Have you got enough supplies?"

"No business of yours."

"I am Muhan cra Neyen…"

"Don't care who you are. Go away. I don't want to speak to you. I've got people to look after."

"Are you a member of a *houln*? I want to speak to the leader of one, I don't mind which."

Another voice called out, "Get rid of him, send him to Yarelk."

"Yarelk," said Muhan. "I've heard of him. Stone Grasshoppers, right?"

"If you want him, go down the hill, cross the south bridge. Second archway on the right and shout his name. Now get out of here."

Muhan followed the directions, leading his party to the courtyard beyond the second arch. The group's Feeler raised a hand and told him, "There's more than fifty people here and they're not friendly."

"Yarelk. Are you there?"

There was no response.

"Yarelk, I want to talk to you."

"But do I want to talk to you? Who are you anyway?"

"I'm Muhan cra Neyen. I'd like us to work together to save the city."

"What do you mean?"

"Help us find the sources of contamination and my

Aquamancers will purify the water and stop the infection."

"Why would you do that? You never have before."

"True, but there's been a change of policy. I've been elected Leader and that means I rule the inner city. I say this antagonism between the inner and outer cities has to stop."

"Why should I believe you?"

"I can't think of a good reason except that together we could save hundreds of lives, if not thousands."

There was a long pause during which Muhan could hear voices but they weren't loud enough for him to follow the conversation. He wished there was a Voyanter among his companions and resigned himself to waiting.

Eventually Yarelk said, "If you're willing to come with me I'll take you to the worst affected place."

"I'll come."

Yarelk stepped forward from a door at the back of the courtyard, followed by eight big men festooned with knives. "This way."

He led Muhan to the tanneries. They were deserted. "This is where the first deaths happened. I'm told they started soaking a new batch of hides day before yesterday. Don't know for sure but one of my people said they might have been infected. I'm told cows get Greenwater flux same as people."

Muhan looked at Sahnes cra Colnis and asked him, "What do you think?"

"Can't do it by myself. There's too much of it, but I'll give you an example of what can be done." He walked to the edge of one of the smaller pools, gazed into its murky depths and made a stirring gesture. Slowly the water in the pool started rotating. It got faster. The greenish colouration gradually moved out to the edges of the pool leaving clear water in the centre. The change slowly spread through the rest until it all looked completely clean.

He bent down, scooped some water into his hand and drank it.

Yarelk gasped.

"Got to prove I believe it's safe, don't I," said Sahnes. "Do you want to try it?"

Muhan followed Sahnes' example and turned to Yarelk. "Are you satisfied?"

Yarelk glanced at his escort and swallowed several times before dipping his hand in the water and licking it dry. "It tastes fine."

"I'm glad you approve," replied Sahnes. "I'll bring every Aquamancer I can find here tomorrow and together we'll deal with the rest."

"There's still a lot of work to do cleaning up the rest of the city," said Muhan, "But we can do it."

THE ROYAL PALACE
AND HOUSE NEYEN

"Are you there, Baram?" asked Sulereath. "Show yourself."

"Yes, Your Majesty," replied Baram, allowing himself to become visible. He was standing close to the king, between him and the two priests who had just been admitted to the king's study.

"I don't need protection from Rupesc and Grovaen so stay visible if there is nobody else here but them."

"Yes, Your Majesty," said Baram. He dipped his head, acknowledging the others and received similar nods in return.

"Please sit and make yourselves comfortable," said Sulereath, adding, "you too, Baram," when he remained standing.

Baram frowned. He took his duties as royal protector seriously; he didn't want to sit in case having to get up slowed his response to any threat. Not that Rupesc and Grovaen were a potential danger, but he didn't want to fall into bad habits.

"I am comfortable standing," he said.

"Do as you're told, Baram. Sit down."

"Yes, Your Majesty." He pulled a chair across the room until he could sit next to the king.

"What did you want to discuss, Your Reverence?"

"The news from Jotuk, Your Majesty. The Brotherhood is distressed by the death of Desern. Can Baram tell us what is happening there now?"

"Not really," said Baram. "You've heard how we can communicate through the wood stained with Caseir's blood. Well, it's not as clear as usual. Caseir seems to be busy with something. I can reach the others from time to time but never for long enough to get fully up to date."

"That's disappointing," Rupesc commented. "Do you think you could make enough contact to tell Anarya to collect you and take you to Jotuk?"

"Probably."

"We," said Rupesc, gesturing to include himself and Grovaen, "think that His Majesty is safe, at least for the moment. It is unlikely that anyone will be plotting against him with Latisec's execution as an example and deterrent."

"Why do you want me to go to Jotuk? If Anarya comes here she can give you all the news."

"It's not just the news we are interested in. We want you to go there as a bodyguard for the priests and priestesses who are there."

"There are a lot of powerfully talented people among the Families who will protect them," said Baram, "including some Stealthers. What difference can I make?"

"Two of them died despite that level of protection. It may be that you can't really add to it. However, with His Majesty's agreement, we would like you to try."

Sulereath nodded. "These are my subjects, Baram. I need to protect them as much as possible. So, whatever the odds against you making a significant difference are, I would like you to try."

Baram stood, bowed and said, "As you wish, Your Majesty."

Grovaen added, "Also, Baram, we want you to take Raifen to Jotuk. We need a member of the Brotherhood there to replace Desern."

"I'm sure Anarya will be willing to take him when she takes me."

O

"I need a bath," said Yisul. "I feel grubby after that. It was horrible."

"I wish I had been with you," said Anarya, "but Muhan wouldn't hear of it. He insisted it would be too dangerous for me to go into the outer city."

"I know," said Yisul. "I persuaded him that it would be better if you stayed here. I didn't want to risk you in the company of people who still believe in The God, or the Confined Ones. There are too many ways you could have an 'accident' out there."

"Yisa! I don't need looking after like a baby."

"You've been overprotective of me before so you can't grumble when it's my turn to look after you."

"Me, overprotective! What do you mean? I don't do that!"

"Yes, you do," said Yisul. "You didn't want me to go with you into the Darkworld because you were afraid for me."

"That was different."

"Was it? Be honest now. Was it really?"

"Well …"

"Never mind. I'm going to have a bath."

"Can I come and scrub your back?" Anarya asked in a small voice.

"I'd love that," replied Yisul with a smile. "It was awful out there. I didn't have to handle any bodies, just use my talent to find them but it got to me. Some of them were crowded into tiny spaces. I showed you something of the crowding in the outer city but I hadn't realised myself quite how bad it was. Squalid doesn't begin to describe it."

They moved from the reception room of Anarya's suite into the room with a sunken bath, stripped off and splashed happily into the water. The liberal use of verbena-scented soap on each other's backs quickly led to something more intimate.

"Wait!" gasped Anarya.

"What is it?" asked Yisul, rubbing her fingers over Anarya's nipples.

"I think Baram's trying to talk to me."

"Are you sure?" said Yisul. "I haven't heard from him for days."

"Baram? Is that you?"

"… me … come … Carregis … need … Jotuk."

"You want me to bring you to Jotuk?"

"… es."

"Fine. I'll get there soon."

"Anarya … hear."

"I caught some of that," said Yisul. "I wonder what he wants."

"Fragments are all I heard too. Why can't we hear him more clearly?"

"You know how different time can be in the Darkworld. Perhaps that's the problem."

"Could be. We'll find out what he wants when I go and fetch him."

"You're not going yet," said Yisul, nuzzling Anarya's neck and letting one hand fondle her breasts while the other slid down between her thighs. "He'll have to wait until we're done."

O

"Do you want to come to Carregis with me to fetch Baram?" asked Anarya.

Yisul nodded vigorously.

"We'll just be there long enough to find him and come back."

"I know, but I'm pleased you didn't try to exclude me."

"I'm not going to do that again."

"Thank you, my love."

Anarya tried to open the portal somewhere close to Baram. She found him alone, in surroundings she didn't recognise and was about to open the portal when somebody came into the room where he was. The man was a priest of Huler and she caught a glimpse of ornate statuary and hangings through the door he opened. She panicked and slammed the portal shut. *Holy Quarenna bless me, I almost walked into the temple!*

With her heart in her throat she told Yisul what had happened.

"Don't worry about it," said Yisul. "You stopped in

time. Now you know it's possible it just becomes something else to be careful about."

"But I could have killed you!"

"At least we would have been together," replied Yisul. "I wouldn't want to live if you were dead. That's why I want to be with you, so that whatever happens to you happens to me too."

Anarya wrapped her arms around Yisul and they stood there for about a twelfth making consoling noises to each other.

"What do we do now?" asked Anarya.

"Baram won't be in the temple forever. Why don't we go to Carregis and the arranged meeting point in Gatt Street?"

"Will he go there?"

"I'd think he would. Particularly if we both keep trying to talk to him through the wood and tell him that's where we're going."

"Hold my hand, Yisa. We're going to Carregis."

The portal opened in the familiar surroundings of Anarya's room. "Nothing odd happened to me this time," she said. "What about you?"

"No, nothing."

"Let's go to Gatt Street. I fancy one of those cakes."

O

"Well, Baram. What's so urgent that you need to go to Jotuk?"

"The king wants me there to help protect the teachers."

"What does the king think you can accomplish that the Families can't?" asked Yisul.

"He wants to feel he's doing something to protect his subjects. Will you take me, Anarya?"

"Yes, of course I will, although I don't know what good it will do."

"Will you also take Raifen? He's the replacement for Desern."

"Yes, he can come too. Where is he?"

"He's waiting in the temple. Stay here and I'll go get him."

Anarya and Yisul had time to finish their tea and cakes before Baram brought Raifen to meet them. They found a suitably quiet alley behind the temple where nobody could see them and Anarya opened the portal.

HOUSE NEYEN

In House Neyen once again, Anarya smiled to herself at the awed look on Raifen's face. Everyone seemed to react the same way to their first trip through the portal. She looked at the others and told them, "I got a message from Caseir as we came through."

"So did I," said Yisul.

"I didn't hear anything," Raifen sounded puzzled.

"You wouldn't," commented Anarya. "You don't have a piece of the wood where his spirit lives."

"I heard him," said Baram. "It was sort of broken up. I think he wants us to get as many of the pieces of wood together in the same place as we can."

"I got that too," agreed Yisul. "He didn't say why."

"I got a little more than that," said Anarya. "He wants to tell us what he's learned from the daimons. Where are all the bits of wood?"

"Let's see." Yisul started counting on her fingers. "You, Baram and I each have one; Tilua has another; and I think my father has the piece Desern had. The only other piece was the one Yarelk burned."

"That's them all accounted for," said Anarya. "Will you ask your father if we can get together after dinner?"

O

"Does anyone else want something to drink?" asked Yisul after dinner when they gathered in Anarya's suite.

Anarya took a glass of pomegranate liqueur, as did Tilua on her recommendation. Muhan and Raifen accepted wine. Lias and Baram settled for greenberry tea and Yisul poured a fragrant apple and mint cordial for herself.

"There isn't enough wood for everyone," said Anarya. "Lady Lias, will you share with Tilua? And Lord Muhan, you with Raifen?"

When they were all settled and touching wood, Anarya carried on to say, "Let me take the lead and ask the questions, at least at first." She looked around and saw everyone nodding.

"Caseir, can you hear me?"

"Yes, quite clearly."

"Good. We haven't been able to hear you at all well for the last few days. Is that because of the time difference?"

"Yes. The daimons seem to have been stretching time for me. Just as well because they can be difficult to understand, as Anarya can testify. Getting used to their way of speaking has been a slow process. They've wanted to tell me a lot and thought extra time would help. It's been about seventeen days for me."

"Seventeen! It's only been four here. Has it helped? Are you well?"

"Apart from being dead, you mean," said Caseir with a chuckle. "Yes, I'm all right. I've learned quite a bit about the way daimons think. Part of the problem is that they don't talk to each other as such, they use some different form of communication that I don't really understand. However, I've spoken to them enough that I have a pretty good idea of what they mean."

"So, do you know why they want you there in the Darkworld?"

"Yes, they're impressed with how stubborn I am. They need power and they can use my tenacity to augment their own strength."

"What do they need power for?"

"They're worried. That's why I wanted to talk to everyone, and you in particular, Anarya."

"Why me especially?"

"I think maybe I'd better start at the beginning. You'll understand better if I do that. By the way, everyone can ask questions. I can cope with that."

"We're listening," said Anarya.

"Hmm! Where, or rather when, is the beginning?" asked Caseir. "It's long, long ago. The daimons don't think in terms of years so I can't put a number on how long they've been around. I get the impression from them that it's almost as long as the world has been in existence. I've spoken to the oldest of them and it remembers its entry into the Darkworld when there was nothing there."

"What do you mean 'when there was nothing there'? That describes what it's like now. It's as empty as you could imagine," said Anarya.

Caseir disagreed, "It's not really. They see with a different sort of light. Don't ask me to explain it because I can't. Anyway, the oldest told me it was once one of many entities trying to establish themselves as powers in the world. It didn't succeed because two great gods combined forces and banished it, along with many others, into the Darkworld."

"Two great gods!" said Raifen. "Do you mean Huler and Quarenna?"

"I believe so," replied Caseir, "but the daimons never gave them names when they were talking to me."

"Who else could it be?" asked Tilua. "The story you're telling us fits with what the Inner Circle knows of the early history of the gods."

"You said 'many others'. How many daimons are there?" asked Baram.

"I don't know for sure. I've met about twenty and I got the impression there were at least twice as many I haven't met. Saying I saw them everywhere I looked doesn't make sense when talking of the Darkworld, but it does convey something of the way I feel about them now. I was a Daimoner when I was alive and I regarded them differently then. I didn't often use the talent but I sort of looked down on them for submitting so easily to my commands."

"And they've all been around since the beginning?" asked Baram.

"Yes."

"Amazing," said Raifen. "I have to admit I've never

been comfortable around Daimoners. I don't like the idea of powerful and dangerous entities like daimons being so close to us."

"They're not really that dangerous," said Caseir. "They live, if that's the right word, at peace with each other. The only thing they hate is being compelled to work for a Daimoner. That's why Anarya has been able to bargain with them. It's so unusual for anybody except a Daimoner to interact with them that they didn't know what to make of her and treated her almost as one of them."

"You mean they thought I was a daimon!"

"Not exactly. Just someone who was prepared to interact with them as they do with each other. They're great dealers, traders and negotiators."

Anarya shook her head in puzzlement. "I still don't understand them. If they're so powerful why are they subject to coercion by a Daimoner?"

"That's the next part of the story," said Caseir. "When the great gods had finished banishing the daimons there were still six other gods they couldn't get rid of."

"The Confined Ones?"

"Yes, Tilua, they became the Confined Gods. For a long time, probably hundreds of years if not thousands, there was an ongoing struggle between the two and the six. Neither group could gain the ascendancy until the great gods decided to take a risk. They gifted some of their worshippers with the powers we now call talents. Then they offered to release the daimons from the Darkworld if they would work with them and with the talented men and women to fight the six."

"I don't understand," said Raifen. "They formed an alliance to imprison the Confined Gods…"

"Yes."

"…and it was successful…"

"Yes."

"… but the daimons are still in the Darkworld. What happened?"

"The Confined Gods were trapped one at a time but the

gods reneged on their agreement about releasing the daimons from the Darkworld. Daimoners were supposed to be liaison between man and daimon but the gods gave them enough strength to dominate and compel daimons to do their will."

Tilua complained, "No! Holy Quarenna wouldn't do that."

"I'm afraid she did," said Caseir.

"Are you sure you're not just repeating what the daimons want you to believe?" asked Raifen.

"I don't think so. The daimon I spent most time with – the same one you've negotiated with, Anarya – told me that gods and daimons are related to each other and behave the same way. It admitted they would have cheated if they had had the power to do so."

Anarya shivered. "I don't understand. The one I spoke to won't change a bargain unilaterally. It's always tried to make agreements that are advantageous to it, but that's what bargaining is all about, and I was doing the same. The only time it's come close to deceiving me was when it wouldn't let me take the table out of the Darkworld. Even then the discussion we had was a sort of negotiation."

"That," said Caseir, "is because their response to being cheated by the gods was to make bargains sacrosanct. It's very difficult for them to even speak of breaking a promise. It was, probably, the hardest thing for me to understand about them."

Raifen shook his head saying, "I think they've been lying to you, Caseir. You know Huler won't tolerate an oathbreaker – think of the parable of the Deceitful Twins and how the Avenger punished them. He wouldn't break a promise, even one to a defeated enemy."

"Holy Quarenna despises untruths and broken promises," said Tilua. "The daimons aren't being honest with you, Caseir."

"All I can do is tell you what the daimons said. Give me a moment and I'll try to get one of them to repeat what they told me."

Everyone waited for Caseir to speak again. They looked at each other, seeing puzzled and worried looks on every face except those of Muhan and Lias.

"This is upsetting you, isn't it?" said Lias to Tilua.

"Yes, very much. It's so at odds with what we believe about Holy Quarenna. Truth and honesty are attributes we associate with her and her worship. What does it mean if the gods can lie to us?"

"It doesn't affect me so greatly," said Lias. "I admit it's surprising. However, I don't have the commitment to Quarenna that you do." She gestured at everyone sitting stunned into silence. "I'm going to be very prosaic and serve more refreshments while we wait for Caseir."

Some waved Lias away when she offered more drinks, others accepted refills or, in the case of Raifen and Baram, a stronger drink in the shape of a glass of brandy.

"Can everyone hear me?" asked Caseir and they all quickly made sure they were touching one of the shards of wood.

"I've just spoken to one of the daimons. It's here, ready to answer questions. It can't speak to you directly but I will pass on whatever it says. I hope all of you are happy with that."

There was a mutter of agreement, then Caseir spoke again, "I asked about truth and the gods and this is what it told me, '*World is. Truth is. Human lies trivial, god lies risk truth of world. Did once, never more. Dangerous.*' I know it's not easy to follow but it sounds to me as if the gods can't tell lies now because doing so would endanger the world."

"I'd say your interpretation sounds about right," said Tilua.

"Yes," agreed Raifen, "and I must say I'm relieved. The idea that the gods have lied to us is frightening…"

"Not just frightening, horrifying," Tilua admitted. "It undermines all we think we know."

"But," said Raifen, "although they may have lied once, now they are as honest as we've always believed."

"Yes. Thinking about it gives me shivers, but it was the

daimons they lied to, not us. I think I can accept that, more or less – although it's going to take some time to assimilate."

"All of this is very interesting," Muhan observed, "however, it doesn't explain why the daimons are worried."

"Or," said Anarya, "why you wanted me in particular to hear it."

"I haven't got there yet, Anarya. Be patient. I've got a bit more to say before we do."

"Get on with it then. You're starting to worry me."

"Right. The daimons have always been aware of the Confined Gods. Their prison isn't actually part of the Darkworld although it does seem to be linked to it in some way." Caseir paused briefly. "The important thing is that there aren't six of them any more."

"One of them's escaped!" gasped Raifen, signing himself with the thunderbolt.

"No. At least not yet." Caseir continued talking over the exclamations of shock and horror from his audience. "The weakest of them gradually got weaker over the years until she became prey for the strongest. That started a struggle for survival among the others. It's got to the stage where there is now only one left, and he has absorbed all the residual strength of the other five. He's trying to escape and has enough power that he would probably make it if the daimons weren't resisting his efforts. That's why they wanted the additional power my stubbornness provided."

"What about Huler and Quarenna? They won't want him free."

"I'm sure they don't. It took a combination of daimons, talented and gods to imprison the Confined Ones in the first place. The daimons think it will take the same again to deal with the power Kehsieh has accumulated."

"Kehsieh!"

"Yes. I didn't know when I used his name that I was impersonating the last of the Confined Gods"

"Could using his name be considered a form of

worship," wondered Raifen. "Did saying it give him a little bit of extra power?"

"Honestly, I have no idea."

"What can we do?" asked Anarya.

"I think it's not so much 'we' as 'you', Anarya. The daimons are puzzled by your reluctance to be what they call a Gatherer."

"They've called me that several times."

The daimon who's here has just told me, '*Must Gather. Gatherer collect all powers. Link we. Link gods. Fight. Must fight.*' It's not the first time one of them has said something similar to me. If I understand them correctly, they want you to use your talent to collect every other talent. Then you can link with the daimons and use all the talents combined as a weapon against Kehsieh."

"I can't do that. All the talents at once! It's impossible. I've never been able to hold more than two borrowed talents at the same time."

"Forgive me, Anarya," said Tilua. "I think it's time to let everyone know your secret. It might make a difference."

"Do you think so?" asked Anarya in a voice that was close to tears.

"I do."

Anarya swallowed a few times then, holding on to Yisul's arm, said, "Some of you know this already. I hope those who don't will pardon me for concealing the truth." She paused to look at Lias and Muhan and took another deep breath. "I told you I was a Sponger – and that was true, I was. The thing is, my battle with The God burnt out my talent. It left me a Thiever like him because I used his own talent against him and was left holding it when Muhan killed him."

Anarya paused and Tilua filled the silence, saying, "Whenever she isn't holding another talent she has a deep need, almost amounting to a compulsion, to Thieve one. With a couple of exceptions when she was learning about being a Thiever she has only done so in controlled circumstances."

"So that's why you're always wrapped up in a glyph," Muhan nodded slowly. "I had wondered."

"It never occurred to me that you would notice that," said Anarya.

"I can see it quite easily," replied Muhan, "I can't identify the glyph without seeing it being cast but I can tell it's there. I've assumed it was the treatment you once told us you needed."

Tilua asked, "I don't think you've ever tried to hold more than one talent at a time since you became a Thiever, have you?"

"I haven't."

"Now's your chance. There are two Voyanters, a Scratcher, a Stealther and a Feeler here as well as another Sponger. Thieve them. Find out how many you can hold and for how long."

Anarya looked at the faces watching her. "Are you sure? Yisul and Baram know what it feels like to have your talent Thieved. Ask them about it. I don't want to take from anybody who is unwilling."

Yisul and Baram described the shock of losing their talents and the empty, powerless sensation that accompanied the loss. "It's an awful feeling," said Yisul. "Despite that, I am willing to have Anarya take my talent. I don't know how she can stand feeling empty all the time, even with a glyph to help her withstand the void."

"I confess I don't like the idea," admitted Raifen, looking around and catching everyone's eyes, "However, the idea of an unconfined deity taking vengeance on us and our gods – well, it's terrifying. We have to do what we can to help." He looked straight at Anarya and said, "You may take my talent."

Anarya thumbed her forehead and said, "Holy Quarenna aid me," before taking the least familiar of the available talents first. She saw a green stain travelling along the thread linking her aura to Raifen's. When it reached her she felt a quiet confidence, much like the sensation she had experienced on the rare occasions she had borrowed a Feeler's ability before. It had never been a particularly good skill for her as a Sponger, but now it fitted her well and felt comfortable.

Raifen shuddered and seemed to collapse on himself, looking much less of the commanding figure he usually presented himself as. "How long will this last?" he asked.

"I don't know," said Anarya. "I was never a strong Feeler when I borrowed that skill as a Sponger. I could hold it for about a chime, but there doesn't seem to be any correlation between what I could do before and what I can do now."

Who next? I don't think I want to take Tilua's talent. It'll remind me too much of what I've lost.

She looked at Yisul and became a Voyanter. It felt different to her previous experience of holding two talents. Then they had stayed separate, now they sort of wrapped around each other to form something new.

"Thats odd," she said, reporting the new sensation.

"It sounds promising," said Tilua. "That matches what I can see in your aura. I wonder… Try using them both at the same time."

Anarya did what Tilua suggested. It was easy enough to use either of them, much as she had handled two talents in the past. Using both together was difficult. Then she had a momentary glimpse of herself seen through Tilua's eyes. Her aura was a swirling mix of black, green and orange with the colours blending slightly into each other. The vision was brief. When it disappeared, she had double vision for a moment.

"How do you feel?" asked Tilua.

"I can cope with this," said Anarya. "It's a combination I could never have held before. Let's see what happens if I add a third." She reached out to Baram's brown aura. When she made contact it felt wrong. Instead of the colour flowing towards her spontaneously she felt she had to pull it across the gap. The third talent seemed to surround the others. She didn't invoke the Stealther's ability but her vision dimmed as if she had. Seeing the way the others reacted she realised she had become invisible without meaning to.

She gasped from the impact of a sudden headache. Flashing lights obscured her sight, she felt she was about to vomit, then everything went dark.

"Anra, my love, wake up. Please wake up."

Yisul's plea brought Anarya back to consciousness. She was lying on the floor, her head cradled in Yisul's lap. Tears were dripping on to her face.

"What?"

"You vanished. Then you reappeared, unconscious," said Tilua. "I think you lost all the Thieved talents at once."

"I have mine back," Raifen stated."

"So do I," said Baram, "and much too soon if what happened before is anything to go by."

Anarya struggled to sit up. Gratefully, she took several gulps of the water Lias provided. "It didn't work. I remember The God holding five talents at once during the battle I had with him but I can't even hold three. That's a long way from all thirteen. What are we to do?"

"I've no idea," said Tilua in a dispirited voice.

Caseir broke in saying, "Wait a moment. You can't just give up."

"There speaks the Unconquered," Baram muttered. Then he had to explain Caseir's arena nickname to a puzzled Muhan and Lias.

"He's right," said Tilua and Raifen at almost the same moment.

"There must be something we can do," Tilua continued. "Caseir, have the daimons anything to suggest?"

"I'll ask."

With Caseir's attention elsewhere, Anarya got to her feet, walked around for a bit then sat next to Yisul. She took a glass of stargrass tea and let the warm, fragrant, peppery brew ease the tension in her chest. She did her best to describe what she had felt, with little success. Only Tilua had any experience of holding two talents at the same time and she had never tried using them both at once.

People sharing a piece of wood scrambled to make

contact with it when Baram announced Caseir's return.

"Well?" asked Tilua.

"The daimon told me, '*Gatherer must Gather. Sequence. Do right, Gatherer hold. Do wrong dangerous.*'"

"We know it's dangerous," Yisul said. "What does it mean 'sequence'?"

"I won't quote it direct any more. It would take too long. It played with time again and it's taken me about five chimes to understand as much as I think I do."

"Five chimes! It's only been about a third for us," said Raifen. "Oh, sorry, Caseir, I shouldn't interrupt. Stretching time is one of the weirdest things we've heard today."

"That's all right. It gets to me too. Anyway, assuming I'm interpreting it right, I think it means that the Gatherer has to collect the talents in the correct order for them to fit and work together."

"So what's the right order?"

"It doesn't know. It remembers once seeing a Gatherer use the combined talents during the war against the six gods. Unfortunately, it couldn't describe exactly what she did. All I managed to get out of it was that she built a basic foundation; added what it described as senses; then weapons; and finished binding it all together with the ability to interact with the daimons. Unfortunately, it's not clear about which talent falls into which category."

"I can guess part of it," said Anarya. "I saw out of Tilua's eyes for a moment when I combined Feeler and Voyanter. They must be the 'senses'."

"Some of them at least," agreed Tilua. "I'd imagine Whisperer might be a sense too."

"Could be. And maybe Seeker as well."

"I'll have to try again," said Anarya.

Yisul objected, "No, you can't. The daimon told Caseir the wrong sequence is dangerous."

"I have to, you know that, Yisa. The possible threat from Kehsieh is too great."

"Best not to say his name in case we are giving him

strength by doing so," said Tilua. "I'm very much afraid you're right about needing to try again."

"But not right now." Anarya shuddered. "Not that I could anyway. My head's still throbbing from that last attempt. I'll take it cautiously, one step at a time, and I won't add another until I'm certain what I'm doing is right."

"We will need to let more people into your secret," Tilua commented. "We don't have all the talents between us and you're going to need them all." She looked around the serious faces and added, "Based on what we've heard everybody needs to think about what the right order might be."

"I don't think we need all the talents available immediately," said Anarya. "Let's get the 'basic foundation' sorted out first. That's got to be earth, air, fire and water, doesn't it?"

"I'd think so," agreed Raifen. "I also think you're going to need the strongest possible talents."

"We do have a very strong Terromancer," said Tilua. "Trenyas showed just how strong she is after the ambush."

"Ilhas, the Head of House Dunish, is a powerful Pyromancer," offered Muhan, "and I think she could tolerate hearing the truth about Anarya's talent – as could Sahnes cra Colnis who is a very strong Aquamancer."

Raifen wanted to know if Anarya could take him back to Carregis, saying, " I can recruit a very good Aeromancer from among the Brotherhood. And there's a particularly strong Seeker as well. I'm sure they would be willing to come."

"First thing tomorrow," said Anarya. "I've got too much of a headache to do it now."

THE GREAT SQUARE
AND THE TEMPLE OF HULER

The portal opened into the alley behind the temple of Huler. Anarya, Baram and Raifen stepped through and looked around; Anarya wasn't surprised to see it was deserted. Before opening the portal she had previewed the destination to make sure there was nobody there to witness their arrival.

"Gatt Street, fourteenth chime?" she asked.

"That should give me enough time," Raifen agreed as he turned out of the alley into the Great Square and headed towards one of the side entrances to the temple.

"I thought you'd go with him," said Anarya when Baram didn't follow him.

"No, he doesn't need me. He knows as much as I do about the daimons, the last of the Confined Gods and what we need. Also, he's got much more influence with the Brotherhood than I'm ever likely to have. What are you going to do?"

"I think I'll take a look at the stalls then take a trip to the top of the Rock. It's a lovely day and the view downriver should be good. Want to come?"

They set out into the bustle of the square but didn't get far before a junior priest caught up with them and told Baram that Raifen wanted him.

"Oh, well," he said, turning back towards the temple. "I guess I was wrong. Enjoy your day."

Anarya continued on by herself, stopping at various stalls whenever she saw something interesting. *Must buy something for Yisa to make up for not bringing her with me today. I wonder what she'd like? Something simple, I think. It's not as if she needs jewellery or clothes.*

She remembered Yisa's first visit to the square at the Arenafest and her comment about liking candy, so she headed towards the southwest corner where the candymaker was usually to be found.

He was there and, as always, had a delicious looking display of various toffees and flavoured gelatine sweetmeats. *Aniseed for Yisa, obviously, and what else? Rose? Lemon? Mint? I've never seen anything like this in Jotuk, so maybe some for Lias and Muhan too.* When she left the stall, she had spent four and a half bits on a selection of mixed sweets to take back to Jotuk. It made a rather clumsy package. She stopped at another stall to buy a pretty bag with multicoloured beads sewn all over it in a spiral pattern; it held her purchases with ease. She slung it over her shoulder and headed for the Rock. On the way she passed close to the shrine of Quarenna. She didn't expect there to be a message waiting for her but, more out of habit than anything, she detoured to speak to the warden.

She was surprised to find a message addressed to her asking her to deliver the letter enclosed with it to Tilua. She tucked it into her bag.

O

Baram couldn't help wondering why Raifen needed him as he followed the messenger into the temple. He was taken to the Brotherhood's meeting room where Rupesc welcomed him. "Raifen has asked for your presence. He says he wants to make sure he doesn't forget anything and asks you to fill in anything he leaves out. Please, make yourself comfortable."

Baram signed himself with the lightning bolt before taking the seat he had used before, in front of the image of the Avenger.

He sat quietly while Raifen told the Brotherhood about the threat from the last of the Confined Gods and finished by saying, "I'm certain Anarya will need the help of the strongest talents we can find. That's why I hope Druciel and Jimoth will be willing to come to Jotuk and help."

Two of the Brotherhood nodded vigorously. "We will

come, of course," said one of them.

"Have you anything to add, Baram?"

"No, Your Reverences. I can't think of anything."

"I don't disbelieve anything you have told us, Raifen," said Rupesc "I am sure you have reported accurately. However, I would rather we had a direct source of information. Now that we know it is possible for a Daimoner to negotiate with daimons, rather than command them, I would like to have one talk to them about this situation. We might learn more rather than hearing what they say second hand."

Baram interrupted saying, "Your pardon, Your Reverence. I'm not sure if that's possible. The daimons will talk to Caseir because they have already been revenged on him, and he isn't a Daimoner any more so he can't command them. I think they might want to punish, rather than talk to, any other Daimoner."

Rupesc frowned. "You may be right. We can't ask anyone to take that risk. Thank you, Baram. You have saved us from a grave error."

HOUSE NEYEN

On her way through the portal Anarya felt a slight hesitation in the usual rush of movement. A daimon's voice told her, {*Must Gather*}, and movement resumed.

The portal opened in the wing of House Neyen now dedicated to housing the priests and priestesses who had come to Jotuk as teachers. She gave the letter addressed to Tilua to a servant, asked him to deliver it and took the two members of the Brotherhood to meet Muhan.

Leaving them with him she went to her suite looking for Yisul.

"I'm glad you're back," said Yisul. "I missed you."

"You're not angry that I couldn't take you with me today?"

"No, I'm not angry, Anra my love. I admit I'm disappointed I couldn't come, but I'm sure you'll be safer with strong talents to take and that's more important than a temporary separation. You can only bring a few people at a time through the portal and you didn't know how many you would have to move."

"Good. I've got something for you." She rummaged in the bag and gave Yisul the aniseed toffee. "Perhaps this will make up for not being with me."

"It doesn't, but it does help a bit," Yisul replied.

Moments later Anarya had to apologise for laughing at the faces Yisul made trying to unstick her teeth from the very chewy toffee.

O

"Are you sure you're ready to try again?" asked Tilua.

"Yes," replied Anarya. "I've been thinking about it a lot. It's occurred to me that whenever anyone names the elements they're always mentioned in the same order; earth, air, fire and water. Do you suppose that's because it's a memory of how to construct the 'basic foundation'?"

"I suppose it's possible."

"It's the only clue we have so I'll try that order." Anarya looked at Trenyas, said, "You first," and reached towards her violet aura. The sensation that accompanied Terromancy was one of solidity, security and strength. It felt right.

Anarya said, "Now Aeromancy," as she reached for Druciel's white aura. She wondered if the order was wrong because the feeling that came with the talent at first was one of constant change. Then the two talents merged and she felt firmly anchored, as if she was leaning into a strong wind with a firm support behind her.

"How do you feel?" asked Tilua.

"Good. Yes, good so far. I'm ready for fire."

The purple aura of Ilhas cra Dunish blazed with power as Anarya reached for it. It was the brightest Pyromancer's aura she had ever seen. The warmth and comfort of fire greeted her, but the structure she was building felt unstable. There was an awareness of possible danger. She decided she had had better add the Aquamancer's ability quickly and reached out to Sahnes cra Colnis.

The last of the elements brought a mixture of quiet, calm contemplation and strength with its pale blue aura, producing a feeling of restrained power that merged with and modified the threat from fire.

Anarya got the impression that all four talents shifted, wriggled a bit and fitted around and through each other to combine into a strong, secure platform for her.

"It's worked," she said. "This feels like a good foundation. I think I'm ready to move on. Where do I go from here?"

Perhaps one of the 'senses'," offered Tilua. "The question is which one?"

Muhan suggested Voyanter, saying, "The Gatherer has

got to be able to see at a distance to know where to direct the combined power."

"Sounds reasonable."

Yisul's familiar orange aura attracted Anarya. "I'll try that," she said, but as soon as she touched it she knew it was wrong. Blinded by multicoloured lights, she closed her eyes, but the lights were behind her eyelids. She was deafened by a roaring noise that seemed to come from everywhere. Her head throbbed in time with her pulse. She vomited, fell forward from her chair and felt her head hit something. Then everything went black.

○

Anarya woke slowly, feeling comfortable. *I'm in bed. How did I get here?* Then she remembered what had happened and sat up.

"Rest," Yisul told her. "You must rest. Give yourself time to recover."

"I'm fine," said Anarya. "What happened? Did I faint?"

"It was more dramatic than that. You were shaking as if in a fever. You've been unconscious for almost ten chimes and you have a lump on your head the size of a pigeon's egg."

"I feel fine. Let me up."

"Are you sure?"

"Yes! Apart from still being a Thiever not a Sponger, I'm fine."

"Well, at least have something to eat before you get up."

"All right, if that'll keep you happy. I'll have a piece of toffee."

"Anra! I meant proper food."

"Don't be so serious."

Two chimes later Anarya was polishing off a bowl of syllabub, the last of the three course meal Yisul had insisted she eat, when there was the sound of running footsteps in the corridor.

Tilua burst into the room waving a piece of parchment.

"We've got to go back to Carregis," she gasped. "Can you take me? I heard you've recovered. Are you well enough? It's important. That stupid servant didn't give me the letter you brought until now."

"Why? What's wrong?"

"It's Nuasi. She's dying…"

"Oh, no!"

"… and she wants to see us. Hurry!"

"But we can't go. Not right now. I can't open the portal. I've used all the transits the daimon will allow until tomorrow afternoon."

"Oh!"

"I'm so sorry, Tilua. There's nothing I can do about it."

Tilua crumpled into one of the chairs and started crying. "I've known Nuasi for almost fifty years," she said between sobs. "We've been friends all that time and she was so good to me helping me master my talent. I must see her before she dies, I must."

Yisul stood for a moment with her hand to her mouth, then she said, "I have only met Nuasi once but she struck me as being strong-minded."

"You have no idea how strong."

"Well, if she wants to see you isn't she going to hang on until you can get there?"

"Holy Quarenna's mercy!" said Tilua. "You're right. She'll try, at least."

"We'll go as soon as I can use the portal. That'll be shortly after the twelfth chime tomorrow. With Holy Quarenna's blessing we will be in time."

THE SHRINE OF QUARENNA

Anarya tried to visualise Tilua's study but the image of her destination was blurred and poorly defined.

"We're too early," she said. "I'll keep trying so we can go as soon as possible."

A sixth passed, then another, and another. Still the portal wouldn't open. Anarya was fidgeting with impatience.

"Calm down," Tilua told her.

"How can you stay so relaxed when you know every fraction of a chime might be important?"

"I'm a lot older than you, and I've learned to be patient when there's no alternative. If Holy Quarenna wants me to see Nuasi before she dies then we'll get there in time."

Anarya shook her head, wishing she could achieve that kind of serene acceptance. She tried again to see where she wanted to go. The image was there. Not quite clear; the edges were wavering slightly. *Almost – Just a little bit clearer – There – At last!*

"We can go now," she said to Tilua and Kemeneah. "Take my hand."

As soon as her foot hit the floor of her study Tilua was running for the door. She yanked it open, turned left into the rectangular courtyard and hurried down the long side to the next corner, turned left again into a short passage leading to a closed door and paused for a moment to catch her breath.

Anarya rushed after her, barely noticing the lily pond in the middle of the courtyard, the gentle sounds of wind chimes or the fragrances of the flowers surrounding the water.

Tilua eased the door open, entered and went to her knees next to a chair where Nuasi was sleeping propped up on a pile of cushions. She looked quizzically at Belari who was the only other person in the room.

"Is she… "

"She still lives," said Belari, her accent as thick as ever. "Got her wrapped in a pain-cancelling glyph t' let her sleep comfortably."

"Good."

"She's been in lot of pain for last four days but it's only in last day she's accepted relief ah can give her. She's so stubborn at times."

"Don't I know it," agreed Tilua. "Can I waken her without causing her pain?"

"Yes. Glyph be effective for 'bout 'nother half."

Tilua thumbed her forehead then reached out to take Nuasi's hand.

Nuasi opened her eyes and said, "It's about time you got here."

"I'm sorry."

"Don't be. I didn't give you any warning. I should have. I've known I'm dying for three or four months now."

"Why didn't you say anything?"

"What good would that have done? You'd just have worried and I'm far beyond any help you could give."

"Tell me now," said Tilua.

"I've got a lump in my stomach that's gnawing my guts. My joints have been bad for years but the bones themselves were fine until six or seven days ago. Now they're sore too. I'm sure the tumour has spread to involve them. I can't walk more than a couple of steps without having to stop, afraid that my left leg is going to break under me. I've seen people in this state before, and I'm sure you have too."

Tilua nodded and wiped tears from her eyes.

"I've lost my appetite in the last few days and if I do force myself to eat I'm likely to vomit it all up again. You know as well as I do that means the end is near. I don't expect to last more than another two or three days."

"I do know," confirmed Tilua, "I don't like it but I have to accept it. We'll do everything we can to keep you comfortable."

"I know you will. Don't cry for me. By Holy Quarenna's grace I've lived eighty-three years. They've been good and I have few regrets. There's really only one thing I still have to do."

"What's that?"

"Where's Anarya? Did you bring her?"

Anarya stepped forward and knelt next to Tilua. "I'm here."

"Good," sighed Nuasi. "I want you to do something for me."

"Anything."

"You won't like it, but I don't want an argument. What I want you to do is take my talent."

"But... "

"I said I'm not going to argue about it. Just listen to me. Being a Thiever lets you hold on to a stolen talent after the original holder is dead. Am I right?"

"Yes."

"And you know what I mean by some talents being a better fit for you than others."

Anarya nodded.

"Well, there couldn't be a better fit for you than Sponger, it's your native ability. Take my talent just before I die. I hope it will fit so well you'll be able to keep it for the rest of your life."

Anarya sat stunned into silence.

"Obviously," said Nuasi, "I can't be certain because it's something that's never come up before, but it does make sense."

Anarya couldn't think of anything to say and turned to Tilua for help.

"You're right, Nuasi," Tilua agreed. "It does make sense, but I don't think I would ever have thought of it myself. Offering to give away something that's so much part of you is incredibly generous."

"I won't need it anymore and she deserves it after what she's done, getting rid of The God, and handling her new situation so well."

"Oh, I'm not arguing against it," said Tilua. "I can see

one problem. We don't know how long she can be a Sponger while you're alive. It would be terrible if she lost it just before you die and didn't have time to take it again."

"I don't think you need worry about that," said Nuasi. "I've spoken to Kemeneah about what she feels when Anarya takes her talent. She says losing it is always a sudden shock even although it's happened many times and she knows what to expect."

"Other people I've Thieved from have said it's a shock too," commented Anarya.

"If you wait until I'm very weak the shock might be enough to kill me."

"I don't want to kill you."

"A merciful death can be a blessing," said Nuasi. "You won't begrudge me that if a Feeler tells you that's what I want, will you? You did say you'd do anything for me."

"Yes, but…"

Tilua sent for another member of the Inner Circle who used her Feeler ability to confirm that it's what Nuasi really wanted.

Anarya looked away from Nuasi with tears in her eyes, and some hope in her heart.

O

Anarya took over the care of Nuasi, helping her every way she could. As Nuasi found the chair more comfortable than continual movement into and out of bed she stayed there while Anarya used the bed to stay near her.

Two days passed, then Anarya couldn't rouse Nuasi. Tilua summoned other members of the Inner Circle. Together they watched Nuasi's breathing get shallower and irregular. Tilua kissed Nuasi's forehead and nodded to Anarya.

She reached out to Nuasi's aura and saw the shimmering rainbow flood back along the black thread of her own Thiever's aura. The sensation of being in two bodies at once was even stronger than usual. It let her feel Nuasi's strength of will and her calm, peaceful acceptance. Then she was back in her own body. The Sponger ability from Nuasi was subtly different from what her own had felt like. However, there was no doubt it was real and she relished the almost familiar feeling. She bent to kiss Nuasi, took Tilua's hand and waited. It didn't take long. Within a couple of breaths, they recognised the moment when Nuasi's spirit left the body she no longer needed.

They invoked Quarenna's blessing on her and burst into tears.

About a chime later, when their emotional reaction to Nuasi's death had settled a bit and the Inner Circle had dispersed to make arrangements for the funeral, Tilua said, "I can see you're a Sponger again but your aura is strange."

"What's wrong with it?"

"I don't know I'd call it wrong, just different. You still have the Thiever talent so I'm not surprised to see black as well as the rainbow in your aura. It flickers. Sometimes the black surrounds the colours and sometimes it's the other way round."

"What do you suppose it means?"

"Probably that you can be either a Sponger or a Thiever. The only way to find out is to try it. When are you going to see Kemeneah to take her talent again?

"I don't need to. The hunger has gone."

"When would you be seeing her again if you had to?"

"Oh, I see what you mean. I'll take her talent as a Sponger, not as a Thiever and we'll see what happens."

"Exactly."

O

Anarya found Kemeneah and Belari together.

"How much longer is this going to go on?" asked Belari, her accent so much thicker than usual that Anarya had trouble understanding her. "It's affecting Kemeneah."

Anarya looked more closely at the girl than she had for

a long time. She had got used to just taking her talent without saying much to her. She was shocked to see sunken eyes looking back at her from a face that had become thin and pale. "I'm sorry," she mumbled, "I hadn't realised what depriving you of your talent so often was doing to you. I was selfish and didn't stop to think what effect it was having. Please, can you forgive me?"

Kemeneah produced a wan smile and said, "I can manage. I told you before that I consider helping you a duty, and I meant it. Belari worries too much."

"No," said Anarya, "I don't think she does. Have you looked in a mirror recently?"

"It doesn't matter."

"Yes, it does," said Belari. "Ah'm your tutor, ah've got to look after you. Going to tell Tilua this must stop."

"I agree," said Anarya. "It's not good for your health." She paused before saying, "There is something new I want to try. If you will allow me to take your talent one last time I swear by Holy Quarenna it *will* be the last."

Belari scowled when Kemeneah said, "Of course I will allow it."

"Quarenna bless you," said Anarya. She reached out to Kemeneah's aura. The thread she saw was a rainbow wrapped around a black core. *Is that right? I don't want the black.* She stopped before making contact and started again. This time the black encapsulated the rainbow which was muted. She stopped again. *I guess I've got to have both, but which way round?* She decided the configuration with the brightest colours was the one she wanted and used it. As always she felt resilience and serenity from Kemeneah when she made contact. She withdrew the thread and had the familiar feeling of being a Scratcher again. A glance with the Oversight was enough to tell her she had got it right, Kemeneah still had her talent.

"It worked," she said, producing a small globe of light hovering in the air in front of her.

"How?" asked Kemeneah. "You haven't taken my talent. I've still got it. See." She produced another ball of light to match Anarya's.

Anarya explained what had happened when Nuasi died and added, "I used both Thiever and Sponger in borrowing your talent just now. Since the original holders of both are dead I should be able to keep them. Unless I lose the Sponger ability again for some reason I'll never have to worry about the hunger again. It's gone."

Holy Quarenna be praised," said Belari.

Kemeneah smiled, her pale face lighting up. "Do you think I might ask Blessèd Tilua a question?"

"She's always willing to answer questions," said Anarya. "Let's go find her. I expect she'll be in her study."

She was; and she welcomed Anarya and Kemeneah with the offer of tea, which they declined. "What is it you want?"

"I realised some time ago," said Kemeneah, "that I didn't need to keep letting Anarya Thieve my talent so that she could create the glyph. I could have learned it myself and cast it whenever it was needed."

Anarya gasped. "I'm stupid!" she said. "That never occurred to me!"

Tilua lowered her head and said, in a quiet voice, "And you want to know why we didn't do it that way."

"Not exactly. I assume that it was to keep Anarya involved and feeling that she was contributing to the cure. I would just like to know if I'm right."

"You are, and you deserve an apology from me for putting you through all that stress. Perhaps it wasn't necessary, but it was good for Anarya – and for your progress. That insight confirms the opinion of the Inner Circle that you are someone to watch as a prospective future member."

"Oh!" Kemeneah's hand went to her mouth and she blushed.

Anarya laughed in delight and thanked her again for all she had done.

HOUSE NEYEN

The reception room of Anarya's suite was, once again, where she would try to Gather the talents. People straggled into the room in ones and twos at about the tenth chime, helped themselves to drinks and settled down to wait. Extra chairs had been brought in to the room to accommodate them all.

"Are you sure you're ready to try again?" Muhan's question expressed the concern most of them had.

"Oh, yes," replied Anarya, "very much ready. I feel wonderful."

"It's good to see you so cheerful," said Raifen.

"I have reason to be." She went on to tell those who didn't already know what had happened about taking Nuasi's talent. "Thanks to Quarenna's grace and the goodness of Blessèd Nuasi, I'm a Sponger again. I don't have to worry about the empty feeling, or about Thieving someone else's talent. Shall we begin?"

"Just a moment, Anarya," said Tilua. "I can see you're holding a Scratcher's talent. You'll have to wait for it to fade before starting to make the foundation or it will be out of place and we've been told that could be dangerous."

Anarya frowned. "I don't understand. I had forgotten about it. I can usually be a Scratcher for three or four chimes. I borrowed it from Kemeneah yesterday and it should have faded long ago."

"How, in Quarenna's name, can you forget what talent you're holding?" asked Tilua.

Anarya shrugged. "I don't know. I can tell it's there now that I look for it but, otherwise, I'm no more aware of it than of being a Sponger. What I don't understand is how I can still be holding it after all this time."

"Did you use the Thiever talent to take it?"

"No – not exactly – but it was bound up with Sponger and I couldn't use either alone."

"Hmm, I wonder," muttered Tilua. "Can you let go of the Scratcher talent?"

How do I do that? She concentrated, finding it as difficult as ever to see her own aura. The yellow of a Scratcher in it looked particularly bright. She imagined picking that up and dropping it. There was a bright flash in the Oversight and she blinked.

"Oh dear," said Tilua.

"What's wrong?"

"You didn't just drop the Scratcher's talent, you've removed all the yellow from your aura completely."

"I don't feel any different."

Muhan said, "Pardon me. Am I right in thinking yellow is the colour of a Scratcher's aura?"

"Yes."

"Then why don't you try to take mine and use it to replace the missing yellow?"

Anarya asked, "What do you think, Blessèd Tilua?"

"You know as much as I do about it," Tilua replied. "It's probably worth a try. With one colour missing you don't have a full Sponger's aura anymore but you still have the Thiever's talent so you should be able to use that to take Muhan's."

"Are you sure you want to try?" Anarya asked Muhan. "You might end up talentless."

"If it repairs your aura and lets you do the Gathering then it will be worth it. Go ahead. Do it."

Anarya tried to visualise a multi-coloured thread with a black core connecting her aura to Muhan's. She couldn't. She tried again, and again. Every time the thread was black wrapped around the colours, with yellow conspicuously absent. After several attempts, she let it make contact and the yellow of Muhan's aura flooded back along the thread to replace the missing colour in the rainbow. "That feels good. How does my aura look, Tilua?"

"Normal, again."

"I felt it," said Muhan. "I felt the emptiness you described for a few moments. It didn't last long, thank Huler, and I've still got my talent."

Tilua remarked, "But your aura isn't as bright as it was, Muhan. I think you've lost some strength. It might be a permanent loss."

"That's not important. How do you feel, Anarya?"

"Fine. I'm ready to try Gathering again."

She settled back in her chair, borrowed the skills of Terromancy, Aeromancy, Pyromancy and Aquamancy in quick succession and felt them settle into a strong foundation as they had before.

"That went quickly," remarked Tilua.

"I already knew what's right so it was easy." Anarya licked her lips. "We know Voyanter isn't right, so which of the 'senses' should I try this time?"

"We're not even sure what the 'senses' are," said Tilua.

"They've got to include Seeker and Feeler, don't they?" said Lias. "Do you want to try one of them?"

"Seeker, I think."

"Why that?" asked Tilua.

"No real reason. It just feels right." Anarya added the pink aura of the other newcomer from the Brotherhood to the structure she was building in her mind. It settled into place surrounding the foundation.

"What next?" asked Tilua when Anarya expressed her satisfaction with progress.

"You know what? I believe I can see the way this part of the structure is developing and I think I know what comes next."

She bent forward as she added the bright orange of Yisul's talent, then Raifen's green Feeler's aura and the silvery-grey of a Whisperer. They all fitted into place with only a sight feeling of tension as she manipulated them.

Half a chime later she liftred her head, "It's looking good. The 'senses' are all in place now. I'd like to stop for a bit and think about the 'weapons'. I think this is where the wrong order becomes really dangerous."

"Then it's time to stop," said Tilua. "Now that you've got this far you can do it again tomorrow much faster and then move on."

Anarya nodded. "I could do with some food and a rest. It's more tiring than I imagined it would be, but I don't think we need to wait until tomorrow. Let's start again at the fourteenth chime."

O

Tilua was the first to join Anarya for the next session that afternoon. "I can hardly believe it," she said. "You've still got all the talents you took this morning."

"I know. I'd never have guessed I could hold eight at the same time, especially since some of them are ones I could never hold for long or do much with. I think it's because they're all fitting together into a cohesive structure."

"Makes sense," said Tilua. "I wonder how the people you've taken from are coping with the emptiness."

"Yisul says she's still got her talent. I don't know how."

Tilua looked surprised, then suggested, "Maybe it's because you're not using Thiever alone but combining it with Sponger."

"Could be," Anarya agreed.

Tilua asked, "Have you thought about what the right order for the 'weapons' might be?"

"Not really. I think Stealther must be involved to conceal the weapons from…"

"Don't say his name!"

"I wasn't going to. I think of him as the enemy. Anyway, do I install the weapons behind the Stealther's concealment or do I add it after the others are in place?"

"I think I'd be inclined to add Stealther first."

"That makes sense to me too, but I'm not sure. Just remember the order up to now in case I make a mistake and manage to kill myself. You're the only Sponger and potential Gatherer left if I do."

"Holy Quarenna's mercy! I never thought of that. Don't make a mistake, Anarya, please don't."

"Don't say anything about this to Yisul. She's worried enough already about my part in this. The idea that I'm even thinking about what happens if I fail would really upset her."

Yisul joined them. She was scowling and said, "Anra, my love, don't you dare to even think of failure."

When Anarya looked up in astonishment, Yisul added, "You know what my talent is. I heard your discussion with Tilua."

"Oh!"

"I understand why you would conceal this from me, but I'm angry you feel it necessary. I realise the importance of what you're doing. You have to carry on, much though I dislike it. I would in your position."

"I didn't want to upset you."

"I'll be a lot more than upset if you do it wrong and injure or kill yourself. Be careful, please, be *very* careful."

"I'll try, believe me, I'll try."

The whole group got together again. Anarya told them that the structure she had built had held together during the break. The ones she had taken from confirmed that they still held their talents. "I'm sure Scratcher and Lifter are weapons but I'm not sure how Chemer can be considered a weapon, it doesn't have any range. Any ideas?"

"I've been thinking about the Darkworld and the talents and what people have told me about their experiences coming through the portal," said Tilua. "It strikes me that Scratcher and Chemer are very similar. They both manipulate the substance of the Darkworld, one in air and the other in liquid. They even have similar coloured auras, yellow and gold. I think they're essentially the same. It's just that Scratcher is long-ranged and Chemer short."

Muhan commented, "I wonder if they link to air and

water in the foundation. It might be worth taking them in that order."

"What about Lifter?"

"I'm a Lifter," said Feydis cra Rimled. "I've never been through Anarya's portal so I don't know how my talent relates to the Darkworld but I would guess that it provides strength for all the other talents."

"Right. That helps me decide," Anarya said, "Stealther first, then Lifter, Scratcher and Chemer in that order."

She sat back in her chair, thumbed her forehead – a gesture echoed by Yisul, Lias and the priestesses in the group, while Baram and the priests signed themselves with the lightning bolt. "Holy Quarenna protect me." She closed her eyes.

In her mind she saw the basic elements forming a cylindrical monolith surrounded by concentric swirls of Seeker pink, Voyanter orange, Feeler green and Whisperer grey. She added Baram's brown aura and gasped as the whole structure disappeared behind it. *Does that mean I'm wrong? Maybe Stealther should be the last of the weapons, not the first. Maybe it's a defence and not a weapon at all. Perhaps it should be the last thing added.*

She opened her eyes again to see everyone watching her intently and told them about her predicament.

"Can you remove the Stealther's aura and start again?" asked Tilua.

"I can't even see it."

"I've got an idea," said Baram, and vanished. A moment later and he was visible again. "I can see it. You know how people in Stealth can see each other? Well, I just took a look and I can see the structure you're building."

"He's right," said Tilua a moment later after disappearing briefly and reappearing. "I've just borrowed his talent and I can see it too."

"How does that help?" asked Anarya.

"Baram," said Tilua, "you and I need to examine it carefully for any point of weakness."

Baram nodded, and both of them vanished from view.

Almost a quarter chime later Anarya said, "I can see it again," just as Baram and Tilua reappeared. "What did you do?"

"The Stealther's aura was wrapped around the rest of the structure like a cloak," Tilua told her. "Baram spotted a place where it overlapped and managed to tease it apart at that point. That let both of us get a hold of it and peel it off, like stripping the leaves off an ear of corn. Baram has absorbed it again. I don't think we disturbed anything else."

"I'll check it before I do anything to it," said Anarya. There was a long pause while she examined every aspect of the construction.

Some of the observers were getting restless by the time she reported, "It all looks good. I'm going to try again, in a different order."

She borrowed the Lifter's talent and saw the red aura settle on top of the monolith, pulsating gently in time with her heartbeats.

"That looks threatening," she said, describing what she saw. "I wonder if it's linked to my heart and could stop it if I get the next bit wrong."

She glanced around wishing everybody didn't look so tense.

The yellow aura of a Scratcher fitted snugly against half the circumference of the monolith connecting the Aeromancy in the foundation to the red pulse. *So far, so good.* Anarya held her breath as the Chemer's gold linked the Aquamancy from the base to the Lifter's red in the same way on the other half of the structure. The two blended smoothly; the red core stopped pulsing and settled down to a gentle glow.

Anarya's breath gusted from her as she exhaled in relief. Sweat was pouring off her forehead. "I want to have a rest after that," she said. "The structure looks stable and feels solid and – heavy, if that makes sense. Holding it together is tiring. There's only Daimoner and Stealther left. We'll do them tomorrow."

"I think you deserve a rest," said Tilua and the sentiment was echoed by everyone.

"Tomorrow, then."

O

There was an air of anticipation and tension as the group got together again. They all greeted Anarya as they arrived with questions about her well-being.

"I'm fine," she told them repeatedly, "I'm fine, and the structure looks good too, just the way we left it yesterday. Let's get on with it."

She looked across the room to where Jemol cra Fimigh was sitting. A very tall, gaunt woman, the Head of House Fimigh had been one of the principal members of the conspiracy against The God. She had been watching the proceedings with distaste – she associated the Thiever's talent with The God. Muhan had had a hard time persuading her to join the group when she heard that Anarya was a Thiever. He had persisted because they needed a Daimoner. That talent was uncommon among the Families and she was the strongest, able to command a daimon with a nine-syllable name. She sat glaring at Anarya as if she believed she would try to enslave the Families as The God had.

"With your permission, Lady Jemol," said Anarya, well aware of Jemol's opinions and trying to be conciliatory.

"Get on with it, girl."

Anarya bit her tongue to stop an angry retort. She borrowed the Daimoner's talent and tried to add it to the structure. It slid off. She tried again, with the same result.

Lady Jemol snorted and said, "Don't just sit there, girl, open the dark gate."

Anarya had never heard it called that but she realised what Jemol meant and used the Daimoner's talent to open a way into the Darkworld, a way through which she could summon a daimon if she wanted to. She didn't do that. Instead she moved the dark gate to surround the structure of talents and added Baram's Stealther talent to it.

There was a flash of all colours that dazzled her. Then she was in the Darkworld and was able, for the first time when there, to see something other than darkness. She was standing on a smooth surface at the bottom of a bowl-shaped depression about twenty paces in diameter. Caseir's table stood at eye level near the edge of the bowl but it was standing at an angle and looked as if it should be falling down the slope towards her. Next to it, there was a blurred, difficult to see, mass. *That's got to be the construction, doesn't it?* She started walking towards it and stopped in amazement. One step took her halfway to the table and the next well beyond it. She turned round and saw it on top of a flat peak at least twice as tall as her. Another step and it was hanging from the underside of a breaking wave of land, if what she saw could be called land. *This is weird! How do I get to it?* Several more steps took her farther away from the table, then closer, closer still and then far away again. Sometimes it was in front of her, sometimes behind, or off at an angle. *Distance! There's no distance in the Darkworld.*

She tried walking away from the table and, suddenly, there it was immediately in front of her, close enough that she could reach out and touch it.

As soon as she did she was surrounded by a shrill buzzing noise coming from everywhere. When she concentrated, it resolved into a cacophony of daimon voices, one of which was directed at her.

{*Welcome, Gatherer.*}

"You made it," said Caseir. "Good. I'll tell everyone you're safe."

{*Gatherer good. Done well. Need soon.*}

"What do I do now, Caseir?"

"I believe we have to wait until the last of the Confined Gods manages to break out of his prison. The daimons seem to think this will happen soon."

"What's their idea of soon? They've been stretching time for you."

"Yes, they can stretch time, as you call it, but for short periods only. Otherwise time passes here much like it does in our world. You have to go back to Jotuk and wait until you're needed. I'll let you know when that is."

"How do I get back?"

"How should I know? It's your Gathering."

I can barely see it. Not well enough to take it apart. I guess I could try to open the dark gate from this side.

It worked and she found herself back in Jotuk with Jemol cra Fimigh stifling a scream.

"Oh, it's you!" said Jemol. "You vanished and when you came back I thought you were a daimon coming through a dark gate I didn't control."

"I understand," Anarya acknowledged, "I'd scream too if that happened, but it's only me."

She stood up and closed the gate. Without her needing to do anything the structure disassembled itself bit by bit, but she knew she would be able to put it together again very quickly when it was needed.

"Sit down, quickly," said Tilua and Anarya realised she was very tired and almost falling down.

"That was exhausting. I feel as if I could sleep and slee… "

O

"Waken up! Come on! You can't just lie there."

"What? Oh, Caseir, what's the matter?" Anarya surfaced slowly from sleep, confused, disorientated and uncertain.

"The daimons think it's time. They say they need the Gatherer."

"But I'm not ready! We're not ready."

"You have to be."

"What time is it?"

"First chime, more or less. You've been asleep for more than ten. I woke Yisul and Baram first and they're spreading the word. Everybody will be here soon. I left you to last to give you as much rest as possible. Come on."

Yawning enough that she thought she might dislocate

her jaw, Anarya climbed out of bed and splashed water on her face.

As she started dressing Caseir grumbled, "A robe will do, you're not going to a banquet."

"I'll feel better if I'm properly dressed," Anarya said. "I'll need all the support I can get and that's one way I can help myself."

"I suppose so, but hurry."

She was putting on a cream silk shirt and skirt and an embroidered waistcoat when Yisul ran into the room. She was wearing a lounging robe over her nightdress and looked a bit dishevelled.

"Are you ready yet? Nearly everybody's here. Oh, you're almost dressed, that's good. You look great. I wish I had time to dress too."

"You look fine," said Anarya. She took a deep breath. "Let's go."

A chorus of greetings welcomed her to the reception room. She looked around. Few were fully dressed, most looked as if they had dressed hurriedly and others had simply thrown on robes over their sleepwear. Many were blinking sleep from their eyes.

"Hot drinks will be here soon," said Lias as she entered. Despite her informal dress she managed to look elegant and Anarya had the momentary pang of jealousy again.

Everyone was there, except Jemol cra Fimigh. "Where is she?" asked Muhan. "She was talking about going back to House Fimigh last night but we all need to be here and I thought I talked her into staying in one of the guest rooms, the same as Sahnes and Feydis."

"Actually," said Tilua, "I'm not sure if we do need everybody here. I can see Anarya is holding all the talents at once. It's an incredible sight. Her aura is sparkling with every imaginable colour."

"I'd be much happier with everyone here," said Anarya. "I'm not sure I can put it all together without the original talent holders to draw on."

"Hurry!" said Caseir. "The daimons want you there now."

Anarya started putting the talents together. She got as far as installing the Chemer's skill when Jemol cra Fimigh arrived.

Jemol had taken the time to dress as if for a formal event. Her gown was impeccable and her make-up flawless. The look she gave everyone less well dressed was, at best, condescending.

Anarya finished assembling the construct and opened the dark gate.

IN THE DARKWORLD

Anarya stood beside the construction of talents in the Darkworld and looked around. It was as she remembered seeing it, a mottled brown and black surface stretching as far as she could see in all directions. Pits and peaks were scattered everywhere. They shifted all the time, usually with a slow, writhing movement. The pits filled in or appeared and the peaks collapsed or grew. Occasionally there would be a sudden alteration as the landscape changed in the blink of an eye.

{Welcome, Gatherer}

She turned and looked in the direction the daimon's voice came from. There was nothing to see. "I'm ready," she said. "What do I do?"

{Come}

"Come where? I can't see you."

{Wear Gathered}

"Wear it?"

{Touch.}

She shrugged mentally and turned to look at the construction. It was a little easier to see at close range but it was still difficult. When she went to touch it, her hand sank into it without any sense that it had touched anything. She tried to pull back but couldn't.

"Hurry," said Caseir. "It's almost free."

{Gatherer must wear.}

I guess I don't have a choice. She thumbed her forehead and stepped forward to be engulfed by the construct. Bit by bit she became aware of the talents as they merged into her body more completely than if she was simply holding them. First the red core, then the foundation elements and the senses and lastly the weapons, which were ready for use. The whole thing was much as she imagined a suit of armour would feel like – protective and formidable.

The combination of Voyanter, Feeler and Seeker let her see the daimons for the first time. At first she didn't realise what they were. If asked she would have guessed their form would be menacing and terrifying, but it wasn't. Each one she could see was different although all were sleek, sinuous and elegant. The best description she could give was that they were like elongated seals, twisting and turning in the air around her. Some were as thin as eels, others she wouldn't have been able to put her arms around.

The largest of the daimons approached her and the familiar voice said {*Follow.*}

Anarya discovered that the Aquamancer's talent wasn't only part of the foundation but was also her means of movement. She flowed after the daimon, keeping up with it without difficulty. Everytime she blinked her position relative to the lead daimon changed. She might be above it, behind it, next to it or off to one side. The other daimons stayed together. She would have liked to do the same, but she couldn't work out how to.

Her guide stopped at the edge of a wide pit and said {*Prison.*}

She looked down – and down ... and down. Deep below her an iridescent layer stretched across the pit, closing it off. It was bulging upwards in waves and subsiding again. In places the shimmering had stopped and the membrane, or whatever it was, was a dull, fixed, grey colour that looked rigid and dead.

{*Tell what do.*}

"Fill the hole, I suppose," said Anarya.

{*Try.*} agreed the daimon. It started breaking off bits of the rim and tossing them into the pit. Anarya added power from her Terromancer aspect to break up the surface. More of the daimons joined in and the iridescent layer was buried.

It can't be as easy as that, Anarya thought and looked down into the pit in time to see the dumped material be absorbed by the shimmering layer.

"What do I do now, Caseir? Any ideas?"

"Whenever I faced a stronger opponent in the arena I would make him do all the work. I'd just defend until he exhausted himself. What's happening down there must be tiring. Wait until he gets out of the pit then attack him from all sides and wear him out."

"That makes sense."

She looked into the depths of the pit and saw one of the areas that looked dead enlarge, then rip open. A massive shape, a much bigger version of a daimon, squeezed itself through the tear and started rising. *Holy Quarenna bless me. That must be Kehsieh!*

Although Anarya knew she should be terrified, she felt calmness flow round her like a cloak. *Is that Quarenna's doing?*

"Separate," she told the daimons. "Split into several groups."

The daimons obeyed her.

"Wait until he's at the surface and we can get below him too. Surround him. I'll attack first. Wait for my signal."

Anarya watched the slow rise of Kehsieh.

Not complaining, but why isn't he rising faster? Doesn't he want out of his prison?

The mass of Kehsieh flowed upwards, changing shape with a slow twisting movement.

Quarenna's grace! He's even bigger than I thought.

Anarya pulled strength through the Lifter and gave it to the Scratcher. She used it to make a ball of lightning and tossed it at Kehsieh just as he emerged from the pit.

It hit him, producing a bright yellow flash.

He recoiled. She did it again with the same result.

"Good," she exclaimed and told the daimons to copy her.

Each strike made Kehsieh flinch, but he carried on coming.

She wanted to keep the pressure up and told the daimons, "Don't all attack at once. One group at a time.

Don't let him know where the next attack is coming from. Confuse him."

{Weapon?}

"Try anything. See what works."

A group of daimons swooped in towards Kehsieh. Streams of fire burst from them to hit him.

He ignored the fire.

"Try something else!"

Lightning flared from another group of daimons.

"That's better!" she shouted.

The texture of Kehsieh's surface changed. A dozen or so small protuberances bulged out from the upper half of his body. When they reached the size of an egg they separated from him and sped towards one group of daimons.

Most missed, but there was a shrill screech from one of the daimons.

"Are you injured?" Anarya asked, "How badly?"

{Small part only.}

"You've got to dodge if he tries that again."

Kehsieh's surface wrinkled again. More projectiles erupted from him and flew towards the daimons.

They hit, and there were more screams

One particularly penetrating shriek was followed by the voice of the daimon leader saying *{Gone.}*

"Do you mean one of you is dead?"

{Affirmation. Dispersed. Ended.}

Anarya was surprised to find herself sad about the death of a daimon.

"Be careful," she called. "Don't get too close. Be ready to dodge. You don't have to get near him to attack."

{Must attack.}

"Yes, but take care. Confuse him. Make him chase you."

She threw more lightning of her own at him – he recoiled, but threw off more missiles.

Some of them passed close to her but not near enough for her to think she was the target. *I don't think they're aimed at me. The Stealther is keeping me safe.*

A group of daimons tossed a collection of multicoloured spheres at Kehsieh.

They hit him. Some of them sank into him then erupted in a small explosion. The others did nothing.

"Not bad, but not too good. Try something different!"

Sheets and curtains of shimmering silver wrapped round him. His movements slowed.

"That works! What is it?"

{*Stasis.*}

The reply didn't mean anything to Anarya.

"Whatever it is keep using it!"

Kehsieh changed shape. He became more spherical, with a deep indentation on one side. The floor of the dent started pulsating.

The daimons in front of it scattered.

Holes appeared in the sheets of the stasis effect. They enlarged, and then the whole thing tore apart.

Kehsieh rotated. The dent swung round towards another group of daimons. The focus of his weapon passed over the Gather construct and it started vibrating violently.

Holy Quarenna, I'm losing it!

Then the focus moved on.

Quarenna's mercy! He almost got me by accident. It's a good thing the Stealther's keeping me hidden.

She threw more lightning at Kehsieh. It was effective, but it wasn't enough. The vibration weapon was shredding daimons.

Fire doesn't work. Maybe ice will.

She combined Aquamancy and Pyromancy to send a stream of cold fire towards Kehsieh. It splashed across his side and slopped into the dent that seemed to be the origin of the vibration weapon. It froze and stopped pulsating.

That's got rid of that, but we're not making much impression on him. He's too big.

"More lightning!" she called. "Hit him hard!"

Kehsieh changed shape again. A long spike developed.

Now what? He's too far away for that to be an effective weapon.

Anarya was wrong. The spike suddenly shot forward, instantaneously covering the distance to impale the nearest daimon.

The impaled daimon gave a thin, wavering cry and started shrinking.

He's feeding on it! He'll get stronger! What can I do?

An idea came. She remembered a glyph she knew that caused pain – at least it did in people. *Perhaps it will affect Kehsieh too.*

She formed the pain glyph and released it.

It struck Kehsieh. It had more effect than anything she had tried. She saw him retreat, shrinking slightly.

It worked!

She started to construct the glyph again but couldn't complete it.

I've used too much power. I'm not strong enough on my own!

She realised she was in trouble – uncompleted glyphs were dangerous.

She reached for Caseir. *If his stubbornness can help the daimons it can help me.* Then she realised he was already fully committed to supporting the daimons.

"Help me!" she screamed, feeling the beginnings of panic as the partial glyph started fraying round the edges. "Help me!"

The call sped away from her along the Whispermesh. She felt it touch one node, then three more, then twenty, fifty, eighty, a hundred. She lost count, not that it mattered; every node responded to the urgency of her call.

Power started pouring along the Whispermesh to the red core of the Gather construct. From there it was distributed to every component. Anarya felt she was part of an incredible community of talented who were offering her strength, hope and vitality without asking anything in return.

She turned her attention back to the Darkworld.

Kehsieh had impaled another daimon and was getting bigger again.

The power she was drawing through the Whispermesh made her feel as if she doubled in size, then doubled again and again until she was as large as Kehsieh.

She finished constructing the pain glyph she had abandoned half done and hurled it at him.

"Attack him! Hit him with everything you can. We can beat him!"

Kehsieh released a shower of thousands of bright sparks in all directions.

The ones that hit Anarya faded away without doing any damage.

What was that about?

He threw off more missiles. The combination of Seeker and Voyanter talents showed these ones coming straight at her.

He knows where I am. The gap in that cloud of sparks showed him.

Most of the projectiles thumped into the solidity of Terromancy or were engulfed by the fluidity of the Chemer talent. They did no damage.

She shuddered from the impact of the few that got through her defences. Transient gaps appeared in her armour. It quickly returned to normal.

Kehsieh threw more of his substance at her, enough for her to see a significant reduction in his size.

He's smaller than me now!

She avoided some of the barrage. Some got through.

But he's still dangerous.

Each hit made her twitch.

Some nodes of the Whispermesh flared. A few went dark.

People are dying! How can I stop him?

She remembered what Caseir had told them about the conflict between gods and daimons. It had taken Quarenna and Huler working with daimons and men to imprison the Confined Gods in the first place. *Is it going to take the same to deal with Kehsieh?*

"Holy Quarenna, help us," she shouted as she attacked again. "We need your help."

Kehsieh shrank a little with each attack he launched. He was noticeably smaller than her, and now smaller than some of the daimons. It didn't stop him doing damage.

More of the daimons died.

Anarya was sure that people across the Whispermesh were dying too with each missile that struck home.

"Caseir, ask Huler for help!"

"I don't know if he will respond to a dead man."

"Try!" She took hold of the nearest node of the Whispermesh and said, "Everybody, if you can hear me, pray to the gods for help. We're all in serious trouble."

The Whispermesh was suddenly full of voices – all invoking Huler as the Warrior, or Quarenna as the Warrior Maid.

A strong, benign, fierce, gentle, implacable and supportive presence engulfed Anarya. She felt herself cradled in what had to be Quarenna's embrace and being guided through the twists and turns of constructing a vast three-dimensional glyph.

There are gaps in the glyph! What have I done wrong?

Another presence appeared, as strong as Quarenna's but with a completely different feel. *It's Huler, it must be! How is that possible?*

The gaps in the glyph started filling in. The power was passing through Anarya, but not touching her.

Reassurance flooded from Quarenna. *She's shielding me from contact with Huler!*

The last gap in the glyph vanished. There was a bright, multicoloured flash and the glyph became a closely woven net of light.

Anarya picked it up and threw it over the much reduced body of Kehsieh. He stopped moving.

The daimons moved closer.

Kehsieh didn't react.

The daimons attached themselves to the net, towed it to the pit and dropped it in.

At the bottom of the pit the net solidified into a cage. Surface material poured into the pit, filling it until there was no sign of where it had been.

{Good. All safe now.}

Anarya felt herself shrink to normal size. The Gather construct disassembled itself.

{Go.} said the daimon, and she was back in House Neyen, seated among the talented who had contributed to the Gathering.

She tried to stand up, became very dizzy and felt herself falling forward…

HOUSE NEYEN

Anarya woke up slowly, and reluctantly, as she was feeling very comfortable. She realised she was in bed and looked up to see Yisa standing nearby.

"We've been here before," she said.

"And again it's because you have stretched yourself too far," said Yisul. "You must stop doing that."

"I didn't have a choice, did I? Kehsieh had to be stopped."

"True. How do you feel? Are you fit enough for company?"

"Yes, but I'm not receiving visitors in bed again. Let me up."

"Are you sure? You've been asleep for most of a day."

"Really? I feel fine."

Yisul supported Anarya as she got out of bed and wrapped her up in a shimmering lounging robe of green satin before escorting her to the reception room.

Baram, Muhan, Lias, Tilua and Raifen were waiting for her, all wanting to know how she was feeling.

"I'm fine," she kept saying, "I'm fine. It's all over."

"We know," said Baram. "We were all there with you, all of us who contributed talents to the Gathering."

"It felt as if every other talented person in the world was there too," Tilua added, her voice awed.

"That's right. When I needed help people came," said Anarya. Then she added with awe in her voice, "So did Quarenna and Huler."

"We know. Each of us here had a personal contact with one of them," said Tilua. "It was – indescribable. They left quite quickly once Kesieh was imprisoned but the memory of the contact will be with me forever."

There was a mutter of agreement from everyone else.

"I know what you mean. They guided me at the end, showed me how to imprison Kehsieh again," said Anarya.

"He's imprisoned, not destroyed?" said Muhan.

"He's well buried and very much reduced. Many of the daimons are bigger than him now. I can't see him escaping again. What do you think, Caseir?"

There was no answer.

"Caseir?"

"He hasn't been heard from since the battle," said Yisul. "We think he must be dead."

"I'm not so sure," said Raifen. "I Felt awe and gratitude from him at the same time that Huler left. That was the last time I was aware of him. I think he may have been an avatar of the Warrior, now reabsorbed by Huler."

"That sounds like a suitable reward for him," said Anarya, "but I'll miss him."

"So will I," said Baram.

"What about everyone else?" asked Anarya.

"Everyone you took into the Gathering is well but there have been deaths among others of the talented in House Neyen."

"And, from what we've heard so far, in several of the other Houses," said Muhan. "We have to assume that some of the hits you took killed people who joined you to lend you strength."

"That's not fair," said Anarya. "We all knew there was a risk but the ones who came to support me didn't have a choice. They must have been drawn into the battle whether they wanted to be or not."

"Not so," said Muhan, "They did have a choice. I've spoken to some of those who joined in and they say they weren't forced into battle but were summoned – no not summoned – invited to give help, to join in something dangerous but important. They all say there was no compulsion involved. So far I haven't spoken to anyone who chose not to participate."

"Would they admit to it if they didn't?" asked Baram.

Muhan shrugged.

"You say you feel fine. Does that include your talent?" asked Tilua.

"I don't know. I'm almost afraid to look at my aura."

Anarya concentrated. As always it was difficult to see her own aura. It wasn't until she tried to take Yisul's talent that she got a good look at it. The thread linking her to Yisul was a shimmering rainbow.

"There's no black! Holy Quarenna be praised, there's no black!"

"Yes," confirmed Tilua. "It looks just like it used to with no trace of Thiever, or any of the other talents you held."

Anarya caught hold of Yisul and pulled her into a big hug with tears of joy filling her eyes. "Holy Quarenna has been merciful. I'm a Sponger again and nothing else."

THE END

ACKNOWLEDGEMENTS

Thank you to everyone who was involved in bringing this book to publication:

Elsewhen Press, who first suggested a sequel.

My friends who read and critiqued it while in progress.

And, of course, to my wife for her support and encouragement.

I'm very grateful to all of you.

David M Allan, August 2021

Elsewhen Press

delivering outstanding new talents in speculative fiction

Visit the Elsewhen Press website at elsewhen.press for the latest information on all of our titles, authors and events; to read our blog; find out where to buy our books and ebooks; or to place an order.

Sign up for the Elsewhen Press InFlight Newsletter at elsewhen.press/newsletter

1: THE DEEP AND SHINING DARK
A Locus Recommended Read in 2018

"A rich and memorable tale of political ambition, family and magic, set in an imagined city that feels as vibrant as the characters inhabiting it." **Aliette de Bodard**
Nebula-award winning author of *The Tea Master and the Detective*

You know something's wrong when the cityangel turns up at your door
Magic within the city-state of Marek works without the need for bloodletting, unlike elsewhere in Teren, thanks to an agreement three hundred years ago between an angel and the founding fathers. It also ensures that political stability is protected from magical influence. Now, though, most sophisticates no longer even believe in magic *or* the cityangel.

But magic has suddenly stopped working, discovers Reb, one of the two sorcerers who survived a plague that wiped out virtually all of the rest. Soon she is forced to acknowledge that someone has deposed the cityangel without being able to replace it. Marcia, Heir to House Fereno, and one of the few in high society who is well-aware that magic still exists, stumbles across that same truth. But it is just one part of a much more ambitious plan to seize control of Marek.

Meanwhile, city Council members connive and conspire, unaware that they are being manipulated in a dangerous political game. A game that threatens the peace and security not just of the city, but all the states around the Oval Sea, including the shipboard traders of Salina upon whom Marek relies.

To stop the impending disaster, Reb and Marcia, despite their difference in status, must work together alongside the deposed cityangel and Jonas, a messenger from Salina. But first they must discover who is behind the plot, and each of them must try to decide who they can really trust.

ISBN: 9781911409342 (epub, kindle) / ISBN: 9781911409243 (272pp paperback)
Visit bit.ly/DeepShiningDark

2: SHADOW AND STORM

"never short on adventure and intrigue... the characters are real, full of depth, and richly drawn, and you'll wish you had even more time with them by book's end. A fantastic read." **Rivers Solomon**
Author of *An Unkindness of Ghosts*, Lambda, Tiptree and Locus finalist

Never trust a demon… or a Teren politician
The annual visit by the Teren Throne's representative, the Lord Lieutenant, is merely a symbolic gesture. But this year the Lieutenant has been unexpectedly replaced and Marcia, Heir to House Fereno, suspects a new agenda.

Teren magic is enabled by bloodletting. A Teren magician will invoke a demon and bind them with blood. But demons are devious and if unleashed are sure to create havoc. The Teren way to stop them involves the letting of more of the magician's blood – often terminally. But if a young magician is being sought by an unleashed demon, their only hope may be to escape to Marek where the cityangel can keep the demon at bay. Probably.

Once again Reb, Cato, Jonas and Beckett must deal with a magical problem, while Marcia must tackle a serious political challenge to Marek's future.

ISBN: 9781911409595 (epub, kindle) / ISBN: 9781911409496 (336pp paperback)
Visit bit.ly/ShadowAndStorm

ABOUT DAVID M ALLAN

David M Allan got hooked on reading at a young age by borrowing to the max – 3 books, twice a week – from the public library. He was caught up and transported to fabulous other worlds by the likes of Wells, Verne and Burroughs (and later by Asimov, Bradbury, Clarke, Heinlein, Le Guin, Wyndham…). Alas, the journeys were temporary and he had to return to Earth.

His love affair with science fiction and fantasy had him thinking vaguely about writing but he didn't follow through until after retirement and his relocation, with wife and cat, to a houseboat on the Thames. It was reading one book which he didn't think was very good that led him to say "I could do better than that" and then setting out to prove it. David has since had a number of short stories published in online magazines, and his debut novel *The Empty Throne* published by Elsewhen Press. *Quaestor* was his second novel and *Thiever* is its sequel. They too have been published by Elsewhen Press.

www.ingramcontent.com/pod-product-compliance
Lightning Source LLC
Chambersburg PA
CBHW060732190726
48285CB00001B/178